This is the only complete and authorized U.S. paperbound edition of the trilogy, "The Lord of the Rings," containing all of the original text and maps, a new Foreword, additional Prologue, Glossary and Index by the author, J. R. R. Tolkien.

J. R. R. Tolkien's The Lord of the Rings—*of which this book is the second part*—*is a chronicle of the great War of the Ring, which occurred in the Third Age of Middle-earth. At that time, the One Ring, the Master of all the Rings of Power, had been held for many years by the hobbits, but was eagerly sought by the Enemy who made it. To its wearer, the One Ring gave mastery over every living creature, but since it was devised by an evil power, in the end it inevitably corrupted anyone who attempted to use it. Out of the struggle to possess and control the One Ring, with all its ominous power, there arose a war comparable both in magnitude and in the issues involved to the great wars of our own time. And in that war, the Third Age of Middle-earth came to an end. . . .*

The Two Towers *recounts the further adventures of the band of companions introduced in* The Fellowship of the Ring. *Frodo, unwilling heir to the One Ring, has decided that it is his task and his alone to carry the Ring back to the Fire that will consume its power for evil. Accompanied only by his servant, Sam Gamgee, he is making his way eastward to the ghastly borders of Mordor, the Land of the Enemy. Meanwhile, his companions in the fellowship of the Ring are caught in the strategy of the traitor Saruman and pass on to battle and peril in the West. Secure in his immense power the Enemy marshals his forces. The book ends with the coming of the great Darkness which opens the terrible War of the Rings. How that war was fought, and what became of Frodo and his companions is told in the third and final part,* The Return of the King.

It's been fifteen years at this writing since I first came across THE LORD OF THE RINGS in the stacks at the Carnegie Library in Pittsburgh. I'd been looking for the book for four years, ever since reading W. H. Auden's review in the *New York Times*. I think of that time now—and the years after, when the trilogy continued to be hard to find and hard to explain to most friends—with an undeniable nostalgia. It was a barren era for fantasy, among other things, but a good time for cherishing slighted treasures and mysterious passwords. Long before *Frodo Lives!* began to appear in the New York subways, J. R. R. Tolkien was the magus of my secret knowledge.

I've never thought it an accident that Tolkien's works waited more than ten years to explode into popularity almost overnight. The Sixties were no fouler a decade than the Fifties —they merely reaped the Fifties' foul harvest—but they were the years when millions of people grew aware that the industrial society had become paradoxically unlivable, incalculably immoral, and ultimately deadly. In terms of passwords, the Sixties were the time when the word *progress* lost its ancient holiness, and *escape* stopped being comically obscene. The impulse is being called reactionary now, but lovers of Middle-earth want to go there. I would myself, like a shot.

For in the end it is Middle-earth and its dwellers that we love, not Tolkien's considerable gifts in showing it to us. I said once that the world he charts was there long before him, and I still believe it. He is a great enough magician to tap our most common nightmares, daydreams and twilight fancies, but he never invented them either: he found them a place to live, a green alternative to each day's madness here in a poisoned world. We are raised to honor all the wrong explorers and discoverers—thieves planting flags, murderers carrying crosses. Let us at last praise the colonizers of dreams.

—Peter S. Beagle
Watsonville, California
14 July 1973

THE LORD OF THE RINGS

BY J. R. R. TOLKIEN

PART I
THE FELLOWSHIP OF THE RING

PART II
THE TWO TOWERS

PART III
THE RETURN OF THE KING

The Two Towers

BEING THE SECOND PART OF

THE LORD OF THE RINGS

With a New Foreword by the Author

J. R. R. TOLKIEN

BALLANTINE BOOKS • NEW YORK

ISBN 0-345-27259-5

This edition published by arrangement with
Houghton Mifflin Company

Manufactured in the United States of America

First Ballantine Books Edition: October 1965
Fifty-eighth Printing: October 1977

THE LORD OF THE RINGS

Three Rings for the Elven-kings under the sky,
   Seven for the Dwarf-lords in their halls of stone,
Nine for Mortal Men doomed to die,
   One for the Dark Lord on his dark throne
In the Land of Mordor where the Shadows lie.
   One Ring to rule them all, One Ring to find them,
   One Ring to bring them all and in the darkness bind
      them
In the Land of Mordor where the Shadows lie.

Synopsis

This is the second part of THE LORD OF THE RINGS.

The first part, *The Fellowship of the Ring,* told how Gandalf the Grey discovered that the ring possessed by Frodo the Hobbit was in fact the One Ring, ruler of all the Rings of Power. It recounted the flight of Frodo and his companions from the quiet Shire of their home, pursued by the terror of the Black Riders of Mordor, until at last, with the aid of Aragorn the Ranger of Eriador, they came through desperate perils to the House of Elrond in Rivendell.

There was held the great Council of Elrond, at which it was decided to attempt the destruction of the Ring, and Frodo was appointed the Ring-bearer. The Companions of the Ring were then chosen, who were to aid him in his quest: to come if he could to the Mountain of Fire in Mordor, the land of the Enemy himself, where alone the Ring could be unmade. In this fellowship were Aragorn, and Boromir son of the Lord of Gondor, representing Men; Legolas son of the Elven-king of Mirkwood, for the Elves; Gimli son of Glóin of the Lonely Mountain, for the Dwarves; Frodo with his servant Samwise, and his two young kinsmen Meriadoc and Peregrin, for the Hobbits; and Gandalf the Grey.

The Companions journeyed in secret far from Rivendell in the North, until baffled in their attempt to cross the high pass of Caradhras in winter, they were led by Gandalf through the hidden gate and entered the vast Mines of Moria, seeking a way beneath the mountains. There Gandalf, in battle with a dreadful spirit of the underworld, fell into a dark abyss. But Aragorn, now revealed as the hidden heir of the ancient Kings of the West, led the company on from the East Gate of Moria, through the Elvish land of Lórien, and down the Great River Anduin, until they came to the Falls of Rauros. Already they had become aware that their journey was watched by spies, and that the creature Gollum, who once had possessed the Ring and still lusted for it, was following their trail.

It now became necessary for them to decide whether they should turn east to Mordor; or should go on with Boromir to the aid of Minas Tirith, chief city of Gondor, in the coming war; or should divide. When it became clear that the Ring-bearer was resolved to continue his hopeless journey to the land of the Enemy, Boromir attempted to seize the Ring by force. The first part ended with the fall of Boromir to the lure of the Ring; with the escape and disappearance of Frodo and his servant Samwise; and the scattering of the remainder of the Fellowship by a sudden attack of orc-soldiers, some in the service of the Dark Lord of Mordor, some of the traitor Saruman of Isengard. The Quest of the Ring-bearer seemed already overtaken by disaster.

This second part, *The Two Towers,* now tells how each of the members of the Fellowship of the Ring fared, after the breaking of their fellowship, until the coming of the great Darkness and the outbreak of the War of the Ring, which is to be recounted in the third and last part.

Contents

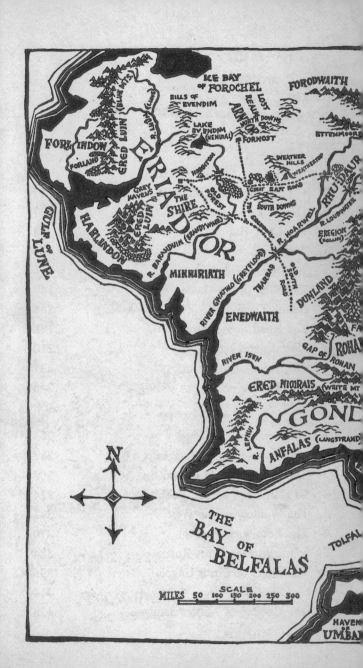

BOOK III

BOOK III

Chapter 1

The Departure of Boromir

Aragorn sped on up the hill. Every now and again he bent to the ground. Hobbits go light, and their footprints are not easy even for a Ranger to read, but not far from the top a spring crossed the path, and in the wet earth he saw what he was seeking.

'I read the signs aright,' he said to himself. 'Frodo ran to the hill-top. I wonder what he saw there? But he returned by the same way, and went down the hill again.'

Aragorn hesitated. He desired to go to the high seat himself, hoping to see there something that would guide him in his perplexities; but time was pressing. Suddenly he leaped forward, and ran to the summit, across the great flag-stones, and up the steps. Then sitting in the high seat he looked out. But the sun seemed darkened, and the world dim and remote. He turned from the North back again to North, and saw nothing save the distant hills, unless it were that far away he could see again a great bird like an eagle high in the air, descending slowly in wide circles down toward the earth.

Even as he gazed his quick ears caught sounds in the woodlands below, on the west side of the River. He stiffened. There were cries, and among them, to his horror, he could distinguish the harsh voices of Orcs. Then suddenly with a deep-throated call a great horn blew, and the blasts of it smote the hills and echoed in the hollows, rising in a mighty shout above the roaring of the falls.

'The horn of Boromir!' he cried. 'He is in need!' He sprang down the steps and away, leaping down the path. 'Alas! An ill fate is on me this day, and all that I do goes amiss. Where is Sam?'

As he ran the cries came louder, but fainter now and desperately the horn was blowing. Fierce and shrill rose the yells of the Orcs, and suddenly the horn-calls ceased.

Aragorn raced down the last slope, but before he could reach the hill's foot, the sounds died away; and as he turned to the left and ran towards them they retreated, until at last he could hear them no more. Drawing his bright sword and crying *Elendil! Elendil!* he crashed through the trees.

A mile, maybe, from Parth Galen in a little glade not far from the lake he found Boromir. He was sitting with his back to a great tree, as if he was resting. But Aragorn saw that he was pierced with many black-feathered arrows; his sword was still in his hand, but it was broken near the hilts; his horn cloven in two was at his side. Many Orcs lay slain, piled all about him and at his feet.

Aragorn knelt beside him. Boromir opened his eyes and strove to speak. At last slow words came. 'I tried to take the Ring from Frodo,' he said. 'I am sorry. I have paid.' His glance strayed to his fallen enemies; twenty at least lay there. 'They have gone: the Halflings: the Orcs have taken them. I think they are not dead. Orcs bound them.' He paused and his eyes closed wearily. After a moment he spoke again.

'Farewell, Aragorn! Go to Minas Tirith and save my people! I have failed.'

'No!' said Aragorn, taking his hand and kissing his brow. 'You have conquered. Few have gained such a victory. Be at peace! Minas Tirith shall not fall!'

Boromir smiled.

'Which way did they go? Was Frodo there?' said Aragorn.

But Boromir did not speak again.

'Alas!' said Aragorn. 'Thus passes the heir of Denethor, Lord of the Tower of Guard! This is a bitter end. Now the Company is all in ruin. It is I that have failed. Vain was Gandalf's trust in me. What shall I do now? Boromir has laid it on me to go to Minas Tirith, and my heart desires it; but where are the Ring and the Bearer? How shall I find them and save the Quest from disaster?'

He knelt for a while, bent with weeping, still clasping

Boromir's hand. So it was that Legolas and Gimli found him. They came from the western slopes of the hill, silently, creeping through the trees as if they were hunting. Gimli had his axe in hand, and Legolas his long knife: all his arrows were spent. When they came into the glade they halted in amazement; and then they stood a moment with heads bowed in grief, for it seemed to them plain what had happened.

'Alas!' said Legolas, coming to Aragorn's side. 'We have hunted and slain many Orcs in the woods, but we should have been of more use here. We came when we heard the horn—but too late, it seems. I fear you have taken deadly hurt.'

'Boromir is dead,' said Aragorn. 'I am unscathed, for I was not here with him. He fell defending the hobbits, while I was away upon the hill.'

'The hobbits!' cried Gimli. 'Where are they then? Where is Frodo?'

'I do not know,' answered Aragorn wearily. 'Before he died Boromir told me that the Orcs had bound them; he did not think that they were dead. I sent him to follow Merry and Pippin; but I did not ask him if Frodo or Sam were with him: not until it was too late. All that I have done to-day has gone amiss. What is to be done now?'

'First we must tend the fallen,' said Legolas. 'We cannot leave him lying like carrion among these foul Orcs.'

'But we must be swift,' said Gimli. 'He would not wish us to linger. We must follow the Orcs, if there is hope that any of our Company are living prisoners.'

'But we do not know whether the Ring-bearer is with them or not,' said Aragorn. 'Are we to abandon him? Must we not seek him first? An evil choice is now before us!'

'Then let us do first what we must do,' said Legolas. 'We have not the time or the tools to bury our comrade fitly, or to raise a mound over him. A cairn we might build.'

'The labour would be hard and long: there are no stones that we could use nearer than the water-side,' said Gimli.

'Then let us lay him in a boat with his weapons, and the

weapons of his vanquished foes,' said Aragorn. 'We will
send him to the Falls of Rauros and give him to Anduin.
The River of Gondor will take care at least that no evil
creature dishonours his bones.'

Quickly they searched the bodies of the Orcs, gathering
their swords and cloven helms and shields into a heap.

'See!' cried Aragorn. 'Here we find tokens!' He picked
out from the pile of grim weapons two knives, leaf-
bladed, damasked in gold and red; and searching further
he found also the sheaths, black, set with small red gems.
'No orc-tools these!' he said. 'They were borne by the
hobbits. Doubtless the Orcs despoiled them, but feared to
keep the knives, knowing them for what they are: work
of Westernesse, wound about with spells for the bane of
Mordor. Well, now, if they still live, our friends are
weaponless. I will take these things, hoping against hope,
to give them back.'

'And I,' said Legolas, 'will take all the arrows that I
can find, for my quiver is empty.' He searched in the pile
and on the ground about and found not a few that were un-
damaged and longer in the shaft than such arrows as the
Orcs were accustomed to use. He looked at them closely.

And Aragorn looked on the slain, and he said: 'Here
lie many that are not folk of Mordor. Some are from the
North, from the Misty Mountains, if I know anything of
Orcs and their kinds. And here are others strange to me.
Their gear is not after the manner of Orcs at all!'

There were four goblin-soldiers of greater stature, swart,
slant-eyed, with thick legs and large hands. They were
armed with short broad-bladed swords, not with the curved
scimitars usual with Orcs; and they had bows of yew, in
length and shape like the bows of Men. Upon their shields
they bore a strange device: a small white hand in the
centre of a black field; on the front of their iron helms was
set an S-rune, wrought of some white metal.

'I have not seen these tokens before,' said Aragorn.
'What do they mean?'

'S is for Sauron,' said Gimli. 'That is easy to read.'

'Nay!' said Legolas. 'Sauron does not use the Elf-runes.'

'Neither does he use his right name, nor permit it to be spelt or spoken,' said Aragorn. 'And he does not use white. The Orcs in the service of Barad-dûr use the sign of the Red Eye.' He stood for a moment in thought. 'S is for Saruman, I guess,' he said at length. 'There is evil afoot in Isengard, and the West is no longer safe. It is as Gandalf feared: by some means the traitor Saruman has had news of our journey. It is likely too that he knows of Gandalf's fall. Pursuers from Moria may have escaped the vigilance of Lórien, or they may have avoided that land and come to Isengard by other paths. Orcs travel fast. But Saruman has many ways of learning news. Do you remember the birds?'

'Well, we have no time to ponder riddles,' said Gimli. 'Let us bear Boromir away!'

'But after that we must guess the riddles, if we are to choose our course rightly,' answered Aragorn.

'Maybe there is no right choice,' said Gimli.

Taking his axe the Dwarf now cut several branches. These they lashed together with bowstrings, and spread their cloaks upon the frame. Upon this rough bier they carried the body of their companion to the shore, together with such trophies of his last battle as they chose to send forth with him. It was only a short way, yet they found it no easy task, for Boromir was a man both tall and strong.

At the water-side Aragorn remained, watching the bier, while Legolas and Gimli hastened back on foot to Parth Galen. It was a mile or more, and it was some time before they came back, paddling two boats swiftly along the shore.

'There is a strange tale to tell!' said Legolas. 'There are only two boats upon the bank. We could find no trace of the other.'

'Have Orcs been there?' asked Aragorn.

'We saw no signs of them,' answered Gimli. 'And Orcs

would have taken or destroyed all the boats, and the baggage as well.'

'I will look at the ground when we come there,' said Aragorn.

Now they laid Boromir in the middle of the boat that was to bear him away. The grey hood and elven-cloak they folded and placed beneath his head. They combed his long dark hair and arrayed it upon his shoulders. The golden belt of Lórien gleamed about his waist. His helm they set beside him, and across his lap they laid the cloven horn and the hilts and shards of his sword; beneath his feet they put the swords of his enemies. Then fastening the prow to the stern of the other boat, they drew him out into the water. They rowed sadly along the shore, and turning into the swift-running channel they passed the green sward of Parth Galen. The steep sides of Tol Brandir were glowing: it was now mid-afternoon. As they went south the fume of Rauros rose and shimmered before them, a haze of gold. The rush and thunder of the falls shook the windless air.

Sorrowfully they cast loose the funeral boat: there Boromir lay, restful, peaceful, gliding upon the bosom of the flowing water. The stream took him while they held their own boat back with their paddles. He floated by them, and slowly his boat departed, waning to a dark spot against the golden light; and then suddenly it vanished. Rauros roared on unchanging. The River had taken Boromir son of Denethor, and he was not seen again in Minas Tirith, standing as he used to stand upon the White Tower in the morning. But in Gondor in after-days it long was said that the elven-boat rode the falls and the foaming pool, and bore him down through Osgiliath, and past the many mouths of Anduin, out into the Great Sea at night under the stars.

For a while the three companions remained silent, gazing after him. Then Aragorn spoke. 'They will look for him from the White Tower,' he said, 'but he will not return from mountain or from sea.' Then slowly he began to sing:

Through Rohan over fen and field where the long grass grows
The West Wind comes walking, and about the walls it goes.
'What news from the West, O wandering wind, do you bring to me tonight?
Have you seen Boromir the Tall by moon or by star-light?'
'I saw him ride over seven streams, over waters wide and grey;
I saw him walk in empty lands, until he passed away
Into the shadows of the North. I saw him then no more.
The North Wind may have heard the horn of the son of Denethor.'
'O Boromir! From the high walls westward I looked afar,
But you came not from the empty lands where no men are.'

Then Legolas sang:

From the mouths of the Sea the South Wind flies, from the sandhills and the stones;
The wailing of the gulls it bears, and at the gate it moans.
'What news from the South, O sighing wind, do you bring to me at eve?
Where now is Boromir the Fair? He tarries and I grieve.'
'Ask not of me where he doth dwell—so many bones there lie
On the white shores and the dark shores under the stormy sky;
So many have passed down Anduin to find the flowing Sea.
Ask of the North Wind news of them the North Wind sends to me!'
'O Boromir! Beyond the gate the seaward road runs south,

But you came not with the wailing gulls from the grey
   sea's mouth.'

Then Aragorn sang again:

From the Gate of Kings the North Wind rides, and past
   the roaring falls;
And clear and cold about the tower its loud horn calls.
'What news from the North, O mighty wind, do you
   bring to me today?
What news of Boromir the Bold? For he is long away.'
'Beneath Amon Hen I heard his cry. There many foes he
   fought.
His cloven shield, his broken sword, they do the water
   brought.
His head so proud, his face so fair, his limbs they laid
   to rest;
And Rauros, golden Rauros-falls, bore him upon its
   breast.'
'O Boromir! The Tower of Guard shall ever northward
   gaze
To Rauros, golden Rauros-falls, until the end of days.'

So they ended. Then they turned their boat and drove
it with all the speed they could against the stream back to
Parth Galen.

'You left the East Wind to me,' said Gimli, 'but I
will say naught of it.'

'That is as it should be,' said Aragorn. 'In Minas Tirith
they endure the East Wind, but they do not ask it for
tidings. But now Boromir has taken his road, and we must
make haste to choose our own.'

He surveyed the green lawn, quickly but thoroughly,
stooping often to the earth. 'No Orcs have been on this
ground,' he said. 'Otherwise nothing can be made out
for certain. All our footprints are here, crossing and re-
crossing. I cannot tell whether any of the hobbits have come
back since the search for Frodo began.' He returned to
the bank, close to where the rill from the spring trickled

out into the River. 'There are some clear prints here,' he said. 'A hobbit waded out into the water and back; but I cannot say how long ago.'

'How then do you read this riddle?' asked Gimli.

Aragorn did not answer at once, but went back to the camping-place and looked at the baggage. 'Two packs are missing,' he said, 'and one is certainly Sam's: it was rather large and heavy. This then is the answer: Frodo has gone by boat, and his servant has gone with him. Frodo must have returned while we were all away. I met Sam going up the hill and told him to follow me; but plainly he did not do so. He guessed his master's mind and came back here before Frodo had gone. He did not find it easy to leave Sam behind!'

'But why should he leave us behind, and without a word?' said Gimli. 'That was a strange deed!'

'And a brave deed,' said Aragorn. 'Sam was right, I think. Frodo did not wish to lead any friend to death with him in Mordor. But he knew that he must go himself. Something happened after he left us that overcame his fear and doubt.'

'Maybe hunting Orcs came on him and he fled,' said Legolas.

'He fled, certainly,' said Aragorn, 'but not, I think, from Orcs.' What he thought was the cause of Frodo's sudden resolve and flight Aragorn did not say. The last words of Boromir he long kept secret.

'Well, so much at least is now clear,' said Legolas: 'Frodo is no longer on this side of the River: only he can have taken the boat. And Sam is with him; only he would have taken his pack.'

'Our choice then,' said Gimli, 'is either to take the remaining boat and follow Frodo, or else to follow the Orcs on foot. There is little hope either way. We have already lost precious hours.'

'Let me think!' said Aragorn. 'And now may I make a right choice, and change the evil fate of this unhappy day!' He stood silent for a moment. 'I will follow the Orcs,' he said at last. 'I would have guided Frodo to Mordor and gone with him to the end; but if I seek him now in the wilderness, I must abandon the captives to torment and death. My heart speaks clearly at last: the fate of the Bearer is in my hands no longer. The Company has played its part. Yet we that remain cannot forsake our companions while we have strength left. Come! We will go now. Leave all that can be spared behind! We will press on by day and dark!'

They drew up the last boat and carried it to the trees. They laid beneath it such of their goods as they did not need and could not carry away. Then they left Parth Galen. The afternoon was fading as they came back to the glade where Boromir had fallen. There they picked up the trail of the Orcs. It needed little skill to find.

'No other folk make such a trampling,' said Legolas. 'It seems their delight to slash and beat down growing things that are not even in their way.'

'But they go with a great speed for all that,' said Aragorn, 'and they do not tire. And later we may have to search for our path in hard bare lands.'

'Well, after them!' said Gimli. 'Dwarves too can go swiftly, and they do not tire sooner than Orcs. But it will be a long chase: they have a long start.'

'Yes,' said Aragorn, 'we shall all need the endurance of Dwarves. But come! With hope or without hope we will follow the trail of our enemies. And woe to them, if we prove the swifter! We will make such a chase as shall be accounted a marvel among the Three Kindreds: Elves, Dwarves, and Men. Forth the Three Hunters!'

Like a deer he sprang away. Through the trees he sped. On and on he led them, tireless and swift, now that his mind was at last made up. The woods about the lake they left behind. Long slopes they climbed, dark, hard-edged against the sky already red with sunset. Dusk came. They passed away, grey shadows in a stony land.

Chapter 2

The Riders of Rohan

Dusk deepened. Mist lay behind them among the trees below, and brooded on the pale margins of the Anduin, but the sky was clear. Stars came out. The waxing moon was riding in the West, and the shadows of the rocks were black. They had come to the feet of stony hills, and their pace was slower, for the trail was no longer easy to follow. Here the highlands of the Emyn Muil ran from North to South in two long tumbled ridges. The western side of each ridge was steep and difficult, but the eastward slopes were gentler, furrowed with many gullies and narrow ravines. All night the three companions scrambled in this bony land, climbing to the crest of the first and tallest ridge, and down again into the darkness of a deep winding valley on the other side.

There in the still cool hour before dawn they rested for a brief space. The moon had long gone down before them, the stars glittered above them; the first light of day had not yet come over the dark hills behind. For the moment Aragorn was at a loss: the orc-trail had descended into the valley, but there it had vanished.

'Which way would they turn, do you think?' said Legolas. 'Northward to take a straighter road to Isengard, or Fangorn, if that is their aim as you guess? Or southward to strike the Entwash?'

'They will not make for the river, whatever mark they aim at,' said Aragorn. 'And unless there is much amiss in Rohan and the power of Saruman is greatly increased, they will take the shortest way that they can find over the fields of the Rohirrim. Let us search northwards!'

The dale ran like a stony trough between the ridged hills, and a trickling stream flowed among the boulders at the bottom. A cliff frowned upon their right; to their left

rose grey slopes, dim and shadowy in the late night. They
went on for a mile or more northwards. Aragorn was
searching, bent towards the ground, among the folds and
gullies leading up into the western ridge. Legolas was some
way ahead. Suddenly the Elf gave a cry and the others
came running towards him.

'We have already overtaken some of those that we are
hunting,' he said. 'Look!' He pointed, and they saw that
what they had at first taken to be boulders lying at the foot
of the slope were huddled bodies. Five dead Orcs lay there.
They had been hewn with many cruel strokes, and two
had been beheaded. The ground was wet with their dark
blood.

'Here is another riddle!' said Gimli. 'But it needs the
light of day, and for that we cannot wait.'

'Yet however you read it, it seems not unhopeful,'
said Legolas. 'Enemies of the Orcs are likely to be our
friends. Do any folk dwell in these hills?'

'No,' said Aragorn. 'The Rohirrim seldom come here,
and it is far from Minas Tirith. It might be that some
company of Men were hunting here for reasons that we do
not know. Yet I think not.'

'What do you think?' said Gimli.

'I think that the enemy brought his own enemy with
him,' answered Aragorn. 'These are Northern Orcs from
far away. Among the slain are none of the great Orcs with
the strange badges. There was a quarrel, I guess: it is no
uncommon thing with these foul folk. Maybe there was
some dispute about the road.'

'Or about the captives,' said Gimli. 'Let us hope that
they, too, did not meet their end here.'

Aragorn searched the ground in a wide circle, but no
other traces of the fight could be found. They went on.
Already the eastward sky was turning pale; the stars were
fading, and a grey light was slowly growing. A little
further north they came to a fold in which a tiny stream,
falling and winding, had cut a stony path down into the

valley. In it some bushes grew, and there were patches of grass upon its sides.

'At last!' said Aragorn. 'Here are the tracks that we seek! Up this water-channel: this is the way that the Orcs went after their debate.'

Swiftly now the pursuers turned and followed the new path. As if fresh from a night's rest they sprang from stone to stone. At last they reached the crest of the grey hill, and a sudden breeze blew in their hair and stirred their cloaks: the chill wind of dawn.

Turning back they saw across the River the far hills kindled. Day leaped into the sky. The red rim of the sun rose over the shoulders of the dark land. Before them in the West the world lay still, formless and grey; but even as they looked, the shadows of night melted, the colours of the waking earth returned: green flowed over the wide meads of Rohan; the white mists shimmered in the water-vales; and far off to the left, thirty leagues or more, blue and purple stood the White Mountains, rising into peaks of jet, tipped with glimmering snows, flushed with the rose of morning.

'Gondor! Gondor!' cried Aragorn. 'Would that I looked on you again in happier hour! Not yet does my road lie southward to your bright streams.

> Gondor! Gondor, between the Mountains and the Sea!
> West Wind blew there; the light upon the Silver Tree
> Fell like bright rain in gardens of the Kings of old.
> O proud walls! White towers! O wingéd crown and
>   throne of gold!
> O Gondor, Gondor! Shall Men behold the Silver Tree,
> Or West Wind blow again between the Mountains and
>   the Sea?

Now let us go!' he said, drawing his eyes away from the South, and looking out west and north to the way that he must tread.

The ridge upon which the companions stood went down

steeply before their feet. Below it twenty fathoms or
more, there was a wide and rugged shelf which ended
suddenly in the brink of a sheer cliff: the East Wall of Rohan. So ended the Emyn Muil, and the green plains of the
Rohirrim stretched away before them to the edge of sight.

'Look!' cried Legolas, pointing up into the pale sky
above them. 'There is the eagle again! He is very high. He
seems to be flying now away, from this land back to the
North. He is going with great speed. Look!'

'No, not even my eyes can see him, my good Legolas,'
said Aragorn. 'He must be far aloft indeed. I wonder what
is his errand, if he is the same bird that I have seen before. But look! I can see something nearer at hand and
more urgent; there is something moving over the plain!'

'Many things,' said Legolas. 'It is a great company
on foot; but I cannot say more, nor see what kind of folk
they may be. They are many leagues away: twelve, I
guess; but the flatness of the plain is hard to measure.'

'I think, nonetheless, that we no longer need any trail
to tell us which way to go,' said Gimli. 'Let us find a path
down to the fields as quick as may be.'

'I doubt if you will find a path quicker than the one that
the Orcs chose,' said Aragorn.

They followed their enemies now by the clear light of
day. It seemed that the Orcs had pressed on with all possible speed. Every now and again the pursuers found
things that had been dropped or cast away: food-bags, the
rings and crusts of hard grey bread, a torn black cloak,
a heavy iron-nailed shoe broken on the stones. The trail
led them north along the top of the escarpment, and at
length they came to a deep cleft carved in the rock by a
stream that splashed noisily down. In the narrow ravine
a rough path descended like a steep stair into the plain.

At the bottom they came with a strange suddenness on
the grass of Rohan. It swelled like a green sea up to the
very foot of the Emyn Muil. The falling stream vanished
into a deep growth of cresses and water-plants, and they
could hear it tinkling away in green tunnels, down long
gentle slopes towards the fens of Entwash Vale far away.

They seemed to have left winter clinging to the hills behind. Here the air was softer and warmer, and faintly scented, as if spring was already stirring and the sap was flowing again in herb and leaf. Legolas took a deep breath, like one that drinks a great draught after long thirst in barren places.

'Ah! the green smell!' he said. 'It is better than much sleep. Let us run!'

'Light feet may run swiftly here,' said Aragorn. 'More swiftly, maybe, than iron-shod Orcs. Now we have a chance to lessen their lead!'

They went in single file, running like hounds on a strong scent, and an eager light was in their eyes. Nearly due west the broad swath of the marching Orcs tramped its ugly slot; the sweet grass of Rohan had been bruised and blackened as they passed. Presently Aragorn gave a cry and turned aside.

'Stay!' he shouted. 'Do not follow me yet!' He ran quickly to the right, away from the main trail; for he had seen footprints that went that way, branching off from the others, the marks of small unshod feet. These, however, did not go far before they were crossed by orc-prints, also coming out from the main trail behind and in front, and then they curved sharply back again and were lost in the trampling. At the furthest point Aragorn stooped and picked up something from the grass; then he ran back.

'Yes,' he said, 'they are quite plain: a hobbit's footprints. Pippin's, I think. He is smaller than the other. And look at this!' He held up a thing that glittered in the sunlight. It looked like the new-opened leaf of a beech-tree, fair and strange in that treeless plain.

'The brooch of an elven-cloak!' cried Legolas and Gimli together.

'Not idly do the leaves of Lórien fall,' said Aragorn. 'This did not drop by chance: it was cast away as a token to any that might follow. I think Pippin ran away from the trail for that purpose.'

'Then he at least was alive,' said Gimli. 'And he had the

use of his wits, and of his legs too. That is heartening. We do not pursue in vain.'

'Let us hope that he did not pay too dearly for his boldness,' said Legolas. 'Come! Let us go on! The thought of those merry young folk driven like cattle burns my heart.'

The sun climbed to the noon and then rode slowly down the sky. Light clouds came up out of the sea in the distant South and were blown away upon the breeze. The sun sank. Shadows rose behind and reached out long arms from the East. Still the hunters held on. One day now had passed since Boromir fell, and the Orcs were yet far ahead. No longer could any sight of them be seen in the level plains.

As nightshade was closing about them Aragorn halted. Only twice in the day's march had they rested for a brief while, and twelve leagues now lay between them and the eastern wall where they had stood at dawn.

'We have come at last to a hard choice,' he said. 'Shall we rest by night, or shall we go on while our will and strength hold?'

'Unless our enemies rest also, they will leave us far behind, if we stay to sleep,' said Legolas.

'Surely even Orcs must pause on the march?' said Gimli.

'Seldom will Orcs journey in the open under the sun, yet these have done so,' said Legolas. 'Certainly they will not rest by night.'

'But if we walk by night, we cannot follow their trail,' said Gimli.

'The trail is straight, and turns neither right nor left, as far as my eyes can see,' said Legolas.

'Maybe, I could lead you at guess in the darkness and hold to the line,' said Aragorn; 'but if we strayed, or they turned aside, then when light came there might be long delay before the trail was found again.'

'And there is this also,' said Gimli: 'only by day can we see if any tracks lead away. If a prisoner should escape, or if one should be carried off, eastward, say, to the Great River, towards Mordor, we might pass the signs and never know it.'

'That is true,' said Aragorn. 'But if I read the signs back yonder rightly, the Orcs of the White Hand prevailed, and the whole company is now bound for Isengard. Their present course bears me out.'

'Yet it would be rash to be sure of their counsels,' said Gimli. 'And what of escape? In the dark we should have passed the signs that led you to the brooch.'

'The Orcs will be doubly on their guard since then, and the prisoners even wearier,' said Legolas. 'There will be no escape again, if we do not contrive it. How that is to be done cannot be guessed, but first we must overtake them.'

'And yet even I, Dwarf of many journeys, and not the least hardy of my folk, cannot run all the way to Isengard without any pause,' said Gimli. 'My heart burns me too, and I would have started sooner; but now I must rest a little to run the better. And if we rest, then the blind night is the time to do so.'

'I said that it was a hard choice,' said Aragorn. 'How shall we end this debate?'

'You are our guide,' said Gimli, 'and you are skilled in the chase. You shall choose.'

'My heart bids me go on,' said Legolas. 'But we must hold together. I will follow your counsel.'

'You give the choice to an ill chooser,' said Aragorn. 'Since we passed through the Argonath my choices have gone amiss.' He fell silent, gazing north and west into the gathering night for a long while.

'We will not walk in the dark,' he said at length. 'The peril of missing the trail or signs of other coming and going seems to me the greater. If the Moon gave enough light, we would use it, but alas! he sets early and is yet young and pale.'

'And tonight he is shrouded anyway,' Gimli murmured. 'Would that the Lady had given us a light, such a gift as she gave to Frodo!'

'It will be more needed where it is bestowed,' said Aragorn. 'With him lies the true Quest. Ours is but a small matter in the great deeds of this time. A vain pursuit from its beginning, maybe, which no choice of mine can mar or mend. Well, I have chosen. So let us use the time as best we may!'

He cast himself on the ground and fell at once into sleep, for he had not slept since their night under the shadow of Tol Brandir. Before dawn was in the sky he woke and rose. Gimli was still deep in slumber, but Legolas was standing, gazing northwards into the darkness, thoughtful and silent as a young tree in a windless night.

'They are far far away,' he said sadly, turning to Aragorn. 'I know in my heart that they have not rested this night. Only an eagle could overtake them now.'

'Nonetheless we will still follow as we may,' said Aragorn. Stooping he roused the Dwarf. 'Come! We must go,' he said. 'The scent is growing cold.'

'But it is still dark,' said Gimli. 'Even Legolas on a hill-top could not see them till the Sun is up.'

'I fear they have passed beyond my sight from hill or plain, under moon or sun,' said Legolas.

'Where sight fails the earth may bring us rumour,' said Aragorn. 'The land must groan under their hated feet.' He stretched himself upon the ground with his ear pressed against the turf. He lay there motionless, for so long a time that Gimli wondered if he had swooned or fallen asleep again. Dawn came glimmering, and slowly a grey light grew about them. At last he rose, and now his friends could see his face: it was pale and drawn, and his look was troubled.

'The rumour of the earth is dim and confused,' he said. 'Nothing walks upon it for many miles about us. Faint and far are the feet of our enemies. But loud are the hoofs of the horses. It comes to my mind that I heard them, even as I lay on the ground in sleep, and they troubled my dreams: horses galloping, passing in the West. But now they are drawing ever further from us, riding northward. I wonder what is happening in this land!'

'Let us go!' said Legolas.

So the third day of their pursuit began. During all its long hours of cloud and fitful sun they hardly paused, now striding, now running, as if no weariness could quench the fire that burned them. They seldom spoke. Over the wide solitude they passed and their elven-cloaks faded against the background of the grey-green fields; even in the cool sunlight of mid-day few but elvish eyes would have marked them, until they were close at hand. Often in their hearts they thanked the Lady of Lórien for the gift of *lembas,* for they could eat of it and find new strength even as they ran.

All day the track of their enemies led straight on, going north-west without a break or turn. As once again the day wore to its end they came to long treeless slopes, where the land rose, swelling up towards a line of low humpbacked downs ahead. The orc-trail grew fainter as it bent north towards them, for the ground became harder and the grass shorter. Far away to the left the river Entwash wound, a silver thread in a green floor. No moving thing could be seen. Often Aragorn wondered that they saw no sign of beast or man. The dwellings of the Rohirrim were for the most part many leagues away to the South, under the wooded eaves of the White Mountains, now hidden in mist and cloud; yet the Horse-lords had formerly kept many herds and studs in the Eastemnet, this easterly region of their realm, and there the herdsmen had wandered much, living in camp and tent, even in winter-time. But now all the land was empty, and there was a silence that did not seem to be the quiet of peace.

At dusk they halted again. Now twice twelve leagues they had passed over the plains of Rohan and the wall of the Emyn Muil was lost in the shadows of the East. The young moon was glimmering in a misty sky, but it gave small light, and the stars were veiled.

'Now do I most grudge a time of rest or any halt in our chase,' said Legolas. 'The Orcs have run before us, as if the very whips of Sauron were behind them. I fear they have already reached the forest and the dark hills, and even now are passing into the shadows of the trees.'

Gimli ground his teeth. 'This is a bitter end to our hope and to all our toil!' he said.

'To hope, maybe, but not to toil,' said Aragorn. 'We shall not turn back here. Yet I am weary.' He gazed back along the way that they had come towards the night gathering in the East. 'There is something strange at work in this land. I distrust the silence. I distrust even the pale Moon. The stars are faint; and I am weary as I have seldom been before, weary as no Ranger should be with a clear trail to follow. There is some will that lends speed to our foes and sets an unseen barrier before us: a weariness that is in the heart more than in the limb.'

'Truly!' said Legolas. 'That I have known since first we came down from the Emyn Muil. For the will is not behind us but before us.' He pointed away over the land of Rohan into the darkling West under the sickle moon.

'Saruman!' muttered Aragorn. 'But he shall not turn us back! Halt we must once more; for, see! even the Moon is falling into gathering cloud. But north lies our road between down and fen when day returns.'

As before Legolas was first afoot, if indeed he had ever slept. 'Awake! Awake!' he cried. 'It is a red dawn. Strange things await us by the eaves of the forest. Good or evil, I do not know; but we are called. Awake!'

The others sprang up, and almost at once they set off again. Slowly the downs drew near. It was still an hour before noon when they reached them: green slopes rising to bare ridges that ran in a line straight towards the North. At their feet the ground was dry and the turf short, but a long strip of sunken land, some ten miles wide, lay between them and the river wandering deep in dim thickets of reed and rush. Just to the West of the southernmost slope there was a great ring, where the turf had been torn and beaten by many trampling feet. From it the orc-trail ran out again, turning north along the dry skirts of the hills. Aragorn halted and examined the tracks closely.

'They rested here a while,' he said, 'but even the outward trail is already old. I fear that your heart spoke truly, Legolas: it is thrice twelve hours, I guess, since the Orcs stood where we now stand. If they held to their pace, then at sundown yesterday they would reach the borders of Fangorn.'

'I can see nothing away north or west but grass dwindling into mist,' said Gimli. 'Could we see the forest, if we climbed the hills?'

'It is still far away,' said Aragorn. 'If I remember rightly, these downs run eight leagues or more to the north, and then north-west to the issuing of the Entwash there lies still a wide land, another fifteen leagues it may be.'

'Well, let us go on,' said Gimli. 'My legs must forget the miles. They would be more willing, if my heart were less heavy.'

The sun was sinking when at last they drew near to the end of the line of downs. For many hours they had marched without rest. They were going slowly now, and Gimli's back was bent. Stone-hard are the Dwarves in labour or journey, but this endless chase began to tell on him, as all hope failed in his heart. Aragorn walked behind him, grim and silent, stooping now and again to scan some print or mark upon the ground. Only Legolas still stepped as lightly as ever, his feet hardly seeming to press the grass, leaving no footprints as he passed; but in the waybread of the Elves he found all the sustenance that he needed, and he could sleep, if sleep it could be called by Men, resting his mind in the strange paths of elvish dreams, even as he walked open-eyed in the light of this world.

'Let us go up on to this green hill!' he said. Wearily they followed him, climbing the long slope, until they came out upon the top. It was a round hill smooth and bare, standing by itself, the most northerly of the downs. The sun sank and the shadows of evening fell like a curtain. They were alone in a grey formless world without mark or measure. Only far away north-west there was a deeper darkness against the dying light: the Mountains of Mist and the forest at their feet.

'Nothing can we see to guide us here,' said Gimli. 'Well, now we must halt again and wear the night away. It is growing cold!'

'The wind is north from the snows,' said Aragorn.

'And ere morning it will be in the East,' said Legolas. 'But rest, if you must. Yet do not cast all hope away. Tomorrow is unknown. Rede oft is found at the rising of the Sun.'

'Three suns already have risen on our chase and brought no counsel,' said Gimli.

The night grew ever colder. Aragorn and Gimli slept fitfully, and whenever they awoke they saw Legolas standing beside them, or walking to and fro, singing softly to himself in his own tongue, and as he sang the white stars opened in the hard black vault above. So the night passed. Together they watched the dawn grow slowly in the sky, now bare and cloudless, until at last the sunrise came. It was pale and clear. The wind was in the East and all the mists had rolled away; wide lands lay bleak about them in the bitter light.

Ahead and eastward they saw the windy uplands of the Wold of Rohan that they had already glimpsed many days ago from the Great River. North-westward stalked the dark forest of Fangorn; still ten leagues away stood its shadowy eaves, and its further slopes faded into the distant blue. Beyond there glimmered far away, as if floating on a grey cloud, the white head of tall Methedras, the last peak of the Misty Mountains. Out of the forest the Entwash flowed to meet them, its stream now swift and narrow, and its banks deep-cloven. The orc-trail turned from the downs towards it.

Following with his keen eyes the trail to the river, and then the river back towards the forest, Aragorn saw a shadow on the distant green, a dark swift-moving blur. He cast himself upon the ground and listened again intently. But Legolas stood beside him, shading his bright elven-eyes with his long slender hand, and he saw not a shadow, nor a blur, but the small figures of horsemen, many horsemen, and the glint of morning on the tips of their spears was like the twinkle of minute stars beyond the edge of mortal sight. Far behind them a dark smoke rose in thin curling threads.

There was a silence in the empty fields, and Gimli could hear the air moving in the grass.

'Riders!' cried Aragorn, springing to his feet. 'Many riders on swift steeds are coming towards us!'

'Yes,' said Legolas, 'there are one hundred and five. Yellow is their hair, and bright are their spears. Their leader is very tall.'

Aragorn smiled. 'Keen are the eyes of the Elves,' he said.

'Nay! The riders are little more than five leagues distant,' said Legolas.

'Five leagues or one,' said Gimli, 'we cannot escape them in this bare land. Shall we wait for them here or go on our way?'

'We will wait,' said Aragorn. 'I am weary, and our hunt has failed. Or at least others were before us; for these horsemen are riding back down the orc-trail. We may get news from them.'

'Or spears,' said Gimli.

'There are three empty saddles, but I see no hobbits,' said Legolas.

'I did not say that we should hear good news,' said Aragorn. 'But evil or good we will await it here.'

The three companions now left the hill-top, where they might be an easy mark against the pale sky, and they walked slowly down the northward slope. A little above the hill's foot they halted, and wrapping their cloaks about them, they sat huddled together upon the faded grass. The time passed slowly and heavily. The wind was thin and searching. Gimli was uneasy.

'What do you know of these horsemen, Aragorn?' he said. 'Do we sit here waiting for sudden death?'

'I have been among them,' answered Aragorn. 'They

are proud and wilful, but they are true-hearted, generous in thought and deed; bold but not cruel; wise but un-learned, writing no books but singing many songs, after the manner of the children of Men before the Dark Years. But I do not know what has happened here of late, nor in what mind the Rohirrim may now be between the traitor Saruman and the threat of Sauron. They have long been the friends of the people of Gondor, though they are not akin to them. It was in forgotten years long ago that Eorl the Young brought them out of the North, and their kinship is rather with the Bardings of Dale, and with the Beornings of the Wood, among whom may still be seen many men tall and fair, as are the Riders of Rohan. At least they will not love the Orcs.'

'But Gandalf spoke of a rumour that they pay tribute to Mordor,' said Gimli.

'I believe it no more than did Boromir,' answered Ara-gorn.

'You will soon learn the truth,' said Legolas. 'Already they approach.'

At length even Gimli could hear the distant beat of galloping hoofs. The horsemen, following the trail, had turned from the river, and were drawing near the downs. They were riding like the wind.

Now the cries of clear strong voices came ringing over the fields. Suddenly they swept up with a noise like thun-der, and the foremost horseman swerved, passing by the foot of the hill, and leading the host back southward along the western skirts of the downs. After him they rode: a long line of mail-clad men, swift, shining, fell and fair to look upon.

Their horses were of great stature, strong and clean-limbed; their grey coats glistened, their long tails flowed in the wind, their manes were braided on their proud necks. The Men that rode them matched them well: tall and long-limbed; their hair, flaxen-pale, flowed under their light helms, and streamed in long braids behind them; their faces were stern and keen. In their hands were tall spears of ash, painted shields were slung at their backs, long swords were at their belts, their burnished shirts of mail hung down upon their knees.

In pairs they galloped by, and though every now and then one rose in his stirrups and gazed ahead and to either side, they appeared not to perceive the three strangers sitting silently and watching them. The host had almost passed when suddenly Aragorn stood up, and called in a loud voice:

'What news from the North, Riders of Rohan?'

With astonishing speed and skill they checked their steeds, wheeled, and came charging round. Soon the three companions found themselves in a ring of horsemen moving in a running circle, up the hill-slope behind them and down, round and round them, and drawing ever inwards. Aragorn stood silent, and the other two sat without moving, wondering what way things would turn.

Without a word or cry, suddenly, the Riders halted. A thicket of spears was pointed towards the strangers; and some of the horsemen had bows in hand, and their arrows were already fitted to the string. Then one rode forward, a tall man, taller than all the rest; from his helm as a crest a white horsetail flowed. He advanced until the point of his spear was within a foot of Aragorn's breast. Aragorn did not stir.

'Who are you, and what are you doing in this land?' said the Rider, using the Common Speech of the West, in manner and tone like to the speech of Boromir, Man of Gondor.

'I am called Strider,' answered Aragorn. 'I came out of the North. I am hunting Orcs.'

The Rider leaped from his horse. Giving his spear to another who rode up and dismounted at his side, he drew his sword and stood face to face with Aragorn, surveying him keenly, and not without wonder. At length he spoke again.

'At first I thought that you yourselves were Orcs,' he said; 'but now I see that it is not so. Indeed you know little of Orcs, if you go hunting them in this fashion. They were swift and well-armed, and they were many. You would have changed from hunters to prey, if ever you had overtaken them. But there is something strange about you, Strider.' He bent his clear bright eyes again upon the Ranger. 'That is no name for a Man that you give. And strange too is your raiment. Have you sprung out of the grass? How did you escape our sight? Are you elvish folk?'

'No,' said Aragorn. 'One only of us is an Elf, Legolas from the Woodland Realm in distant Mirkwood. But we have passed through Lothlórien, and the gifts and favour of the Lady go with us.'

The Rider looked at them with renewed wonder, but his eyes hardened. 'Then there is a Lady in the Golden Wood, as old tales tell!' he said. 'Few escape her nets, they say. These are strange days! But if you have her favour, then you also are net-weavers and sorcerers, maybe.' He turned a cold glance suddenly upon Legolas and Gimli. 'Why do you not speak, silent ones?' he demanded.

Gimli rose and planted his feet firmly apart: his hand gripped the handle of his axe, and his dark eyes flashed. 'Give me your name, horse-master, and I will give you mine, and more besides,' he said.

'As for that,' said the Rider, staring down at the Dwarf, 'the stranger should declare himself first. Yet I am named Éomer son of Éomund, and am called the Third Marshal of Riddermark.'

'Then Éomer son of Éomund, Third Marshal of Riddermark, let Gimli the Dwarf Glóin's son warn you against foolish words. You speak evil of that which is fair beyond the reach of your thought, and only little wit can excuse you.'

Éomer's eyes blazed, and the Men of Rohan murmured angrily, and closed in, advancing their spears. 'I would cut off your head, beard and all, Master Dwarf, it if stood but a little higher from the ground,' said Éomer.

'He stands not alone,' said Legolas, bending his bow and fitting an arrow with hands that moved quicker than sight. 'You would die before your stroke fell.'

Éomer raised his sword, and things might have gone ill, but Aragorn sprang between them, and raised his hand. 'Your pardon, Éomer!' he cried. 'When you know more you will understand why you have angered my companions. We intend no evil to Rohan, nor to any of its folk, neither to man nor to horse. Will you not hear our tale before you strike?'

'I will,' said Éomer lowering his blade. 'But wanderers in the Riddermark would be wise to be less haughty in these days of doubt. First tell me your right name.'

'First tell me whom you serve,' said Aragorn. 'Are you friend or foe of Sauron, the Dark Lord of Mordor?'

'I serve only the Lord of the Mark, Théoden King son of Thengel,' answered Éomer. 'We do not serve the Power of the Black Land far away, but neither are we yet at open war with him; and if you are fleeing from him, then you had best leave this land. There is trouble now on all our borders, and we are threatened; but we desire only to be free, and to live as we have lived, keeping our own, and serving no foreign lord, good or evil. We welcomed guests kindly in the better days, but in these times the unbidden stranger finds us swift and hard. Come! Who are you? Whom do *you* serve? At whose command do you hunt Orcs in our land?'

'I serve no man,' said Aragorn; 'but the servants of Sauron I pursue into whatever land they may go. There are few among mortal Men who know more of Orcs; and I do not hunt them in this fashion out of choice. The Orcs whom we pursued took captive two of my friends. In such need a man that has no horse will go on foot, and he will not ask for leave to follow the trail. Nor will he count the heads of the enemy save with a sword. I am not weaponless.'

Aragorn threw back his cloak. The elven-sheath glittered as he grasped it, and the bright blade of Andúril shone like a sudden flame as he swept it out. 'Elendil!' he cried. 'I am Aragorn son of Arathorn, and am called Elessar, the Elfstone, Dúnadan, the heir of Isildur Elendil's son of Gondor. Here is the Sword that was Broken and is forged again! Will you aid me or thwart me? Choose swiftly!'

Gimli and Legolas looked at their companion in amazement, for they had not seen him in this mood before. He seemed to have grown in stature while Éomer had shrunk; and in his living face they caught a brief vision of the power and majesty of the kings of stone. For a moment it seemed to the eyes of Legolas that a white flame flickered on the brows of Aragorn like a shining crown.

Éomer stepped back and a look of awe was in his face. He cast down his proud eyes. 'These are indeed strange days,' he muttered. 'Dreams and legends spring to life out of the grass.

'Tell me, lord,' he said, 'what brings you here? And what was the meaning of the dark words? Long has Boromir son of Denethor been gone seeking an answer, and the horse that we lent him came back riderless. What doom do you bring out of the North?'

'The doom of choice,' said Aragorn. 'You may say this to Théoden son of Thengel: open war lies before him, with Sauron or against him. None may live now as they have lived, and few shall keep what they call their own. But of these great matters we will speak later. If chance allows, I will come myself to the king. Now I am in great need, and I ask for help, or at least for tidings. You heard that we are pursuing an orc-host that carried off our friends. What can you tell us?'

'That you need not pursue them further,' said Éomer. 'The Orcs are destroyed.'

'And our friends?'

'We found none but Orcs.'

'But that is strange indeed,' said Aragorn. 'Did you search the slain? Were there no bodies other than those of orc-kind? They would be small, only children to your eyes, unshod but clad in grey.'

'There were no dwarves nor children,' said Éomer. 'We counted all the slain and despoiled them, and then we piled the carcasses and burned them, as is our custom. The ashes are smoking still.'

'We do not speak of dwarves or children,' said Gimli. 'Our friends were hobbits.'

'Hobbits?' said Éomer. 'And what may they be? It is a strange name.'

'A strange name for a strange folk,' said Gimli. 'But these were very dear to us. It seems that you have heard in Rohan of the words that troubled Minas Tirith. They spoke of the Halfling. These hobbits are Halflings.'

'Halflings!' laughed the rider that stood beside Éomer. 'Halflings! But they are only a little people in old songs and children's tales out of the North. Do we walk in legends or on the green earth in the daylight?'

'A man may do both,' said Aragorn. 'For not we but those who come after will make the legends of our time. The green earth, say you? That is a mighty matter of legend, though you tread it under the light of day!'

'Time is pressing,' said the rider, not heeding Aragorn. 'We must hasten south, lord. Let us leave these wild-folk to their fancies. Or let us bind them and take them to the king.'

'Peace, Éothain!' said Éomer in his own tongue. 'Leave me a while. Tell the *éored* to assemble on the path, and make ready to ride to the Entwade.'

Muttering Éothain retired, and spoke to the others. Soon they drew off and left Éomer alone with the three companions.

'All that you say is strange, Aragorn,' he said. 'Yet you speak the truth, that is plain: the Men of the Mark do not lie, and therefore they are not easily deceived. But you have not told all. Will you not now speak more fully of your errand, so that I may judge what to do?'

'I set out from Imladris, as it is named in the rhyme, many weeks ago,' answered Aragorn. 'With me went Boromir of Minas Tirith. My errand was to go to that city with the son of Denethor, to aid his folk in their war against Sauron. But the Company that I journeyed with had other business. Of that I cannot speak now. Gandalf the Grey was our leader.'

'Gandalf!' Éomer exclaimed. 'Gandalf Grayhame is known in the Mark; but his name, I warn you, is no longer a password to the king's favour. He has been a guest in the land many times in the memory of men, coming as he will, after a season, or after many years. He is ever the herald of strange events: a bringer of evil, some now say.

'Indeed since his last coming in the summer all things have gone amiss. At that time our trouble with Saruman began. Until then we counted Saruman our friend, but Gandalf came then and warned us that sudden war was preparing in Isengard. He said that he himself had been a prisoner in Orthanc and had hardly escaped, and he begged for help. But Théoden would not listen to him, and he went away. Speak not the name of Gandalf loudly in Théoden's ears! He is wroth. For Gandalf took the horse that is called Shadowfax, the most precious of all the king's steeds, chief of the *Mearas,* which only the Lord of the Mark may ride. For the sire of their race was the great horse of Eorl that knew the speech of Men. Seven nights ago Shadowfax returned; but the king's anger is not less, for now the horse is wild and will let no man handle him.'

'Then Shadowfax has found his way alone from the far North,' said Aragorn; 'for it was there that he and Gandalf parted. But alas! Gandalf will ride no longer. He fell into darkness in the Mines of Moria and comes not again.'

'That is heavy tidings,' said Éomer. 'At least to me, and to many; though not to all, as you may find, if you come to the king.'

'It is tidings more grievous than any in this land can understand, though it may touch them sorely ere the year is much older,' said Aragorn. 'But when the great fall, the less must lead. My part it has been to guide our Company on the long road from Moria. Through Lórien we came— of which it were well that you should learn the truth ere you speak of it again—and thence down the leagues of the Great River to the falls of Rauros. There Boromir was slain by the same Orcs whom you destroyed.'

'Your news is all of woe!' cried Éomer in dismay. 'Great harm is this death to Minas Tirith, and to us all. That was a worthy man! All spoke his praise. He came seldom to the Mark, for he was ever in the wars on the East-borders; but I have seen him. More like to the swift sons of Eorl than to the grave Men of Gondor he seemed to me, and likely to prove a great captain of his people when his time came. But we have had no word of this grief out of Gondor. When did he fall?'

'It is now the fourth day since he was slain,' answered Aragorn; 'and since the evening of that day we have journeyed from the shadow of Tol Brandir.'

'On foot?' cried Éomer.

'Yes, even as you see us.'

Wide wonder came into Éomer's eyes. 'Strider is too poor a name, son of Arathorn,' he said. 'Wingfoot I name you. This deed of the three friends should be sung in many a hall. Forty leagues and five you have measured ere the fourth day is ended! Hardy is the race of Elendil!

'But now, lord, what would you have me do! I must return in haste to Théoden. I spoke warily before my men. It is true that we are not yet at open war with the Black Land, and there are some, close to the king's ear, that speak craven counsels; but war is coming. We shall not forsake our old alliance with Gondor, and while they fight we shall aid them: so say I and all who hold with me. The East-mark is my charge, the ward of the Third Marshal, and I have removed all our herds and herdfolk, withdrawing them beyond Entwash, and leaving none here but guards and swift scouts.'

'Then you do not pay tribute to Sauron?' said Gimli.

'We do not and we never have,' said Éomer with a flash of his eyes; 'though it comes to my ears that that lie has been told. Some years ago the Lord of the Black Land wished to purchase horses of us at great price, but we refused him, for he puts beasts to evil use. Then he sent plundering Orcs, and they carry off what they can, choosing always the black horses: few of these are now left. For that reason our feud with the Orcs is bitter.

'But at this time our chief concern is with Saruman. He has claimed lordship over all this land, and there has been war between us for many months. He has taken Orcs into his service, and Wolf-riders, and evil Men, and he has closed the Gap against us, so that we are likely to be beset both east and west.

'It is ill dealing with such a foe: he is a wizard both cunning and dwimmer-crafty, having many guises. He walks here and there, they say, as an old man hooded and cloaked, very like to Gandalf, as many now recall. His spies slip through every net, and his birds of ill omen are abroad in the sky. I do not know how it will all end, and my heart misgives me; for it seems to me that his friends do not all dwell in Isengard. But if you come to the king's house, you shall see for yourself. Will you not come? Do I hope in vain that you have been sent to me for a help in doubt and need?'

'I will come when I may,' said Aragorn.

'Come now!' said Éomer. 'The Heir of Elendil would be a strength indeed to the Sons of Eorl in this evil tide. There is battle even now upon the Westemnet, and I fear that it may go ill for us.

'Indeed in this riding north I went without the king's leave, for in my absence his house is left with little guard. But scouts warned me of the orc-host coming down out of the East Wall three nights ago, and among them they reported that some bore the white badges of Saruman. So suspecting what I most fear, a league between Orthanc and the Dark Tower, I led forth my *éored,* men of my own household; and we overtook the Orcs at nightfall two days ago, near to the borders of the Entwood. There we surrounded them, and gave battle yesterday at dawn. Fifteen of my men I lost, and twelve horses alas! For the Orcs were greater in number than we counted on. Others joined them, coming out of the East across the Great River: their trail is plain to see a little north of this spot. And others, too, came out of the forest. Great Orcs, who also bore the White Hand of Isengard: that kind is stronger and more fell than all others.

'Nonetheless we put an end to them. But we have been too long away. We are needed south and west. Will you not come? There are spare horses as you see. There is work for the Sword to do. Yes, and we could find a use for Gimli's axe and the bow of Legolas, if they will pardon my rash words concerning the Lady of the Wood. I spoke only as do all men in my land, and I would gladly learn better.'

'I thank you for your fair words,' said Aragorn, 'and my heart desires to come with you; but I cannot desert my friends while hope remains.'

'Hope does not remain,' said Éomer. 'You will not find your friends on the North-borders.'

'Yet my friends are not behind. We found a clear token not far from the East Wall that one at least of them was still alive there. But between the wall and the downs we have found no other trace of them, and no trail has turned aside, this way or that, unless my skill has wholly left me.'

'Then what do you think has become of them?'

'I do not know. They may have been slain and burned among the Orcs; but that you will say cannot be, and I do not fear it. I can only think that they were carried off into the forest before the battle, even before you encircled your foes, maybe. Can you swear that none escaped your net in such a way?'

'I would swear that no Orc escaped after we sighted them,' said Éomer. 'We reached the forest-eaves before them, and if after that any living thing broke through our ring, then it was no Orc and had some elvish power.'

'Our friends were attired even as we are,' said Aragorn; 'and you passed us by under the full light of day.'

'I had forgotten that,' said Éomer. 'It is hard to be sure of anything among so many marvels. The world is all grown strange. Elf and Dwarf in company walk in our daily fields; and folk speak with the Lady of the Wood and yet live; and the Sword comes back to war that was broken in the long ages ere the fathers of our fathers rode into the Mark! How shall a man judge what to do in such times?'

'As he ever has judged,' said Aragorn. 'Good and ill have not changed since yesteryear; nor are they one thing among Elves and Dwarves and another among Men. It is a man's part to discern them, as much in the Golden Wood as in his own house.'

'True indeed,' said Éomer. 'But I do not doubt you, nor the deed which my heart would do. Yet I am not free to do all as I would. It is against our law to let strangers wander at will in our land, until the king himself shall give them leave, and more strict is the command in these days of peril. I have begged you to come back willingly with me, and you will not. Loth am I to begin a battle of one hundred against three.'

'I do not think your law was made for such a chance,' said Aragorn. 'Nor indeed am I a stranger; for I have been in this land before, more than once, and ridden with the host of the Rohirrim, though under other name and in other guise. You I have not seen before, for you are young, but I have spoken with Éomund your father, and with Théoden son of Thengel. Never in former days would any high lord of this land have constrained a man to abandon such a quest as mine. My duty at least is clear, to go on. Come now, son of Éomund, the choice must be made at last. Aid us, or at the worst let us go free. Or seek to carry out your law. If you do so there will be fewer to return to your war or to your king.'

Éomer was silent for a moment, then he spoke. 'We both have need of haste,' he said. 'My company chafes to be away, and every hour lessens your hope. This is my choice. You may go; and what is more, I will lend you horses. This only I ask: when your quest is achieved, or is proved vain, return with the horses over the Entwade to Meduseld, the high house in Edoras where Théoden now sits. Thus you shall prove to him that I have not misjudged. In this I place myself, and maybe my very life, in the keeping of your good faith. Do not fail.'

'I will not,' said Aragorn.

There was great wonder, and many dark and doubtful

glances, among his men, when Éomer gave orders that the
spare horses were to be lent to the strangers, but only
Éothain dared to speak openly.

'It may be well enough for this lord of the race of Gondor, as he claims,' he said, 'but who has heard of a horse
of the Mark being given to a Dwarf?'

'No one,' said Gimli. 'And do not trouble: no one will
ever hear of it. I would sooner walk than sit on the back
of any beast so great, free or begrudged.'

'But you must ride now, or you will hinder us,' said
Aragorn.

'Come, you shall sit behind me, friend Gimli,' said
Legolas. 'Then all will be well, and you need neither
borrow a horse nor be troubled by one.'

A great dark-grey horse was brought to Aragorn, and
he mounted it. 'Hasufel is his name,' said Éomer. 'May he
bear you well and to better fortune than Gárulf, his late
master!'

A smaller and lighter horse, but restive and fiery, was
brought to Legolas. Arod was his name. But Legolas asked
them to take off saddle and rein. 'I need them not,' he
said, and leaped lightly up, and to their wonder Arod was
tame and willing beneath him, moving here and there with
but a spoken word: such was the elvish way with all good
beasts. Gimli was lifted up behind his friend, and he
clung to him, not much more at ease than Sam Gamgee in
a boat.

'Farewell, and may you find what you seek!' cried
Éomer. 'Return with what speed you may, and let our
swords hereafter shine together!'

'I will come,' said Aragorn.

'And I will come, too,' said Gimli. 'The matter of the
Lady Galadriel lies still between us. I have yet to teach
you gentle speech.'

'We shall see,' said Éomer. 'So many strange things
have chanced that to learn the praise of a fair lady under
the loving strokes of a Dwarf's axe will seem no great
wonder. Farewell!'

With that they parted. Very swift were the horses of Rohan. When after a little Gimli looked back, the company of Éomer were already small and far away. Aragorn did not look back: he was watching the trail as they sped on their way, bending low with his head beside the neck of Hasufel. Before long they came to the borders of the Entwash, and there they met the other trail of which Éomer had spoken, coming down from the East out of the Wold.

Aragorn dismounted and surveyed the ground, then leaping back into the saddle, he rode away for some distance eastward, keeping to one side and taking care not to override the footprints. Then he again dismounted and examined the ground, going backwards and forwards on foot.

'There is little to discover,' he said when he returned. 'The main trail is all confused with the passage of the horsemen as they came back; their outward course must have lain nearer the river. But this eastward trail is fresh and clear. There is no sign there of any feet going the other way, back towards Anduin. Now we must ride slower, and make sure that no trace or footstep branches off on either side. The Orcs must have been aware from this point that they were pursued; they may have made some attempt to get their captives away before they were overtaken.'

As they rode forward the day was overcast. Low grey clouds came over the Wold. A mist shrouded the sun. Ever nearer the tree-clad slopes of Fangorn loomed, slowly darkling as the sun went west. They saw no sign of any trail to right or left, but here and there they passed single Orcs, fallen in their tracks as they ran, with grey-feathered arrows sticking in back or throat.

At last as the afternoon was waning they came to the eaves of the forest, and in an open glade among the first trees they found the place of the great burning: the ashes were still hot and smoking. Beside it was a great pile of helms and mail, cloven shields, and broken swords, bows and darts and other gear of war. Upon a stake in the middle was set a great goblin head; upon its shattered helm the white badge could still be seen. Further away, not far from the river, where it came streaming out from the edge of the wood, there was a mound. It was newly raised: the raw earth was covered with freshcut turves: about it were planted fifteen spears.

Aragorn and his companions searched far and wide about the field of battle, but the light faded, and evening soon drew down, dim and misty. By nightfall they had discovered no trace of Merry and Pippin.

'We can do no more,' said Gimli sadly. 'We have been set many riddles since we came to Tol Brandir, but this is the hardest to unravel. I would guess that the burned bones of the hobbits are now mingled with the Orcs'. It will be hard news for Frodo, if he lives to hear it; and hard too for the old hobbit who waits in Rivendell. Elrond was against their coming.'

'But Gandalf was not,' said Legolas.

'But Gandalf chose to come himself, and he was the first to be lost,' answered Gimli. 'His foresight failed him.'

'The counsel of Gandalf was not founded on foreknowledge of safety, for himself or for others,' said Aragorn. 'There are some things that it is better to begin than to refuse, even though the end may be dark. But I shall not depart from this place yet. In any case we must here await the morning-light.'

A little way beyond the battle-field they made their camp under a spreading tree: it looked like a chestnut, and yet it still bore many broad brown leaves of a former year, like dry hands with long splayed fingers; they rattled mournfully in the night-breeze.

Gimli shivered. They had brought only one blanket apiece. 'Let us light a fire,' he said. 'I care no longer for the danger. Let the Orcs come as thick as summer-moths round a candle!'

'If those unhappy hobbits are astray in the woods, it might draw them hither,' said Legolas.

'And it might draw other things, neither Orc nor Hobbit,' said Aragorn. 'We are near to the mountain-marches of the traitor Saruman. Also we are on the very edge of Fangorn, and it is perilous to touch the trees of that wood, it is said.'

'But the Rohirrim made a great burning here yesterday,' said Gimli, 'and they felled trees for the fire, as can be seen. Yet they passed the night after safely here, when their labour was ended.'

'They were many,' said Aragorn, 'and they do not heed the wrath of Fangorn, for they come here seldom, and they do not go under the trees. But our paths are likely to lead us into the very forest itself. So have a care! Cut no living wood!'

'There is no need,' said Gimli. 'The Riders have left chip and bough enough, and there is dead wood lying in plenty.' He went off to gather fuel, and busied himself with building and kindling a fire; but Aragorn sat silent with his back to the great tree, deep in thought; and Legolas stood alone in the open looking towards the profound shadow of the wood, leaning forward, as one who listens to voices calling from a distance.

When the Dwarf had a small bright blaze going, the three companions drew close to it and sat together, shrouding the light with their hooded forms. Legolas looked up at the boughs of the tree reaching out above them.

'Look!' he said. 'The tree is glad of the fire!'

It may have been that the dancing shadows tricked their eyes, but certainly to each of the companions the boughs appeared to be bending this way and that so as to come above the flames, while the upper branches were stooping down; the brown leaves now stood out stiff, and rubbed together like many cold cracked hands taking comfort in the warmth.

There was a silence, for suddenly the dark and unknown forest, so near at hand, made itself felt as a great brooding presence, full of secret purpose. After a while Legolas spoke again.

'Celeborn warned us not to go far into Fangorn,' he said.

'Do you know why, Aragorn? What are the fables of the forest that Boromir had heard?'

'I have heard many tales in Gondor and elsewhere,' said Aragorn, 'but if it were not for the words of Celeborn I should deem them only fables that Men have made as true knowledge fades. I had thought of asking you what was the truth of the matter. And if an Elf of the Wood does not know, how shall a Man answer?'

'You have journeyed further than I,' said Legolas. 'I have heard nothing of this in my own land, save only songs that tell how the Onodrim, that Men call Ents, dwelt there long ago; for Fangorn is old, old even as the Elves would reckon it.'

'Yes, it is old,' said Aragorn, 'as old as the forest by the Barrow-downs, and it is far greater. Elrond says that the two are akin, the last strongholds of the mighty woods of the Elder Days, in which the Firstborn roamed while Men still slept. Yet Fangorn holds some secret of its own. What it is I do not know.'

'And I do not wish to know,' said Gimli. 'Let nothing that dwells in Fangorn be troubled on my account!'

They now drew lots for the watches, and the lot for the first watch fell to Gimli. The others lay down. Almost at once sleep laid hold on them: 'Gimli!' said Aragorn drowsily. 'Remember, it is perilous to cut bough or twig from a living tree in Fangorn. But do not stray far in search of dead wood. Let the fire die rather! Call me at need!'

With that he fell asleep. Legolas already lay motionless, his fair hands folded upon his breast, his eyes unclosed, blending living night and deep dream, as is the way with Elves. Gimli sat hunched by the fire, running his thumb thoughtfully along the edge of his axe. The tree rustled. There was no other sound.

Suddenly Gimli looked up, and there just on the edge of the firelight stood an old bent man, leaning on a staff, and wrapped in a great cloak; his wide-brimmed hat was pulled down over his eyes. Gimli sprang up, too amazed for the moment to cry out, though at once the thought flashed into his mind that Saruman had caught them.

Both Aragorn and Legolas, roused by his sudden movement, sat up and stared. The old man did not speak or make a sign.

'Well, father, what can we do for you?' said Aragorn, leaping to his feet. 'Come and be warm, if you are cold!' He strode forward, but the old man was gone. There was no trace of him to be found near at hand, and they did not dare to wander far. The moon had set and the light was very dark.

Suddenly Legolas gave a cry. 'The horses! The horses!'

The horses were gone. They had dragged their pickets and disappeared. For some time the three companions stood still and silent, troubled by this new stroke of ill fortune. They were under the eaves of Fangorn, and endless leagues lay between them and the Men of Rohan, their only friends in this wide and dangerous land. As they stood, it seemed to them that they heard, far off in the night, the sound of horses whinnying and neighing. Then all was quiet again, except for the cold rustle of the wind.

'Well, they are gone,' said Aragorn at last. 'We cannot find them or catch them; so that if they do not return of their own will, we must do without. We started on our feet, and we have those still.'

'Feet!' said Gimli. 'But we cannot eat them as well as walk on them.' He threw some fuel on the fire and slumped down beside it.

'Only a few hours ago you were unwilling to sit on a horse of Rohan,' laughed Legolas. 'You will make a rider yet.'

'It seems unlikely that I shall have the chance,' said Gimli.

'If you wish to know what I think,' he began again after a while, 'I think it was Saruman. Who else? Remember the words of Éomer: *he walks about like an old man hooded and cloaked*. Those were the words. He has gone off with our horses, or scared them away, and here we are. There is more trouble coming to us, mark my words!'

'I mark them,' said Aragorn. 'But I marked also that this

old man had a hat not a hood. Still I do not doubt that you guess right, and that we are in peril here, by night or day. Yet in the meantime there is nothing that we can do but rest, while we may. I will watch for a while now, Gimli. I have more need of thought than of sleep.'

The night passed slowly. Legolas followed Aragorn, and Gimli followed Legolas, and their watches wore away. But nothing happened. The old man did not appear again, and the horses did not return.

Chapter 3

The Uruk-Hai

Pippin lay in a dark and troubled dream: it seemed that he could hear his own small voice echoing in black tunnels, calling *Frodo, Frodo!* But instead of Frodo hundreds of hideous orc-faces grinned at him out of the shadows, hundreds of hideous arms grasped at him from every side. Where was Merry?

He woke. Cold air blew on his face. He was lying on his back. Evening was coming and the sky above was growing dim. He turned and found that the dream was little worse than the waking. His wrists, legs, and ankles were tied with cords. Beside him Merry lay, white-faced, with a dirty rag bound across his brow. All about them sat or stood a great company of Orcs.

Slowly in Pippin's aching head memory pieced itself together and became separated from dream-shadows. Of course: he and Merry had run off into the woods. What had come over them? Why had they dashed off like that, taking no notice of old Strider? They had run a long way shouting—he could not remember how far or how long; and then suddenly they had crashed right into a group of Orcs: they were standing listening, and they did not appear to see Merry and Pippin until they were almost in their arms. Then they yelled and dozens of other goblins had sprung out of the trees. Merry and he had drawn their swords, but the Orcs did not wish to fight, and had tried only to lay hold of them, even when Merry had cut off several of their arms and hands. Good old Merry!

Then Boromir had come leaping through the trees. He had made them fight. He slew many of them and the rest fled. But they had not gone far on the way back when they were attacked again, by a hundred Orcs at least, some of them very large, and they shot a rain of arrows: always at Boromir. Boromir had blown his great horn till the

woods rang, and at first the Orcs had been dismayed and
had drawn back; but when no answer but the echoes came,
they had attacked more fiercely than ever. Pippin did not
remember much more. His last memory was of Boromir
leaning against a tree, plucking out an arrow; then darkness fell suddenly.

'I suppose I was knocked on the head,' he said to himself. 'I wonder if poor Merry is much hurt. What has happened to Boromir? Why didn't the Orcs kill us? Where
are we, and where are we going?'

He could not answer the questions. He felt cold and
sick. 'I wish Gandalf had never persuaded Elrond to let
us come,' he thought. 'What good have I been? Just a
nuisance: a passenger, a piece of luggage. And now I
have been stolen and I am just a piece of luggage for the
Orcs. I hope Strider or someone will come and claim us!
But ought I to hope for it? Won't that throw out all the
plans? I wish I could get free!'

He struggled a little, quite uselessly. One of the Orcs
sitting near laughed and said something to a companion
in their abominable tongue. 'Rest while you can, little
fool!' he said then to Pippin, in the Common Speech,
which he made almost as hideous as his own language.
'Rest while you can! We'll find a use for your legs before
long. You'll wish you had got none before we get home.'

'If I had my way, you'd wish you were dead now,' said
the other. 'I'd make you squeak, you miserable rat.' He
stooped over Pippin, bringing his yellow fangs close to his
face. He had a black knife with a long jagged blade in his
hand. 'Lie quiet, or I'll tickle you with this,' he hissed.
'Don't draw attention to yourself, or I may forget my
orders. Curse the Isengarders! *Uglúk u bagronk sha push-
dug Saruman-glob búbhosh skai*': he passed into a long
angry speech in his own tongue that slowly died away into
muttering and snarling.

Terrified Pippin lay still, though the pain at his wrists
and ankles was growing, and the stones beneath him were
boring into his back. To take his mind off himself he lis-

tened intently to all that he could hear. There were many
voices round about, and though orc-speech sounded at
all times full of hate and anger, it seemed plain that something like a quarrel had begun, and was getting hotter.

To Pippin's surprise he found that much of the talk
was intelligible; many of the Orcs were using ordinary
language. Apparently the members of two or three quite
different tribes were present, and they could not understand one another's orc-speech. There was an angry debate concerning what they were to do now: which way they
were to take and what should be done with the prisoners.

'There's no time to kill them properly,' said one. 'No
time for play on this trip.'

'That can't be helped,' said another. 'But why not kill
them quick, kill them now? They're a cursed nuisance,
and we're in a hurry. Evening's coming on, and we ought
to get a move on.'

'Orders,' said a third voice in a deep growl. *'Kill all but*
NOT *the Halflings; they are to be brought back* ALIVE
as quickly as possible. That's my orders.'

'What are they wanted for?' asked several voices. 'Why
alive? Do they give good sport?'

'No! I heard that one of them has got something, something that's wanted for the War, some elvish plot or other.
Anyway they'll each be questioned.'

'Is that all you know? Why don't we search them and
find out? We might find something that we could use
ourselves.'

'That is a very interesting remark,' sneered a voice,
softer than the others but more evil. 'I may have to report
that. The prisoners are NOT to be searched or plundered:
those are *my* orders.'

'And mine too,' said the deep voice. *'Alive and as
captured; no spoiling.* That's my orders.'

'Not our orders!' said one of the earlier voices. 'We have
come all the way from the Mines to kill, and avenge our
folk. I wish to kill, and then go back north.'

'Then you can wish again,' said the growling voice. 'I

am Uglúk. I command. I return to Isengard by the shortest road.'

'Is Saruman the master or the Great Eye?' said the evil
voice. 'We should go back at once to Lugbúrz.'

'If we could cross the Great River, we might,' said another voice. 'But there are not enough of us to venture
down to the bridges.'

'I came across,' said the evil voice. 'A winged Nazgûl
awaits us northward on the east-bank.'

'Maybe, maybe! Then you'll fly off with our prisoners,
and get all the pay and praise in Lugbúrz, and leave us to
foot it as best we can through the Horse-country. No, we
must stick together. These lands are dangerous: full of foul
rebels and brigands.'

'Aye, we must stick together,' growled Uglúk. 'I don't
trust you little swine. You've no guts outside your own
sties. But for us you'd all have run away. We are the
fighting Uruk-hai! We slew the great warrior. We took the
prisoners. We are the servants of Saruman the Wise,
the White Hand: the Hand that gives us man's-flesh to eat.
We came out of Isengard, and led you here, and we shall
lead you back by the way we choose. I am Uglúk. I have
spoken.'

'You have spoken more than enough, Uglúk,' sneered
the evil voice. 'I wonder how they would like it in Lugbúrz. They might think that Uglúk's shoulders needed re-
lieving of a swollen head. They might ask where his
strange ideas came from. Did they come from Saruman,
perhaps? Who does *he* think he is, setting up on his own
with his filthy white badges? They might agree with me,
with Grishnákh their trusted messenger; and I Grishnákh
say this: Saruman is a fool, and a dirty treacherous fool.
But the Great Eye is on him.

'*Swine* is it? How do you folk like being called *swine*
by the muck-rakers of a dirty little wizard? It's orc-flesh
they eat, I'll warrant.'

Many loud yells in orc-speech answered him, and the
ringing clash of weapons being drawn. Cautiously Pippin
rolled over, hoping to see what would happen. His guards

had gone to join in the fray. In the twilight he saw a large black Orc, probably Uglúk, standing facing Grishnákh, a short crook-legged creature, very broad and with long arms that hung almost to the ground. Round them were many smaller goblins. Pippin supposed that these were the ones from the North. They had drawn their knives and swords, but hesitated to attack Uglúk.

Uglúk shouted, and a number of other Orcs of nearly his own size ran up. Then suddenly, without warning, Uglúk sprang forwards, and with two swift strokes swept the heads off two of his opponents. Grishnákh stepped aside and vanished into the shadows. The others gave way, and one stepped backwards and fell over Merry's prostrate form with a curse. Yet that probably saved his life, for Uglúk's followers leaped over him and cut down another with their broad-bladed swords. It was the yellow-fanged guard. His body fell right on top of Pippin, still clutching its long saw-edged knife.

'Put up your weapons!' shouted Uglúk. 'And let's have no more nonsense! We go straight west from here, and down the stair. From there straight to the downs, then along the river to the forest. And we march day and night. That clear?'

'Now,' thought Pippin, 'if only it takes that ugly fellow a little while to get his troop under control, I've got a chance.' A gleam of hope had come to him. The edge of the black knife had snicked his arm, and then slid down to his wrist. He felt the blood trickling on to his hand, but he also felt the cold touch of steel against his skin.

The Orcs were getting ready to march again, but some of the Northerners were still unwilling, and the Isen-garders slew two more before the rest were cowed. There was much cursing and confusion. For the moment Pippin was unwatched. His legs were securely bound, but his arms were only tied about the wrists, and his hands were in front of him. He could move them both together, though the bonds were cruelly tight. He pushed the dead Orc to one side, then hardly daring to breathe, he drew the knot of the wrist-cord up and down against the blade of the knife. It was sharp and the dead hand held it fast. The cord was cut! Quickly Pippin took it in his fingers and knotted it again into a loose bracelet of two loops and slipped it over his hands. Then he lay very still.

'Pick up those prisoners!' shouted Uglúk. 'Don't play any tricks with them! If they are not alive when we get back, someone else will die too.'

An Orc seized Pippin like a sack, put its head between his tied hands, grabbed his arms and dragged them down, until Pippin's face was crushed against its neck; then it jolted off with him. Another treated Merry in the same way. The Orc's clawlike hand gripped Pippin's arms like iron; the nails bit into him. He shut his eyes and slipped back into evil dreams.

Suddenly he was thrown on to the stony floor again. It was early night, but the slim moon was already falling westward. They were on the edge of a cliff that seemed to look out over a sea of pale mist. There was a sound of water falling nearby.

'The scouts have come back at last,' said an Orc close at hand.

'Well, what did you discover?' growled the voice of Uglúk.

'Only a single horseman, and he made off westwards. All's clear now.'

'Now, I daresay. But how long? You fools! You should have shot him. He'll raise the alarm. The cursed horse-breeders will hear of us by morning. Now we'll have to leg it double quick.'

A shadow bent over Pippin. It was Uglúk. 'Sit up!' said the Orc. 'My lads are tired of lugging you about. We have got to climb down, and you must use your legs. Be helpful now. No crying out, no trying to escape. We have ways of paying for tricks that you won't like, though they won't spoil your usefulness for the Master.'

He cut the thongs round Pippin's legs and ankles, picked him up by his hair and stood him on his feet. Pippin fell down, and Uglúk dragged him up by his hair again. Several Orcs laughed. Uglúk thrust a flask between his teeth and poured some burning liquid down his throat: he felt a hot fierce glow flow through him. The pain in his legs and ankles vanished. He could stand.

'Now for the other!' said Uglúk. Pippin saw him go to Merry, who was lying close by, and kick him. Merry groaned. Seizing him roughly Uglúk pulled him into a sitting position, and tore the bandage off his head. Then he smeared the wound with some dark stuff out of a small wooden box. Merry cried out and struggled wildly.

The Orcs clapped and hooted. 'Can't take his medicine,' they jeered. 'Doesn't know what's good for him. Ai! We shall have some fun later.'

But at the moment Uglúk was not engaged in sport. He needed speed and had to humour unwilling followers. He was healing Merry in orc-fashion; and his treatment worked swiftly. When he had forced a drink from his flask down the hobbit's throat, cut his leg-bonds, and dragged him to his feet, Merry stood up, looking pale but grim and defiant, and very much alive. The gash in his forehead gave him no more trouble, but he bore a brown scar to the end of his days.

'Hullo, Pippin!' he said. 'So you've come on this little expedition, too? Where do we get bed and breakfast?'

'Now then!' said Uglúk. 'None of that! Hold your tongues. No talk to one another. Any trouble will be reported at the other end, and He'll know how to pay you. You'll get bed and breakfast all right: more than you can stomach.'

The orc-band began to descend a narrow ravine leading down into the misty plain below. Merry and Pippin, separated by a dozen Orcs or more, climbed down with them. At the bottom they stepped onto grass, and the hearts of the hobbits rose.

'Now straight on!' shouted Uglúk. 'West and a little north. Follow Lugdush.'

'But what are we going to do at sunrise?' said some of the Northerners.

'Go on running,' said Uglúk. 'What do you think? Sit on the grass and wait for the Whiteskins to join the picnic?'

'But we can't run in the sunlight.'

'You'll run with me behind you,' said Uglúk. 'Runt! Or you'll never see your beloved holes again. By the White Hand! What's the use of sending out mountain-maggots on a trip, only half trained. Run, curse you! Run while night lasts!'

Then the whole company began to run with the long loping strides of Orcs. They kept no order, thrusting, jostling, and cursing; yet their speed was very great. Each hobbit had a guard of three. Pippin was far back in the line. He wondered how long he would be able to go on at this pace: he had had no food since the morning. One of his guards had a whip. But at present the orc-liquor was still hot in him. His wits, too, were wide-awake.

Every now and again there came into his mind unbidden a vision of the keen face of Strider bending over a dark trail, and running, running behind. But what could even a Ranger see except a confused trail of orc-feet? His own little prints and Merry's were overwhelmed by the trampling of the iron-shod shoes before them and behind them and about them.

They had gone only a mile or so from the cliff when the land sloped down into a wide shallow depression, where the ground was soft and wet. Mist lay there, pale-glimmering in the last rays of the sickle moon. The dark shapes of the Orcs in front grew dim, and then were swallowed up.

'Ai! Steady now!' shouted Uglúk from the rear.

A sudden thought leaped into Pippin's mind, and he acted on it at once. He swerved aside to the right, and dived out of the reach of his clutching guard, headfirst into the mist; he landed sprawling on the grass.

'Halt!' yelled Uglúk.

There was for a moment turmoil and confusion. Pippin sprang up and ran. But the Orcs were after him. Some suddenly loomed up right in front of him.

'No hope of escape!' thought Pippin. 'But there is a hope that I have left some of my own marks unspoilt on the wet ground.' He groped with his two tied hands at his throat, and unclasped the brooch of his cloak. Just as long arms and hard claws seized him, he let it fall. 'There I suppose it will lie until the end of time,' he thought. 'I don't know why I did it. If the others have escaped, they've probably all gone with Frodo.'

A whip-thong curled round his legs, and he stifled a cry.

'Enough!' shouted Uglúk running up. 'He's still got to run a long way yet. Make 'em both run! Just use the whip as a reminder.'

'But that's not all,' he snarled, turning to Pippin. 'I shan't forget. Payment is only put off. Leg it!'

Neither Pippin nor Merry remembered much of the later part of the journey. Evil dreams and evil waking were blended into a long tunnel of misery, with hope growing ever fainter behind. They ran, and they ran, striving to keep up the pace set by the Orcs, licked every now and again with a cruel thong cunningly handled. If they halted or stumbled, they were seized and dragged for some distance.

The warmth of the orc-draught had gone. Pippin felt cold and sick again. Suddenly he fell face downward on the turf. Hard hands with rending nails gripped and lifted him. He was carried like a sack once more, and darkness grew about him: whether the darkness of another night, or a blindness of his eyes, he could not tell.

Dimly he became aware of voices clamouring: it seemed that many of the Orcs were demanding a halt. Uglúk was shouting. He felt himself flung to the ground, and he lay as he fell, till black dreams took him. But he did not long escape from pain; soon the iron grip of merciless hands was on him again. For a long time he was tossed and shaken, and then slowly the darkness gave way, and he came back to the waking world and found that it was morning. Orders were shouted and he was thrown roughly on the grass.

There he lay for a while, fighting with despair. His head swam, but from the heat in his body he guessed that he had been given another draught. An Orc stooped over him, and flung him some bread and a strip of raw dried flesh. He ate the stale grey bread hungrily, but not the meat. He was famished but not yet so famished as to eat flesh flung to him by an Orc, the flesh of he dared not guess what creature.

He sat up and looked about. Merry was not far away. They were by the banks of a swift narrow river. Ahead mountains loomed: a tall peak was catching the first rays of the sun. A dark smudge of forest lay on the lower slopes before them.

There was much shouting and debating among the Orcs; a quarrel seemed on the point of breaking out again between the Northerners and the Isengarders. Some were pointing back away south, and some were pointing eastward.

'Very well,' said Uglúk. 'Leave them to me then! No killing, as I've told you before; but if you want to throw away what we've come all the way to get, throw it away! I'll look after it. Let the fighting Uruk-hai do the work, as usual. If you're afraid of the Whiteskins, run! Run! There's the forest,' he shouted, pointing ahead. 'Get to it! It's your best hope. Off you go! And quick, before I knock a few more heads off, to put some sense into the others.'

There was some cursing and scuffling, and then most of the Northerners broke away and dashed off, over a hundred of them, running wildly along the river towards the mountains. The hobbits were left with the Isengarders: a grim dark band, four score at least of large, swart, slant-eyed Orcs with great bows and short broad-bladed swords. A few of the larger and bolder Northerners remained with them.

'Now we'll deal with Grishnákh,' said Uglúk; but some even of his own followers were looking uneasily southwards.

'I know,' growled Uglúk. 'The cursed horse-boys have got wind of us. But that's all your fault, Snaga. You and the other scouts ought to have your ears cut off. But we are the fighters. We'll feast on horseflesh yet, or something better.'

At that moment Pippin saw why some of the troop had been pointing eastward. From that direction there now came hoarse cries, and there was Grishnákh again, and at his back a couple of score of others like him: long-armed crook-legged Orcs. They had a red eye painted on their shields. Uglúk stepped forward to meet them.

'So you've come back?' he said. 'Thought better of it, eh?'

'I've returned to see that Orders are carried out and the prisoners safe,' answered Grishnákh.

'Indeed!' said Uglúk. 'Waste of effort. I'll see that orders are carried out in my command. And what else did you come back for? You went in a hurry. Did you leave anything behind?'

'I left a fool,' snarled Grishnákh. 'But there were some stout fellows with him that are too good to lose. I knew you'd lead them into a mess. I've come to help them.'

'Splendid!' laughed Uglúk. 'But unless you've got some guts for fighting, you've taken the wrong way. Lugbúrz was your road. The Whiteskins are coming. What's happened to your precious Nazgûl? Has he had another mount shot under him? Now, if you'd brought him along, that might have been useful—if these Nazgûl are all they make out.'

'*Nazgûl, Nazgûl,*' said Grishnákh, shivering and licking his lips, as if the word had a foul taste that he savoured painfully. 'You speak of what is deep beyond the reach of your muddy dreams, Uglúk,' he said. '*Nazgûl!* Ah! All that they make out! One day you'll wish that you had not said that. Ape!' he snarled fiercely. 'You ought to know that they're the apple of the Great Eye. But the winged Nazgûl: not yet, not yet. He won't let them show themselves across the Great River yet, not too soon. They're for the War—and other purposes.'

'You seem to know a lot,' said Uglúk. 'More than is good for you, I guess. Perhaps those in Lugbúrz might wonder how, and why. But in the meantime the Uruk-hai of Isengard can do the dirty work, as usual. Don't stand slavering there! Get your rabble together! The other swine are legging it to the forest. You'd better follow. You wouldn't get back to the Great River alive. Right off the mark! Now! I'll be on your heels.'

The Isengarders seized Merry and Pippin again and slung them on their backs. Then the troop started off. Hour after hour they ran, pausing now and again only to sling the hobbits to fresh carriers. Either because they were quicker and hardier, or because of some plan of Grishnákh's, the Isengarders gradually passed through the Orcs of Mordor, and Grishnákh's folk closed in behind. Soon they were gaining also on the Northerners ahead. The forest began to draw nearer.

Pippin was bruised and torn, his aching head was grated by the filthy jowl and hairy ear of the Orc that held him. Immediately in front were bowed backs, and tough thick legs going up and down, up and down, unresting, as if they were made of wire and horn, beating out the nightmare seconds of an endless time.

In the afternoon Uglúk's troop overtook the Northerners. They were flagging in the rays of the bright sun, winter sun shining in a pale cool sky though it was; their heads were down and their tongues lolling out.

'Maggots!' jeered the Isengarders. 'You're cooked. The Whiteskins will catch you and eat you. They're coming!'

A cry from Grishnákh showed that this was not mere jest. Horsemen, riding very swiftly, had indeed been sighted: still far behind, but gaining on the Orcs, gaining on them like a tide over the flats on folk straying in a quicksand.

The Isengarders began to run with a redoubled pace that astonished Pippin, a terrific spurt it seemed for the end of a race. Then he saw that the sun was sinking, falling behind the Misty Mountains; shadows reached over the land. The soldiers of Mordor lifted their heads and also began to put on speed. The forest was dark and close. Already they had passed a few outlying trees. The land

was beginning to slope upwards, ever more steeply; but
the Orcs did not halt. Both Uglúk and Grishnákh shouted,
spurring them on to a last effort.

'They will make it yet. They will escape,' thought Pippin. And then he managed to twist his neck, so as to glance
back with one eye over his shoulder. He saw that riders
away eastward were already level with the Orcs, galloping
over the plain. The sunset gilded their spears and helmets,
and glinted in their pale flowing hair. They were hemming
the Orcs in, preventing them from scattering, and driving
them along the line of the river.

He wondered very much what kind of folk they were.
He wished now that he had learned more in Rivendell, and
looked more at maps and things; but in those days the
plans for the journey seemed to be in more competent
hands, and he had never reckoned with being cut off
from Gandalf, or from Strider, and even from Frodo.
All that he could remember about Rohan was that Gandalf's horse, Shadowfax, had come from that land. That
sounded hopeful, as far as it went.

'But how will they know that we are not Orcs?' he
thought. 'I don't suppose they've ever heard of hobbits
down here. I suppose I ought to be glad that the beastly
Orcs look like being destroyed, but I would rather be saved
myself.' The chances were that he and Merry would be
killed together with their captors, before ever the Men of
Rohan were aware of them.

A few of the riders appeared to be bowmen, skilled at
shooting from a running horse. Riding swiftly into range
they shot arrows at the Orcs that straggled behind, and
several of them fell; then the riders wheeled away out of
the range of the answering bows of their enemies, who shot
wildly, not daring to halt. This happened many times, and
on one occasion arrows fell among the Isengarders. One of
them, just in front of Pippin, stumbled and did not get up
again.

Night came down without the Riders closing in for battle. Many Orcs had fallen, but fully two hundred remained. In the early darkness the Orcs came to a hillock. The eaves of the forest were very near, probably no more than three furlongs away, but they could go no further. The horsemen had encircled them. A small band disobeyed Uglúk's command, and ran on towards the forest: only three returned.

'Well, here we are,' sneered Grishnákh. 'Fine leadership! I hope the great Uglúk will lead us out again.'

'Put those Halflings down!' ordered Uglúk, taking no notice of Grishnákh. 'You, Lugdush, get two others and stand guard over them. They're not to be killed, unless the filthy Whiteskins break through. Understand? As long as I'm alive, I want 'em. But they're not to cry out, and they're not to be rescued. Bind their legs!'

The last part of the order was carried out mercilessly. But Pippin found that for the first time he was close to Merry. The Orcs were making a great deal of noise, shouting and clashing their weapons, and the hobbits managed to whisper together for a while.

'I don't think much of this,' said Merry. 'I feel nearly done in. Don't think I could crawl away far, even if I was free.'

'*Lembas!*' whispered Pippin. '*Lembas*: I've got some. Have you? I don't think they've taken anything but our swords.'

'Yes, I had a packet in my pocket,' answered Merry, 'but it must be battered to crumbs. Anyway I can't put my mouth in my pocket!'

'You won't have to. I've——'; but just then a savage kick warned Pippin that the noise had died down, and the guards were watchful.

The night was cold and still. All round the knoll on which the Orcs were gathered little watch-fires sprang up, golden-red in the darkness, a complete ring of them. They were within a long bowshot, but the riders did not show themselves against the light, and the Orcs wasted many arrows shooting at the fires, until Uglúk stopped them.

The riders made no sound. Later in the night when the moon came out of the mist, then occasionally they could be seen, shadowy shapes that glinted now and again in the white light, as they moved in ceaseless patrol.

'They'll wait for the Sun, curse them!' growled one of the guards. 'Why don't we get together and charge through? What's old Uglúk think he's doing, I should like to know?'

'I daresay you would,' snarled Uglúk stepping up from behind. 'Meaning I don't think at all, eh? Curse you! You're as bad as the other rabble: the maggots and the apes of Lugbúrz. No good trying to charge with them. They'd just squeal and bolt, and there are more than enough of these filthy horse-boys to mop up our lot on the flat.

'There's only one thing those maggots can do: they can see like gimlets in the dark. But these Whiteskins have better night-eyes than most Men, from all I've heard; and don't forget their horses! They can see the night-breeze, or so it's said. Still there's one thing the fine fellows don't know! Mauhúr and his lads are in the forest, and they should turn up any time now.'

Uglúk's words were enough, apparently, to satisfy the Isengarders; but the other Orcs were both dispirited and rebellious. They posted a few watchers, but most of them lay on the ground, resting in the pleasant darkness. It did indeed become very dark again; for the moon passed westward into thick cloud, and Pippin could not see anything a few feet away. The fires brought no light to the hillock. The riders were not, however, content merely to wait for the dawn and let their enemies rest. A sudden outcry on the east side of the knoll showed that something was wrong. It seemed that some of the Men had ridden in close, slipped off their horses, crawled to the edge of the camp and killed several Orcs, and then had faded away again. Uglúk dashed off to stop a stampede.

Pippin and Merry sat up. Their guards, Isengarders, had gone with Uglúk. But if the hobbits had any thought of escape, it was soon dashed. A long hairy arm took each of them by the neck and drew them close together. Dimly

they were aware of Grishnákh's great head and hideous
face between them; his foul breath was on their cheeks.
He began to paw them and feel them. Pippin shuddered
as hard cold fingers groped down his back.

'Well, my little ones!' said Grishnákh in a soft whisper.
'Enjoying your nice rest? Or not? A little awkwardly
placed perhaps: swords and whips on one side, and nasty
spears on the other! Little people should not meddle in
affairs that are too big for them.' His fingers continued to
grope. There was a light like a pale but hot fire behind his
eyes.

The thought came suddenly into Pippin's mind, as if
caught direct from the urgent thought of his enemy:
'Grishnákh knows about the Ring! He's looking for it, while
Uglúk is busy: he probably wants it for himself.' Cold fear
was in Pippin's heart, yet at the same time he was wondering what use he could make of Grishnákh's desire.

'I don't think you will find it that way,' he whispered.
'It isn't easy to find.'

'*Find it?*' said Grishnákh: his fingers stopped crawling
and gripped Pippin's shoulder. 'Find what? What are you
talking about, little one?'

For a moment Pippin was silent. Then suddenly in the
darkness he made a noise in his throat: *gollum, gollum.*
'Nothing, my precious,' he added.

The hobbits felt Grishnákh's fingers twitch. 'O ho!'
hissed the goblin softly. 'That's what he means, is it? O ho!
Very ve-ry dangerous, my little ones.'

'Perhaps,' said Merry, now alert and aware of Pippin's
guess. 'Perhaps; and not only for us. Still you know your
own business best. Do you want it, or not? And what would
you give for it?'

'Do I want it? Do I want it?' said Grishnákh, as if
puzzled; but his arms were trembling. 'What would I give
for it? What do you mean?'

'We mean,' said Pippin, choosing his words carefully,
'that it's no good groping in the dark. We could save you
time and trouble. But you must untie our legs first, or we'll
do nothing, and say nothing.'

'My dear tender little fools,' hissed Grishnákh, 'everything you have, and everything you know, will be got out of you in due time: everything! You'll wish there was more than you could tell to satisfy the Questioner, indeed you will: quite soon. We shan't hurry the enquiry. Oh dear no! What do you think you've been kept alive for? My dear little fellows, please believe me when I say that it was not out of kindness: that's not even one of Uglúk's faults.'

'I find it quite easy to believe,' said Merry. 'But you haven't got your prey home yet. And it doesn't seem to be going your way, whatever happens. If we come to Isengard, it won't be the great Grishnákh that benefits: Saruman will take all that he can find. If you want anything for yourself, now's the time to do a deal.'

Grishnákh began to lose his temper. The name of Saruman seemed specially to enrage him. Time was passing and the disturbance was dying down. Uglúk or the Isengarders might return at any minute. 'Have you got it —either of you?' he snarled.

'*Gollum, gollum!*' said Pippin.

'Untie our legs!' said Merry.

They felt the Orc's arms trembling violently. 'Curse you, you filthy little vermin!' he hissed. 'Untie your legs? I'll untie every string in your bodies. Do you think I can't search you to the bones? Search you! I'll cut you both to quivering shreds. I don't need the help of your legs to get you away—and have you all to myself!'

Suddenly he seized them. The strength in his long arms and shoulders was terrifying. He tucked them one under each armpit, and crushed them fiercely to his sides; a great stifling hand was clapped over each of their mouths. Then he sprang forward, stooping low. Quickly and silently he went, until he came to the edge of the knoll. There, choosing a gap between the watchers, he passed like an evil shadow out into the night, down the slope and away westward towards the river that flowed out of the forest. In that direction there was a wide open space with only one fire.

After going a dozen yards he halted, peering and listening. Nothing could be seen or heard. He crept slowly on, bent almost double. Then he squatted and listened again. Then he stood up, as if to risk a sudden dash. At that very moment the dark form of a rider loomed up right in front of him. A horse snorted and reared. A man called out.

Grishnákh flung himself on the ground flat, dragging the hobbits under him; then he drew his sword. No doubt he meant to kill his captives, rather than allow them to escape or to be rescued; but it was his undoing. The sword rang faintly, and glinted a little in the light of the fire away to his left. An arrow came whistling out of the gloom: it was aimed with skill, or guided by fate, and it pierced his right hand. He dropped the sword and shrieked. There was a quick beat of hoofs, and even as Grishnákh leaped up and ran, he was ridden down and a spear passed through him. He gave a hideous shivering cry and lay still.

The hobbits remained flat on the ground, as Grishnákh had left them. Another horseman came riding swiftly to his comrade's aid. Whether because of some special keenness of sight, or because of some other sense, the horse lifted and sprang lightly over them; but its rider did not see them, lying covered in their elven-cloaks, too crushed for the moment, and too afraid to move.

At last Merry stirred and whispered softly: 'So far so good; but how are *we* to avoid being spitted?'

The answer came almost immediately. The cries of Grishnákh had roused the Orcs. From the yells and screeches that came from the knoll the hobbits guessed that their disappearance had been discovered: Uglúk was probably knocking off a few more heads. Then suddenly the answering cries of orc-voices came from the right, outside the circle of watch-fires, from the direction of the forest and the mountains. Mauhúr had apparently arrived and was attacking the besiegers. There was the sound of galloping horses. The Riders were drawing in their ring close round the knoll, risking the orc-arrows, so as to prevent any sortie, while a company rode off to deal with

the newcomers. Suddenly Merry and Pippin realized that
without moving they were now outside the circle: there was
nothing between them and escape.

'Now,' said Merry, 'if only we had our legs and hands
free, we might get away. But I can't touch the knots, and I
can't bite them.'

'No need to try,' said Pippin. 'I was going to tell you:
I've managed to free my hands. These loops are only left
for show. You'd better have a bit of *lembas* first.'

He slipped the cords off his wrists, and fished out a
packet. The cakes were broken, but good, still in their leaf-
wrappings. The hobbits each ate two or three pieces. The
taste brought back to them the memory of fair faces, and
laughter, and wholesome food in quiet days now far away.
For a while they ate thoughtfully, sitting in the dark,
heedless of the cries and sounds of battle nearby. Pippin
was the first to come back to the present.

'We must be off,' he said. 'Half a moment!' Grishnákh's
sword was lying close at hand, but it was too heavy and
clumsy for him to use; so he crawled forward, and finding
the body of the goblin he drew from its sheath a long
sharp knife. With this he quickly cut their bonds.

'Now for it!' he said. 'When we've warmed up a bit, perhaps we shall be able to stand again, and walk. But in any
case we had better start by crawling.'

They crawled. The turf was deep and yielding, and that
helped them; but it seemed a long slow business. They
gave the watch-fire a wide berth, and wormed their
way forward bit by bit, until they came to the edge of the
river, gurgling away in the black shadows under its deep
banks. Then they looked back.

The sounds had died away. Evidently Mauhúr and his
'lads' had been killed or driven off. The Riders had returned to their silent, ominous vigil. It would not last very
much longer. Already the night was old. In the East,
which had remained unclouded, the sky was beginning to
grow pale.

'We must get under cover,' said Pippin, 'or we shall be
seen. It will not be any comfort to us, if these riders dis-

cover that we are not Orcs after we are dead.' He got up and stamped his feet. 'Those cords have cut me like wires; but my feet are getting warm again. I could stagger on now. What about you, Merry?'

Merry got up. 'Yes,' he said, 'I can manage it. *Lembas* does put heart into you! A more wholesome sort of feeling, too, than the heat of that orc-draught. I wonder what it was made of. Better not to know, I expect. Let's get a drink of water to wash away the thought of it!'

'Not here, the banks are too steep,' said Pippin. 'Forward now!'

They turned and walked side by side slowly along the line of the river. Behind them the light grew in the East. As they walked they compared notes, talking lightly in hobbit-fashion of the things that had happened since their capture. No listener would have guessed from their words that they had suffered cruelly, and been in dire peril, going without hope towards torment and death; or that even now, as they knew well, they had little chance of ever finding friend or safety again.

'You seem to have been doing well, Master Took,' said Merry. 'You will get almost a chapter in old Bilbo's book, if ever I get a chance to report to him. Good work: especially guessing that hairy villain's little game, and playing up to him. But I wonder if anyone will ever pick up your trail and find that brooch. I should hate to lose mine, but I am afraid yours is gone for good.

'I shall have to brush up my toes, if I am to get level with you. Indeed Cousin Brandybuck is going in front now. This is where he comes in. I don't suppose you have much notion where we are; but I spent my time at Rivendell rather better. We are walking west along the Entwash. The butt-end of the Misty Mountains is in front, and Fangorn Forest.'

Even as he spoke the dark edge of the forest loomed up straight before them. Night seemed to have taken refuge under its great trees, creeping away from the coming Dawn.

'Lead on, Master Brandybuck!' said Pippin. 'Or lead

back! We have been warned against Fangorn. But one
so knowing will not have forgotten that.'

'I have not,' answered Merry; 'but the forest seems
better to me, all the same, than turning back into the middle of a battle.'

He led the way in under the huge branches of the trees.
Old beyond guessing, they seemed. Great trailing beards
of lichen hung from them, blowing and swaying in the
breeze. Out of the shadows the hobbits peeped, gazing back
down the slope: little furtive figures that in the dim light
looked like elf-children in the deeps of time peering out of
the Wild Wood in wonder at their first Dawn.

Far over the Great River, and the Brown Lands, leagues
upon grey leagues away, the Dawn came, red as flame.
Loud rang the hunting-horns to greet it. The Riders of
Rohan sprang suddenly to life. Horn answered horn again.

Merry and Pippin heard, clear in the cold air, the neighing of war-horses, and the sudden singing of many men.
The Sun's limb was lifted, an arc of fire, above the mar-
gin of the world. Then with a great cry the Riders
charged from the East; the red light gleamed on mail and
spear. The Orcs yelled and shot all the arrows that remained to them. The hobbits saw several horsemen fall; but
their line held on up the hill and over it, and wheeled
round and charged again. Most of the raiders that were
left alive then broke and fled, this way and that, pursued
one by one to the death. But one band, holding together in
a black wedge, drove forward resolutely in the direction
of the forest. Straight up the slope they charged towards
the watchers. Now they were drawing near, and it seemed
certain that they would escape: they had already hewn
down three Riders that barred their way.

'We have watched too long,' said Merry. 'There's Uglúk! I don't want to meet him again.' The hobbits turned
and fled deep into the shadows of the wood.

So it was that they did not see the last stand, when
Uglúk was overtaken and brought to bay at the very edge
of Fangorn. There he was slain at last by Éomer, the Third

Marshal of Rohan, who dismounted and fought him sword to sword. And over the wide fields the keen-eyed Riders hunted down the few Orcs that had escaped and still had strength to fly.

Then when they had laid their fallen comrades in a mound and had sung their praises, the Riders made a great fire and scattered the ashes of their enemies. So ended the raid, and no news of it came ever back either to Mordor or to Isengard; but the smoke of the burning rose high to heaven and was seen by many watchful eyes.

Chapter 4

Treebeard

Meanwhile the hobbits went with as much speed as the dark and tangled forest allowed, following the line of the running stream, westward and up towards the slopes of the mountains, deeper and deeper into Fangorn. Slowly their fear of the Orcs died away, and their pace slackened. A queer stifling feeling came over them, as if the air were too thin or too scanty for breathing.

At last Merry halted. 'We can't go on like this,' he panted. 'I want some air.'

'Let's have a drink at any rate,' said Pippin. 'I'm parched.' He clambered onto a great tree-root that wound down into the stream, and stooping drew up some water in his cupped hands. It was clear and cold, and he took many draughts. Merry followed him. The water refreshed them and seemed to cheer their hearts; for a while they sat together on the brink of the stream, dabbling their sore feet and legs, and peering round at the trees that stood silently about them, rank upon rank, until they faded away into grey twilight in every direction.

'I suppose you haven't lost us already?' said Pippin, leaning back against a great tree-trunk. 'We can at least follow the course of this stream, the Entwash or whatever you call it, and get out again the way we came.'

'We could, if our legs would do it,' said Merry; 'and if we could breathe properly.'

'Yes, it is all very dim, and stuffy, in here,' said Pippin. 'It reminds me, somehow, of the old room in the Great Place of the Tooks away back in the Smials at Tuckborough: a huge place, where the furniture has never been moved or changed for generations. They say the Old Took lived in it year after year, while he and the room got older and shabbier together—and it has never been changed since he died, a century ago. And Old Gerontius

was my great-great-grandfather: that puts it back a bit.
But that is nothing to the old feeling of this wood. Look
at all those weeping, trailing, beards and whiskers of
lichen! And most of the trees seem to be half covered with
ragged dry leaves that have never fallen. Untidy. I can't
imagine what spring would look like here, if it ever comes;
still less a spring-cleaning.'

'But the Sun at any rate must peep in sometimes,' said
Merry. 'It does not look or feel at all like Bilbo's description of Mirkwood. That was all dark and black, and the
home of dark black things. This is just dim, and frightfully
tree-ish. You can't imagine *animals* living here at all, or
staying for long.'

'No, nor hobbits,' said Pippin. 'And I don't like the
thought of trying to get through it either. Nothing to eat
for a hundred miles, I should guess. How are our supplies?'

'Low,' said Merry. 'We ran off with nothing but a couple
of spare packets of *lembas,* and left everything else behind.' They looked at what remained of the elven-cakes:
broken fragments for about five meagre days, that was all.
'And not a wrap or a blanket,' said Merry. 'We shall be
cold tonight, whichever way we go.'

'Well, we'd better decide on the way now,' said Pippin.
'The morning must be getting on.'

Just then they became aware of a yellow light that had
appeared, some way further on into the wood: shafts of
sunlight seemed suddenly to have pierced the forest-roof.

'Hullo!' said Merry. 'The Sun must have run into a
cloud while we've been under these trees, and now she has
run out again; or else she has climbed high enough to look
down through some opening. It isn't far—let's go and in-
vestigate!'

They found it was further than they thought. The
ground was rising steeply still, and it was becoming in-
creasingly stony. The light grew broader as they went on,
and soon they saw that there was a rock-wall before them:
the side of a hill, or the abrupt end of some long root
thrust out by the distant mountains. No trees grew on it,

and the sun was falling full on its stony face. The twigs of
the trees at its foot were stretched out stiff and still, as
if reaching out to the warmth. Where all had looked so
shabby and grey before, the wood now gleamed with rich
browns, and with the smooth black-greys of bark like
polished leather. The boles of the trees glowed with a soft
green like young grass: early spring or a fleeting vision
of it was about them.

In the face of the stony wall there was something like a
stair: natural perhaps, and made by the weathering and
splitting of the rock, for it was rough and uneven. High up,
almost level with the tops of forest-trees, there was a shelf
under a cliff. Nothing grew there but a few grasses and
weeds at its edge, and one old stump of a tree with only
two bent branches left: it looked almost like the figure of
some gnarled old man, standing there, blinking in the
morning-light.

'Up we go!' said Merry joyfully. 'Now for a breath of
air, and a sight of the land!'

They climbed and scrambled up the rock. If the stair
had been made it was for bigger feet and longer legs than
theirs. They were too eager to be surprised at the remark-
able way in which the cuts and sores of their captivity
had healed and their vigour had returned. They came at
length to the edge of the shelf almost at the feet of the old
stump; then they sprang up and turned round with their
backs to the hill, breathing deep, and looking out eastward.
They saw that they had only come some three or four
miles into the forest: the heads of the trees marched
down the slopes towards the plain. There, near the fringe
of the forest, tall spires of curling black smoke went up,
wavering and floating towards them.

'The wind's changing,' said Merry. 'It's turned east
again. It feels cool up here.'

'Yes,' said Pippin; 'I'm afraid this is only a passing
gleam, and it will all go grey again. What a pity! This
shaggy old forest looked so different in the sunlight. I almost felt I liked the place.'

'Almost felt you liked the Forest! That's good! That's

uncommonly kind of you,' said a strange voice. 'Turn round and let me have a look at your faces. I almost feel that I dislike you both, but do not let us be hasty. Turn round!' A large knob-knuckled hand was laid on each of their shoulders, and they were twisted round, gently but irresistibly; then two great arms lifted them up.

They found that they were looking at a most extraordinary face. It belonged to a large Man-like, almost Troll-like, figure, at least fourteen feet high, very sturdy, with a tall head, and hardly any neck. Whether it was clad in stuff like green and grey bark, or whether that was its hide, was difficult to say. At any rate the arms, at a short distance from the trunk, were not wrinkled, but covered with a brown smooth skin. The large feet had seven toes each. The lower part of the long face was covered with a sweeping grey beard, bushy, almost twiggy at the roots, thin and mossy at the ends. But at the moment the hobbits noted little but the eyes. These deep eyes were now surveying them, slow and solemn, but very penetrating. They were brown, shot with a green light. Often afterwards Pippin tried to describe his first impression of them.

'One felt as if there was an enormous well behind them, filled up with ages of memory and long, slow, steady thinking; but their surface was sparkling with the present: like sun shimmering on the outer leaves of a vast tree, or on the ripples of a very deep lake. I don't know, but it felt as if something that grew in the ground—asleep, you might say, or just feeling itself as something between root-tip and leaf-tip, between deep earth and sky—had suddenly waked up, and was considering you with the same slow care that it had given to its own inside affairs for endless years.'

'Hrum, Hoom,' murmured the voice, a deep voice like a very deep woodwind instrument. 'Very odd indeed! Do not be hasty, that is my motto. But if I had seen you, before I heard your voices—I liked them: nice little voices; they reminded me of something I cannot remember—if I had seen you before I heard you, I should have just trodden on you, taking you for little Orcs, and found out my mistake afterwards. Very odd you are, indeed. Root and twig, very odd!'

Pippin, though still amazed, no longer felt afraid. Under those eyes he felt a curious suspense, but not fear. 'Please,' he said, 'who are you? And what are you?'

A queer look came into the old eyes, a kind of wariness; the deep wells were covered over. 'Hrum, now,' answered the voice; 'well, I am an Ent, or that's what they call me. Yes, Ent is the word. *The* Ent, I am, you might say, in your manner of speaking. *Fangorn* is my name according to some, *Treebeard* others make it. *Treebeard* will do.'

'An *Ent*?' said Merry. 'What's that? But what do you call yourself? What's your real name?'

'Hoo now!' replied Treebeard. 'Hoo! Now that would be telling! Not so hasty. And *I* am doing the asking. You are in *my* country. What are *you*, I wonder? I cannot place you. You do not seem to come in the old lists that I learned when I was young. But that was a long, long time ago, and they may have made new lists. Let me see! Let me see! How did it go?

> *Learn now the lore of Living Creatures!*
> *First name the four, the free peoples:*
> *Eldest of all, the elf-children;*
> *Dwarf the delver, dark are his houses;*
> *Ent the earthborn, old as mountains;*
> *Man the mortal, master of horses:*

Hm, hm, hm.

> *Beaver the builder, buck the leaper,*
> *Bear bee-hunter, boar the fighter;*
> *Hound is hungry, hare is fearful . . .*

hm, hm.

> *Eagle in eyrie, ox in pasture,*
> *Hart horn-crownéd; hawk is swiftest,*
> *Swan the whitest, serpent coldest. . . .*

Hoom, hm; hoom, hm, how did it go? Room tum, room tum, roomty toom tum. It was a long list. But anyway you do not seem to fit in anywhere!'

'We always seem to have got left out of the old lists, and the old stories,' said Merry. 'Yet we've been about for quite a long time. We're *hobbits*.'

'Why not make a new line?' said Pippin.

Half-grown hobbits, the hole-dwellers.

Put us in amongst the four, next to Man (the Big People) and you've got it.'

'Hm! Not bad, not bad,' said Treebeard. 'That would do. So you live in holes, eh? It sounds very right and proper. Who calls you *hobbits,* though? That does not sound elvish to me. Elves made all the old words: they began it.'

'Nobody else calls us hobbits; we call ourselves that,' said Pippin.

'Hoom, hmm! Come now! Not so hasty! You call *yourselves* hobbits? But you should not go telling just anybody. You'll be letting out your own right names if you're not careful.'

'We aren't careful about that,' said Merry. 'As a matter of fact I'm a Brandybuck, Meriadoc Brandybuck, though most people call me just Merry.'

'And I'm a Took, Peregrin Took, but I'm generally called Pippin, or even Pip.'

'Hm, but you *are* hasty folk, I see,' said Treebeard. 'I am honoured by your confidence; but you should not be too free all at once. There are Ents and Ents, you know; or there are Ents and things that look like Ents but ain't, as you might say. I'll call you Merry and Pippin, if you please —nice names. For I am not going to tell you *my* name, not yet at any rate.' A queer half-knowing, half-humorous look came with a green flicker into his eyes. 'For one thing it would take a long while: my name is growing all the time, and I've lived a very long, long time; so *my* name is like a story. Real names tell you the story of the things they belong to in my language, in the Old Entish as you might say. It is a lovely language, but it takes a very long time to say anything in it, because we do not say anything in it, unless it is worth taking a long time to say, and to listen to.

'But now,' and the eyes became very bright and 'present', seeming to grow smaller and almost sharp, 'what is going on? What are you doing in it all? I can see and hear (*and* smell *and* feel) a great deal from this, from this, from this *a-lalla-lalla-rumba-kamanda-lind-or-burúmë*. Excuse me: that is a part of my name for it; I do not know what the word is in the outside languages: you know, the thing we are on, where I stand and look out on fine mornings, and think about the Sun, and the grass beyond the wood, and the horses, and the clouds, and the unfolding of the world. What is going on? What is Gandalf up to? And these—*burárum*,' he made a deep rumbling noise like a discord on a great organ—'these Orcs, and young Saruman down at Isengard? I like news. But not too quick now.'

'There is quite a lot going on,' said Merry; 'and even if we tried to be quick, it would take a long time to tell. But you told us not to be hasty. Ought we to tell you anything so soon? Would you think it rude, if we asked what you are going to do with us, and which side you are on? And did you know Gandalf?'

'Yes, I do know him: the only wizard that really cares about trees,' said Treebeard. 'Do you know him?'

'Yes,' said Pippin sadly, 'we did. He was a great friend, and he was our guide.'

'Then I can answer your other questions,' said Treebeard. 'I am not going to do anything *with* you; not if you mean by that "do something *to* you" without your leave. We might do some things together. I don't know about *sides*. I go my own way; but your way may go along with mine for a while. But you speak of Master Gandalf, as if he was in a story that had come to an end.'

'Yes, we do,' said Pippin sadly. 'The story seems to be going on, but I am afraid Gandalf has fallen out of it.'

'Hoo, come now!' said Treebeard. 'Hoom, hm, ah well.' He paused, looking long at the hobbits. 'Hoom, ah, well I do not know what to say. Come now!'

'If you would like to hear more,' said Merry, 'we will tell you. But it will take some time. Wouldn't you like to put us down? Couldn't we sit here together in the sun, while it lasts? You must be getting tired of holding us up.'

'Hm, *tired*? No, I am not tired. I do not easily get tired. And I do not sit down. I am not very, hm, bendable. But there, the Sun *is* going in. Let us leave this—did you say what you call it?'

'Hill?' suggested Pippin. 'Shelf? Step?' suggested Merry.

Treebeard repeated the words thoughtfully. 'Hill. Yes, that was it. But it is a hasty word for a thing that has stood here ever since this part of the world was shaped. Never mind. Let us leave it, and go.'

'Where shall we go?' asked Merry.

'To my home, or one of my homes,' answered Treebeard.

'Is it far?'

'I do not know. You might call it far, perhaps. But what does that matter?'

'Well, you see, we have lost all our belongings,' said Merry. 'We have only a little food.'

'O! Hm! You need not trouble about that,' said Treebeard. 'I can give you a drink that will keep you green and growing for a long, long while. And if we decide to part company, I can set you down outside my country at any point you choose. Let us go!'

Holding the hobbits gently but firmly, one in the crook of each arm, Treebeard lifted up first one large foot and then the other, and moved them to the edge of the shelf. The rootlike toes grasped the rocks. Then carefully and solemnly, he stalked down from step to step, and reached the floor of the Forest.

At once he set off with long deliberate strides through the trees, deeper and deeper into the wood, never far from the stream, climbing steadily up towards the slopes of the mountains. Many of the trees seemed asleep, or as unaware of him as of any other creature that merely passed by; but some quivered, and some raised up their branches above his head as he approached. All the while, as he walked, he talked to himself in a long running stream of musical sounds.

The hobbits were silent for some time. They felt, oddly enough, safe and comfortable, and they had a great deal to think and wonder about. At last Pippin ventured to speak again.

'Please, Treebeard,' he said, 'could I ask you something? Why did Celeborn warn us against your forest? He told us not to risk getting entangled in it.'

'Hmm, did he now?' rumbled Treebeard. 'And I might have said much the same, if you had been going the other way. Do not risk getting entangled in the woods of *Laurelindórinan*! That is what the Elves used to call it, but now they make the name shorter: *Lothlórien* they call it. Perhaps they are right: maybe it is fading, not growing. Land of the Valley of Singing Gold, that was it, once upon a time. Now it is the Dreamflower. Ah well! But it is a queer place, and not for just anyone to venture in. I am surprised that you ever got out, but much more surprised that you ever got in: that has not happened to strangers for many a year. It is a queer land.

'And so is this. Folk have come to grief here. Aye, they have, to grief. *Laurelindórinan lindelorendor malinornélion ornemalin,*' he hummed to himself. 'They are falling rather behind the world in there, I guess,' he said. 'Neither this country, nor anything else outside the Golden Wood, is what it was when Celeborn was young. Still:

Taurelilómëa-tumbalemorna Tumbaletaurëa Lómëanor,

that is what they used to say. Things have changed, but it is still true in places.'

'What do you mean?' said Pippin. 'What is true?'

'The trees and the Ents,' said Treebeard. 'I do not understand all that goes on myself, so I cannot explain it to you. Some of us are still true Ents, and lively enough in our fashion, but many are growing sleepy, going tree-ish, as you might say. Most of the trees are just trees, of course; but many are half awake. Some are quite wide awake, and a few are, well, ah, well, getting *Entish*. That is going on all the time.

'When that happens to a tree, you find that some have *bad* hearts. Nothing to do with their wood: I do not mean that. Why, I knew some good old willows down the Entwash, gone long ago, alas! They were quite hollow, indeed they were falling all to pieces, but as quiet and sweet-spoken as a young leaf. And then there are some trees in the valleys under the mountains, sound as a bell, and bad right through. That sort of thing seems to spread. There used to be some very dangerous parts in this country. There are still some very black patches.'

'Like the Old Forest away to the north, do you mean?' asked Merry.

'Aye, aye, something like, but much worse. I do not doubt there is some shadow of the Great Darkness lying there still away north; and bad memories are handed down. But there are hollow dales in this land where the Darkness has never been lifted, and the trees are older than I am. Still, we do what we can. We keep off strangers and the foolhardy; and we train and we teach, we walk and we weed.

'We are tree-herds, we old Ents. Few enough of us are left now. Sheep get like shepherds, and shepherds like sheep, it is said; but slowly, and neither have long in the world. It is quicker and closer with trees and Ents, and they walk down the ages together. For Ents are more like Elves: less interested in themselves than Men are, and better at getting inside other things. And yet again Ents are more like Men, more changeable than Elves are, and quicker at taking the colour of the outside, you might say. Or better than both: for they are steadier and keep their minds on things longer.

'Some of my kin look just like trees now, and need something great to rouse them; and they speak only in whispers. But some of my trees are limb-lithe, and many can talk to me. Elves began it, of course, waking trees up and teaching them to speak and learning their tree-talk. They always wished to talk to everything, the old Elves did. But then the Great Darkness came, and they passed away over the Sea, or fled into far valleys, and hid themselves, and made songs about days that would never come again. Never again. Aye, aye, there was all one wood once upon a time from here to the Mountains of Lune, and this was just the East End.

'Those were the broad days! Time was when I could walk and sing all day and hear no more than the echo of my own voice in the hollow hills. The woods were like the woods of Lothlórien, only thicker, stronger, younger. And the smell of the air! I used to spend a week just breathing.'

Treebeard fell silent, striding along, and yet making hardly a sound with his great feet. Then he began to hum again, and passed into a murmuring chant. Gradually the hobbits became aware that he was chanting to them:

> In the willow-meads of Tasarinan I walked in the
> Spring.
> Ah! the sight and the smell of the Spring in Nan-
> tasarion!
> And I said that was good.
> I wandered in Summer in the elm-woods of Ossiriand.
> Ah! the light and the music in the Summer by the
> Seven Rivers of Ossir!
> And I thought that was best.
> To the beeches of Neldoreth I came in the Autumn.
> Ah! the gold and the red and the sighing of leaves in the
> Autumn in Taur-na-neldor!
> It was more than my desire.
> To the pine-trees upon the highland of Dorthonion I
> climbed in the Winter.
> Ah! the wind and the whiteness and the black branches
> of Winter upon Orod-na-Thôn!
> My voice went up and sang in the sky.
> And now all those lands lie under the wave,

And I walk in Ambarona, in Tauremorna, in Aldalómë,
In my own land, in the country of Fangorn,
Where the roots are long,
And the years lie thicker than the leaves
In Tauremornalómë.

He ended, and strode on silently, and in all the wood, as far as ear could reach, there was not a sound.

The day waned, and dusk was twined about the boles of the trees. At last the hobbits saw, rising dimly before them, a steep dark land: they had come to the feet of the mountains, and to the green roots of tall Methedras. Down the hillside the young Entwash, leaping from its springs high above, ran noisily from step to step to meet them. On the right of the stream there was a long slope, clad with grass, now grey in the twilight. No trees grew there and it was open to the sky; stars were shining already in lakes between shores of cloud.

Treebeard strode up the slope, hardly slackening his pace. Suddenly before them the hobbits saw a wide opening. Two great trees stood there, one on either side, like living gate-posts; but there was no gate save their crossing and interwoven boughs. As the old Ent approached, the trees lifted up their branches, and all their leaves quivered and rustled. For they were evergreen trees, and their leaves were dark and polished, and gleamed in the twilight. Beyond them was a wide level space, as though the floor of a great hall had been cut in the side of the hill. On either hand the walls sloped upwards, until they were fifty feet high or more, and along each wall stood an aisle of trees that also increased in height as they marched inwards.

At the far end the rock-fall was sheer, but at the bottom it had been hollowed back into a shallow bay with an arched roof: the only roof of the hall, save the branches of the trees, which at the inner end overshadowed all the ground leaving only a broad open path in the middle. A little stream escaped from the springs above, and

leaving the main water, fell tinkling down the sheer face
of the wall, pouring in silver drops, like a fine curtain in
front of the arched bay. The water was gathered again into
a stone basin in the floor between the trees, and thence
it spilled and flowed away beside the open path, out to
rejoin the Entwash in its journey through the forest.

'Hm! Here we are!' said Treebeard, breaking his long
silence. 'I have brought you about seventy thousand ent-
strides, but what that comes to in the measurement of your
land I do not know. Anyhow we are near the roots of the
Last Mountain. Part of the name of this place might be
Wellinghall, if it were turned into your language. I like it.
We will stay here tonight.' He set them down on the
grass between the aisles of the trees, and they followed
him towards the great arch. The hobbits now noticed that
as he walked his knees hardly bent, but his legs opened in
a great stride. He planted his big toes (and they were
indeed big, and very broad) on the ground first, before
any part of his feet.

For a moment Treebeard stood under the rain of the
falling spring, and took a deep breath; then he laughed,
and passed inside. A great stone table stood there, but no
chairs. At the back of the bay it was already quite dark.
Treebeard lifted two great vessels and stood them on the
table. They seemed to be filled with water; but he held his
hands over them, and immediately they began to glow,
one with a golden and the other with a rich green light; and
the blending of the two lights lit the bay, as if the sun
of summer was shining through a roof of young leaves.
Looking back, the hobbits saw that the trees in the court
had also begun to glow, faintly at first, but steadily quickening, until every leaf was edged with light: some green,
some gold, some red as copper; while the tree-trunks
looked like pillars moulded out of luminous stone.

'Well, well, now we can talk again,' said Treebeard.
'You are thirsty, I expect. Perhaps you are also tired.
Drink this!' He went to the back of the bay, and then they
saw that several tall stone jars stood there, with heavy

lids. He removed one of the lids, and dipped in a great ladle, and with it filled three bowls, one very large bowl, and two smaller ones.

'This is an ent-house,' he said, 'and there are no seats, I fear. But you may sit on the table.' Picking up the hobbits he set them on the great stone slab, six feet above the ground, and there they sat dangling their legs, and drinking in sips.

The drink was like water, indeed very like the taste of the draughts they had drunk from the Entwash near the borders of the forest, and yet there was some scent or savour in it which they could not describe: it was faint, but it reminded them of the smell of a distant wood borne from afar by a cool breeze at night. The effect of the draught began at the toes, and rose steadily through every limb, bringing refreshment and vigour as it coursed upwards, right to the tips of the hair. Indeed the hobbits felt that the hair on their heads was actually standing up, waving and curling and growing. As for Treebeard, he first laved his feet in the basin beyond the arch, and then he drained his bowl at one draught, one long, slow draught. The hobbits thought he would never stop.

At last he set the bowl down again. 'Ah—ah,' he sighed. 'Hm, hoom, now we can talk easier. You can sit on the floor, and I will lie down; that will prevent this drink from rising to my head and sending me to sleep.'

On the right side of the bay there was a great bed on low legs, not more than a couple of feet high, covered deep in dried grass and bracken. Treebeard lowered himself slowly onto this (with only the slightest sign of bending at his middle), until he lay at full length, with his arms behind his head, looking up at the ceiling, upon which lights were flickering, like the play of leaves in the sunshine. Merry and Pippin sat beside him on pillows of grass.

'Now tell me your tale, and do not hurry!' said Treebeard.

The hobbits began to tell him the story of their adven-

tures ever since they left Hobbiton. They followed no very
clear order, for they interrupted one another continually,
and Treebeard often stopped the speaker, and went back
to some earlier point, or jumped forward asking questions
about later events. They said nothing whatever about the
Ring, and did not tell him why they set out or where they
were going to; and he did not ask for any reasons.

He was immensely interested in everything: in the Black
Riders, in Elrond, and Rivendell, in the Old Forest, and
Tom Bombadil, in the Mines of Moria, and in Lothlórien
and Galadriel. He made them describe the Shire and its
country over and over again. He said an odd thing at this
point. 'You never see any, hm, any Ents round there, do
you?' he asked. 'Well, not Ents, *Entwives* I should really
say.'

'*Entwives?*' said Pippin. 'Are they like you at all?'

'Yes, hm, well no: I do not really know now,' said
Treebeard thoughtfully. 'But they would like your country, so I just wondered.'

Treebeard was however especially interested in everything that concerned Gandalf; and most interested of all
in Saruman's doings. The hobbits regretted very much that
they knew so little about them: only a rather vague report by Sam of what Gandalf had told the Council. But
they were clear at any rate that Uglúk and his troop
came from Isengard, and spoke of Saruman as their master.

'Hm, hoom!' said Treebeard, when at last their story had
wound and wandered down to the battle of the Orcs and
the Riders of Rohan. 'Well, well! That is a bundle of news
and no mistake. You have not told me all, no indeed,
not by a long way. But I do not doubt that you are doing
as Gandalf would wish. There is something very big going
on, that I can see, and what it is maybe I shall learn in
good time, or in bad time. By root and twig, but it is a
strange business: up sprout a little folk that are not in the
old lists, and behold! the Nine forgotten Riders reappear
to hunt them, and Gandalf takes them on a great journey, and Galadriel harbours them in Caras Galadon, and

Orcs pursue them down all the leagues of Wilderland: indeed they seem to be caught up in a great storm. I hope they weather it!'

'And what about yourself?' asked Merry.

'Hoom, hm, I have not troubled about the Great Wars,' said Treebeard; 'they mostly concern Elves and Men. That is the business of wizards: wizards are always troubled about the future. I do not like worrying about the future. I am not altogether on anybody's *side,* because nobody is altogether on my *side,* if you understand me: nobody cares for the woods as I care for them, not even Elves nowadays. Still, I take more kindly to Elves than to others: it was the Elves that cured us of dumbness long ago, and that was a great gift that cannot be forgotten, though our ways have parted since. And there are some things, of course, whose side I am altogether *not* on; I am against them altogether: these—*burárum'* (he again made a deep rumble of disgust) '—these Orcs, and their masters.

'I used to be anxious when the shadow lay on Mirkwood, but when it removed to Mordor, I did not trouble for a while: Mordor is a long way away. But it seems that the wind is setting East, and the withering of all woods may be drawing near. There is naught that an old Ent can do to hold back that storm: he must weather it or crack.

'But Saruman now! Saruman is a neighbour: I cannot overlook him. I must do something, I suppose. I have often wondered lately what I should do about Saruman.'

'Who is Saruman?' asked Pippin. 'Do you know anything about his history?'

'Saruman is a wizard,' answered Treebeard. 'More than that I cannot say. I do not know the history of wizards. They appeared first after the Great Ships came over the Sea; but if they came with the Ships I never can tell. Saruman was reckoned great among them, I believe. He gave up wandering about and minding the affairs of Men and Elves, some time ago—you would call it a very long time ago; and he settled down at Angrenost, or Isengard as the Men of Rohan call it. He was very quiet to begin with, but his fame began to grow. He was chosen to be the head of the White Council, they say; but that did not turn out too well. I wonder now if even then Saruman was not turning to evil ways. But at any rate he used to give no trouble to his neighbours. I used to talk to him. There was a time when he was always walking about my woods. He was polite in those days, always asking my leave (at least when he met me); and always eager to listen. I told him many things that he would never have found out by himself; but he never repaid me in like kind. I cannot remember that he ever told me anything. And he got more and more like that; his face, as I remember it—I have not seen it for many a day—became like windows in a stone wall: windows with shutters inside.

'I think that I now understand what he is up to. He is plotting to become a Power. He has a mind of metal and wheels; and he does not care for growing things, except as far as they serve him for the moment. And now it is clear that he is a black traitor. He has taken up with foul folk, with the Orcs. Brm, hoom! Worse than that: he has been doing something to them; something dangerous. For these Isengarders are more like wicked Men. It is a mark of evil things that came in the Great Darkness that they cannot abide the Sun; but Saruman's Orcs can endure it, even if they hate it. I wonder what he has done? Are they Men he has ruined, or has he blended the races of Orcs and Men? That would be a black evil!'

Treebeard rumbled for a moment, as if he were pronouncing some deep, subterranean Entish malediction. 'Some time ago I began to wonder how Orcs dared to pass through my woods so freely,' he went on. 'Only lately did I guess that Saruman was to blame, and that long ago he had been spying out all the ways, and discovering my secrets. He and his foul folk are making havoc now. Down on the borders they are felling trees—good trees. Some of the trees they just cut down and leave to rot—orc-mischief that, but most are hewn up and carried off to feed the fires of Orthanc. There is always a smoke rising from Isengard these days.

'Curse him, root and branch! Many of those trees

were my friends, creatures I had known from nut and acorn; many had voices of their own that are lost forever now. And there are wastes of stump and bramble where once there were singing groves. I have been idle. I have let things slip. It must stop!'

Treebeard raised himself from his bed with a jerk, stood up, and thumped his hand on the table. The vessels of light trembled and sent up two jets of flame. There was a flicker like green fire in his eyes, and his beard stood out stiff as a great besom.

'I will stop it!' he boomed. 'And you shall come with me. You may be able to help me. You will be helping your own friends that way, too; for if Saruman is not checked Rohan and Gondor will have an enemy behind as well as in front. Our roads go together—to Isengard!'

'We will come with you,' said Merry. 'We will do what we can.'

'Yes!' said Pippin. 'I should like to see the White Hand overthrown. I should like to be there, even if I could not be of much use: I shall never forget Uglúk and the crossing of Rohan.'

'Good! Good!' said Treebeard. 'But I spoke hastily. We must not be hasty. I have become too hot. I must cool myself and think; for it is easier to shout *stop*! than to do it!'

He strode to the archway and stood for some time under the falling rain of the spring. Then he laughed and shook himself, and wherever the drops of water fell glittering from him to the ground they glinted like red and green sparks. He came back and laid himself on the bed again and was silent.

After some time the hobbits heard him murmuring again. He seemed to be counting on his fingers. 'Fangorn, Finglas, Fladrif, aye, aye,' he sighed. 'The trouble is that there are so few of us left,' he said turning toward the hobbits. 'Only three remain of the first Ents that walked in the woods before the Darkness: only myself, Fangorn, and Finglas and Fladrif—to give them their Elvish names;

you may call them Leaflock and Skinbark if you like that
better. And of us three, Leaflock and Skinbark are not
much use for this business. Leaflock has grown sleepy, almost tree-ish, you might say: he has taken to standing by
himself half-asleep all through the summer with the deep
grass of the meadows round his knees. Covered with leafy
hair he is. He used to rouse up in winter; but of late he
has been too drowsy to walk far even then. Skinbark lived
on the mountain-slopes west of Isengard. That is where
the worst trouble has been. He was wounded by the Orcs,
and many of his folk and his tree-herds have been murdered and destroyed. He has gone up into the high places,
among the birches that he loves best, and he will not
come down. Still, I daresay I could get together a fair
company of our younger folks—if I could make them
understand the need; if I could rouse them: we are not a
nasty folk. What a pity there are so few of us!'

'Why are there so few, when you have lived in this
country so long?' asked Pippin. 'Have a great many died?'

'Oh, no!' said Treebeard. 'None have died from inside,
as you might say. Some have fallen in the evil chambers of
the long years, of course; and more have grown tree-ish.
But there were never many of us and we have not increased. There have been no Entings—no children, you
would say, not for a terrible long count of years. You
see, we lost the Entwives.'

'How very sad!' said Pippin. 'How was it that they all
died?'

'They did not *die*!' said Treebeard. 'I never said *died*.
We lost them, I said. We lost them and we cannot find
them.' He sighed. 'I thought most folk knew that. There
were songs about the hunt of the Ents for the Entwives
sung among Elves and Men from Mirkwood to Gondor.
They cannot be quite forgotten.'

'Well, I am afraid the songs have not come west over
the Mountains to the Shire,' said Merry. 'Won't you tell
us some more, or sing us one of the songs?'

'Yes, I will indeed,' said Treebeard, seeming pleased
with the request. 'But I cannot tell it properly, only in

short; and then we must end our talk: tomorrow we have councils to call, and work to do, and maybe a journey to begin.'

'It is rather a strange and sad story,' he went on after a pause. 'When the world was young, and the woods were wide and wild, the Ents and the Entwives—and there were Entmaidens then: ah! the loveliness of Fimbrethil, of Wandlimb the lightfooted, in the days of our youth!—they walked together and they housed together. But our hearts did not go on growing in the same way: the Ents gave their love to things that they met in the world, and the Entwives gave their thought to other things, for the Ents loved the great trees, and the wild woods, and the slopes of the high hills; and they drank of the mountain-streams, and ate only such fruit as the trees let fall in their path; and they learned of the Elves and spoke with the Trees. But the Entwives gave their minds to the lesser trees, and to the meads in the sunshine beyond the feet of the forests; and they saw the sloe in the thicket, and the wild apple and the cherry blossoming in spring, and the green herbs in the waterlands in summer, and the seeding grasses in the autumn fields. They did not desire to speak with these things; but they wished them to hear and obey what was said to them. The Entwives ordered them to grow according to their wishes, and bear leaf and fruit to their liking; for the Entwives desired order, and plenty, and peace (by which they meant that things should remain where they had set them). So the Entwives made gardens to live in. But we Ents went on wandering, and we only came to the gardens now and again. Then when the Darkness came in the North, the Entwives crossed the Great River, and made new gardens, and tilled new fields, and we saw them more seldom. After the Darkness was over-thrown the land of the Entwives blossomed richly, and their fields were full of corn. Many men learned the crafts of the Entwives and honoured them greatly; but we were only a legend to them, a secret in the heart of the forest. Yet here we still are, while all the gardens of the

Entwives are wasted: Men call them the Brown Lands now.

'I remember it was long ago—in the time of the war between Sauron and the Men of the Sea—desire came over me to see Fimbrethil again. Very fair she was still in my eyes, when I had last seen her, though little like the Entmaiden of old. For the Entwives were bent and browned by their labour; their hair parched by the sun to the hue of ripe corn and their cheeks like red apples. Yet their eyes were still the eyes of our own people. We crossed over Anduin and came to their land; but we found a desert: it was all burned and uprooted, for war had passed over it. But the Entwives were not there. Long we called, and long we searched; and we asked all folk that we met which way the Entwives had gone. Some said they had never seen them; and some said that they had seen them walking away west, and some said east, and others south. But nowhere that we went could we find them. Our sorrow was very great. Yet the wild wood called, and we returned to it. For many many years we used to go out every now and again and look for the Entwives, walking far and wide and calling them by their beautiful names. But as time passed we went more seldom and wandered less far. And now the Entwives are only a memory for us, and our beards are long and grey. The Elves made many songs concerning the Search of the Ents, and some of the songs passed into the tongues of Men. But we made no songs about it, being content to chant their beautiful names when we thought of the Entwives. We believe that we may meet again in a time to come, and perhaps we shall find somewhere a land where we can live together and both be content. But it is foreboded that that will only be when we have both lost all that we now have. And it may well be that that time is drawing near at last. For if Sauron of old destroyed the gardens, the Enemy today seems likely to wither all the woods.

'There was an Elvish song that spoke of this, or at least so I understand it. It used to be sung up and down the

Great River. It was never an Entish song, mark you: it would have been a very long song in Entish! But we know it by heart, and hum it now and again. This is how it runs in your tongue:

ENT.

> *When Spring unfolds the beechen leaf, and*
> *   sap is in the bough;*
> *When light is on the wild-wood stream, and*
> *   wind is on the brow;*
> *When stride is long, and breath is deep, and*
> *   keen the mountain-air,*
> *Come back to me! Come back to me, and*
> *   say my land is fair!*

ENTWIFE.

> *When Spring is come to garth and field,*
> *   and corn is in the blade;*
> *When blossom like a shining snow is on the*
> *   orchard laid;*
> *When shower and Sun upon the Earth with*
> *   fragrance fill the air,*
> *I'll linger here, and will not come, because*
> *   my land is fair.*

ENT.

> *When Summer lies upon the world, and in a*
> *   noon of gold,*
> *Beneath the roof of sleeping leaves the*
> *   dreams of trees unfold;*
> *When woodland halls are green and cool,*
> *   and wind is in the West,*
> *Come back to me! Come back to me, and*
> *   say my land is best!*

ENTWIFE.

> *When Summer warms the hanging fruit and*
> *   burns the berry brown;*
> *When straw is gold, and ear is white, and*
> *   harvest comes to town;*
> *When honey spills, and apple swells, though*
> *   wind be in the West,*

*I'll linger here beneath the Sun, because my
land is best!*

ENT.

*When Winter comes, the winter wild that
hill and wood shall slay;
When trees shall fall and starless night devour the sunless day;
When wind is in the deadly East, then in
the bitter rain
I'll look for thee, and call to thee; I'll come
to thee again!*

ENTWIFE.

*When Winter comes, and singing ends;
when darkness falls at last;
When broken is the barren bough, and light
and labour past;
I'll look for thee, and wait for thee, until we
meet again:
Together we will take the road beneath the
bitter rain!*

BOTH.

*Together we will take the road that leads
into the West.
And far away will find a land where both
our hearts may rest.*

Treebeard ended his song. 'That is how it goes,' he said.
'It's Elvish, of course: lighthearted, quickworded, and
soon over. I daresay it is fair enough. But the Ents could
say more on their side, if they had time! But now I am
going to stand up and take a little sleep. Where will you
stand?'

'We usually lie down to sleep,' said Merry. 'We shall be
all right where we are.'

'Lie down to sleep!' said Treebeard. 'Why of course
you do! Hm, hoom: I was forgetting: singing that song put
me in mind of old times: almost thought that I was talking
to young Entings, I did. Well, you can lie on the bed.
I am going to stand in the rain. Good night!'

Merry and Pippin climbed onto the bed and curled up in the soft grass and fern. It was fresh, and sweet-scented, and warm. The lights died down, and the glow of the trees faded; but outside under the arch they could see old Treebeard standing, motionless, with his arms raised above his head. The bright stars peered out of the sky, and lit the falling water as it spilled onto his fingers and head, and dripped, dripped, in hundreds of silver drops onto his feet. Listening to the tinkling of the drops the hobbits fell asleep.

They woke to find a cool sun shining into the great court, and onto the floor of the bay. Shreds of high cloud were overheard, running on a stiff easterly wind. Treebeard was not to be seen; but while Merry and Pippin were bathing in the basin by the arch, they heard him humming and singing, as he came up the path between the trees.

'Hoo, ho! Good morning, Merry and Pippin!' he boomed, when he saw them. 'You sleep long. I have been many a hundred strides already today. Now we will have a drink, and go to Entmoot.'

He poured them out two full bowls from a stone jar; but from a different jar. The taste was not the same as it had been the night before: it was earthier and richer, more sustaining and food-like, so to speak. While the hobbits drank, sitting on the edge of the bed, and nibbling small pieces of elf-cake (more because they felt that eating was a necessary part of breakfast than because they felt hungry), Treebeard stood, humming in Entish or Elvish or some strange tongue, and looking up at the sky.

'Where is Entmoot?' Pippin ventured to ask.

'Hoo, eh? Entmoot?' said Treebeard, turning round. 'It is not a place, it is a gathering of Ents—which does not often happen nowadays. But I have managed to make a fair number promise to come. We shall meet in the place where we have always met: Derndingle Men call it. It is away south from here. We must be there before noon.'

Before long they set off. Treebeard carried the hobbits in his arms as on the previous day. At the entrance to the court he turned to the right, stepped over the stream, and strode away southwards along the feet of great tumbled slopes where trees were scanty. Above these the hobbits saw thickets of birch and rowan, and beyond them dark climbing pinewoods. Soon Treebeard turned a little away from the hills and plunged into deep groves, where the trees were larger, taller, and thicker than any that the hobbits had ever seen before. For a while they felt faintly the sense of stifling which they had noticed when they first ventured into Fangorn, but it soon passed. Treebeard did not talk to them. He hummed to himself deeply and thoughtfully, but Merry and Pippin caught no proper words: it sounded like *boom, boom, rumboom, boorar, boom boom, dahrar boom boom, dahrar boom,* and so on with a constant change of note and rhythm. Now and again they thought they heard an answer, a hum or a quiver of sound, that seemed to come out of the earth, or from boughs above their heads, or perhaps from the boles of the trees; but Treebeard did not stop or turn his head to either side.

They had been going for a long while—Pippin had tried to keep count of the 'ent-strides' but had failed, getting lost at about three thousand—when Treebeard began to slacken his pace. Suddenly he stopped, put the hobbits down, and raised his curled hands to his mouth so that they made a hollow tube; then he blew or called through them. A great *hoom, hom* rang out like a deep-throated horn in the woods, and seemed to echo from the trees. Far off there came from several directions a similar *hoom, hom, hoom* that was not an echo but an answer.

Treebeard now perched Merry and Pippin on his shoulders and strode on again, every now and then sending out another horn-call, and each time the answers came louder and nearer. In this way they came at last to what looked like an impenetrable wall of dark evergreen trees, trees of a kind that the hobbits had never seen before: they branched out right from the roots, and were densely clad in dark glossy leaves like thornless holly, and they bore many stiff upright flower-spikes with large shining olive-coloured buds.

Turning to the left and skirting this huge hedge Treebeard came in a few strides to a narrow entrance. Through it a worn path passed and dived suddenly down a long steep slope. The hobbits saw that they were descending into a great dingle, almost as round as a bowl, very wide and deep, crowned at the rim with the high dark evergreen hedge. It was smooth and grassclad inside, and there were no trees except three very tall and beautiful silver-birches that stood at the bottom of the bowl. Two other paths led down into the dingle: from the west and from the east.

Several Ents had already arrived. More were coming in down the other paths, and some were now following Treebeard. As they drew near the hobbits gazed at them. They had expected to see a number of creatures as much like Treebeard as one hobbit is like another (at any rate to a stranger's eye); and they were very much surprised to see nothing of the kind. The Ents were as different from one another as trees from trees: some as different as one tree is from another of the same name but quite different growth and history; and some as different as one tree-kind from another, as birch from beech, oak from fir. There were a few older Ents, bearded and gnarled like hale but ancient trees (though none looked as ancient as Treebeard); and there were tall strong Ents, clean-limbed and smooth-skinned like forest-trees in their prime; but there were no young Ents, no saplings. Altogether there were about two dozen standing on the wide grassy floor of the dingle, and as many more were marching in.

At first Merry and Pippin were struck chiefly by the variety that they saw: the many shapes, and colours, the differences in girth, and height, and length of leg and arm; and in the number of toes and fingers (anything from three to nine). A few seemed more or less related to Treebeard, and reminded them of beech-trees or oaks. But there were other kinds. Some recalled the chestnut: brown-skinned Ents with large splayfingered hands, and short thick legs. Some recalled the ash: tall straight grey Ents with many-fingered hands and long legs; some the fir (the tallest Ents), and others the birch, the rowan, and the linden. But when the Ents all gathered round Treebeard, bowing their heads slightly, murmuring in their slow musical voices, and looking long and intently at the strangers, then the hobbits saw that they were all of the same kindred, and all had the same eyes: not all so old or so deep as Treebeard's, but all with the same slow, steady, thoughtful expression, and the same green flicker.

As soon as the whole company was assembled, standing in a wide circle round Treebeard, a curious and unintelligible conversation began. The Ents began to murmur slowly: first one joined and then another, until they were all chanting together in a long rising and falling rhythm, now louder on one side of the ring, now dying away there and rising to a great boom on the other side. Though he could not catch or understand any of the words—he supposed the language was Entish—Pippin found the sound very pleasant to listen to at first; but gradually his attention wavered. After a long time (and the chant showed no signs of slackening) he found himself wondering, since Entish was such an 'unhasty' language, whether they had yet got further than *Good Morning*; and if Treebeard was to call the roll, how many days it would take to sing all their names. 'I wonder what the Entish is for *yes* or *no*,' he thought. He yawned.

Treebeard was immediately aware of him. 'Hm, ha, hey, my Pippin!' he said, and the other Ents all stopped their chant. 'You are a hasty folk, I was forgetting; and anyway it is wearisome listening to a speech you do not understand. You may get down now. I have told your names to the Entmoot, and they have seen you, and they have agreed that you are not Orcs, and that a new line shall be put in the old lists. We have got no further yet, but that is quick work for an Entmoot. You and Merry can stroll about in the dingle, if you like. There is a well of good water, if you need refreshing, away yonder in the north bank. There are still some words to speak before the Moot

really begins. I will come and see you again, and tell you
how things are going.'

He put the hobbits down. Before they walked away,
they bowed low. This feat seemed to amuse the Ents very
much, to judge by the tone of their murmurs, and the
flicker of their eyes; but they soon turned back to their own
business. Merry and Pippin climbed up the path that came
in from the west, and looked through the opening in the
great hedge. Long tree-clad slopes rose from the lip of the
dingle, and away beyond them, above the fir-trees of
the furthest ridge there rose, sharp and white, the peak of a
high mountain. Southwards to their left they could see the
forest falling away down into the grey distance. There far
away there was a pale green glimmer that Merry guessed
to be a glimpse of the plains of Rohan.

'I wonder where Isengard is?' said Pippin.

'I don't know quite where we are,' said Merry; 'but that
peak is probably Methedras, and as far as I can remember
the ring of Isengard lies in a fork or deep cleft at the
end of the mountains. It is probably down behind this
great ridge. There seems to be a smoke or haze over there,
left of the peak, don't you think?'

'What is Isengard like?' said Pippin. 'I wonder what
Ents can do about it anyway.'

'So do I,' said Merry. 'Isengard is a sort of ring of rocks
or hills, I think, with a flat space inside and an island or
pillar of rock in the middle, called Orthanc. Saruman has
a tower on it. There is a gate, perhaps more than one, in the
encircling wall, and I believe there is a stream running
through it; it comes out of the mountains, and flows
on across the Gap of Rohan. It does not seem the
sort of place for Ents to tackle. But I have an odd feeling
about these Ents: somehow I don't think they are quite as
safe and, well, funny as they seem. They seem slow,
queer, and patient, almost sad; and yet I believe they
could be roused. If that happened, I would rather not be
on the other side.'

'Yes!' said Pippin. 'I know what you mean. There might

be all the difference between an old cow sitting and thoughtfully chewing, and a bull charging; and the change might come suddenly. I wonder if Treebeard will rouse them. I am sure he means to try. But they don't like being roused. Treebeard got roused himself last night, and then bottled it up again.'

The hobbits turned back. The voices of the Ents were still rising and falling in their conclave. The sun had now risen high enough to look over the high hedge: it gleamed on the tops of the birches and lit the northward side of the dingle with a cool yellow light. There they saw a little glittering fountain. They walked along the rim of the great bowl at the feet of the evergreens—it was pleasant to feel cool grass about their toes again, and not to be in a hurry —and then they climbed down to the gushing water. They drank a little, a clean, cold, sharp draught, and sat down on a mossy stone, watching the patches of sun on the grass and the shadows of the sailing clouds passing over the floor of the dingle. The murmur of the Ents went on. It seemed a very strange and remote place, outside their world, and far from everything that had ever happened to them. A great longing came over them for the faces and voices of their companions, especially for Frodo and Sam, and for Strider.

At last there came a pause in the Ent-voices; and looking up they saw Treebeard coming towards them, with another Ent at his side.

'Hm, hoom, here I am again,' said Treebeard. 'Are you getting weary, or feeling impatient, hmm, eh? Well, I am afraid that you must not get impatient yet. We have finished the first stage now; but I have still got to explain things again to those that live a long way off, far from Isengard, and those that I could not get round to before the Moot, and after that we shall have to decide what to do. However, deciding what to do does not take Ents so long as going over all the facts and events that they have to make up their minds about. Still, it is no use denying, we shall be here a long time yet: a couple of days very likely. So I have brought you a companion. He

has an ent-house nearby. Bregalad is his Elvish name. He
says he has already made up his mind and does not need
to remain at the Moot. Hm, hm, he is the nearest thing
among us to a hasty Ent. You ought to get on together.
Good bye!' Treebeard turned and left them.

Bregalad stood for some time surveying the hobbits
solemnly; and they looked at him, wondering when he
would show any signs of 'hastiness'. He was tall, and
seemed to be one of the younger Ents; he had smooth
shining skin on his arms and legs; his lips were ruddy, and
his hair was grey-green. He could bend and sway like a
slender tree in the wind. At last he spoke, and his voice
though resonant was higher and clearer than Treebeard's.

'Ha, hmm, my friends, let us go for a walk!' he said. 'I
am Bregalad, that is Quickbeam in your language. But it
is only a nickname, of course. They have called me that
ever since I said *yes* to an elder Ent before he had finished
his question. Also I drink quickly, and go out while some
are still wetting their beards. Come with me!'

He reached down two shapely arms and gave a long-
fingered hand to each of the hobbits. All that day they
walked about in the woods with him, singing, and laughing; for Quickbeam often laughed. He laughed if the
sun came out from behind a cloud, he laughed if they
came upon a stream or spring: then he stooped and
splashed his feet and head with water; he laughed sometimes at some sound or whisper in the trees. Whenever he
saw a rowan-tree he halted a while with his arms stretched
out, and sang, and swayed as he sang.

At nightfall he brought them to his ent-house: nothing
more than a mossy stone set upon turves under a green
bank. Rowan-trees grew in a circle about it, and there
was water (as in all ent-houses), a spring bubbling out
from the bank. They talked for a while as darkness fell on
the forest. Not far away the voices of the Entmoot could
be heard still going on; but now they seemed deeper and
less leisurely, and every now and again one great voice
would rise in a high and quickening music, while all the
others died away. But beside them Bregalad spoke gently

in their own tongue, almost whispering; and they learned that he belonged to Skinbark's people, and the country where they had lived had been ravaged. That seemed to the hobbits quite enough to explain his 'hastiness', at least in the matter of Orcs.

'There were rowan-trees in my home,' said Bregalad, softly and sadly, 'rowan-trees that took root when I was an Enting, many many years ago in the quiet of the world. The oldest were planted by the Ents to try and please the Entwives; but they looked at them and smiled and said that they knew where whiter blossom and richer fruit were growing. Yet there are no trees of all that race, the people of the Rose, that are so beautiful to me. And these trees grew, and grew, till the shadow of each was like a green hall, and their red berries in the autumn were a burden, and a beauty and a wonder. Birds used to flock there. I like birds, even when they chatter; and the rowan has enough and to spare. But the birds became unfriendly and greedy and tore at the trees, and threw the fruit down and did not eat it. Then Orcs came with axes and cut down my trees. I came and called them by their long names, but they did not quiver, they did not hear or answer: they lay dead.

O Orofarnë, Lassemista, Carnimírië!
O rowan fair, upon your hair how white the blossom lay!
O rowan mine, I saw you shine upon a summer's day,
Your rind so bright, your leaves so light, your voice so cool
*   and soft:*
Upon your head how golden-red the crown you bore aloft!
O rowan dead, upon your head your hair is dry and grey;
Your crown is spilled, your voice is stilled for ever and a
*   day.*
O Orofarnë, Lassemista, Carnimírië!

The hobbits fell asleep to the sound of the soft singing of Bregalad, that seemed to lament in many tongues the fall of trees that he had loved.

The next day they spent also in his company, but they

did not go far from his 'house'. Most of the time they sat silent under the shelter of the bank; for the wind was colder, and the clouds closer and greyer; there was little sunshine, and in the distance the voices of the Ents at the Moot still rose and fell, sometimes loud and strong, sometimes low and sad, sometimes quickening, sometimes slow and solemn as a dirge. A second night came and still the Ents held conclave under hurrying clouds and fitful stars.

The third day broke, bleak and windy. At sunrise the Ents' voices rose to a great clamour and then died down again. As the morning wore on the wind fell and the air grew heavy with expectancy. The hobbits could see that Bregalad was now listening intently, although to them, down in the dell of his ent-house, the sound of the Moot was faint.

The afternoon came, and the sun, going west towards the mountains, sent out long yellow beams between the cracks and fissures of the clouds. Suddenly they were aware that everything was very quiet; the whole forest stood in listening silence. Of course, the Ent-voices had stopped. What did that mean? Bregalad was standing up erect and tense, looking back northwards towards Derndingle.

Then with a crash came a great ringing shout: *rahoom-rah!* The trees quivered and bent as if a gust had struck them. There was another pause, and then a marching music began like solemn drums, and above the rolling beats and booms there welled voices singing high and strong.

We come, we come with roll of drum: ta-runda runda
runda rom!

The Ents were coming: ever nearer and louder rose their song:

We come, we come with horn and drum: ta-rūna rūna
rūna rom!

Bregalad picked up the hobbits and strode from his house.

Before long they saw the marching line approaching: the Ents were swinging along with great strides down the slope towards them. Treebeard was at their head, and some fifty followers were behind him, two abreast, keeping step with their feet and beating time with their hands upon their flanks. As they drew near the flash and flicker of their eyes could be seen.

'Hoom, hom! Here we come with a boom, here we come at last!' called Treebeard when he caught sight of Bregalad and the hobbits. 'Come, join the Moot! We are off. We are off to Isengard!'

'To Isengard!' the Ents cried in many voices.

'To Isengard!'

> To Isengard! Though Isengard be ringed and barred with
>   doors of stone;
> Though Isengard be strong and hard, as cold as stone and
>   bare as bone,
> We go, we go, we go to war, to hew the stone and break
>   the door;
> For bole and bough are burning now, the furnace roars—
>   we go to war!
> To land of gloom with tramp of doom, with roll of drum,
>   we come, we come;
>   To Isengard with doom we come!
>   With doom we come, with doom we come!

So they sang as they marched southwards.

Bregalad, his eyes shining, swung into the line beside Treebeard. The old Ent now took the hobbits back, and set them on his shoulders again, and so they rode proudly at the head of the singing company with beating hearts and heads held high. Though they had expected something to happen eventually, they were amazed at the change that had come over the Ents. It seemed now as

sudden as the bursting of a flood that had long been held
back by a dike.

'The Ents made up their minds rather quickly, after all,
didn't they?' Pippin ventured to say after some time,
when for a moment the singing paused, and only the beating of hands and feet was heard.

'Quickly?' said Treebeard. 'Hoom! Yes, indeed. Quicker
than I expected. Indeed I have not seen them roused like
this for many an age. We Ents do not like being roused;
and we never are roused unless it is clear to us that our
trees and our lives are in great danger. That has not happened in this Forest since the wars of Sauron and the Men
of the Sea. It is the orc-work, the wanton hewing—*rárum*
—without even the bad excuse of feeding the fires, that
has so angered us; and the treachery of a neighbour, who
should have helped us. Wizards ought to know better:
they do know better. There is no curse in Elvish, Entish, or
the tongues of Men bad enough for such treachery. Down
with Saruman!'

'Will you really break the doors of Isengard?' asked
Merry.

'Ho, hm, well, we could, you know! You do not know,
perhaps, how strong we are. Maybe you have heard of
Trolls? They are mighty strong. But Trolls are only counterfeits, made by the Enemy in the Great Darkness, in
mockery of Ents, as Orcs were of Elves. We are stronger
than Trolls. We are made of the bones of the earth. We
can split stone like the roots of trees, only quicker, far
quicker, if our minds are roused! If we are not hewn down,
or destroyed by fire or blast or sorcery, we could split
Isengard into splinters and crack its walls into rubble.'

'But Saruman will try to stop you, won't he?'

'Hm, ah, yes, that is so. I have not forgotten it. Indeed
I have thought long about it. But, you see, many of the
Ents are younger than I am, by many lives of trees. They
are all roused now, and their mind is all on one thing:
breaking Isengard. But they will start thinking again before long; they will cool down a little, when we take our
evening drink. What a thirst we shall have! But let them

march now and sing! We have a long way to go, and there is time ahead for thought. It is something to have started.'

Treebeard marched on, singing with the others for a while. But after a time his voice died to a murmur and fell silent again. Pippin could see that his old brow was wrinkled and knotted. At last he looked up, and Pippin could see a sad look in his eyes, sad but not unhappy. There was a light in them, as if the green flame had sunk deeper into the dark wells of his thought.

'Of course, it is likely enough, my friends,' he said slowly, 'likely enough that we are going to *our* doom: the last march of the Ents. But if we stayed at home and did nothing, doom would find us anyway, sooner or later. That thought has long been growing in our hearts; and that is why we are marching now. It was not a hasty resolve. Now at least the last march of the Ents may be worth a song. Aye,' he sighed, 'we may help the other peoples before we pass away. Still, I should have liked to see the songs come true about the Entwives. I should dearly have liked to see Fimbrethil again. But there, my friends, songs like trees bear fruit only in their own time and their own way: and sometimes they are withered untimely.'

The Ents went striding on at a great pace. They had descended into a long fold of the land that fell away southward; now they began to climb up, and up, onto the high western ridge. The woods fell away and they came to scattered groups of birch, and then to bare slopes where only a few gaunt pine-trees grew. The sun sank behind the dark hill-back in front. Grey dusk fell.

Pippin looked behind. The number of the Ents had grown—or what was happening? Where the dim bare slopes that they had crossed should lie, he thought he saw groves of trees. But they were moving! Could it be that the trees of Fangorn were awake, and the forest was rising, marching over the hills to war? He rubbed his eyes wondering if sleep and shadow had deceived him; but the great grey shapes moved steadily onward. There was

a noise like wind in many branches. The Ents were drawing near the crest of the ridge now, and all song had
ceased. Night fell, and there was silence: nothing was to
be heard save a faint quiver of the earth beneath the
feet of the Ents, and a rustle, the shade of a whisper as to
many drifting leaves. At last they stood upon the summit,
and looked down into a dark pit: the great cleft at the end
of the mountains: Nan Curunír, the Valley of Saruman.

'Night lies over Isengard,' said Treebeard.

Chapter 5

The White Rider

'My very bones are chilled,' said Gimli, flapping his arms and stamping his feet. Day had come at last. At dawn the companions had made such breakfast as they could; now in the growing light they were getting ready to search the ground again for signs of the hobbits.

'And do not forget that old man!' said Gimli. 'I should be happier if I could see the print of a boot.'

'Why would that make you happy?' said Legolas.

'Because an old man with feet that leave marks might be no more than he seemed,' answered the Dwarf.

'Maybe,' said the Elf; 'but a heavy boot might leave no print here: the grass is deep and springy.'

'That would not baffle a Ranger,' said Gimli. 'A bent blade is enough for Aragorn to read. But I do not expect him to find any traces. It was an evil phantom of Saruman that we saw last night. I am sure of it, even under the light of morning. His eyes are looking out on us from Fangorn even now, maybe.'

'It is likely enough,' said Aragorn; 'yet I am not sure. I am thinking of the horses. You said last night, Gimli, that they were scared away. But I did not think so. Did you hear them, Legolas? Did they sound to you like beasts in terror?'

'No,' said Legolas. 'I heard them clearly. But for the darkness and our own fear I should have guessed that they were beasts wild with some sudden gladness. They spoke as horses will when they meet a friend that they have long missed.'

'So I thought,' said Aragorn; 'but I cannot read the riddle, unless they return. Come! The light is growing fast. Let us look first and guess later! We should begin here, near to our own camping-ground, searching carefully all about, and working up the slope towards the forest. To find the hobbits is our errand, whatever we may think of our visitor in the night. If they escaped by some chance, then they must have hidden in the trees, or they would have been seen. If we find nothing between here and the eaves of the wood, then we will make a last search upon the battle-field and among the ashes. But there is little hope there: the horsemen of Rohan did their work too well.'

For some time the companions crawled and groped upon the ground. The tree stood mournfully above them, its dry leaves now hanging limp, and rattling in the chill easterly wind. Aragorn moved slowly away. He came to the ashes of the watch-fire near the river-bank, and then began to retrace the ground back towards the knoll where the battle had been fought. Suddenly he stooped and bent low with his face almost in the grass. Then he called to the others. They came running up.

'Here at last we find news!' said Aragorn. He lifted up a broken leaf for them to see, a large pale leaf of golden hue, now fading and turning brown. 'Here is a mallorn-leaf of Lórien, and there are small crumbs on it, and a few more crumbs in the grass. And see! there are some pieces of cut cord lying nearby!'

'And here is the knife that cut them!' said Gimli. He stooped and drew out of a tussock, into which some heavy foot had trampled it, a short jagged blade. The haft from which it had been snapped was beside it. 'It was an orc-weapon,' he said, holding it gingerly, and looking with disgust at the carved handle: it had been shaped like a hideous head with squinting eyes and leering mouth.

'Well, here is the strangest riddle that we have yet found!' exclaimed Legolas. 'A bound prisoner escapes both from the Orcs and from the surrounding horsemen. He then stops, while still in the open, and cuts his bonds with an orc-knife. But how and why? For if his legs were tied, how did he walk? And if his arms were tied, how did he use the knife? And if neither were tied, why did he cut the cords at all? Being pleased with his skill, he then sat down and

quietly ate some waybread! That at least is enough to show
that he was a hobbit, without the mallorn-leaf. After that,
I suppose, he turned his arms into wings and flew away
singing into the trees. It should be easy to find him: we
only need wings ourselves!'

'There was sorcery here right enough,' said Gimli. 'What
was that old man doing? What have you to say, Aragorn,
to the reading of Legolas? Can you better it?'

'Maybe, I could,' said Aragorn, smiling. 'There are some
other signs near at hand that you have not considered. I
agree that the prisoner was a hobbit and must have had
either legs or hands free, before he came here. I guess that
it was hands, because the riddle then becomes easier, and
also because, as I read the marks, he was *carried* to this
point by an Orc. Blood was spilled there, a few paces
away, orc-blood. There are deep prints of hoofs all about
this spot, and signs that a heavy thing was dragged away.
The Orc was slain by horsemen, and later his body was
hauled to the fire. But the hobbit was not seen: he was not
"in the open", for it was night and he still had his elven-
cloak. He was exhausted and hungry, and it is not to
be wondered at that, when he had cut his bonds with the
knife of his fallen enemy, he rested and ate a little before
he crept away. But it is a comfort to know that he had
some *lembas* in his pocket, even though he ran away
without gear or pack; that, perhaps, is like a hobbit. I say
he, though I hope and guess that both Merry and Pippin
were here together. There is, however, nothing to show
that for certain.'

'And how do you suppose that either of our friends came
to have a hand free?' asked Gimli.

'I do not know how it happened,' answered Aragorn.
'Nor do I know why an Orc was carrying them away. Not
to help them to escape, we may be sure. Nay, rather I
think that I now begin to understand a matter that has
puzzled me from the beginning: Why when Boromir had
fallen were the Orcs content with the capture of Merry and
Pippin? They did not seek out the rest of us, nor attack
our camp; but instead they went with all speed towards

Isengard. Did they suppose they had captured the Ring-bearer and his faithful comrade? I think not. Their masters would not dare to give such plain orders to Orcs, even if they knew so much themselves; they would not speak openly to them of the Ring; they are not trusty servants. But I think the Orcs had been commanded to capture *hobbits,* alive, at all costs. An attempt was made to slip out with the precious prisoners before the battle. Treachery perhaps, likely enough with such folk; some large and bold Orc may have been trying to escape with the prize alone, for his own ends. There, that is my tale. Others might be devised. But on this we may count in any case: one at least of our friends escaped. It is our task to find him and help him before we return to Rohan. We must not be daunted by Fangorn, since need drove him into that dark place.'

'I do not know which daunts me more: Fangorn, or the thought of the long road through Rohan on foot,' said Gimli.

'Then let us go to the forest,' said Aragorn.

It was not long before Aragorn found fresh signs. At one point, near the bank of the Entwash he came upon footprints: hobbit-prints, but too light for much to be made of them. Then again beneath the bole of a great tree on the very edge of the wood more prints were discovered. The earth was bare and dry, and did not reveal much.

'One hobbit at least stood here for a while and looked back; and then he turned away into the forest,' said Aragorn.

'Then we must go in, too,' said Gimli. 'But I do not like the look of this Fangorn; and we were warned against it. I wish the chase had led anywhere else!'

'I do not think the wood feels evil, whatever tales may say,' said Legolas. He stood under the eaves of the forest, stooping forward, as if he were listening, and peering with wide eyes into the shadows. 'No, it is not evil; or what evil is in it is far away. I catch only the faintest echoes of dark places where the hearts of the trees are black. There is no malice near us; but there is watchfulness, and anger.'

'Well, it has no cause to be angry with me,' said Gimli. 'I have done it no harm.'

'That is just as well,' said Legolas. 'But nonetheless it has suffered harm. There is something happening inside, or going to happen. Do you not feel the tenseness? It takes my breath.'

'I feel the air is stuffy,' said the Dwarf. 'This wood is lighter than Mirkwood, but it is musty and shabby.'

'It is old, very old,' said the Elf. 'So old that almost I feel young again, as I have not felt since I journeyed with you children. It is old and full of memory. I could have been happy here, if I had come in days of peace.'

'I dare say you could,' snorted Gimli. 'You are a Wood-elf, anyway, though Elves of any kind are strange folk. Yet you comfort me. Where you go, I will go. But keep your bow ready to hand, and I will keep my axe loose in my belt. Not for use on trees,' he added hastily, looking up at the tree under which they stood. 'I do not wish to meet that old man at unawares without an argument ready to hand, that is all. Let us go!'

With that the three hunters plunged into the forest of Fangorn. Legolas and Gimli left the tracking to Aragorn. There was little for him to see. The floor of the forest was dry and covered with a drift of leaves; but guessing that the fugitives would stay near the water, he returned often to the banks of the stream. So it was that he came upon the place where Merry and Pippin had drunk and bathed their feet. There plain for all to see were the footprints of two hobbits, one somewhat smaller than the other.

'This is good tidings,' said Aragorn. 'Yet the marks are two days old. And it seems that at this point the hobbits left the water-side.'

'Then what shall we do now?' said Gimli. 'We cannot pursue them through the whole fastness of Fangorn. We have come ill supplied. If we do not find them soon, we shall be of no use to them, except to sit down beside them and show our friendship by starving together.'

'If that is indeed all we can do, then we must do that,' said Aragorn. 'Let us go on.'

They came at length to the steep abrupt end of Treebeard's Hill, and looked up at the rock-wall with its rough steps leading to the high shelf. Gleams of sun were striking through the hurrying clouds, and the forest now looked less grey and drear.

'Let us go up and look about us!' said Legolas. 'I still feel my breath short. I should like to taste a freer air for a while.'

The companions climbed up. Aragorn came last, moving slowly: he was scanning the steps and ledges closely.

'I am almost sure that the hobbits have been up here,' he said. 'But there are other marks, very strange marks, which I do not understand. I wonder if we can see anything from this ledge which will help us to guess which way they went next?'

He stood up and looked about, but he saw nothing that was of any use. The shelf faced southward and eastward; but only on the east was the view open. There he could see the heads of the trees descending in ranks towards the plain from which they had come.

'We have journeyed a long way round,' said Legolas. 'We could have all come here safe together, if we had left the Great River on the second or third day and struck west. Few can foresee whither their road will lead them, till they come to its end.'

'But we did not wish to come to Fangorn,' said Gimli.

'Yet here we are—and nicely caught in the net,' said Legolas. 'Look!'

'Look at what?' said Gimli.

'There in the trees.'

'Where? I have not elf-eyes.'

'Hush! Speak more softly! Look!' said Legolas pointing. 'Down in the wood, back in the way that we have just come. It is he. Cannot you see him, passing from tree to tree?'

'I see, I see now!' hissed Gimli. 'Look, Aragorn! Did I not warn you? There is the old man. All in dirty grey rags: that is why I could not see him at first.'

Aragorn looked and beheld a bent figure moving slowly. It was not far away. It looked like an old beggar-man, walking wearily, leaning on a rough staff. His head was bowed, and he did not look towards them. In other lands they would have greeted him with kind words; but now they stood silent, each feeling a strange expectancy: something was approaching that held a hidden power—or menace.

Gimli gazed with wide eyes for a while, as step by step the figure drew nearer. Then suddenly, unable to contain himself longer, he burst out: 'Your bow, Legolas! Bend it! Get ready! It is Saruman. Do not let him speak, or put a spell upon us! Shoot first!'

Legolas took his bow and bent it, slowly and as if some other will resisted him. He held an arrow loosely in his hand but did not fit it to the string. Aragorn stood silent; his face was watchful and intent.

'Why are you waiting? What is the matter with you?' said Gimli in a hissing whisper.

'Legolas is right,' said Aragorn quietly. 'We may not shoot an old man so, at unawares and unchallenged, whatever fear or doubt be on us. Watch and wait!'

At that moment the old man quickened his pace and came with surprising speed to the foot of the rock-wall. Then suddenly he looked up, while they stood motionless looking down. There was no sound.

They could not see his face: he was hooded, and above the hood he wore a wide-brimmed hat, so that all his features were overshadowed, except for the end of his nose and his grey beard. Yet it seemed to Aragorn that he caught the gleam of eyes keen and bright from within the shadow of the hooded brows.

At last the old man broke the silence. 'Well met indeed, my friends,' he said in a soft voice. 'I wish to speak to you.

Will you come down, or shall I come up?' Without waiting for an answer he began to climb.

'Now!' cried Gimli. 'Stop him, Legolas!'

'Did I not say that I wished to speak to you?' said the old man. 'Put away that bow, Master Elf!'

The bow and arrow fell from Legolas' hands, and his arms hung loose at his sides.

'And you, Master Dwarf, pray take your hand from your axe-haft, till I am up! You will not need such arguments.'

Gimli started and then stood still as stone, staring while the old man sprang up the rough steps as nimbly as a goat. All weariness seemed to have left him. As he stepped up on the shelf there was a gleam, too brief for certainty, a quick glint of white, as if some garment shrouded by the grey rags had been for an instant revealed. The intake of Gimli's breath could be heard as a loud hiss in the silence.

'Well met, I say again!' said the old man, coming towards them. When he was a few feet away, he stood, stooping over his staff, with his head thrust forward, peering at them from under his hood. 'And what may you be doing in these parts? An Elf, a Man, and a Dwarf, all clad in elvish fashion. No doubt there is a tale worth hearing behind it all. Such things are not often seen here.'

'You speak as one that knows Fangorn well,' said Aragorn. 'Is that so?'

'Not well,' said the old man: 'that would be the study of many lives. But I come here now and again.'

'Might we know your name, and then hear what it is that you have to say to us?' said Aragorn. 'The morning passes, and we have an errand that will not wait.'

'As for what I wished to say, I have said it: What may you be doing, and what tale can you tell of yourselves? As for my name!' He broke off, laughing long and softly. Aragorn felt a shudder run through him at the sound, a strange cold thrill; and yet it was not fear or terror that he felt: rather it was like the sudden bite of a keen air, or the slap of a cold rain that wakes an uneasy sleeper.

'My name!' said the old man again. 'Have you not guessed it already? You have heard it before, I think. Yes, you have heard it before. But come now, what of your tale?'

The three companions stood silent and made no answer.

'There are some who would begin to doubt whether your errand is fit to tell,' said the old man. 'Happily I know something of it. You are tracking the footsteps of two young hobbits, I believe. Yes, hobbits. Don't stare, as if you had never heard the strange name before. You have, and so have I. Well, they climbed up here the day before yesterday; and they met someone that they did not expect. Does that comfort you? And now you would like to know where they were taken? Well, well, maybe I can give you some news about that. But why are we standing? Your errand, you see, is no longer as urgent as you thought. Let us sit down and be more at ease.'

The old man turned away and went towards a heap of fallen stones and rock at the foot of the cliff behind. Immediately, as if a spell had been removed, the others relaxed and stirred. Gimli's hand went at once to his axe-haft. Aragorn drew his sword. Legolas picked up his bow.

The old man took no notice, but stopped and sat himself on a low flat stone. Then his grey cloak drew apart, and they saw, beyond doubt, that he was clothed beneath all in white.

'Saruman!' cried Gimli, springing towards him with axe in hand. 'Speak! Tell us where you have hidden our friends! What have you done with them? Speak, or I will make a dint in your hat that even a wizard will find it hard to deal with!'

The old man was too quick for him. He sprang to his feet and leaped to the top of a large rock. There he stood, grown suddenly tall, towering above them. His hood and his grey rags were flung away. His white garments shone. He lifted up his staff, and Gimli's axe leaped from his grasp and fell ringing on the ground. The sword of Aragorn, stiff in his motionless hand, blazed with a sudden fire. Legolas gave a great shout and shot an arrow high into the air: it vanished in a flash of flame.

'Mithrandir!' he cried. 'Mithrandir!'

'Well met, I say to you again, Legolas!' said the old man.

They all gazed at him. His hair was white as snow in the sunshine; and gleaming white was his robe; the eyes under his deep brows were bright, piercing as the rays of the sun; power was in his hand. Between wonder, joy, and fear they stood and found no words to say.

At last Aragorn stirred. 'Gandalf!' he said. 'Beyond all hope you return to us in our need! What veil was over my sight? Gandalf!' Gimli said nothing, but sank to his knees, shading his eyes.

'Gandalf,' the old man repeated, as if recalling from old memory a long disused word. 'Yes, that was the name. I was Gandalf.'

He stepped down from the rock, and picking up his grey cloak wrapped it about him: it seemed as if the sun had been shining, but now was hid in cloud again. 'Yes, you may still call me Gandalf,' he said, and the voice was the voice of their old friend and guide. 'Get up, my good Gimli! No blame to you, and no harm done to me. Indeed my friends, none of you has any weapon that could hurt me. Be merry! We meet again. At the turn of the tide. The great storm is coming, but the tide has turned.'

He laid his hand on Gimli's head, and the Dwarf looked up and laughed suddenly. 'Gandalf!' he said. 'But you are all in white!'

'Yes, I am in white now,' said Gandalf. 'Indeed I *am* Saruman, one might almost say, Saruman as he should have been. But come now, tell me of yourselves! I have passed through fire and deep water, since we parted. I have forgotten much that I thought I knew, and learned again much that I had forgotten. I can see many things far off, but many things that are close at hand I cannot see. Tell me of yourselves!'

'What do you wish to know?' said Aragorn. 'All that has happened since we parted on the bridge would be a long tale. Will you not first give us news of the hobbits? Did you find them, and are they safe?'

'No, I did not find them,' said Gandalf. 'There was a darkness over the valleys of the Emyn Muil, and I did not know of their captivity, until the eagle told me.'

'The eagle!' said Legolas. 'I have seen an eagle high and far off: the last time was three days ago, above the Emyn Muil.'

'Yes,' said Gandalf, 'that was Gwaihir the Windlord, who rescued me from Orthanc. I sent him before me to watch the River and gather tidings. His sight is keen, but he cannot see all that passes under hill and tree. Some things he has seen, and others I have seen myself. The Ring now has passed beyond my help, or the help of any of the Company that set out from Rivendell. Very nearly it was revealed to the Enemy, but it escaped. I had some part in that: for I sat in a high place, and I strove with the Dark Tower; and the Shadow passed. Then I was weary, very weary; and I walked long in dark thought.'

'Then you know about Frodo!' said Gimli. 'How do things go with him?'

'I cannot say. He was saved from a great peril, but many lie before him still. He resolved to go alone to Mordor, and he set out: that is all that I can say.'

'Not alone,' said Legolas. 'We think that Sam went with him.'

'Did he!' said Gandalf, and there was a gleam in his eye and a smile on his face. 'Did he indeed? It is news to me, yet it does not surprise me. Good! Very good! You lighten my heart. You must tell me more. Now sit by me and tell me the tale of your journey.'

The companions sat on the ground at his feet, and Aragorn took up the tale. For a long while Gandalf said nothing, and he asked no questions. His hands were spread upon his knees, and his eyes were closed. At last when Aragorn spoke of the death of Boromir and of his last journey upon the Great River, the old man sighed.

'You have not said all that you know or guess, Aragorn

my friend,' he said quietly. 'Poor Boromir! I could not see what happened to him. It was a sore trial for such a man: a warrior, and a lord of men. Galadriel told me that he was in peril. But he escaped in the end. I am glad. It was not in vain that the young hobbits came with us, if only for Boromir's sake. But that is not the only part they have to play. They were brought to Fangorn, and their coming was like the falling of small stones that starts an avalanche in the mountains. Even as we talk here, I hear the first rumblings. Saruman had best not be caught away from home when the dam bursts!'

'In one thing you have not changed, dear friend,' said Aragorn: 'you still speak in riddles.'

'What? In riddles?' said Gandalf. 'No! For I was talking aloud to myself. A habit of the old: they choose the wisest person present to speak to; the long explanations needed by the young are wearying.' He laughed, but the sound now seemed warm and kindly as a gleam of sunshine.

'I am no longer young even in the reckoning of Men of the Ancient Houses,' said Aragorn. 'Will you not open your mind more clearly to me?'

'What then shall I say?' said Gandalf, and paused for a while in thought. 'This in brief is how I see things at the moment, if you wish to have a piece of my mind as plain as possible. The Enemy, of course, has long known that the Ring is abroad, and that it is borne by a hobbit. He knows now the number of our Company that set out from Rivendell, and the kind of each of us. But he does not yet perceive our purpose clearly. He supposes that we were all going to Minas Tirith; for that is what he would himself have done in our place. And according to his wisdom it would have been a heavy stroke against his power. Indeed he is in great fear, not knowing what mighty one may suddenly appear, wielding the Ring, and assailing him with war, seeking to cast him down and take his place. That we should wish to cast him down and have *no* one in his place is not a thought that occurs to his mind. That we should try to destroy the Ring itself has not yet entered into his darkest dream. In which no doubt you will see our good fortune and our hope. For imagining war he has let loose war, believing that he has no time to waste; for he that strikes the first blow, if he strikes it hard enough, may need to strike no more. So the forces that he has long been preparing he is now setting in motion, sooner than he intended. Wise fool. For if he had used all his power to guard Mordor, so that none could enter, and bent all his guile to the hunting of the Ring, then indeed hope would have faded: neither Ring nor bearer could long have eluded him. But now his eye gazes abroad rather than near at home; and mostly he looks towards Minas Tirith. Very soon now his strength will fall upon it like a storm.

'For already he knows that the messengers that he sent to waylay the Company have failed again. They have not found the Ring. Neither have they brought away any hobbits as hostages. Had they done even so much as that, it would have been a heavy blow to us, and it might have been fatal. But let us not darken our hearts by imagining the trial of their gentle loyalty in the Dark Tower. For the Enemy has failed—so far. Thanks to Saruman.'

'Then is not Saruman a traitor?' said Gimli.

'Indeed yes,' said Gandalf. 'Doubly. And is not that strange? Nothing that we have endured of late has seemed so grievous as the treason of Isengard. Even reckoned as a lord and captain Saruman has grown very strong. He threatens the Men of Rohan and draws off their help from Minas Tirith, even as the main blow is approaching from the East. Yet a treacherous weapon is ever a danger to the hand. Saruman also had a mind to capture the Ring, for himself, or at least to snare some hobbits for his evil purposes. So between them our enemies have contrived only to bring Merry and Pippin with marvellous speed, and in the nick of time, to Fangorn, where otherwise they would never have come at all!

'Also they have filled themselves with new doubts that disturb their plans. No tidings of the battle will come to Mordor, thanks to the horsemen of Rohan; but the Dark Lord knows that two hobbits were taken in the Emyn Muil and borne away towards Isengard against the will of his own servants. He now has Isengard to fear as well as Minas Tirith. If Minas Tirith falls, it will go ill with Saruman.'

'It is a pity that our friends lie in between,' said Gimli. 'If no land divided Isengard and Mordor, then they could fight while we watched and waited.'

'The visitor would emerge stronger than either, and free from doubt,' said Gandalf. 'But Isengard cannot fight Mordor, unless Saruman first obtains the Ring. That he will never do now. He does not yet know his peril. There is much that he does not know. He was so eager to lay his hands on his prey that he could not wait at home, and he came forth to meet and to spy on his messengers. But he came too late, for once, and the battle was over and beyond his help before he reached these parts. He did not remain here long. I look into his mind and I see his doubt. He has no woodcraft. He believes that the horsemen slew and burned all upon the field of battle; but he does not know whether the Orcs were bringing any prisoners or not. And he does not know of the quarrel between his servants and the Orcs of Mordor; nor does he know of the Winged Messenger.'

'The Winged Messenger!' cried Legolas. 'I shot at him with the bow of Galadriel above Sarn Gebir, and I felled him from the sky. He filled us all with fear. What new terror is this?'

'One that you cannot slay with arrows,' said Gandalf. 'You only slew his steed. It was a good deed; but the Rider was soon horsed again. For he was a Nazgûl, one of the Nine, who ride now upon winged steeds. Soon their terror will overshadow the last armies of our friends, cutting off the sun. But they have not yet been allowed to cross the River, and Saruman does not know of this new shape in which the Ringwraiths have been clad. His thought is ever on the Ring. Was it present in the battle? Was it found? What if Théoden, Lord of the Mark, should come by it and learn of its power? That is the danger that he sees, and he has fled back to Isengard to double and treble his assault on Rohan. And all the time there is another danger, close at hand, which he does not see, busy with his fiery thoughts. He has forgotten Treebeard.'

'Now you speak to yourself again,' said Aragorn with a smile. 'Treebeard is not known to me. And I have guessed part of Saruman's double treachery; yet I do not see in what way the coming of two hobbits to Fangorn has served, save to give us a long and fruitless chase.'

'Wait a minute!' cried Gimli. 'There is another thing that I should like to know first. Was it you, Gandalf, or Saruman that we saw last night?'

'You certainly did not see me,' answered Gandalf, 'therefore I must guess that you saw Saruman. Evidently we look so much alike that your desire to make an incurable dent in my hat must be excused.'

'Good, good!' said Gimli. 'I am glad that it was not you.'

Gandalf laughed again. 'Yes, my good Dwarf,' he said, 'it is a comfort not to be mistaken at all points. Do I not know it only too well! But of course, I never blamed you for your welcome of me. How could I do so, who have so often counselled my friends to suspect even their own hands when dealing with the Enemy. Bless you, Gimli, son of Glóin! Maybe you will see us both together one day and judge between us!'

'But the hobbits!' Legolas broke in. 'We have come far to seek them, and you seem to know where they are. Where are they now?'

'With Treebeard and the Ents,' said Gandalf.

'The Ents!' exclaimed Aragorn. 'Then there is truth in the old legends about dwellers in the deep forests and the giant shepherds of the trees? Are there still Ents in the world? I thought they were only a memory of ancient days, if indeed they were ever more than a legend of Rohan.'

'A legend of Rohan!' cried Legolas. 'Nay, every Elf in Wilderland has sung songs of the old Onodrim and their long sorrow. Yet even among us they are only a memory. If I were to meet one still walking in this world, then indeed I should feel young again! But Treebeard: that is only a rendering of Fangorn into the Common Speech; yet you seem to speak of a person. Who is this Treebeard?'

'Ah! now you are asking much,' said Gandalf. 'The little that I know of his long slow story would make a tale for which we have no time now. Treebeard is Fangorn, the guardian of the forest; he is the oldest of the Ents, the oldest living thing that still walks beneath the Sun upon this Middle-earth. I hope indeed, Legolas, that you may yet meet him. Merry and Pippin have been fortunate: they met him here, even where we sit. For he came here two days ago and bore them away to his dwelling far off by the roots of the mountains. He often comes here, especially when his mind is uneasy, and rumours of the world outside trouble him. I saw him four days ago striding among the trees, and I think he saw me, for he paused; but I did not speak, for I was heavy with thought, and weary after my struggle with the Eye of Mordor; and he did not speak either, nor call my name.'

'Perhaps he also thought that you were Saruman,' said Gimli. 'But you speak of him as if he was a friend. I thought Fangorn was dangerous.'

'Dangerous!' cried Gandalf. 'And so am I, very dangerous: more dangerous than anything you will ever meet, unless you are brought alive before the seat of the Dark Lord. And Aragorn is dangerous, and Legolas is dangerous. You are beset with dangers, Gimli son of Glóin; for you are dangerous yourself, in your own fashion. Certainly the forest of Fangorn is perilous—not least to those that are too ready with their axes; and Fangorn himself, he is perilous too; yet he is wise and kindly nonetheless. But now his long slow wrath is brimming over, and all the forest is filled with it. The coming of the hobbits and the tidings that they brought have spilled it: it will soon be running like a flood; but its tide is turned against Saruman and the axes of Isengard. A thing is about to happen which has not happened since the Elder Days: the Ents are going to wake up and find that they are strong.'

'What will they do?' asked Legolas in astonishment.

'I do not know,' said Gandalf. 'I do not think they know

themselves. I wonder.' He fell silent, his head bowed in thought.

The others looked at him. A gleam of sun through fleeting clouds fell on his hands, which lay now upturned on his lap: they seemed to be filled with light as a cup is with water. At last he looked up and gazed straight at the sun.

'The morning is wearing away,' he said. 'Soon we must go.'

'Do we go to find our friends and to see Treebeard?' asked Aragorn.

'No,' said Gandalf. 'That is not the road that you must take. I have spoken words of hope. But only of hope. Hope is not victory. War is upon us and all our friends, a war in which only the use of the Ring could give us surety of victory. It fills me with great sorrow and great fear: for much shall be destroyed and all may be lost. I am Gandalf, Gandalf the White, but Black is mightier still.'

He rose and gazed out eastward, shading his eyes, as if he saw things far away that none of them could see. Then he shook his head. 'No,' he said in a soft voice, 'it has gone beyond our reach. Of that at least let us be glad. We can no longer be tempted to use the Ring. We must go down to face a peril near despair, yet that deadly peril is removed.'

He turned. 'Come, Aragorn son of Arathorn!' he said. 'Do not regret your choice in the valley of the Emyn Muil, nor call it a vain pursuit. You chose amid doubts the path that seemed right: the choice was just, and it has been rewarded. For so we have met in time, who otherwise might have met too late. But the quest of your companions is over. Your next journey is marked by your given word. You must go to Edoras and seek out Théoden in his hall. For you are needed. The light of Andúril must now be uncovered in the battle for which it has so long waited. There is war in Rohan, and worse evil: it goes ill with Théoden.'

'Then are we not to see the merry young hobbits again?' said Legolas.

'I did not say so,' said Gandalf. 'Who knows? Have patience. Go where you must go, and hope! To Edoras! I go thither also.'

'It is a long way for a man to walk, young or old,' said Aragorn. 'I fear the battle will be over long ere I come there.'

'We shall see, we shall see,' said Gandalf. 'Will you come now with me?'

'Yes, we will set out together,' said Aragorn. 'But I do not doubt that you will come there before me, if you wish.' He rose and looked long at Gandalf. The others gazed at them in silence as they stood there facing one another. The grey figure of the Man, Aragorn son of Arathorn, was tall, and stern as stone, his hand upon the hilt of his sword; he looked as if some king out of the mists of the sea had stepped upon the shores of lesser men. Before him stooped the old figure, white, shining now as if with some light kindled within, bent, laden with years, but holding a power beyond the strength of kings.

'Do I not say truly, Gandalf,' said Aragorn at last, 'that you could go whithersoever you wished quicker than I? And this I also say you are our captain and our banner. The Dark Lord has Nine: But we have One, mightier than they: the White Rider. He has passed through the fire and the abyss, and they shall fear him. We will go where he leads.'

'Yes, together we will follow you,' said Legolas. 'But first it would ease my heart, Gandalf, to hear what befell you in Moria. Will you not tell us? Can you not stay even to tell your friends how you were delivered?'

'I have stayed already too long,' answered Gandalf. 'Time is short. But if there were a year to spend, I would not tell you all.'

'Then tell us what you will, and time allows!' said Gimli. 'Come, Gandalf, tell us how you fared with the Balrog!'

'Name him not!' said Gandalf, and for a moment it

seemed that a cloud of pain passed over his face, and he sat silent, looking old as death. 'Long time I fell,' he said at last, slowly, as if thinking back with difficulty. 'Long I fell, and he fell with me. His fire was about me. I was burned. Then we plunged into the deep water and all was dark. Cold it was as the tide of death: almost it froze my heart.'

'Deep is the abyss that is spanned by Durin's Bridge, and none has measured it,' said Gimli.

'Yet it has a bottom, beyond light and knowledge,' said Gandalf. 'Thither I came at last, to the uttermost foundations of stone. He was with me still. His fire was quenched, but now he was a thing of slime, stronger than a strangling snake.

'We fought far under the living earth, where time is not counted. Ever he clutched me, and ever I hewed him, till at last he fled into dark tunnels. They were not made by Durin's folk, Gimli son of Glóin. Far, far below the deepest delvings of the Dwarves, the world is gnawed by nameless things. Even Sauron knows them not. They are older than he. Now I have walked there, but I will bring no report to darken the light of day. In that despair my enemy was my only hope, and I pursued him, clutching at his heel. Thus he brought me back at last to the secret ways of Khazad-dûm: too well he knew them all. Ever up now we went, until we came to the Endless Stair.'

'Long has that been lost,' said Gimli. 'Many have said that it was never made save in legend, but others say that it was destroyed.'

'It was made, and it had not been destroyed,' said Gandalf. 'From the lowest dungeon to the highest peak it climbed, ascending in unbroken spiral in many thousand steps, until it issued at last in Durin's Tower carved in the living rock of Zirakzigil, the pinnacle of the Silvertine.

'There upon Celebdil was a lonely window in the snow, and before it lay a narrow space, a dizzy eyrie above the mists of the world. The sun shone fiercely there, but all below was wrapped in cloud. Out he sprang, and even as I came behind, he burst into new flame. There was none to see, or perhaps in after ages songs would still be sung of the Battle of the Peak.' Suddenly Gandalf laughed. 'But what would they say in song? Those that looked up from afar thought that the mountain was crowned with storm. Thunder they heard, and lightning, they said, smote upon Celebdil, and leaped back broken into tongues of fire. Is not that enough? A great smoke rose about us, vapour and steam. Ice fell like rain. I threw down my enemy, and he fell from the high place and broke the mountain-side where he smote it in his ruin. Then darkness took me, and I strayed out of thought and time, and I wandered far on roads that I will not tell.

'Naked I was sent back—for a brief time, until my task was done. And naked I lay upon the mountain-top. The tower behind was crumbled into dust, the window gone; the ruined stair was choked with burned and broken stone. I was alone, forgotten, without escape upon the hard horn of the world. There I lay staring upward, while the stars wheeled over, and each day was as long as a life-age of the earth. Faint to my ears came the gathered rumour of all lands: the springing and the dying, the song and the weeping, and the slow everlasting groan of over-burdened stone. And so at the last Gwaihir the Windlord found me again, and he took me up and bore me away.

' "Ever am I fated to be your burden, friend at need," I said.

' "A burden you have been," he answered, "but not so now. Light as a swan's feather in my claw you are. The Sun shines through you. Indeed I do not think you need me any more: were I to let you fall, you would float upon the wind."

' "Do not let me fall!" I gasped, for I felt life in me again. "Bear me to Lothlórien!"

' "That indeed is the command of the Lady Galadriel who sent me to look for you," he answered.

'Thus it was that I came to Caras Galadon and found you but lately gone. I tarried there in the ageless time of that land where days bring healing not decay. Healing I found, and I was clothed in white. Counsel I gave and counsel took. Thence by strange roads I came, and messages I bring to some of you. To Aragorn I was bidden to say this:

> *Where now are the Dúnedain, Elessar, Elessar?*
> *Why do thy kinsfolk wander afar?*
> *Near is the hour when the Lost should come forth,*
> *And the Grey Company ride from the North.*
> *But dark is the path appointed for thee:*
> *The Dead watch the road that leads to the Sea.*

To Legolas she sent this word:

> *Legolas Greenleaf long under tree*
> *In joy thou hast lived. Beware of the Sea!*
> *If thou hearest the cry of the gull on the shore,*
> *Thy heart shall then rest in the forest no more.'*

Gandalf fell silent and shut his eyes.

'Then she sent me no message?' said Gimli and bent his head.

'Dark are her words,' said Legolas, 'and little do they mean to those that receive them.'

'That is no comfort,' said Gimli.

'What then?' said Legolas. 'Would you have her speak openly to you of your death?'

'Yes, if she had nought else to say.'

'What is that?' said Gandalf, opening his eyes. 'Yes, I think I can guess what her words may mean. Your pardon, Gimli! I was pondering the messages once again. But indeed she sent words to you, and neither dark nor sad.

' "To Gimli son of Glóin," she said, "give his Lady's greeting. Lockbearer, wherever thou goest my thought goes with thee. But have a care to lay thine axe to the right tree!" '

'In happy hour you have returned to us, Gandalf,' cried the Dwarf, capering as he sang loudly in the strange dwarf-tongue. 'Come, come!' he shouted, swinging his axe.

'Since Gandalf's head is now sacred, let us find one that is right to cleave!'

'That will not be far to seek,' said Gandalf, rising from his seat. 'Come! We have spent all the time that is allowed to a meeting of parted friends. Now there is need of haste.'

He wrapped himself again in his old tattered cloak, and led the way. Following him they descended quickly from the high shelf and made their way back through the forest, down the bank of the Entwash. They spoke no more words, until they stood again upon the grass beyond the eaves of Fangorn. There was no sign of their horses to be seen.

'They have not returned,' said Legolas. 'It will be a weary walk!'

'I shall not walk. Time presses,' said Gandalf. Then lifting up his head he gave a long whistle. So clear and piercing was the note that the others stood amazed to hear such a sound come from those old bearded lips. Three times he whistled; and then faint and far off it seemed to them that they heard the whinny of a horse borne up from the plains upon the eastern wind. They waited wondering. Before long there came the sound of hoofs, at first hardly more than a tremor of the ground perceptible only to Aragorn as he lay upon the grass, then growing steadily louder and clearer to a quick beat.

'There is more than one horse coming,' said Aragorn.

'Certainly,' said Gandalf. 'We are too great a burden for one.'

'There are three,' said Legolas, gazing out over the plain. 'See how they run! There is Hasufel, and there is my friend Arod beside him! But there is another that strides ahead: a very great horse. I have not seen his like before.'

'Nor will you again,' said Gandalf. 'That is Shadowfax. He is the chief of the *Mearas*, lords of horses, and not even Théoden, King of Rohan, has ever looked on a better. Does he not shine like silver, and run as smoothly as a swift stream? He has come for me: the horse of the White Rider. We are going to battle together.'

Even as the old wizard spoke, the great horse came striding up the slope towards them; his coat was glistening and his mane flowing in the wind of his speed. The two others followed, now far behind. As soon as Shadowfax saw Gandalf, he checked his pace and whinnied loudly; then trotting gently forward he stooped his proud head and nuzzled his great nostrils against the old man's neck.

Gandalf caressed him. 'It is a long way from Rivendell, my friend,' he said; 'but you are wise and swift and come at need. Far let us ride now together, and part not in this world again!'

Soon the other horses came up and stood quietly by, as if awaiting orders. 'We go at once to Meduseld, the hall of your master, Théoden,' said Gandalf, addressing them gravely. They bowed their heads. 'Time presses, so with your leave, my friends, we will ride. We beg you to use all the speed that you can. Hasufel shall bear Aragorn and Arod Legolas. I will set Gimli before me, and by his leave Shadowfax shall bear us both. We will wait now only to drink a little.'

'Now I understand a part of last night's riddle,' said Legolas as he sprang lightly upon Arod's back. 'Whether they fled at first in fear, or not, our horses met Shadowfax, their chieftain, and greeted him with joy. Did you know that he was at hand, Gandalf?'

'Yes, I knew,' said the wizard. 'I bent my thought upon him, bidding him to make haste; for yesterday he was far away in the south of this land. Swiftly may he bear me back again!'

Gandalf spoke now to Shadowfax, and the horse set off at a good pace, yet not beyond the measure of the others. After a little while he turned suddenly, and choosing a place where the banks were lower, he waded the river, and then led them away due south into a flat land, treeless and wide. The wind went like grey waves through the endless miles of grass. There was no sign of road or track, but Shadowfax did not stay or falter.

'He is steering a straight course now for the hall of

Théoden under the slopes of the White Mountains,' said Gandalf. 'It will be quicker so. The ground is firmer in the Eastemnet, where the chief northward track lies, across the river, but Shadowfax knows the way through every fen and hollow.'

For many hours they rode on through the meads and riverlands. Often the grass was so high that it reached above the knees of the riders, and their steeds seemed to be swimming in a grey-green sea. They came upon many hidden pools, and broad acres of sedge waving above wet and treacherous bogs; but Shadowfax found the way, and the other horses followed in his swath. Slowly the sun fell from the sky down in the West. Looking out over the great plain, far away the riders saw it for a moment like a red fire sinking into the grass. Low upon the edge of sight shoulders of the mountains glinted red upon either side. A smoke seemed to rise up and darken the sun's disc to the hue of blood, as if it had kindled the grass as it passed down under the rim of earth.

'There lies the Gap of Rohan,' said Gandalf. 'It is now almost due west of us. That way lies Isengard.'

'I see a great smoke,' said Legolas. 'What may that be?'

'Battle and war!' said Gandalf. 'Ride on!'

Chapter 6

The King of the Golden Hall

They rode on through sunset, and slow dusk, and gathering night. When at last they halted and dismounted, even Aragorn was stiff and weary. Gandalf only allowed them a few hours' rest. Legolas and Gimli slept, and Aragorn lay flat, stretched upon his back; but Gandalf stood, leaning on his staff, gazing into the darkness, east and west. All was silent, and there was no sign or sound of living thing. The night was barred with long clouds, fleeting on a chill wind, when they arose again. Under the cold moon they went on once more, as swift as by the light of day.

Hours passed and still they rode on. Gimli nodded and would have fallen from his seat, if Gandalf had not clutched and shaken him. Hasufel and Arod, weary but proud, followed their tireless leader, a grey shadow before them hardly to be seen. The miles went by. The waxing moon sank into the cloudy West.

A bitter chill came into the air. Slowly in the East the dark faded to a cold grey. Red shafts of light leapt above the black walls of the Emyn Muil far away upon their left. Dawn came clear and bright; a wind swept across their path, rushing through the bent grasses. Suddenly Shadowfax stood still and neighed. Gandalf pointed ahead.

'Look!' he cried, and they lifted their tired eyes. Before them stood the mountains of the South: white-tipped and streaked with black. The grass-lands rolled against the hills that clustered at their feet, and flowed up into many valleys still dim and dark, untouched by the light of dawn, winding their way into the heart of the great mountains. Immediately before the travellers the widest of these glens opened like a long gulf among the hills. Far inward they glimpsed a tumbled mountain-mass with one tall peak; at the mouth of the vale there stood like a sentinel a lonely height. About its feet there flowed, as a thread of silver, the stream that issued from the dale; upon its brow they caught, still far away, a glint in the rising sun, a glimmer of gold.

'Speak, Legolas!' said Gandalf. 'Tell us what you see there before us!'

Legolas gazed ahead, shading his eyes from the level shafts of the new-risen sun. 'I see a white stream that comes down from the snows,' he said. 'Where it issues from the shadow of the vale a green hill rises upon the east. A dike and mighty wall and thorny fence encircle it. Within there rise the roofs of houses; and in the midst, set upon a green terrace, there stands aloft a great hall of Men. And it seems to my eyes that it is thatched with gold. The light of it shines far over the land. Golden, too, are the posts of its doors. There men in bright mail stand; but all else within the courts are yet asleep.'

'Edoras those courts are called,' said Gandalf, 'and Meduseld is that golden hall. There dwells Théoden son of Thengel, King of the Mark of Rohan. We are come with the rising of the day. Now the road lies plain to see before us. But we must ride more warily; for war is abroad, and the Rohirrim, the Horse-lords, do not sleep, even if it seem so from afar. Draw no weapon, speak no haughty word, I counsel you all, until we are come before Théoden's seat.'

The morning was bright and clear about them, and birds were singing, when the travellers came to the stream. It ran down swiftly into the plain, and beyond the feet of the hills turned across their path in a wide bend, flowing away east to feed the Entwash far off in its reed-choked beds. The land was green: in the wet meads and along the grassy borders of the stream grew many willow-trees. Already in this southern land they were blushing red at their fingertips, feeling the approach of spring. Over the stream there was a ford between low banks much trampled by the passage of horses. The travellers passed over and

came upon a wide rutted track leading towards the up-
lands.

At the foot of the walled hill the way ran under the
shadow of many mounds, high and green. Upon their
western sides the grass was white as with a drifted snow:
small flowers sprang there like countless stars amid the
turf.

'Look!' said Gandalf. 'How fair are the bright eyes in
the grass! Evermind they are called, Simbelmynë in this
land of Men, for they blossom in all the season of the
year, and grow where dead men rest. Behold! We are
come to the great barrows where the sires of Théoden
sleep.'

'Seven mounds upon the left, and nine upon the right,'
said Aragorn. 'Many long lives of men it is since the golden
hall was built.'

'Five hundred times have the red leaves fallen in Mirkwood in my home since then,' said Legolas, 'and but a little
while does that seem to us.'

'But to the Riders of the Mark it seems so long ago,'
said Aragorn, 'that the raising of this house is but a
memory of song, and the years before are lost in the mist
of time. Now they call this land their home, their own, and
their speech is sundered from their northern kin.' Then he
began to chant softly in a slow tongue unknown to the
Elf and Dwarf; yet they listened, for there was a strong
music in it.

'That, I guess, is the language of the Rohirrim,' said
Legolas; 'for it is like to this land itself; rich and rolling in
part, and else hard and stern as the mountains. But I cannot guess what it means, save that it is laden with the
sadness of Mortal Men.'

'It runs thus in the Common Speech,' said Aragorn, 'as
near as I can make it.

Where now the horse and the rider? Where is the horn that
  was blowing?
Where is the helm and the hauberk, and the bright hair
  flowing?

Where is the hand on the harpstring, and the red fire
* glowing?*
Where is the spring and the harvest and the tall corn
* growing?*
They have passed like rain on the mountain, like a wind
* in the meadow;*
The days have gone down in the West behind the hills
* into shadow.*
Who shall gather the smoke of the dead wood burning,
Or behold the flowing years from the Sea returning?

Thus spoke a forgotten poet long ago in Rohan, recalling how tall and fair was Eorl the Young, who rode down out of the North; and there were wings upon the feet of his steed, Felaróf, father of horses. So men still sing in the evening.'

With these words the travellers passed the silent mounds. Following the winding way up the green shoulders of the hills, they came at last to the wide wind-swept walls and the gates of Edoras.

There sat many men in bright mail, who sprang at once to their feet and barred the way with spears. 'Stay, strangers here unknown!' they cried in the tongue of the Riddermark, demanding the names and errand of the strangers. Wonder was in their eyes but little friendliness; and they looked darkly upon Gandalf.

'Well do I understand your speech,' he answered in the same language; 'yet few strangers do so. Why then do you not speak in the Common Tongue, as is the custom in the West, if you wish to be answered?'

'It is the will of Théoden King that none should enter his gates, save those who know our tongue and are our friends,' replied one of the guards. 'None are welcome here in days of war but our own folk, and those that come from Mundburg in the land of Gondor. Who are you that come heedless over the plain thus strangely clad, riding horses like to our own horses? Long have we kept guard here, and we have watched you from afar. Never have we seen other riders so strange, nor any horse more proud than is one of these that bear you. He is one of the *Mearas,* unless our eyes are cheated by some spell. Say, are you not a wizard, some spy from Saruman, or phantoms of his craft? Speak now and be swift!'

'We are no phantoms,' said Aragorn, 'nor do your eyes cheat you. For indeed these are your own horses that we ride, as you knew well ere you asked, I guess. But seldom does thief ride home to the stable. Here are Hasufel and Arod, that Éomer, the Third Marshal of the Mark, lent to us, only two days ago. We bring them back now, even as we promised him. Has not Éomer then returned and given warning of our coming?'

A troubled look came into the guard's eyes. 'Of Éomer I have naught to say,' he answered. 'If what you tell me is truth, then doubtless Théoden will have heard of it. Maybe your coming was not wholly unlooked-for. It is but two nights ago that Wormtongue came to us and said that by the will of Théoden no stranger should pass these gates.'

'Wormtongue?' said Gandalf, looking sharply at the guard. 'Say no more! My errand is not to Wormtongue, but to the Lord of the Mark himself. I am in haste. Will you not go or send to say that we are come?' His eyes glinted under his deep brows as he bent his gaze upon the man.

'Yes, I will go,' he answered slowly. 'But what names shall I report? And what shall I say of you? Old and weary you seem now, and yet you are fell and grim beneath, I deem.'

'Well do you see and speak,' said the wizard. 'For I am Gandalf. I have returned. And behold! I too bring back a horse. Here is Shadowfax the Great, whom no other hand can tame. And here beside me is Aragorn son of Arathorn, the heir of Kings, and it is to Mundburg that he goes. Here also are Legolas the Elf and Gimli the Dwarf, our comrades. Go now and say to your master that we are at his gates and would have speech with him, if he will permit us to come into his hall.'

'Strange names you give indeed! But I will report them as you bid, and learn my master's will,' said the guard.

'Wait here a little while, and I will bring you such answer as seems good to him. Do not hope too much! These are dark days.' He went swiftly away, leaving the strangers in the watchful keeping of his comrades.

After some time he returned. 'Follow me!' he said. 'Théoden gives you leave to enter; but any weapon that you bear, be it only a staff, you must leave on the threshold. The doorwardens will keep them.'

The dark gates were swung open. The travellers entered, walking in file behind their guide. They found a broad path, paved with hewn stones, now winding upward, now climbing in short flights of well-laid steps. Many houses built of wood and many dark doors they passed. Beside the way in a stone channel a stream of clear water flowed, sparkling and chattering. At length they came to the crown of the hill. There stood a high platform above a green terrace, at the foot of which a bright spring gushed from a stone carved in the likeness of a horse's head; beneath was a wide basin from which the water spilled and fed the falling stream. Up the green terrace went a stair of stone, high and broad, and on either side of the topmost step were stone-hewn seats. There sat other guards, with drawn swords laid upon their knees. Their golden hair was braided on their shoulders; the sun was blazoned upon their green shields, their long corslets were burnished bright, and when they rose taller they seemed than mortal men.

'There are the doors before you,' said the guide. 'I must return now to my duty at the gate. Farewell! And may the Lord of the Mark be gracious to you!'

He turned and went swiftly back down the road. The others climbed the long stair under the eyes of the tall watchmen. Silent they stood now above and spoke no word, until Gandalf stepped out upon the paved terrace at the stair's head. Then suddenly with clear voices they spoke a courteous greeting in their own tongue.

'Hail, comers from afar!' they said, and they turned the

hilts of their swords towards the travellers in token of peace. Green gems flashed in the sunlight. Then one of the guards stepped forward and spoke in the Common Speech.

'I am the Doorward of Théoden,' he said. 'Háma is my name. Here I must bid you lay aside your weapons before you enter.'

Then Legolas gave into his hand his silver-hafted knife, his quiver, and his bow. 'Keep these well,' he said, 'for they come from the Golden Wood and the Lady of Lothlórien gave them to me.'

Wonder came into the man's eyes, and he laid the weapons hastily by the wall, as if he feared to handle them. 'No man will touch them, I promise you,' he said.

Aragorn stood a while hesitating. 'It is not my will,' he said, 'to put aside my sword or to deliver Andúril to the hand of any other Man.'

'It is the will of Théoden,' said Háma.

'It is not clear to me that the will of Théoden son of Thengel, even though he be lord of the Mark, should prevail over the will of Aragorn son of Arathorn, Elendil's heir of Gondor.'

'This is the house of Théoden, not of Aragorn, even were he King of Gondor in the seat of Denethor,' said Háma, stepping swiftly before the doors and barring the way. His sword was now in his hand and the point towards the strangers.

'This is idle talk,' said Gandalf. 'Needless is Théoden's demand, but it is useless to refuse. A king will have his way in his own hall, be it folly or wisdom.'

'Truly,' said Aragorn. 'And I would do as the master of the house bade me, were this only a woodman's cot, if I bore now any sword but Andúril.'

'Whatever its name may be,' said Háma, 'here you shall lay it, if you would not fight alone against all the men in Edoras.'

'Not alone!' said Gimli, fingering the blade of his axe, and looking darkly up at the guard, as if he were a young tree that Gimli had a mind to fell. 'Not alone!'

'Come, come!' said Gandalf. 'We are all friends here.

Or should be; for the laughter of Mordor will be our only reward, if we quarrel. My errand is pressing. Here at least is *my* sword, goodman Háma. Keep it well. Glamdring it is called, for the Elves made it long ago. Now let me pass. Come, Aragorn!'

Slowly Aragorn unbuckled his belt and himself set his sword upright against the wall. 'Here I set it,' he said; 'but I command you not to touch it, nor to permit any other to lay hand on it. In this elvish sheath dwells the Blade that was Broken and has been made again. Telchar first wrought it in the deeps of time. Death shall come to any man that draws Elendil's sword save Elendil's heir.'

The guard stepped back and looked with amazement on Aragorn. 'It seems that you are come on the wings of song out of the forgotten days,' he said. 'It shall be, lord, as you command.'

'Well,' said Gimli, 'if it has Andúril to keep it company, my axe may stay here, too, without shame'; and he laid it on the floor. 'Now then, if all is as you wish, let us go and speak with your master.'

The guard still hesitated. 'Your staff,' he said to Gandalf. 'Forgive me, but that too must be left at the doors.'

'Foolishness!' said Gandalf. 'Prudence is one thing, but discourtesy is another. I am old. If I may not lean on my stick as I go, then I will sit out here, until it pleases Théoden to hobble out himself to speak with me.'

Aragorn laughed. 'Every man has something too dear to trust to another. But would you part an old man from his support? Come, will you not let us enter?'

'The staff in the hand of a wizard may be more than a prop for age,' said Háma. He looked hard at the ash-staff on which Gandalf leaned. 'Yet in doubt a man of worth will trust to his own wisdom. I believe you are friends and folk worthy of honour, who have no evil purpose. You may go in.'

The guards now lifted the heavy bars of the doors and swung them slowly inwards grumbling on their great hinges. The travellers entered. Inside it seemed dark and

warm after the clear air upon the hill. The hall was long
and wide and filled with shadows and half lights; mighty
pillars upheld its lofty roof. But here and there bright sun-
beams fell in glimmering shafts from the eastern windows,
high under the deep eaves. Through the louver in the roof,
above the thin wisps of issuing smoke, the sky showed
pale and blue. As their eyes changed, the travellers perceived that the floor was paved with stones of many
hues; branching runes and strange devices intertwined beneath their feet. They saw now that the pillars were richly
carved, gleaming dully with gold and half-seen colours.
Many woven cloths were hung upon the walls, and over
their wide spaces marched figures of ancient legend, some
dim with years, some darkling in the shade. But upon one
form the sunlight fell: a young man upon a white horse. He
was blowing a great horn, and his yellow hair was flying in
the wind. The horse's head was lifted, and its nostrils were
wide and red as it neighed, smelling battle afar. Foaming
water, green and white, rushed and curled about its
knees.

'Behold Eorl the Young!' said Aragorn. 'Thus he rode
out of the North to the Battle of the Field of Celebrant.'

Now the four companions went forward, past the clear
wood-fire burning upon the long hearth in the midst of the
hall. Then they halted. At the far end of the house, beyond the hearth and facing north towards the doors, was
a dais with three steps; and in the middle of the dais was a
great gilded chair. Upon it sat a man so bent with age
that he seemed almost a dwarf; but his white hair was
long and thick and fell in great braids from beneath a
thin golden circlet set upon his brow. In the centre upon
his forehead shone a single white diamond. His beard
was laid like snow upon his knees; but his eyes still
burned with a bright light, glinting as he gazed at the
strangers. Behind his chair stood a woman clad in white.
At his feet upon the steps sat a wizened figure of a man,
with a pale wise face and heavy-lidded eyes.

There was a silence. The old man did not move in his

chair. At length Gandalf spoke. 'Hail, Théoden son of Thengel! I have returned. For behold! the storm comes, and now all friends should gather together, lest each singly be destroyed.'

Slowly the old man rose to his feet, leaning heavily upon a short black staff with a handle of white bone; and now the strangers saw that, bent though he was, he was still tall and must in youth have been high and proud indeed.

'I greet you,' he said, 'and maybe you look for welcome. But truth to tell your welcome is doubtful here, Master Gandalf. You have ever been a herald of woe. Troubles follow you like crows, and ever the oftener the worse. I will not deceive you: when I heard that Shadowfax had come back riderless, I rejoiced at the return of the horse, but still more at the lack of the rider; and when Éomer brought the tiding that you had gone at last to your long home, I did not mourn. But news from afar is seldom sooth. Here you come again! And with you come evils worse than before, as might be expected. Why should I welcome you, Gandalf Stormcrow? Tell me that.' Slowly he sat down again in his chair.

'You speak justly, lord,' said the pale man sitting upon the steps of the dais. 'It is not yet five days since the bitter tidings came that Théodred your son was slain upon the West Marches: your right hand, Second Marshal of the Mark. In Éomer there is little trust. Few men would be left to guard your walls, if he had been allowed to rule. And even now we learn from Gondor that the Dark Lord is stirring in the East. Such is the hour in which this wanderer chooses to return. Why indeed should we welcome you, Master Stormcrow? *Láthspell* I name you, Ill-news; and ill news is an ill guest they say.' He laughed grimly, as he lifted his heavy lids for a moment and gazed on the strangers with dark eyes.

'You are held wise, my friend Wormtongue, and are doubtless a great support to your master,' answered Gandalf in a soft voice. 'Yet in two ways may a man come with evil tidings. He may be a worker of evil; or he may be such as leaves well alone, and comes only to bring aid in time of need.'

'That is so,' said Wormtongue; 'but there is a third kind: pickers of bones, meddlers in other men's sorrows, carrion-fowl that grow fat on war. What aid have you ever brought, Stormcrow? And what aid do you bring now? It was aid from us that you sought last time that you were here. Then my lord bade you choose any horse that you would and be gone; and to the wonder of all you took Shadowfax in your insolence. My lord was sorely grieved; yet to some it seemed that to speed you from the land the price was not too great. I guess that it is likely to turn out the same once more: you will seek aid rather than render it. Do you bring men? Do you bring horses, swords, spears? That I would call aid; that is our present need. But who are these that follow at your tail? Three ragged wanderers in grey, and you yourself the most beggar-like of the four!'

'The courtesy of your hall is somewhat lessened of late, Théoden son of Thengel,' said Gandalf. 'Has not the messenger from your gate reported the names of my companions? Seldom has any lord of Rohan received three such guests. Weapons they have laid at your doors that are worth many a mortal man, even the mightiest. Grey is their raiment, for the Elves clad them, and thus they have passed through the shadow of great perils to your hall.'

'Then it is true, as Éomer reported, that you are in league with the Sorceress of the Golden Wood?' said Wormtongue. 'It is not to be wondered at: webs of deceit were ever woven in Dwimordene.'

Gimli strode a pace forward, but felt suddenly the hand of Gandalf clutch him by the shoulder, and he halted, standing stiff as stone.

> In Dwimordene, in Lórien
> Seldom have walked the feet of Men,
> Few mortal eyes have seen the light
> That lies there ever, long and bright.
> Galadriel! Galadriel!

Clear is the water of your well;
White is the star in your white hand;
Unmarred, unstained is leaf and land
In Dwimordene, in Lórien
More fair than thoughts of Mortal Men.

Thus Gandalf softly sang, and then suddenly he changed. Casting his tattered cloak aside, he stood up and leaned no longer on his staff; and he spoke in a clear cold voice.

'The wise speak only of what they know, Gríma son of Gálmód. A witless worm have you become. Therefore be silent, and keep your forked tongue behind your teeth. I have not passed through fire and death to bandy crooked words with a serving-man till the lightning falls.'

He raised his staff. There was a roll of thunder. The sunlight was blotted out from the eastern windows; the whole hall became suddenly dark as night. The fire faded to sullen embers. Only Gandalf could be seen, standing white and tall before the blackened hearth.

In the gloom they heard the hiss of Wormtongue's voice: 'Did I not counsel you, lord, to forbid his staff? That fool, Háma, has betrayed us!' There was a flash as if lightning had cloven the roof. Then all was silent. Wormtongue sprawled on his face.

'Now Théoden son of Thengel, will you hearken to me?' said Gandalf. 'Do you ask for help?' He lifted his staff and pointed to a high window. There the darkness seemed to clear, and through the opening could be seen, high and far, a patch of shining sky. 'Not all is dark. Take courage, Lord of the Mark; for better help you will not find. No counsel have I to give to those that despair. Yet counsel I could give, and words I could speak to you. Will you hear them? They are not for all ears. I bid you come out before your doors and look abroad. Too long have you sat in shadows and trusted to twisted tales and crooked promptings.'

Slowly Théoden left his chair. A faint light grew in the

hall again. The woman hastened to the king's side, taking
his arm, and with faltering steps the old man came down
from the dais and paced softly through the hall. Wormtongue remained lying on the floor. They came to the doors
and Gandalf knocked.

'Open!' he cried. 'The Lord of the Mark comes forth!'

The doors rolled back and a keen air came whistling in.
A wind was blowing on the hill.

'Send your guards down to the stairs' foot,' said Gandalf. 'And you, lady, leave him a while with me. I will
care for him.'

'Go, Éowyn sister-daughter!' said the old king. 'The
time for fear is past.'

The woman turned and went slowly into the house. As
she passed the doors she turned and looked back. Grave
and thoughtful was her glance, as she looked on the king
with cool pity in her eyes. Very fair was her face, and her
long hair was like a river of gold. Slender and tall she
was in her white robe girt with silver; but strong she
seemed and stern as steel, a daughter of kings. Thus Aragorn for the first time in the full light of day beheld
Éowyn, lady of Rohan, and thought her fair, fair and
cold, like a morning of pale spring that is not yet come to
womanhood. And she now was suddenly aware of him:
tall heir of kings, wise with many winters, greycloaked,
hiding a power that yet she felt. For a moment still as
stone she stood, then turning swiftly she was gone.

'Now, lord,' said Gandalf, 'look out upon your land!
Breathe the free air again!'

From the porch upon the top of the high terrace they
could see beyond the stream the green fields of Rohan
fading into distant grey. Curtains of wind-blown rain were
slanting down. The sky above and to the west was still dark
with thunder, and lightning far away flickered among the
tops of hidden hills. But the wind had shifted to the north,
and already the storm that had come out of the East
was receding, rolling away southward to the sea. Suddenly through a rent in the clouds behind them a shaft
of sun stabbed down. The falling showers gleamed like

silver, and far away the river glittered like a shimmering glass.

'It is not so dark here,' said Théoden.

'No,' said Gandalf. 'Nor does age lie so heavily on your shoulders as some would have you think. Cast aside your prop!'

From the king's hand the black staff fell clattering on the stones. He drew himself up, slowly, as a man that is stiff from long bending over some dull toil. Now tall and straight he stood, and his eyes were blue as he looked into the opening sky.

'Dark have been my dreams of late,' he said, 'but I feel as one new-awakened. I would now that you had come before, Gandalf. For I fear that already you have come too late, only to see the last days of my house. Not long now shall stand the high hall which Brego son of Eorl built. Fire shall devour the high seat. What is to be done?'

'Much,' said Gandalf. 'But first send for Éomer. Do I not guess rightly that you hold him prisoner, by the counsel of Gríma, of him that all save you name the Wormtongue?'

'It is true,' said Théoden. 'He had rebelled against my commands, and threatened death to Gríma in my hall.'

'A man may love you and yet not love Wormtongue or his counsels,' said Gandalf.

'That may be. I will do as you ask. Call Háma to me. Since he proved untrusty as a doorward, let him become an errand-runner. The guilty shall bring the guilty to judgement,' said Théoden, and his voice was grim, yet he looked at Gandalf and smiled and as he did so many lines of care were smoothed away and did not return.

When Háma had been summoned and had gone, Gandalf led Théoden to a stone seat, and then sat himself before the king upon the topmost stair. Aragorn and his companions stood nearby.

'There is no time to tell all that you should hear,' said Gandalf. 'Yet if my hope is not cheated, a time will come

ere long when I can speak more fully. Behold! you are
come into a peril greater even than the wit of Wormtongue could weave into your dreams. But see! you dream
no longer. You live. Gondor and Rohan do not stand
alone. The enemy is strong beyond our reckoning, yet we
have hope at which he has not guessed.'

Quickly now Gandalf spoke. His voice was low and
secret, and none save the king heard what he said. But
ever as he spoke the light shone brighter in Théoden's eye,
and at the last he rose from his seat to his full height,
and Gandalf beside him, and together they looked out
from the high place towards the East.

'Verily,' said Gandalf, now in a loud voice, keen and
clear, 'that way lies our hope, where sits our greatest fear.
Doom hangs still on a thread. Yet hope there is still, if we
can but stand unconquered for a little while.'

The others too now turned their eyes eastward. Over the
sundering leagues of land, far away they gazed to the edge
of sight, and hope and fear bore their thoughts still on,
beyond dark mountains to the Land of Shadow. Where now
was the Ring-bearer? How thin indeed was the thread upon
which doom still hung! It seemed to Legolas, as he strained
his farseeing eyes, that he caught a glint of white: far
away perchance the sun twinkled on a pinnacle of the
Tower of Guard. And further still, endlessly remote and
yet a present threat, there was a tiny tongue of flame.

Slowly Théoden sat down again, as if weariness still
struggled to master him against the will of Gandalf. He
turned and looked at his great house. 'Alas!' he said, 'that
these evil days should be mine, and should come in my
old age instead of that peace which I have earned. Alas
for Boromir the brave! The young perish and the old linger, withering.' He clutched his knees with his wrinkled
hands.

'Your fingers would remember their old strength better,
if they grasped a sword-hilt,' said Gandalf.

Théoden rose and put his hand to his side; but no sword
hung at his belt. 'Where has Gríma stowed it?' he muttered under his breath.

'Take this, dear lord!' said a clear voice. 'It was ever at your service.' Two men had come softly up the stair and stood now a few steps from the top. Éomer was there. No helm was on his head, no mail was on his breast, but in his hand he held a drawn sword; and as he knelt he offered the hilt to his master.

'How comes this?' said Théoden sternly. He turned towards Éomer, and the men looked in wonder at him, standing now proud and erect. Where was the old man whom they had left crouching in his chair or leaning on his stick?

'It is my doing, lord,' said Háma, trembling. 'I understood that Éomer was to be set free. Such joy was in my heart that maybe I have erred. Yet, since he was free again, and he a marshal of the Mark, I brought him his sword as he bade me.'

'To lay at your feet, my lord,' said Éomer.

For a moment of silence Théoden stood looking down at Éomer as he knelt still before him. Neither moved.

'Will you not take the sword?' said Gandalf.

Slowly Théoden stretched forth his hand. As his fingers took the hilt, it seemed to the watchers that firmness and strength returned to his thin arm. Suddenly he lifted the blade and swung it shimmering and whistling in the air. Then he gave a great cry. His voice rang clear as he chanted in the tongue of Rohan a call to arms.

> *Arise now, arise, Riders of Théoden!*
> *Dire deeds awake, dark is it eastward.*
> *Let horse be bridled, horn be sounded!*
> *Forth Eorlingas!*

The guards, thinking that they were summoned, sprang up the stair. They looked at their lord in amazement, and then as one man they drew their swords and laid them at his feet. 'Command us!' they said.

'*Westu Théoden hál!*' cried Éomer. 'It is a joy to us to see you return into your own. Never again shall it be said, Gandalf, that you come only with grief!'

'Take back your sword, Éomer, sister-son!' said the king. 'Go, Háma, and seek my own sword! Gríma has it in his keeping. Bring him to me also. Now, Gandalf, you said that you had counsel to give, if I would hear it. What is your counsel?'

'You have yourself already taken it,' answered Gandalf. 'To put your trust in Éomer, rather than in a man of crooked mind. To cast aside regret and fear. To do the deed at hand. Every man that can ride should be sent west at once, as Éomer counselled you: we must first destroy the threat of Saruman, while we have time. If we fail, we fall. If we succeed—then we will face the next task. Meanwhile your people that are left, the women and the children and the old, should fly to the refuges that you have in the mountains. Were they not prepared against just such an evil day as this? Let them take provision, but delay not, nor burden themselves with treasures, great or small. It is their lives that are at stake.'

'This counsel seems good to me now,' said Théoden. 'Let all my folk get ready! But you my guests—truly you said, Gandalf, that the courtesy of my hall is lessened. You have ridden through the night, and the morning wears away. You have had neither sleep nor food. A guest-house shall be made ready: there you shall sleep, when you have eaten.'

'Nay, lord,' said Aragorn. 'There is no rest yet for the weary. The men of Rohan must ride forth today, and we will ride with them, axe, sword, and bow. We did not bring them to rest against your wall, Lord of the Mark. And I promised Éomer that my sword and his should be drawn together.'

'Now indeed there is hope of victory!' said Éomer.

'Hope, yes,' said Gandalf. 'But Isengard is strong. And other perils draw ever nearer. Do not delay, Théoden, when we are gone. Lead your people swiftly to the Hold of Dunharrow in the hills!'

'Nay, Gandalf!' said the king. 'You do not know your own skill in healing. It shall not be so. I myself will go to war, to fall in the front of the battle, if it must be. Thus shall I sleep better.'

'Then even the defeat of Rohan will be glorious in song,' said Aragorn. The armed men that stood near clashed their weapons, crying: 'The Lord of the Mark will ride! Forth Eorlingas!'

'But your people must not be both unarmed and shepherdless,' said Gandalf. 'Who shall guide them and govern them in your place?'

'I will take thought for that ere I go,' answered Théoden. 'Here comes my counsellor.'

At that moment Háma came again from the hall. Behind him cringing between two other men, came Gríma the Wormtongue. His face was very white. His eyes blinked in the sunlight. Háma knelt and presented to Théoden a long sword in a scabbard clasped with gold and set with green gems.

'Here, lord, is Herugrim, your ancient blade,' he said. 'It was found in his chest. Loth was he to render up the keys. Many other things are there which men have missed.'

'You lie,' said Wormtongue. 'And this sword your master himself gave into my keeping.'

'And he now required it of you again,' said Théoden. 'Does that displease you?'

'Assuredly not, lord,' said Wormtongue. 'I care for you and yours as best I may. But do not weary yourself, or tax too heavily your strength. Let others deal with these irksome guests. Your meat is about to be set on the board. Will you not go to it?'

'I will,' said Théoden. 'And let food for my guests be set on the board beside me. The host rides today. Send the heralds forth! Let them summon all who dwell nigh! Every man and strong lad able to bear arms, all who have horses, let them be ready in the saddle at the gate ere the second hour from noon!'

'Dear lord!' cried Wormtongue. 'It is as I feared. This wizard has bewitched you. Are none to be left to defend

the Golden Hall of your fathers, and all your treasure?
None to guard the Lord of the Mark?'

'If this is bewitchment,' said Théoden, 'it seems to me
more wholesome than your whisperings. Your leechcraft
ere long would have had me walking on all fours like a
beast. No, not one shall be left, not even Gríma. Gríma
shall ride too. Go! You have yet time to clean the rust
from your sword.'

'Mercy, lord!' whined Wormtongue, grovelling on the
ground. 'Have pity on one worn out in your service. Send
me not from your side! I at least will stand by you when
all others have gone. Do not send your faithful Gríma
away!'

'You have my pity,' said Théoden. 'And I do not send
you from my side. I go myself to war with my men. I bid
you come with me and prove your faith.'

Wormtongue looked from face to face. In his eyes was
the hunted look of a beast seeking some gap in the ring
of his enemies. He licked his lips with a long pale tongue.
'Such a resolve might be expected from a lord of the House
of Eorl, old though he be,' he said. 'But those who truly
love him would spare his failing years. Yet I see that I
come too late. Others, whom the death of my lord would
perhaps grieve less, have already persuaded him. If I cannot undo their work, hear me at least in this, lord! One who
knows your mind and honours your commands should be
left in Edoras. Appoint a faithful steward. Let your counsellor Gríma keep all things till your return—and I pray
that we may see it, though no wise man will deem it hopeful.'

Éomer laughed. 'And if that plea does not excuse you
from war, most noble Wormtongue,' he said, 'what office
of less honour would you accept? To carry a sack of meal
up into the mountains—if any man would trust you with
it?'

'Nay, Éomer, you do not fully understand the mind of
Master Wormtongue,' said Gandalf, turning his piercing
glance upon him. 'He is bold and cunning. Even now he
plays a game with peril and wins a throw. Hours of my

precious time he has wasted already. Down snake!' he said suddenly in a terrible voice. 'Down on your belly! How long is it since Saruman bought you? What was the promised price? When all the men were dead, you were to pick your share of the treasure, and take the woman you desire? Too long have you watched her under your eyelids and haunted her steps.'

Éomer grasped his sword. 'That I knew already,' he muttered. 'For that reason I would have slain him before, forgetting the law of the hall. But there are other reasons.' He stepped forward, but Gandalf stayed him with his hand.

'Éowyn is safe now,' he said. 'But you, Wormtongue, you have done what you could for your true master. Some reward you have earned at least. Yet Saruman is apt to overlook his bargains. I should advise you to go quickly and remind him, lest he forget your faithful service.'

'You lie,' said Wormtongue.

'That word comes too oft and easy from your lips,' said Gandalf. 'I do not lie. See, Théoden, here is a snake! With safety you cannot take it with you, nor can you leave it behind. To slay it would be just. But it was not always as it now is. Once it was a man, and did you service in its fashion. Give him a horse and let him go at once, wherever he chooses. By his choice you shall judge him.'

'Do you hear this, Wormtongue?' said Théoden. 'This is your choice: to ride with me to war, and let us see in battle whether you are true; or to go now, whither you will. But then, if ever we meet again, I shall not be merciful.'

Slowly Wormtongue rose. He looked at them with half-closed eyes. Last of all he scanned Théoden's face and opened his mouth as if to speak. Then suddenly he drew himself up. His hands worked. His eyes glittered. Such malice was in them that men stepped back from him. He bared his teeth; and then with a hissing breath he spat before the king's feet, and darting to one side, he fled down the stair.

'After him!' said Théoden. 'See that he does no harm to any, but do not hurt him or hinder him. Give him a horse, if he wishes it.'

'And if any will bear him,' said Éomer.

One of the guards ran down the stair. Another went to the well at the foot of the terrace and in his helm drew water. With it he washed clean the stones that Wormtongue had defiled.

'Now my guests, come!' said Théoden. 'Come and take such refreshment as haste allows.'

They passed back into the great house. Already they heard below them in the town the heralds crying and the war-horns blowing. For the king was to ride forth as soon as the men of the town and those dwelling near could be armed and assembled.

At the king's board sat Éomer and the four guests, and there also waiting upon the king was the lady Éowyn. They ate and drank swiftly. The others were silent while Théoden questioned Gandalf concerning Saruman.

'How far back his treachery goes, who can guess?' said Gandalf. 'He was not always evil. Once I do not doubt that he was the friend of Rohan; and even when his heart grew colder, he found you useful still. But for long now he has plotted your ruin, wearing the mask of friendship, until he was ready. In those years Wormtongue's task was easy, and all that you did was swiftly known in Isengard; for your land was open, and strangers came and went. And ever Wormtongue's whispering was in your ears, poisoning your thought, chilling your heart, weakening your limbs, while others watched and could do nothing, for your will was in his keeping.

'But when I escaped and warned you, then the mask was torn, for those who would see. After that Wormtongue played dangerously, always seeking to delay you, to prevent your full strength being gathered. He was crafty: dulling men's wariness, or working on their fears, as served the occasion. Do you not remember how eagerly he urged that no man should be spared on a wildgoose chase northward, when the immediate peril was westward? He persuaded you to forbid Éomer to pursue the raiding Orcs. If Éomer had not defied Wormtongue's voice

speaking with your mouth, those Orcs would have reached
Isengard by now, bearing a great prize. Not indeed that
prize which Saruman desires above all else, but at the least
two members of my Company, sharers of a secret hope, of
which even to you, lord, I cannot yet speak openly. Dare
you think of what they might now be suffering, or what
Saruman might have learned to our destruction?'

'I owe much to Éomer,' said Théoden. 'Faithful heart
may have froward tongue.'

'Say also,' said Gandalf, 'that to crooked eyes truth may
wear a wry face.'

'Indeed my eyes were almost blind,' said Théoden. 'Most
of all I owe to you, my guest. Once again you have come in
time. I would give you a gift ere we go, at your own choosing. You have only to name aught that is mine. I reserve
now only my sword!'

'Whether I came in time or not is yet to be seen,' said
Gandalf. 'But as for your gift, lord, I will choose one that
will fit my need: swift and sure. Give me Shadowfax! He
was only lent before, if loan we may call it. But now I shall
ride him into great hazard, setting silver against black: I
would not risk anything that is not my own. And already
there is a bond of love between us.'

'You choose well,' said Théoden; 'and I give him now
gladly. Yet it is a great gift. There is none like to Shadowfax. In him one of the mighty steeds of old has returned.
None such shall return again. And to you my other guests
I will offer such things as may be found in my armoury.
Swords you do not need, but there are helms and coats
of mail of cunning work, gifts to my fathers out of Gondor. Choose from these ere we go, and may they serve
you well!'

Now men came bearing raiment of war from the king's
hoard, and they arrayed Aragorn and Legolas in shining
mail. Helms too they chose, and round shields: their bosses
were overlaid with gold and set with gems, green and red
and white. Gandalf took no armour; and Gimli needed no
coat of rings, even if one had been found to match his

stature, for there was no hauberk in the hoards of Edoras of better make than his short corslet forged beneath the Mountain in the North. But he chose a cap of iron and leather that fitted well upon his round head; and a small shield he also took. It bore the running horse, white upon green, that was the emblem of the house of Eorl.

'May it keep you well!' said Théoden. 'It was made for me in Thengel's day, while still I was a boy.'

Gimli bowed. 'I am proud, Lord of the Mark, to bear your device,' he said. 'Indeed sooner would I bear a horse than be borne by one. I love my feet better. But, maybe, I shall come yet where I can stand and fight.'

'It may well be so,' said Théoden.

The king now rose, and at once Éowyn came forward bearing wine. *'Ferthu Théoden hál!'* she said. 'Receive now this cup and drink in happy hour. Health be with thee at thy going and coming!'

Théoden drank from the cup, and she then proffered it to the guests. As she stood before Aragorn she paused suddenly and looked upon him, and her eyes were shining. And he looked down upon her fair face and smiled; but as he took the cup, his hand met hers, and he knew that she trembled at the touch. 'Hail Aragorn son of Arathorn!' she said. 'Hail Lady of Rohan!' he answered, but his face now was troubled and he did not smile.

When they had all drunk, the king went down the hall to the doors. There the guards awaited him, and heralds stood, and all the lords and chiefs were gathered together that remained in Edoras or dwelt nearby.

'Behold! I go forth, and it seems like to be my last riding,' said Théoden. 'I have no child. Théodred my son is slain. I name Éomer my sister-son to be my heir. If neither of us return, then choose a new lord as you will. But to someone I must now entrust my people that I leave behind, to rule them in my place. Which of you will stay?'

No man spoke.

'Is there none whom you would name? In whom do my people trust?'

'In the House of Eorl,' answered Háma.

'But Éomer I cannot spare, nor would he stay,' said the king; 'and he is the last of that House.'

'I said not Éomer,' answered Háma. 'And he is not the last. There is Éowyn, daughter of Éomund, his sister. She is fearless and high-hearted. All love her. Let her be as lord to the Eorlingas, while we are gone.'

'It shall be so,' said Théoden. 'Let the heralds announce to the folk that the Lady Éowyn will lead them!'

Then the king sat upon a seat before his doors, and Éowyn knelt before him and received from him a sword and a fair corslet. 'Farewell sister-daughter!' he said. 'Dark is the hour, yet maybe we shall return to the Golden Hall. But in Dunharrow the people may long defend themselves, and if the battle go ill, thither will come all who escape.'

'Speak not so!' she answered. 'A year shall I endure for every day that passes until your return.' But as she spoke her eyes went to Aragorn who stood nearby.

'The king shall come again,' he said. 'Fear not! Not West but East does our doom await us.'

The king now went down the stair with Gandalf beside him. The others followed. Aragorn looked back as they passed towards the gate. Alone Éowyn stood before the doors of the house at the stair's head; the sword was set upright before her, and her hands were laid upon the hilt. She was clad now in mail and shone like silver in the sun.

Gimli walked with Legolas, his axe on his shoulder. 'Well, at last we set off!' he said. 'Men need many words before deeds. My axe is restless in my hands. Though I doubt not that these Rohirrim are fell-handed when they come to it. Nonetheless this is not the warfare that suits me. How shall I come to the battle? I wish I could walk and not bump like a sack at Gandalf's saddlebow.'

'A safer seat than many, I guess,' said Legolas. 'Yet doubtless Gandalf will gladly put you down on your feet when blows begin; or Shadowfax himself. An axe is no weapon for a rider.'

'And a Dwarf is no horseman. It is orc-necks I would hew, not shave the scalps of Men,' said Gimli, patting the haft of his axe.

At the gate they found a great host of men, old and young, all ready in the saddle. More than a thousand were there mustered. Their spears were like a springing wood. Loudly and joyously they shouted as Théoden came forth. Some held in readiness the king's horse, Snowmane, and others held the horses of Aragorn and Legolas. Gimli stood ill at ease, frowning, but Éomer came up to him, leading his horse.

'Hail, Gimli Glóin's son!' he cried. 'I have not had time to learn gentle speech under your rod, as you promised. But shall we not put aside our quarrel? At least I will speak no evil again of the Lady of the Wood.'

'I will forget my wrath for a while, Éomer son of Éomund,' said Gimli; 'but if ever you chance to see the Lady Galadriel with your eyes, then you shall acknowledge her the fairest of ladies, or our friendship will end.'

'So be it!' said Éomer. 'But until that time pardon me, and in token of pardon ride with me, I beg. Gandalf will be at the head with the Lord of the Mark; but Firefoot, my horse, will bear us both, if you will.'

'I thank you indeed,' said Gimli greatly pleased. 'I will gladly go with you, if Legolas, my comrade, may ride beside us.'

'It shall be so,' said Éomer. 'Legolas upon my left, and Aragorn upon my right, and none will dare to stand before us!'

'Where is Shadowfax?' said Gandalf.

'Running wild over the grass,' they answered. 'He will let no man handle him. There he goes, away down by the ford, like a shadow among the willows.'

Gandalf whistled and called aloud the horse's name, and far away he tossed his head and neighed, and turning sped towards the host like an arrow.

'Were the breath of the West Wind to make a body visible, even so would it appear,' said Éomer, as the great horse ran up, until he stood before the wizard.

'The gift seems already to be given,' said Théoden. 'But hearken all! Here now I name my guest, Gandalf Greyhame, wisest of counsellors, most welcome of wanderers, a lord of the Mark, a chieftain of the Eorlingas while our kin shall last; and I give to him Shadowfax, prince of horses.'

'I thank you, Théoden King,' said Gandalf. Then suddenly he threw back his grey cloak, and cast aside his hat, and leaped to horseback. He wore no helm nor mail. His snowy hair flew free in the wind, his white robes shone dazzling in the sun.

'Behold the White Rider!' cried Aragorn, and all took up the words.

'Our King and the White Rider!' they shouted. 'Forth Eorlingas!'

The trumpets sounded. The horses reared and neighed. Spear clashed on shield. Then the king raised his hand, and with a rush like the sudden onset of a great wind the last host of Rohan rode thundering into the West.

Far over the plain Éowyn saw the glitter of their spears, as she stood still, alone before the doors of the silent house.

Chapter 7

Helm's Deep

The sun was already westering as they rode from Edoras, and the light of it was in their eyes, turning all the rolling fields of Rohan to a golden haze. There was a beaten way, north-westward along the foot-hills of the White Mountains, and this they followed, up and down in a green country, crossing small swift streams by many fords. Far ahead and to their right the Misty Mountains loomed; ever darker and taller they grew as the miles went by. The sun went slowly down before them. Evening came behind.

The host rode on. Need drove them. Fearing to come too late, they rode with all the speed they could, pausing seldom. Swift and enduring were the steeds of Rohan, but there were many leagues to go. Forty leagues and more it was, as a bird flies, from Edoras to the fords of the Isen, where they hoped to find the king's men that held back the hosts of Saruman.

Night closed about them. At last they halted to make their camp. They had ridden for some five hours and were far out upon the western plain, yet more than half their journey lay still before them. In a great circle, under the starry sky and the waxing moon, they now made their bivouac. They lit no fires, for they were uncertain of events; but they set a ring of mounted guards about them, and scouts rode out far ahead, passing like shadows in the folds of the land. The slow night passed without tidings or alarm. At dawn the horns sounded, and within an hour they took the road again.

There were no clouds overhead yet, but a heaviness was in the air; it was hot for the season of the year. The rising sun was hazy, and behind it, following it slowly up the sky, there was a growing darkness, as of a great storm moving out of the East. And away in the North-west there seemed to be another darkness brooding about the feet of the Misty Mountains, a shadow that crept down slowly from the Wizard's Vale.

Gandalf dropped back to where Legolas rode beside Éomer. 'You have the keen eyes of your fair kindred, Legolas,' he said; 'and they can tell a sparrow from a finch a league off. Tell me, can you see anything away yonder towards Isengard?'

'Many miles lie between,' said Legolas, gazing thither and shading his eyes with his long hand. 'I can see a darkness. There are shapes moving in it, great shapes far away upon the bank of the river; but what they are I cannot tell. It is not mist or cloud that defeats my eyes: there is a veiling shadow that some power lays upon the land, and it marches slowly down stream. It is as if the twilight under endless trees were flowing downwards from the hills.'

'And behind us comes a very storm of Mordor,' said Gandalf. 'It will be a black night.'

As the second day of their riding drew on, the heaviness in the air increased. In the afternoon the dark clouds began to overtake them: a sombre canopy with great billowing edges flecked with dazzling light. The sun went down, blood-red in a smoking haze. The spears of the Riders were tipped with fire as the last hafts of light kindled the steep faces of the peaks of Thrihyrne: now very near they stood on the northernmost arm of the White Mountains, three jagged horns staring at the sunset. In the last red glow men in the vanguard saw a black speck, a horseman riding back towards them. They halted awaiting him.

He came, a weary man with dinted helm and cloven shield. Slowly he climbed from his horse and stood there a while gasping. At length he spoke. 'Is Éomer here?' he asked. 'You come at last, but too late, and with too little strength. Things have gone evilly since Théodred fell. We were driven back yesterday over the Isen with great loss; many perished at the crossing. Then at night fresh forces came over the river against our camp. All Isengard must be emptied; and Saruman has armed the wild hillmen and herd-folk of Dunland beyond the rivers, and these also he loosed upon us. We were overmastered. The shieldwall was broken. Erkenbrand of Westfold has drawn off those men he could gather towards his fastness in Helm's Deep. The rest are scattered.

'Where is Éomer? Tell him there is no hope ahead. He should return to Edoras before the wolves of Isengard come there.'

Théoden had sat silent, hidden from the man's sight behind his guards; now he urged his horse forward. 'Come, stand before me, Ceorl!' he said. 'I am here. The last host of the Eorlingas has ridden forth. It will not return without battle.'

The man's face lightened with joy and wonder. He drew himself up. Then he knelt, offering his notched sword to the king. 'Command me, lord!' he cried. 'And pardon me! I thought——'

'You thought I remained in Meduseld bent like an old tree under winter snow. So it was when you rode to war. But a west wind has shaken the boughs,' said Théoden. 'Give this man a fresh horse! Let us ride to the help of Erkenbrand!'

While Théoden was speaking, Gandalf rode a short way ahead, and he sat there alone, gazing north to Isengard and west to the setting sun. Now he came back.

'Ride, Théoden!' he said. 'Ride to Helm's Deep! Go not to the Fords of Isen, and do not tarry in the plain! I must leave you for a while. Shadowfax must bear me now on a swift errand.' Turning to Aragorn and Éomer and the men of the king's household, he cried: 'Keep well the Lord of the Mark, till I return. Await me at Helm's Gate! Farewell!'

He spoke a word to Shadowfax, and like an arrow from the bow the great horse sprang away. Even as they looked he was gone: a flash of silver in the sunset, a wind over the grass, a shadow that fled and passed from sight. Snow-

mane snorted and reared, eager to follow; but only a swift
bird on the wing could have overtaken him.

'What does that mean?' said one of the guard to Háma.

'That Gandalf Greyhame has need of haste,' answered
Háma. 'Ever he goes and comes unlooked-for.'

'Wormtongue, were he here, would not find it hard to
explain,' said the other.

'True enough,' said Háma; 'but for myself, I will wait
until I see Gandalf again.'

'Maybe you will wait long,' said the other.

The host turned away now from the road to the Fords of
Isen and bent their course southward. Night fell, and still
they rode on. The hills drew near, but the tall peaks of
Thrihyrne were already dim against the darkening sky.
Still some miles away, on the far side of the Westfold
Vale, lay a green coomb, a great bay in the mountains,
out of which a gorge opened in the hills. Men of that land
called it Helm's Deep, after a hero of old wars who had
made his refuge there. Ever steeper and narrower it
wound inward from the north under the shadow of the
Thrihyrne, till the crowhaunted cliffs rose like mighty
towers on either side, shutting out the light.

At Helm's Gate, before the mouth of the Deep, there
was a heel of rock thrust outward by the northern cliff.
There upon its spur stood high walls of ancient stone, and
within them was a lofty tower. Men said that in the far-off
days of the glory of Gondor the sea-kings had built here
this fastness with the hands of giants. The Hornburg it
was called, for a trumpet sounded upon the tower echoed
in the Deep behind, as if armies long-forgotten were issuing to war from caves beneath the hills. A wall, too,
the men of old had made from the Hornburg to the
southern cliff, barring the entrance to the gorge. Beneath
it by a wide culvert the Deeping Stream passed out. About
the feet of the Hornrock it wound, and flowed then in a
gully through the midst of a wide green gore, sloping
gently down from Helm's Gate to Helm's Dike. Thence it

fell into the Deeping Coomb and out into the Westfold Vale. There in the Hornburg at Helm's Gate Erkenbrand, master of Westfold on the borders of the Mark, now dwelt. As the days darkened with threat of war, being wise, he had repaired the wall and made the fastness strong.

The Riders were still in the low valley before the mouth of the Coomb, when cries and hornblasts were heard from their scouts that went in front. Out of the darkness arrows whistled. Swiftly a scout rode back and reported that wolf-riders were abroad in the valley, and that a host of Orcs and wild men were hurrying southward from the Fords of Isen and seemed to be making for Helm's Deep.

'We have found many of our folk lying slain as they fled thither,' said the scout. 'And we have met scattered companies, going this way and that, leaderless. What has become of Erkenbrand none seem to know. It is likely that he will be overtaken ere he can reach Helm's Gate, if he has not already perished.'

'Has aught been seen of Gandalf?' asked Théoden.

'Yes, lord. Many have seen an old man in white upon a horse, passing hither and thither over the plains like wind in the grass. Some thought he was Saruman. It is said that he went away ere nightfall towards Isengard. Some say also that Wormtongue was seen earlier, going north-ward with a company of Orcs.'

'It will go ill with Wormtongue, if Gandalf comes upon him,' said Théoden. 'Nonetheless I miss now both my counsellors, the old and the new. But in this need we have no better choice than to go on, as Gandalf said, to Helm's Gate, whether Erkenbrand be there or no. Is it known how great is the host that comes from the North?'

'It is very great,' said the scout. 'He that flies counts every foeman twice, yet I have spoken to stouthearted men, and I do not doubt that the main strength of the enemy is many times as great as all that we have here.'

'Then let us be swift,' said Éomer. 'Let us drive through such foes as are already between us and the fastness.

There are caves in Helm's Deep where hundreds may lie hid; and secret ways lead thence up onto the hills.'

'Trust not to secret ways,' said the king. 'Saruman has long spied out this land. Still in that place our defence may last long. Let us go!'

Aragorn and Legolas went now with Éomer in the van. On through the dark night they rode, ever slower as the darkness deepened and their way climbed southward, higher and higher into the dim folds about the mountains' feet. They found few of the enemy before them. Here and there they came upon roving bands of Orcs; but they fled ere the Riders could take or slay them.

'It will not be long I fear,' said Éomer, 'ere the coming of the king's host will be known to the leader of our enemies, Saruman or whatever captain he has sent forth.'

The rumour of war grew behind them. Now they could hear, borne over the dark, the sound of harsh singing. They had climbed far up into the Deeping Coomb when they looked back. Then they saw torches, countless points of fiery light upon the black fields behind, scattered like red flowers, or winding up from the lowlands in long flickering lines. Here and there a larger blaze leapt up.

'It is a great host and follows us hard,' said Aragorn.

'They bring fire,' said Théoden, 'and they are burning as they come, rick, cot, and tree. This was a rich vale and had many homesteads. Alas for my folk!'

'Would that day was here and we might ride down upon them like a storm out of the mountains!' said Aragorn. 'It grieves me to fly before them.'

'We need not fly much further,' said Éomer. 'Not far ahead now lies Helm's Dike, an ancient trench and rampart scored across the coomb, two furlongs below Helm's Gate. There we can turn and give battle.'

'Nay, we are too few to defend the Dike,' said Théoden. 'It is a mile long or more, and the breach in it is wide.'

'At the breach our rearguard must stand, if we are pressed,' said Éomer.

There was neither star nor moon when the Riders came to the breach in the Dike, where the stream from above passed out, and the road beside it ran down from the Hornburg. The rampart loomed suddenly before them, a high shadow beyond a dark pit. As they rode up a sentinel challenged them.

'The Lord of the Mark rides to Helm's Gate,' Éomer answered. 'I, Éomund, speak.'

'This is good tidings beyond hope,' said the sentinel. 'Hasten! The enemy is on your heels.'

The host passed through the breach and halted on the sloping sward above. They now learned to their joy that Erkenbrand had left many men to hold Helm's Gate, and more had since escaped thither.

'Maybe, we have a thousand fit to fight on foot,' said Gamling, an old man, the leader of those that watched the Dike. 'But most of them have seen too many winters, as I have, or too few, as my son's son here. What news of Erkenbrand? Word came yesterday that he was retreating hither with all that is left of the best riders of Westfold. But he has not come.'

'I fear that he will not come now,' said Éomer. 'Our scouts have gained no news of him, and the enemy fills all the valley behind us.'

'I would that he had escaped,' said Théoden. 'He was a mighty man. In him lived again the valour of Helm the Hammerhand. But we cannot await him here. We must draw all our forces now behind the walls. Are you well stored? We bring little provision, for we rode forth to open battle, not to a siege.'

'Behind us in the caves of the Deep are three parts of the folk of Westfold, old and young, children and women,' said Gamling. 'But great store of food, and many beasts and their fodder, have also been gathered there.'

'That is well,' said Éomer. 'They are burning or despoiling all that is left in the vale.'

'If they come to bargain for our goods at Helm's Gate, they will pay a high price,' said Gamling.

The king and his Riders passed on. Before the causeway that crossed the stream they dismounted. In a long file they led their horses up the ramp and passed within the gates of the Hornburg. There they were welcomed again with joy and renewed hope; for now there were men enough to man both the burg and the barrier wall.

Quickly Éomer set his men in readiness. The king and the men of his household were in the Hornburg, and there also were many of the Westfold-men. But on the Deeping Wall and its tower, and behind it, Éomer arrayed most of the strength that he had, for here the defence seemed more doubtful, if the assault were determined and in great force. The horses were led far up the Deep under such guard as could be spared.

The Deeping Wall was twenty feet high, and so thick that four men could walk abreast along the top, sheltered by a parapet over which only a tall man could look. Here and there were clefts in the stone through which men could shoot. This battlement could be reached by a stair running down from a door in the outer court of the Hornburg; three flights of steps led also up onto the wall from the Deep behind; but in front it was smooth, and the great stones of it were set with such skill that no foothold could be found at their joints, and at the top they hung over like a sea-delved cliff.

Gimli stood leaning against the breastwork upon the wall. Legolas sat above on the parapet, fingering his bow, and peering out into the gloom.

'This is more to my liking,' said the dwarf, stamping on the stones. 'Ever my heart rises as we draw near the mountains. There is good rock here. This country has tough bones. I felt them in my feet as we came up from the dike. Give me a year and a hundred of my kin and I would make this a place that armies would break upon like water.'

'I do not doubt it,' said Legolas. 'But you are a dwarf, and dwarves are strange folk. I do not like this place, and I shall like it no more by the light of day. But you comfort

me, Gimli, and I am glad to have you standing nigh
with your stout legs and your hard axe. I wish there were
more of your kin among us. But even more would I give
for a hundred good archers of Mirkwood. We shall need
them. The Rohirrim have good bowmen after their fashion,
but there are too few here, too few.'

'It is dark for archery,' said Gimli. 'Indeed it is time
for sleep. Sleep! I feel the need of it, as never I thought
any dwarf could. Riding is tiring work. Yet my axe is
restless in my hand. Give me a row of orc-necks and room
to swing and all weariness will fall from me!'

A slow time passed. Far down in the valley scattered
fires still burned. The hosts of Isengard were advancing in
silence now. Their torches could be seen winding up the
coomb in many lines.

Suddenly from the Dike yells and screams, and the
fierce battle-cries of men broke out. Flaming brands appeared over the brink and clustered thickly at the breach.
Then they scattered and vanished. Men came galloping
back over the field and up the ramp to the gate of the
Hornburg. The rearguard of the Westfolders had been
driven in.

'The enemy is at hand!' they said. 'We loosed every arrow that we had, and filled the Dike with Orcs. But it will
not halt them long. Already they are scaling the bank at
many points, thick as marching ants. But we have taught
them not to carry torches.'

It was now past midnight. The sky was utterly dark, and
the stillness of the heavy air foreboded storm. Suddenly
the clouds were seared by a blinding flash. Branched
lightning smote down upon the eastward hills. For a staring
moment the watchers on the walls saw all the space between them and the Dike lit with white light: it was boiling and crawling with black shapes, some squat and broad,
some tall and grim, with high helms and sable shields.
Hundreds and hundreds more were pouring over the Dike
and through the breach. The dark tide flowed up to the

walls from cliff to cliff. Thunder rolled in the valley. Rain came lashing down.

Arrows thick as the rain came whistling over the battlements, and fell clinking and glancing on the stones. Some found a mark. The assault on Helm's Deep had begun, but no sound or challenge was heard within; no answering arrows came.

The assailing hosts halted, foiled by the silent menace of rock and wall. Ever and again the lightning tore aside the darkness. Then the Orcs screamed, waving spear and sword, and shooting a cloud of arrows at any that stood revealed upon the battlements; and the men of the Mark amazed looked out as it seemed to them, upon a great field of dark corn, tossed by a tempest of war, and every ear glinted with barbed light.

Brazen trumpets sounded. The enemy surged forward, some against the Deeping Wall, others towards the causeway and the ramp that led up to the Hornburg-gates. There the hugest Orcs were mustered, and the wild men of the Dunland fells. A moment they hesitated and then on they came. The lightning flashed, and blazoned upon every helm and shield the ghastly hand of Isengard was seen. They reached the summit of the rock; they drove towards the gates.

Then at last an answer came: a storm of arrows met them, and a hail of stones. They wavered, broke, and fled back; and then charged again, broke and charged again; and each time, like the incoming sea, they halted at a higher point. Again trumpets rang, and a press of roaring men leaped forth. They held their great shields above them like a roof, while in their midst they bore two trunks of mighty trees. Behind them orc-archers crowded, sending a hail of darts against the bowmen on the walls. They gained the gates. The trees, swung by strong arms, smote the timbers with a rending boom. If any man fell, crushed by a stone hurtling from above, two others sprang to take his place. Again and again the great rams swung and crashed.

Éomer and Aragorn stood together on the Deeping

Wall. They heard the roar of voices and the thudding of the rams; and then in a sudden flash of light they beheld the peril of the gates.

'Come!' said Aragorn. 'This is the hour when we draw swords together!'

Running like fire, they sped along the wall, and up the steps, and passed into the outer court upon the Rock. As they ran they gathered a handful of stout swordsmen. There was a small postern-door that opened in an angle of the burg-wall on the west, where the cliff stretched out to meet it. On that side a narrow path ran round towards the great gate, between the wall and the sheer brink of the Rock. Together Éomer and Aragorn sprang through the door, their men close behind. The two swords flashed from the sheath as one.

'Gúthwinë!' cried Éomer. 'Gúthwinë for the Mark!'

'Andúril!' cried Aragorn. 'Andúril for the Dúnedain!'

Charging from the side, they hurled themselves upon the wild men. Andúril rose and fell, gleaming with white fire. A shout went up from wall and tower: 'Andúril! Andúril goes to war. The Blade that was Broken shines again!'

Dismayed the rammers let fall the trees and turned to fight; but the wall of their shields was broken as by a lightning-stroke, and they were swept away, hewn down, or cast over the Rock into the stony stream below. The orc-archers shot wildly and then fled.

For a moment Éomer and Aragorn halted before the gates. The thunder was rumbling in the distance now. The lightning flickered still, far off among the mountains in the South. A keen wind was blowing from the North again. The clouds were torn and drifting, and stars peeped out; and above the hills of the Coomb-side the westering moon rode, glimmering yellow in the storm-wrack.

'We did not come too soon,' said Aragorn, looking at the gates. Their great hinges and iron bars were wrenched and bent; many of their timbers were cracked.

'Yet we cannot stay here beyond the walls to defend

them,' said Éomer. 'Look!' He pointed to the causeway. Already a great press of Orcs and Men were gathering again beyond the stream. Arrows whined, and skipped on the stones about them. 'Come! We must get back and see what we can do to pile stone and beam across the gates within. Come now!'

They turned and ran. At that moment some dozen Orcs that had lain motionless among the slain leaped to their feet, and came silently and swiftly behind. Two flung themselves to the ground at Éomer's heels, tripped him, and in a moment they were on top of him. But a small dark figure that none had observed sprang out of the shadows and gave a hoarse shout: *Baruk Khazâd! Khazâd ai-mênu!* An axe swung and swept back. Two Orcs fell headless. The rest fled.

Éomer struggled to his feet, even as Aragorn ran back to his aid.

The postern was closed again, the iron door was barred and piled inside with stones. When all were safe within, Éomer turned: 'I thank you, Gimli son of Glóin!' he said. 'I did not know that you were with us in the sortie. But oft the unbidden guest proves the best company. How came you there?'

'I followed you to shake off sleep,' said Gimli; 'but I looked on the hillmen and they seemed overlarge for me, so I sat beside a stone to see your sword-play.'

'I shall not find it easy to repay you,' said Éomer.

'There may be many a chance ere the night is over,' laughed the Dwarf. 'But I am content. Till now I have hewn naught but wood since I left Moria.'

'Two!' said Gimli, patting his axe. He had returned to his place on the wall.

'Two?' said Legolas. 'I have done better, though now I must grope for spent arrows; all mine are gone. Yet I make my tale twenty at the least. But that is only a few leaves in a forest.'

The sky now was quickly clearing and the sinking moon was shining brightly. But the light brought little hope to the Riders of the Mark. The enemy before them seemed to have grown rather than diminished, and still more were pressing up from the valley through the breach. The sortie upon the Rock gained only a brief respite. The assault on the gates was redoubled. Against the Deeping Wall the hosts of Isengard roared like a sea. Orcs and hill-men swarmed about its feet from end to end. Ropes with grappling hooks were hurled over the parapet faster than men could cut them or fling them back. Hundreds of long ladders were lifted up. Many were cast down in ruin, but many more replaced them, and Orcs sprang up them like apes in the dark forests of the South. Before the wall's foot the dead and broken were piled like shingle in a storm; ever higher rose the hideous mounds, and still the enemy came on.

The men of Rohan grew weary. All their arrows were spent, and every shaft was shot; their swords were notched, and their shields were riven. Three times Aragorn and Éomer rallied them, and three times Andúril flamed in a desperate charge that drove the enemy from the wall.

Then a clamour arose in the Deep behind. Orcs had crept like rats through the culvert through which the stream flowed out. There they had gathered in the shadow of the cliffs, until the assault above was hottest and nearly all the men of the defence had rushed to the wall's top. Then they sprang out. Already some had passed into the jaws of the Deep and were among the horses, fighting with the guards.

Down from the wall leapt Gimli with a fierce cry that echoed in the cliffs. *'Khazâd! Khazâd!'* He soon had work enough.

'Ai-oi!' he shouted. 'The Orcs are behind the wall. Ai-oi! Come, Legolas! There are enough for us both. *Khazâd ai-mênu!'*

Gamling the Old looked down from the Hornburg, hearing the great voice of the dwarf above all the tumult.

'The Orcs are in the Deep!' he cried. 'Helm! Helm! Forth Helmingas!' he shouted as he leaped down the stair from the Rock with many men of Westfold at his back.

Their onset was fierce and sudden, and the Orcs gave way before them. Ere long they were hemmed in in the narrows of the gorge, and all were slain or driven shrieking into the chasm of the Deep to fall before the guardians of the hidden caves.

'Twenty-one!' cried Gimli. He hewed a two-handed stroke and laid the last Orc before his feet. 'Now my count passes Master Legolas again.'

'We must stop this rat-hole,' said Gamling. 'Dwarves are said to be cunning folk with stone. Lend us your aid, master!'

'We do not shape stone with battle-axes, nor with our finger-nails,' said Gimli. 'But I will help as I may.'

They gathered such small boulders and broken stones as they could find to hand, and under Gimli's direction the Westfold-men blocked up the inner end of the culvert, until only a narrow outlet remained. Then the Deeping Stream, swollen by the rain, churned and fretted in its choked path, and spread slowly in cold pools from cliff to cliff.

'It will be drier above,' said Gimli. 'Come, Gamling, let us see how things go on the wall!'

He climbed up and found Legolas beside Aragorn and Éomer. The elf was whetting his long knife. There was for a while a lull in the assault, since the attempt to break in through the culvert had been foiled.

'Twenty-one!' said Gimli.

'Good!' said Legolas. 'But my count is now two dozen. It has been knife-work up here.'

Éomer and Aragorn leant wearily on their swords. Away on the left the crash and clamour of the battle on the Rock rose loud again. But the Hornburg still held fast, like an island in the sea. Its gates lay in ruin; but over the barricade of beams and stones within no enemy as yet had passed.

Aragorn looked at the pale stars, and at the moon, now sloping behind the western hills that enclosed the valley. 'This is a night as long as years,' he said. 'How long will the day tarry?'

'Dawn is not far off,' said Gamling, who had now climbed up beside him. 'But dawn will not help us, I fear.'

'Yet dawn is ever the hope of men,' said Aragorn.

'But these creatures of Isengard, these half-orcs and goblin-men that the foul craft of Saruman has bred, they will not quail at the sun,' said Gamling. 'And neither will the wild men of the hills. Do you not hear their voices?'

'I hear them,' said Éomer; 'but they are only the scream of birds and the bellowing of beasts to my ears.'

'Yet there are many that cry in the Dunland tongue,' said Gamling. 'I know that tongue. It is an ancient speech of men, and once was spoken in many western valleys of the Mark. Hark! They hate us, and they are glad; for our doom seems certain to them. "The king, the king!" they cry. "We will take their king. Death to the Forgoil! Death to the Strawheads! Death to the robbers of the North!" Such names they have for us. Not in half a thousand years have they forgotten their grievance that the lords of Gondor gave the Mark to Eorl the Young and made alliance with him. That old hatred Saruman has inflamed. They are fierce folk when roused. They will not give way now for dusk or dawn, until Théoden is taken, or they themselves are slain.'

'Nonetheless day will bring hope to me,' said Aragorn. 'Is it not said that no foe has ever taken the Hornburg, if men defended it?'

'So the minstrels say,' said Éomer.

'Then let us defend it, and hope!' said Aragorn.

Even as they spoke there came a blare of trumpets. Then there was a crash and a flash of flame and smoke. The waters of the Deeping Stream poured out hissing and foaming: they were choked no longer, a gaping hole was blasted in the wall. A host of dark shapes poured in.

'Devilry of Saruman!' cried Aragorn. 'They have crept in

the culvert again, while we talked, and they have lit the
fire of Orthanc beneath our feet. Elendil, Elendil!' he
shouted, as he leaped down into the breach; but even as
he did so a hundred ladders were raised against the battlements. Over the wall and under the wall the last assault
came sweeping like a dark wave upon a hill of sand. The
defence was swept away. Some of the Riders were driven
back, further and further into the Deep, falling and fighting as they gave way, step by step, towards the caves.
Others cut their way back towards the citadel.

A broad stairway climbed from the Deep up to the Rock
and the rear-gate of the Hornburg. Near the bottom stood
Aragorn. In his hand still Andúril gleamed, and the terror
of the sword for a while held back the enemy, as one by
one all who could gain the stair passed up towards the
gate. Behind on the upper steps knelt Legolas. His bow was
bent, but one gleaned arrow was all that he had left,
and he peered out now, ready to shoot the first Orc that
should dare to approach the stair.

'All who can have now got safe within, Aragorn,' he
called. 'Come back!'

Aragorn turned and sped up the stair; but as he ran he
stumbled in his weariness. At once his enemies leapt forward. Up came the Orcs, yelling, with their long arms
stretched out to seize him. The foremost fell with Legolas'
last arrow in his throat, but the rest sprang after him.
Then a great boulder, cast from the outer wall above,
crashed down upon the stair, and hurled them back into
the Deep. Aragorn gained the door, and swiftly it clanged
to behind him.

'Things go ill, my friends,' he said, wiping the sweat
from his brow with his arm.

'Ill enough,' said Legolas, 'but not yet hopeless, while
we have you with us. Where is Gimli?'

'I do not know,' said Aragorn. 'I last saw him fighting on
the ground behind the wall, but the enemy swept us apart.'

'Alas! That is evil news,' said Legolas.

'He is stout and strong,' said Aragorn. 'Let us hope that
he will escape back to the caves. There he would be safe

for a while. Safer than we. Such a refuge would be to the liking of a dwarf.'

'That must be my hope,' said Legolas. 'But I wish that he had come this way. I desired to tell Master Gimli that my tale is now thirty-nine.'

'If he wins back to the caves, he will pass your count again,' laughed Aragorn. 'Never did I see an axe so wielded.'

'I must go and seek some arrows,' said Legolas. 'Would that this night would end, and I could have better light for shooting.'

Aragorn now passed into the citadel. There to his dismay he learned that Éomer had not reached the Hornburg.

'Nay, he did not come to the Rock,' said one of the Westfold-men. 'I last saw him gathering men about him and fighting in the mouth of the Deep. Gamling was with him, and the dwarf; but I could not come to them.'

Aragorn strode on through the inner court, and mounted to a high chamber in the tower. There stood the king, dark against a narrow window, looking out upon the vale.

'What is the news, Aragorn?' he said.

'The Deeping Wall is taken, lord, and all the defence swept away; but many have escaped hither to the Rock.'

'Is Éomer here?'

'No, lord. But many of your men retreated into the Deep; and some say that Éomer was amongst them. In the narrows they may hold back the enemy and come within the caves. What hope they may have then I do not know.'

'More than we. Good provision, it is said. And the air is wholesome there because of the outlets through fissures in the rock far above. None can force an entrance against determined men. They may hold out long.'

'But the Orcs have brought a devilry from Orthanc,' said Aragorn. 'They have a blasting fire, and with it they took the Wall. If they cannot come in the caves, they may seal up those that are inside. But now we must turn all our thought to our own defence.'

'I fret in this prison,' said Théoden. 'If I could have set a spear in rest, riding before my men upon the field, maybe I could have felt again the joy of battle, and so ended. But I serve little purpose here.'

'Here at least you are guarded in the strongest fastness of the Mark,' said Aragorn. 'More hope we have to defend you in the Hornburg than in Edoras, or even at Dunharrow in the mountains.'

'It is said that the Hornburg has never fallen to assault,' said Théoden; 'but now my heart is doubtful. The world changes, and all that once was strong now proves unsure. How shall any tower withstand such numbers and such reckless hate? Had I known that the strength of Isengard was grown so great, maybe I should not so rashly have ridden forth to meet it, for all the arts of Gandalf. His counsel seems not now so good as it did under the morning sun.'

'Do not judge the counsel of Gandalf, until all is over, lord,' said Aragorn.

'The end will not be long,' said the king. 'But I will not end here, taken like an old badger in a trap. Snowmane and Hasufel and the horses of my guard are in the inner court. When dawn comes, I will bid men sound Helm's horn, and I will ride forth. Will you ride with me then, son of Arathorn? Maybe we shall cleave a road, or make such an end as will be worth a song—if any be left to sing of us hereafter.'

'I will ride with you,' said Aragorn.

Taking his leave, he returned to the walls, and passed round all their circuit, enheartening the men, and lending aid wherever the assault was hot. Legolas went with him. Blasts of fire leaped up from below shaking the stones. Grappling-hooks were hurled, and ladders raised. Again and again the Orcs gained the summit of the outer wall, and again the defenders cast them down.

At last Aragorn stood above the great gates, heedless of the darts of the enemy. As he looked forth he saw the eastern sky grow pale. Then he raised his empty hand, palm outward in token of parley.

The Orcs yelled and jeered. 'Come down! Come down!' they cried. 'If you wish to speak to us, come down! Bring out your king! We are the fighting Uruk-hai. We will fetch him from his hole, if he does not come. Bring out your skulking king!'

'The king stays or comes at his own will,' said Aragorn.

'Then what are you doing here?' they answered. 'Why do you look out? Do you wish to see the greatness of our army? We are the fighting Uruk-hai.'

'I looked out to see the dawn,' said Aragorn.

'What of the dawn?' they peered. 'We are the Uruk-hai: we do not stop the fight for night or day, for fair weather or for storm. We come to kill, by sun or moon. What of the dawn?'

'None knows what the new day shall bring him,' said Aragorn. 'Get you gone, ere it turn to your evil.'

'Get down or we will shoot you from the wall,' they cried. 'This is no parley. You have nothing to say.'

'I have still this to say,' answered Aragorn. 'No enemy has yet taken the Hornburg. Depart, or not one of you will be spared. Not one will be left alive to take back tidings to the North. You do not know your peril.'

So great a power and royalty was revealed in Aragorn, as he stood there alone above the ruined gates before the host of his enemies, that many of the wild men paused, and looked back over their shoulders to the valley, and some looked up doubtfully at the sky. But the Orcs laughed with loud voices; and a hail of darts and arrows whistled over the wall, as Aragorn leaped down.

There was a roar and a blast of fire. The archway of the gate above which he had stood a moment before crumbled and crashed in smoke and dust. The barricade was scattered as if by a thunderbolt. Aragorn ran to the king's tower.

But even as the gate fell, and the Orcs about it yelled, preparing to charge, a murmur arose behind them, like a wind in the distance, and it grew to a clamour of many voices crying strange news in the dawn. The Orcs upon the Rock, hearing the rumour of dismay, wavered and looked back. And then, sudden and terrible, from the tower above, the sound of the great horn of Helm rang out.

All that heard that sound trembled. Many of the Orcs cast themselves on their faces and covered their ears with their claws. Back from the Deep the echoes came, blast upon blast, as if on every cliff and hill a mighty herald stood. But on the walls men looked up, listening with wonder; for the echoes did not die. Ever the hornblasts wound on among the hills; nearer now and louder they answered one to another, blowing fierce and free.

'Helm! Helm!' the Riders shouted. 'Helm is arisen and comes back to war. Helm for Théoden King!'

And with that shout the king came. His horse was white as snow, golden was his shield, and his spear was long. At his right hand was Aragorn, Elendil's heir, behind him rode the lords of the House of Eorl the Young. Light sprang in the sky. Night departed.

'Forth Eorlingas!' With a cry and a great noise they charged. Down from the gates they roared, over the causeway they swept, and they drove through the hosts of Isengard as a wind among grass. Behind them from the Deep came the stern cries of men issuing from the caves, driving forth the enemy. Out poured all the men that were left upon the Rock. And ever the sound of blowing horns echoed in the hills.

On they rode, the king and his companions. Captains and champions fell or fled before them. Neither orc nor man withstood them. Their backs were to the swords and spears of the Riders, and their faces to the valley. They cried and wailed, for fear and great wonder had come upon them with the rising of the day.

So King Théoden rode from Helm's Gate and clove his path to the great Dike. There the company halted. Light grew bright about them. Shafts of the sun flared above the eastern hills and glimmered on their spears. But they sat

silent on their horses, and they gazed down upon the
Deeping Coomb.

The land had changed. Where before the green dale
had lain, its grassy slopes lapping the ever-mounting hills,
there now a forest loomed. Great trees, bare and silent,
stood, rank on rank, with tangled bough and hoary head;
their twisted roots were buried in the long green grass.
Darkness was under them. Between the Dike and the
eaves of that nameless wood only two open furlongs lay.
There now cowered the proud hosts of Saruman, in terror
of the king and in terror of the trees. They streamed down
from Helm's Gate until all above the Dike was empty of
them, but below it they were packed like swarming flies.
Vainly they crawled and clambered about the walls of the
coomb, seeking to escape. Upon the east too sheer and
stony was the valley's side; upon the left, from the west,
their final doom approached.

There suddenly upon a ridge appeared a rider, clad in
white, shining in the rising sun. Over the low hills the horns
were sounding. Behind him, hastening down the long
slopes, were a thousand men on foot; their swords were in
their hands. Amid them strode a man tall and strong. His
shield was red. As he came to the valley's brink, he set
to his lips a great black horn and blew a ringing blast.

'Erkenbrand!' the Riders shouted. 'Erkenbrand!'

'Behold the White Rider!' cried Aragorn. 'Gandalf is
come again!'

'Mithrandir, Mithrandir!' said Legolas. 'This is wizardry
indeed! Come! I would look on this forest, ere the spell
changes.'

The hosts of Isengard roared, swaying this way and that,
turning from fear to fear. Again the horn sounded from
the tower. Down through the breach of the Dike charged
the king's company. Down from the hills leaped Erkenbrand, lord of Westfold. Down leaped Shadowfax, like a
deer that runs surefooted in the mountains. The White
Rider was upon them, and the terror of his coming filled
the enemy with madness. The wild men fell on their faces

before him. The Orcs reeled and screamed and cast aside both sword and spear. Like a black smoke driven by a mounting wind they fled. Wailing they passed under the waiting shadow of the trees; and from that shadow none ever came again.

Chapter 8

The Road to Isengard

So it was that in the light of a fair morning King Théoden and Gandalf the White Rider met again upon the green grass beside the Deeping Stream. There was also Aragorn son of Arathorn, and Legolas the Elf, and Erkenbrand of Westfold, and the lords of the Golden House. About them were gathered the Rohirrim, the Riders of the Mark: wonder overcame their joy in victory, and their eyes were turned towards the wood.

Suddenly there was a great shout, and down from the Dike came those who had been driven back into the Deep. There came Gamling the Old, and Éomer son of Éomund, and beside them walked Gimli the dwarf. He had no helm, and about his head was a linen band stained with blood; but his voice was loud and strong.

'Forty-two, Master Legolas!' he cried. 'Alas! My axe is notched: the forty-second had an iron collar on his neck. How is it with you?'

'You have passed my score by one,' answered Legolas. 'But I do not grudge you the game, so glad am I to see you on your legs!'

'Welcome, Éomer, sister-son!' said Théoden. 'Now that I see you safe, I am glad indeed.'

'Hail, Lord of the Mark!' said Éomer. 'The dark night has passed, and day has come again. But the day has brought strange tidings.' He turned and gazed in wonder, first at the wood and then at Gandalf. 'Once more you come in the hour of need, unlooked-for,' he said.

'Unlooked-for?' said Gandalf. 'I said that I would return and meet you here.'

'But you did not name the hour, nor foretell the manner of your coming. Strange help you bring. You are mighty in wizardry, Gandalf the White!'

'That may be. But if so, I have not shown it yet. I have

but given good counsel in peril, and made use of the speed of Shadowfax. Your own valour has done more, and the stout legs of the Westfoldmen marching through the night.'

Then they all gazed at Gandalf with still greater wonder. Some glanced darkly at the wood, and passed their hands over their brows, as if they thought their eyes saw otherwise than his.

Gandalf laughed long and merrily. 'The trees?' he said. 'Nay, I see the wood as plainly as do you. But that is no deed of mine. It is a thing beyond the counsel of the wise. Better than my design, and better even than my hope the event has proved.'

'Then if not yours, whose is the wizardry?' said Théoden. 'Not Saruman's, that is plain. Is there some mightier sage, of whom we have yet to learn?'

'It is not wizardry, but a power far older,' said Gandalf: 'a power that walked the earth, ere elf sang or hammer rang.

> *Ere iron was found or tree was hewn,*
> *When young was mountain under moon;*
> *Ere ring was made, or wrought was woe,*
> *It walked the forests long ago.'*

'And what may be the answer to your riddle?' said Théoden.

'If you would learn that, you should come with me to Isengard,' answered Gandalf.

'To Isengard?' they cried.

'Yes,' said Gandalf. 'I shall return to Isengard, and those who will may come with me. There we may see strange things.'

'But there are not men enough in the Mark, not if they were all gathered together and healed of wounds and weariness, to assault the stronghold of Saruman,' said Théoden.

'Nevertheless to Isengard I go,' said Gandalf. 'I shall not stay there long. My way lies now eastward. Look for me in Edoras, ere the waning of the moon!'

'Nay!' said Théoden. 'In the dark hour before dawn I doubted, but we will not part now. I will come with you, if that is your counsel.'

'I wish to speak with Saruman, as soon as may be now,' said Gandalf, 'and since he has done you great injury, it would be fitting if you were there. But how soon and how swiftly will you ride?'

'My men are weary with battle,' said the King; 'and I am weary also. For I have ridden far and slept little. Alas! My old age is not feigned nor due only to the whisperings of Wormtongue. It is an ill that no leech can wholly cure, not even Gandalf.'

'Then let all who are to ride with me rest now,' said Gandalf. 'We will journey under the shadow of evening. It is as well; for it is my counsel that all our comings and goings should be as secret as may be, henceforth. But do not command many men to go with you, Théoden. We go to a parley not to a fight.'

The King then chose men that were unhurt and had swift horses, and he sent them forth with tidings of the victory into every vale of the Mark; and they bore his summons also, bidding all men, young and old, to come in haste to Edoras. There the Lord of the Mark would hold an assembly of all that could bear arms, on the second day after the full moon. To ride with him to Isengard the King chose Éomer and twenty men of his household. With Gandalf would go Aragorn, and Legolas, and Gimli. In spite of his hurt the dwarf would not stay behind.

'It was only a feeble blow and the cap turned it,' he said. 'It would take more than such an orc-scratch to keep me back.'

'I will tend it, while you rest,' said Aragorn.

The king now returned to the Hornburg, and slept, such a sleep of quiet as he had not known for many years, and the remainder of his chosen company rested also. But the others, all that were not hurt or wounded, began a great labour; for many had fallen in the battle and lay dead upon the field or in the Deep.

No Orcs remained alive; their bodies were uncounted. But a great many of the hillmen had given themselves up; and they were afraid, and cried for mercy.

The Men of the Mark took their weapons from them, and set them to work.

'Help now to repair the evil in which you have joined,' said Erkenbrand; 'and afterwards you shall take an oath never again to pass the Fords of Isen in arms, nor to march with the enemies of Men; and then you shall go free back to your land. For you have been deluded by Saruman. Many of you have got death as the reward of your trust in him; but had you conquered, little better would your wages have been.'

The men of Dunland were amazed, for Saruman had told them that the men of Rohan were cruel and burned their captives alive.

In the midst of the field before the Hornburg two mounds were raised, and beneath them were laid all the Riders of the Mark who fell in the defence, those of the East Dales upon one side, and those of Westfold upon the other. In a grave alone under the shadow of the Hornburg lay Háma, captain of the King's guard. He fell before the Gate.

The Orcs were piled in great heaps, away from the mounds of Men, not far from the eaves of the forest. And the people were troubled in their minds; for the heaps of carrion were too great for burial or for burning. They had little wood for firing, and none would have dared to take an axe to the strange trees, even if Gandalf had not warned them to hurt neither bark nor bough at their great peril.

'Let the Orcs lie,' said Gandalf. 'The morning may bring new counsel.'

In the afternoon the King's company prepared to depart. The work of burial was then but beginning; and Théoden mourned for the loss of Háma, his captain, and cast the first earth upon his grave. 'Great injury indeed has

Saruman done to me and all this land,' he said; 'and I will remember it, when we meet.'

The sun was already drawing near the hills upon the west of the Coomb, when at last Théoden and Gandalf and their companions rode down from the Dike. Behind them were gathered a great host, both of the Riders and of the people of Westfold, old and young, women and children, who had come out from the caves. A song of victory they sang with clear voices; and then they fell silent, wondering what would chance, for their eyes were on the trees and they feared them.

The Riders came to the wood, and they halted; horse and man, they were unwilling to pass in. The trees were grey and menacing, and a shadow or a mist was about them. The ends of their long sweeping boughs hung down like searching fingers, their roots stood up from the ground like the limbs of strange monsters, and dark caverns opened beneath them. But Gandalf went forward, leading the company, and where the road from the Hornburg met the trees they saw now an opening like an arched gate under mighty boughs; and through it Gandalf passed, and they followed him. Then to their amazement they found that the road ran on, and the Deeping Stream beside it; and the sky was open above and full of golden light. But on either side the great aisles of the wood were already wrapped in dusk, stretching away into impenetrable shadows; and there they heard the creaking and groaning of boughs, and far cries, and a rumour of wordless voices, murmuring angrily. No Orc or other living creature could be seen.

Legolas and Gimli were now riding together upon one horse; and they kept close beside Gandalf, for Gimli was afraid of the wood.

'It is hot in here,' said Legolas to Gandalf. 'I feel a great wrath about me. Do you not feel the air throb in your ears?'

'Yes,' said Gandalf.

'What has become of the miserable Orcs?' said Legolas.

'That, I think, no one will ever know,' said Gandalf.

They rode in silence for a while; but Legolas was ever glancing from side to side, and would often have halted to listen to the sounds of the wood, if Gimli had allowed it.

'These are the strangest trees that ever I saw,' he said; 'and I have seen many an oak grow from acorn to ruinous age. I wish that there were leisure now to walk among them: they have voices, and in time I might come to understand their thought.'

'No, no!' said Gimli. 'Let us leave them! I guess their thought already: hatred of all that go on two legs; and their speech is of crushing and strangling.'

'Not of all that go on two legs,' said Legolas. 'There I think you are wrong. It is Orcs that they hate. For they do not belong here and know little of Elves and Men. Far away are the valleys where they sprang. From the deep dales of Fangorn, Gimli, that is whence they come, I guess.'

'Then that is the most perilous wood in Middle-earth,' said Gimli. 'I should be grateful for the part they have played, but I do not love them. You may think them wonderful, but I have seen a greater wonder in this land, more beautiful than any grove or glade that ever grew: my heart is still full of it.

'Strange are the ways of Men, Legolas! Here they have one of the marvels of the Northern World, and what do they say of it? Caves, they say! Caves! Holes to fly to in time of war, to store fodder in! My good Legolas, do you know that the caverns of Helm's Deep are vast and beautiful? There would be an endless pilgrimage of Dwarves, merely to gaze at them, if such things were known to be. Aye indeed, they would pay pure gold for a brief glance!'

'And I would give gold to be excused,' said Legolas; 'and double to be let out, if I strayed in!'

'You have not seen, so I forgive your jest,' said Gimli. 'But you speak like a fool. Do you think those halls are fair, where your King dwells under the hill in Mirkwood, and Dwarves helped in their making long ago? They are but hovels compared with the caverns I have seen here: immeasurable halls, filled with an everlasting music of water that tinkles into pools, as fair as Kheled-zâram in the starlight.

'And, Legolas, when the torches are kindled and men walk on the sandy floors under the echoing domes, ah! then, Legolas, gems and crystals and veins of precious ore glint in the polished walls; and the light glows through folded marbles, shell-like, translucent as the living hands of Queen Galadriel. There are columns of white and saffron and dawn-rose, Legolas, fluted and twisted into dreamlike forms; they sprung up from many-coloured floors to meet the glistening pendants of the roof: wings, ropes, curtains fine as frozen clouds; spears, banners, pinnacles of suspended palaces! Still lakes mirror them: a glimmering world looks up from dark pools covered with clear glass; cities, such as the mind of Durin could scarce have imagined in his sleep, stretch on through avenues and pillared courts, on into the dark recesses where no light can come. And plink! a silver drop falls, and the round wrinkles in the glass make all the towers bend and waver like weeds and corals in a grotto of the sea. Then evening comes: they fade and twinkle out; the torches pass on into another chamber and another dream. There is chamber after chamber, Legolas; hall opening out of hall, dome after dome, stair beyond stair; and still the winding paths lead on into the mountains' heart. Caves! The Caverns of Helm's Deep! Happy was the chance that drove me there! It makes me weep to leave them.'

'Then I will wish you this fortune for your comfort, Gimli,' said the Elf, 'that you may come safe from war and return to see them again. But do not tell all your kindred! There seems little left for them to do, from your account. Maybe the men of this land are wise to say little: one family of busy dwarves with hammer and chisel might mar more than they made.'

'No, you do not understand,' said Gimli. 'No dwarf could be unmoved by such loveliness. None of Durin's race would mine those caves for stones or ore, not if diamonds and gold could be got there. Do you cut down groves of blossoming trees in the springtime for firewood? We would tend these glades of flowering stone, not quarry them. With cautious skill, tap by tap—a small chip of rock and no more, perhaps, in a whole anxious day—so we could work, and as the years went by, we should open up new ways, and display far chambers that are still dark, glimpsed only as a void beyond fissures in the rock. And lights, Legolas! We should make lights, such lamps as once shone in Khazad-dûm; and when we wished we would drive away the night that has lain there since the hills were made; and when we desired rest, we would let the night return.'

'You move me, Gimli,' said Legolas. 'I have never heard you speak like this before. Almost you make me regret that I have not seen these caves. Come! Let us make this bargain—if we both return safe out of the perils that await us, we will journey for a while together. You shall visit Fangorn with me, and then I will come with you to see Helm's Deep.'

'That would not be the way of return that I should choose,' said Gimli. 'But I will endure Fangorn, if I have your promise to come back to the caves and share their wonder with me.'

'You have my promise,' said Legolas. 'But alas! Now we must leave behind both cave and wood for a while. See! We are coming to the end of the trees. How far is it to Isengard, Gandalf?'

'About fifteen leagues, as the crows of Saruman make it,' said Gandalf: 'five from the mouth of Deeping Coomb to the Fords; and ten more from there to the gates of Isengard. But we shall not ride all the way this night.'

'And when we come there, what shall we see?' asked Gimli. 'You may know, but I cannot guess.'

'I do not know myself for certain,' answered the wizard. 'I was there at nightfall yesterday, but much may have happened since. Yet I think that you will not say that the journey was in vain—not though the Glittering Caves of Aglarond be left behind.'

At last the company passed through the trees, and found that they had come to the bottom of the Coomb,

where the road from Helm's Deep branched, going one
way east to Edoras, and the other north to the Fords of
Isen. As they rode from under the eaves of the wood,
Legolas halted and looked back with regret. Then he gave
a sudden cry.

'There are eyes!' he said. 'Eyes looking out from the
shadows of the boughs! I never saw such eyes before.'

The others, surprised by his cry, halted and turned; but
Legolas started to ride back.

'No, no!' cried Gimli. 'Do as you please in your madness, but let me first get down from this horse! I wish to
see no eyes!'

'Stay, Legolas Greenleaf!' said Gandalf. 'Do not go
back into the wood, not yet! Now is not your time.'

Even as he spoke, there came forward out of the trees
three strange shapes. As tall as trolls they were, twelve
feet or more in height; their strong bodies, stout as young
trees, seemed to be clad with raiment or with hide of
close-fitting grey and brown. Their limbs were long, and
their hands had many fingers; their hair was stiff, and
their beards grey-green as moss. They gazed out with
solemn eyes, but they were not looking at the riders: their
eyes were bent northwards. Suddenly they lifted their long
hands to their mouths, and sent forth ringing calls, clear as
notes of a horn, but more musical and various. The calls
were answered; and turning again, the riders saw other
creatures of the same kind approaching, striding through
the grass. They came swiftly from the North, walking like
wading herons in their gait, but not in their speed; for
their legs in their long paces beat quicker than the heron's
wings. The riders cried aloud in wonder, and some set
their hands upon their sword-hilts.

'You need no weapons,' said Gandalf. 'These are but
herdsmen. They are not enemies, indeed they are not concerned with us at all.'

So it seemed to be; for as he spoke the tall creatures,
without a glance at the riders, strode into the wood and
vanished.

'Herdsmen!' said Théoden. 'Where are their flocks?

What are they, Gandalf? For it is plain that to you, at any rate, they are not strange.'

'They are the shepherds of the trees,' answered Gandalf. 'Is it so long since you listened to tales by the fireside? There are children in your land who, out of the twisted threads of story, could pick the answer to your question. You have seen Ents, O King, Ents of Fangorn Forest, which in your tongue you call the Entwood. Did you think that the name was given only in idle fancy? Nay, Théoden, it is otherwise: to them you are but the passing tale; all the years from Eorl the Young to Théoden the Old are of little count to them; and all the deeds of your house but a small matter.'

The king was silent. 'Ents!' he said at length. 'Out of the shadows of legend I begin a little to understand the marvel of the trees, I think. I have lived to see strange days. Long we have tended our beasts and our fields, built our houses, wrought our tools, or ridden away to help in the wars of Minas Tirith. And that we called the life of Men, the way of the world. We cared little for what lay beyond the borders of our land. Songs we have that tell of these things, but we are forgetting them, teaching them only to children, as a careless custom. And now the songs have come down among us out of strange places, and walk visible under the Sun.'

'You should be glad, Théoden King,' said Gandalf. 'For not only the little life of Men is now endangered, but the life also of those things which you have deemed the matter of legend. You are not without allies, even if you know them not.'

'Yet also I should be sad,' said Théoden, 'for however the fortune of war shall go, may it not so end that much that was fair and wonderful shall pass forever out of Middle-earth?'

'It may,' said Gandalf. 'The evil of Sauron cannot be wholly cured, nor made as if it had not been. But to such days we are doomed. Let us now go on with the journey we have begun!'

The company turned then away from the coomb and from the wood and took the road towards the Fords. Legolas followed reluctantly. The sun had set, already it had sunk behind the rim of the world; but as they rode out from the shadow of the hills and looked west to the Gap of Rohan the sky was still red, and a burning light was under the floating clouds. Dark against it there wheeled and flew many black-winged birds. Some passed overhead with mournful cries, returning to their homes among the rocks.

'The carrion-fowl have been busy about the battle-field,' said Éomer.

They rode now at an easy pace and dark came down upon the plains about them. The slow moon mounted, now waxing towards the full, and in its cold silver light the swelling grass-lands rose and fell like a wide grey sea. They had ridden for some four hours from the branching of the roads when they drew near to the Fords. Long slopes ran swiftly down to where the river spread in stony shoals between high grassy terraces. Borne upon the wind they heard the howling of wolves. Their hearts were heavy, remembering the many men that had fallen in battle in this place.

The road dipped between rising turf-banks, carving its way through the terraces of the river's edge, and up again upon the further side. There were three lines of flat stepping-stones across the stream, and between them fords for horses, that went from either brink to a bare eyot in the midst. The riders looked down upon the crossings, and it seemed strange to them; for the Fords had ever been a place full of the rush and chatter of water upon stones; but now they were silent. The beds of the stream were almost dry, a bare waste of shingles and grey sand.

'This is become a dreary place,' said Éomer. 'What sickness has befallen the river? Many fair things Saruman has destroyed: has he devoured the springs of Isen too?'

'So it would seem,' said Gandalf.

'Alas!' said Théoden. 'Must we pass this way, where the carrion-beasts devour so many good Riders of the Mark?'

'This is our way,' said Gandalf. 'Grievous is the fall of your men; but you shall see that at least the wolves of the mountains do not devour them. It is with their friends, the Orcs, that they hold their feast: such indeed is the friendship of their kind. Come!'

They rode down to the river, and as they came the wolves ceased their howling and slunk away. Fear fell on them seeing Gandalf in the moon, and Shadowfax his horse shining like silver. The riders passed over to the islet, and glittering eyes watched them wanly from the shadows of the banks.

'Look!' said Gandalf. 'Friends have laboured here.'

And they saw that in the midst of the eyot a mound was piled, ringed with stones, and set about with many spears.

'Here lie all the Men of the Mark that fell near this place,' said Gandalf.

'Here let them rest!' said Éomer. 'And when their spears have rotted and rusted, long still may their mound stand and guard the Fords of Isen!'

'Is this your work also, Gandalf, my friend?' said Théoden. 'You accomplished much in an evening and a night!'

'With the help of Shadowfax—and others,' said Gandalf. 'I rode fast and far. But here beside the mound I will say this for your comfort: many fell in the battles of the Fords, but fewer than rumour made them. More were scattered than were slain; I gathered together all that I could find. Some of them I sent to join Erkenbrand; some I set to this labour that you see, and they by now have gone back to Edoras. Many others also I sent thither before to guard your house. Saruman I knew had despatched his full strength against you, and his servants had turned aside from all other errands and gone to Helm's Deep: the lands seemed empty of enemies; yet I feared that wolf-riders and plunderers might ride nonetheless to Meduseld, while it was undefended. But now I think you need not fear: you will find your house to welcome your return.'

'And glad shall I be to see it again,' said Théoden,

'though brief now, I doubt not, shall be my abiding there.'

With that the company said farewell to the island and the mound, and passed over the river, and climbed the further bank. Then they rode on, glad to have left the mournful Fords. As they went the howling of the wolves broke out anew.

There was an ancient highway that ran down from Isengard to the crossings. For some way it took its course beside the river, bending with it east and then north; but at the last it turned away and went straight towards the gates of Isengard; and these were under the mountain-side in the west of the valley, sixteen miles or more from its mouth. This road they followed but they did not ride upon it; for the ground beside it was firm and level, covered for many miles about with short springing turf. They rode now more swiftly, and by midnight the Fords were nearly five leagues behind. Then they halted, ending their night's journey, for the King was weary. They were come to the feet of the Misty Mountains, and the long arms of Nan Curunír stretched down to meet them. Dark lay the vale before them, for the moon had passed into the West, and its light was hidden by the hills. But out of the deep shadow of the dale rose a vast spire of smoke and vapour; as it mounted, it caught the rays of the sinking moon, and spread in shimmering billows, black and silver, over the starry sky.

'What do you think of that, Gandalf?' asked Aragorn. 'One would say that all the Wizard's Vale was burning.'

'There is ever a fume above that valley in these days,' said Éomer: 'but I have never seen aught like this before. These are steams rather than smokes. Saruman is brewing some devilry to greet us. Maybe he is boiling all the waters of Isen, and that is why the river runs dry.'

'Maybe he is,' said Gandalf. 'Tomorrow we shall learn what he is doing. Now let us rest for a while, if we can.'

They camped beside the bed of the Isen river; it was still silent and empty. Some of them slept a little. But late in the night the watchmen cried out, and all awoke. The moon was gone. Stars were shining above; but over the ground there crept a darkness blacker than the night. On both sides of the river it rolled towards them, going northward.

'Stay where you are!' said Gandalf. 'Draw no weapons! Wait! and it will pass you by!'

A mist gathered about them. Above them a few stars still glimmered faintly; but on either side there arose walls of impenetrable gloom; they were in a narrow lane between moving towers of shadow. Voices they heard, whisperings and groanings and an endless rustling sigh; the earth shook under them. Long it seemed to them that they sat and were afraid; but at last the darkness and the rumour passed, and vanished between the mountain's arms.

Away south upon the Hornburg, in the middle night men heard a great noise, as a wind in the valley, and the ground trembled; and all were afraid and no one ventured to go forth. But in the morning they went out and were amazed; for the slain Orcs were gone, and the trees also. Far down into the valley of the Deep the grass was crushed and trampled brown, as if giant herdsmen had pastured great droves of cattle there; but a mile below the Dike a huge pit had been delved in the earth, and over it stones were piled into a hill. Men believed that the Orcs whom they had slain were buried there; but whether those who had fled into the wood were with them, none could say, for no man ever set foot upon that hill. The Death Down it was afterwards called, and no grass would grow there. But the strange trees were never seen in Deeping Coomb again; they had returned at night, and had gone far away to the dark dales of Fangorn. Thus they were revenged upon the Orcs.

The king and his company slept no more that night; but they saw and heard no other strange thing, save one: the voice of the river beside them suddenly awoke. There was a rush of water hurrying down among the stones; and

when it had passed, the Isen flowed and bubbled in its
bed again, as it had ever done.

At dawn they made ready to go on. The light came grey
and pale, and they did not see the rising of the sun. The
air above was heavy with fog, and a reek lay on the land
about them. They went slowly, riding now upon the highway. It was broad and hard, and well-tended. Dimly
through the mists they could descry the long arm of the
mountains rising on their left. They had passed into Nan
Curunír, the Wizard's Vale. That was a sheltered valley,
open only to the South. Once it had been fair and green,
and through it the Isen flowed, already deep and strong
before it found the plains; for it was fed by many springs
and lesser streams among the rain-washed hills, and all
about it there had lain a pleasant, fertile land.

It was not so now. Beneath the walls of Isengard there
still were acres tilled by the slaves of Saruman; but most
of the valley had become a wilderness of weeds and
thorns. Brambles trailed upon the ground, or clambering
over bush and bank, made shaggy caves where small
beasts housed. No trees grew there; but among the rank
grasses could still be seen the burned and axe-hewn stumps
of ancient groves. It was a sad country, silent now but for
the stony noise of quick waters. Smokes and steams
drifted in sullen clouds and lurked in the hollows. The riders did not speak. Many doubted in their hearts, wondering
to what dismal end their journey led.

After they had ridden for some miles, the highway
became a wide street, paved with great flat stones,
squared and laid with skill; no blade of grass was seen in
any joint. Deep gutters, filled with trickling water, ran
down on either side. Suddenly a tall pillar loomed up before them. It was black; and set upon it was a great stone,
carved and painted in the likeness of a long White
Hand. Its fingers pointed north. Not far now they knew
that the gates of Isengard must stand, and their hearts were
heavy; but their eyes could not pierce the mists ahead.

Beneath the mountain's arm within the Wizard's Vale

through years uncounted had stood that ancient place
that Men called Isengard. Partly it was shaped in the making of the mountains, but mighty works the Men of Westernesse had wrought there of old; and Saruman had dwelt
there long and had not been idle.

This was its fashion, while Saruman was at his height,
accounted by many the chief of wizards. A great ring-wall
of stone, like towering cliffs, stood out from the shelter
of the mountain-side, from which it ran and then returned
again. One entrance only was there made in it, a great arch
delved in the southern wall. Here through the black rock
a long tunnel had been hewn, closed at either end with
mighty doors of iron. They were so wrought and poised
upon their huge hinges, posts of steel driven into the living
stone, that when unbarred they could be moved with a light
thrust of the arms, noiselessly. One who passed in and came
at length out of the echoing tunnel, beheld a plain, a great
circle, somewhat hollowed like a vast shallow bowl: a
mile it measured from rim to rim. Once it had been green
and filled with avenues, and groves of fruitful trees, watered
by streams that flowed from the mountains to a lake. But
no green thing grew there in the latter days of Saruman.
The roads were paved with stone-flags, dark and hard;
and beside their borders instead of trees there marched
long lines of pillars, some of marble, some of copper and
of iron, joined by heavy chains.

Many houses there were, chambers, halls and passages, cut and tunnelled back into the walls upon their inner side, so that all the open circle was overlooked by
countless windows and dark doors. Thousands could dwell
there, workers, servants, slaves, and warriors with great
store of arms; wolves were fed and stabled in deep dens
beneath. The plain, too, was bored and delved. Shafts
were driven deep into the ground; their upper ends were
covered by low mounds and domes of stone, so that in the
moonlight the Ring of Isengard looked like a graveyard of
unquiet dead. For the ground trembled. The shafts ran
down by many slopes and spiral stairs to caverns far under;
there Saruman had treasuries, store-houses, armouries,

smithies, and great furnaces. Iron wheels revolved there
endlessly, and hammers thudded. At night plumes of
vapour steamed from the vents, lit from beneath with red
light, or blue, or venomous green.

To the centre all the roads ran between their chains.
There stood a tower of marvellous shape. It was fashioned
by the builders of old, who smoothed the Ring of Isengard,
and yet it seemed a thing not made by the craft of Men,
but riven from the bones of the earth in the ancient torment
of the hills. A peak and isle of rock it was, black and
gleaming hard: four mighty piers of many-sided stone were
welded into one, but near the summit they opened into
gaping horns, their pinnacles sharp as the points of
spears, keen-edged as knives. Between them was a narrow
space, and there upon a floor of polished stone, written
with strange signs, a man might stand five hundred feet
above the plain. This was Orthanc, the citadel of Saruman, the name of which had (by design or chance) a
twofold meaning; for in the Elvish speech *orthanc* signifies
Mount Fang, but in the language of the Mark of old the
Cunning Mind.

A strong place and wonderful was Isengard, and long
it had been beautiful; and there great lords had dwelt, the
wardens of Gondor upon the West, and wise men that
watched the stars. But Saruman had slowly shaped it to
his shifting purposes, and made it better, as he thought,
being deceived—for all those arts and subtle devices, for
which he forsook his former wisdom, and which fondly
he imagined were his own, came but from Mordor; so
that what he made was naught, only a little copy, a child's
model or a slave's flattery, of that vast fortress, armoury,
prison, furnace of great power, Barad-dûr, the Dark
Tower, which suffered no rival, and laughed at flattery,
biding its time, secure in its pride and its immeasurable
strength.

This was the stronghold of Saruman, as fame reported
it; for within living memory the men of Rohan had not
passed its gates, save perhaps a few, such as Worm-

tongue, who came in secret and told no man what they saw.

Now Gandalf rode to the great pillar of the Hand, and passed it; and as he did so the Riders saw to their wonder that the Hand appeared no longer white. It was stained as with dried blood; and looking closer they perceived that its nails were red. Unheeding Gandalf rode on into the mist, and reluctantly they followed him. All about them now, as if there had been a sudden flood, wide pools of water lay beside the road, filling the hollows, and rills went trickling down among the stones.

At last Gandalf halted and beckoned to them; and they came, and saw that beyond him the mists had cleared, and a pale sunlight shone. The hour of noon had passed. They were come to the doors of Isengard.

But the doors lay hurled and twisted on the ground. And all about, stone, cracked and splintered into countless jagged shards, was scattered far and wide, or piled in ruinous heaps. The great arch still stood, but it opened now upon a roofless chasm: the tunnel was laid bare, and through the cliff-like walls on either side great rents and breaches had been torn; their towers were beaten into dust. If the Great Sea had risen in wrath and fallen on the hills with storm, it could have worked no greater ruin.

The ring beyond was filled with steaming water: a bubbling cauldron, in which there heaved and floated a wreckage of beams and spars, chests and casks and broken gear. Twisted and leaning pillars reared their splintered stems above the flood, but all the roads were drowned. Far off, it seemed, half veiled in winding cloud, there loomed the island rock. Still dark and tall, unbroken by the storm, the tower of Orthanc stood. Pale waters lapped about its feet.

The king and all his company sat silent on their horses, marvelling, perceiving that the power of Saruman was overthrown; but how they could not guess. And now they turned their eyes towards the archway and the ruined

gates. There they saw close beside them a great rubble-
heap; and suddenly they were aware of two small figures
lying on it at their ease, grey-clad, hardly to be seen
among the stones. There were bottles and bowls and
platters laid beside them, as if they had just eaten well,
and now rested from their labour. One seemed asleep; the
other, with crossed legs and arms behind his head, leaned
back against a broken rock and sent from his mouth long
wisps and little rings of thin blue smoke.

For a moment Théoden and Éomer and all his men
stared at them in wonder. Amid all the wreck of Isengard
this seemed to them the strangest sight. But before the
king could speak, the small smoke-breathing figure became
suddenly aware of them, as they sat there silent on the edge
of the mist. He sprang to his feet. A young man he
looked, or like one, though not much more than half a
man in height; his head of brown curling hair was uncovered, but he was clad in a travel-stained cloak of the
same hue and shape as the companions of Gandalf had
worn when they rode to Edoras. He bowed very low,
putting his hand upon his breast. Then, seeming not to
observe the wizard and his friends, he turned to Éomer
and the king.

'Welcome, my lords, to Isengard!' he said. 'We are the
door-wardens. Meriadoc, son of Saradoc is my name; and
my companion, who, alas! is overcome with weariness'—
here he gave the other a dig with his foot—'is Peregrin,
son of Paladin, of the house of Took. Far in the North is
our home. The Lord Saruman is within; but at the moment
he is closeted with one Wormtongue, or, doubtless he
would be here to welcome such honourable guests.'

'Doubtless he would!' laughed Gandalf. 'And was it Saruman that ordered you to guard his damaged doors,
and watch for the arrival of guests, when your attention
could be spared from plate and bottle?'

'No, good sir, the matter escaped him,' answered Merry
gravely. 'He has been much occupied. Our orders came
from Treebeard, who has taken over the management of

Isengard. He commanded me to welcome the Lord of Rohan with fitting words. I have done my best.'

'And what about your companions? What about Legolas and me?' cried Gimli, unable to contain himself longer. 'You rascals, you woolly-footed and wool-pated truants! A fine hunt you have led us! Two hundred leagues, through fen and forest, battle and death, to rescue you! And here we find you feasting and idling—and smoking! Smoking! Where did you come by the weed, you villains? Hammer and tongs! I am so torn between rage and joy, that if I do not burst, it will be a marvel!'

'You speak for me, Gimli,' laughed Legolas. 'Though I would sooner learn how they came by the wine.'

'One thing you have not found in your hunting, and that's brighter wits,' said Pippin, opening an eye. 'Here you find us sitting on a field of victory, amid the plunder of armies, and you wonder how we came by a few well-earned comforts!'

'Well-earned?' said Gimli. 'I cannot believe that!'

The Riders laughed. 'It cannot be doubted that we witness the meeting of dear friends,' said Théoden. 'So these are the lost ones of your company, Gandalf? The days are fated to be filled with marvels. Already I have seen many since I left my house; and now here before my eyes stand yet another of the folk of legend. Are not these the Halflings, that some among us call the Holbytlan?'

'Hobbits, if you please, lord,' said Pippin.

'Hobbits?' said Théoden. 'Your tongue is strangely changed; but the name sounds not unfitting so. Hobbits! No report that I have heard does justice to the truth.'

Merry bowed; and Pippin got up and bowed low. 'You are gracious, lord; or I hope that I may so take your words,' he said. 'And here is another marvel! I have wandered in many lands, since I left my home, and never till now have I found people that knew any story concerning hobbits.'

'My people came out of the North long ago,' said Théoden. 'But I will not deceive you: we know no tales about hobbits. All that is said among us is that far away, over many hills and rivers, live the halfling folk that dwell in holes in sand-dunes. But there are no legends of their deeds, for it is said that they do little, and avoid the sight of men, being able to vanish in a twinkling; and they can change their voices to resemble the piping of birds. But it seems that more could be said.'

'It could indeed, lord,' said Merry.

'For one thing,' said Théoden, 'I had not heard that they spouted smoke from their mouths.'

'That is not surprising,' answered Merry; 'for it is an art which we have not practised for more than a few generations. It was Tobold Hornblower, of Longbottom in the Southfarthing, who first grew the true pipe-weed in his gardens, about the year 1070 according to our reckoning. How old Toby came by the plant . . .'

'You do not know your danger, Théoden,' interrupted Gandalf. 'These hobbits will sit on the edge of ruin and discuss the pleasures of the table, or the small doings of their fathers, grandfathers, and great-grandfathers, and remoter cousins to the ninth degree, if you encourage them with undue patience. Some other time would be more fitting for the history of smoking. Where is Treebeard, Merry?'

'Away on the north side, I believe. He went to get a drink—of clean water. Most of the other Ents are with him, still busy at their work—over there.' Merry waved his hand towards the steaming lake; and as they looked, they heard a distant rumbling and rattling, as if an avalanche was falling from the mountain-side. Far away came a *hoom-hom*, as of horns blowing triumphantly.

'And is Orthanc then left unguarded?' asked Gandalf.

'There is the water,' said Merry. 'But Quickbeam and some others are watching it. Not all those posts and pillars in the plain are of Saruman's planting. Quickbeam, I think, is by the rock, near the foot of the stair.'

'Yes, a tall grey Ent is there,' said Legolas, 'but his arms are at his sides, and he stands as still as a door-tree.'

'It is past noon,' said Gandalf, 'and we at any rate have not eaten since early morning. Yet I wish to see Treebeard as soon as may be. Did he leave me no message, or has plate and bottle driven it from your mind?'

'He left a message,' said Merry, 'and I was coming to it, but I have been hindered by many other questions. I was to say that, if the Lord of the Mark and Gandalf will ride to the northern wall they will find Treebeard there, and he will welcome them. I may add that they will also find food of the best there; it was discovered and selected by your humble servants.' He bowed.

Gandalf laughed. 'That is better!' he said. 'Well, Théoden, will you ride with me to find Treebeard? We must go round about, but it is not far. When you see Treebeard, you will learn much. For Treebeard is Fangorn, and the eldest and chief of the Ents, and when you speak with him you will hear the speech of the oldest of all living things.'

'I will come with you,' said Théoden. 'Farewell, my hobbits! May we meet again in my house! There you shall sit beside me and tell me all that your hearts desire: the deeds of your grandsires, as far as you can reckon them; and we will speak also of Tobold the Old and his herb-lore. Farewell!'

The hobbits bowed low. 'So that is the King of Rohan!' said Pippin in an undertone. 'A fine old fellow. Very polite.'

Chapter 9

Flotsam and Jetsam

Gandalf and the King's company rode away, turning eastward to make the circuit of the ruined walls of Isengard.
But Aragorn, Gimli, and Legolas remained behind. Leaving Arod and Hasufel to stray in search of grass, they came
and sat beside the hobbits.

'Well, well! The hunt is over, and we meet again at
last, where none of us ever thought to come,' said Aragorn.

'And now that the great ones have gone to discuss high
matters,' said Legolas, 'the hunters can perhaps learn the
answers to their own small riddles. We tracked you as
far as the forest, but there are still many things that I
should like to know the truth of.'

'And there is a great deal, too, that we want to know
about you,' said Merry. 'We have learnt a few things
through Treebeard, the Old Ent, but that is not nearly
enough.'

'All in good time,' said Legolas. 'We were the hunters,
and you should give an account of yourselves to us first.'

'Or second,' said Gimli. 'It would go better after a meal.
I have a sore head, and it is past mid-day. You truants
might make amends by finding us some of the plunder
that you spoke of. Food and drink would pay off some of
my score against you.'

'Then you shall have it,' said Pippin. 'Will you have it
here, or in more comfort in what's left of Saruman's guard-
house—over there under the arch? We had to picnic out
here, so as to keep an eye on the road.'

'Less than an eye!' said Gimli. 'But I will not go into
any orc-house; nor touch Orcs' meat or anything that they
have mauled.'

'We wouldn't ask you to,' said Merry. 'We have had
enough of Orcs ourselves to last a life-time. But there were
many other folk in Isengard. Saruman kept enough wis-

dom not to trust his Orcs. He had Men to guard his gates: some of his most faithful servants, I suppose. Anyway they were favoured and got good provisions.'

'And pipe-weed?' asked Gimli.

'No, I don't think so,' Merry laughed. 'But that is another story, which can wait until after lunch.'   ◆

'Well let us go and have lunch then!' said the Dwarf.

The hobbits led the way; and they passed under the arch and came to a wide door upon the left, at the top of a stair. It opened direct into a large chamber, with other smaller doors at the far end, and a hearth and chimney at one side. The chamber was hewn out of the stone; and it must once have been dark, for its windows looked out only into the tunnel. But light came in now through the broken roof. On the hearth wood was burning.

'I lit a bit of fire,' said Pippin. 'It cheered us up in the fogs. There were few faggots about, and most of the wood we could find was wet. But there is a great draught in the chimney: it seems to wind away up through the rock, and fortunately it has not been blocked. A fire is handy. I will make you some toast. The bread is three or four days old, I am afraid.'

Aragorn and his companions sat themselves down at one end of a long table, and the hobbits disappeared through one of the inner doors.

'Store-room in there, and above the floods, luckily,' said Pippin, as they came back laden with dishes, bowls, cups, knives, and food of various sorts.

'And you need not turn up your nose at the provender, Master Gimli,' said Merry. 'This is not orc-stuff, but man-food, as Treebeard calls it. Will you have wine or beer? There's a barrel inside there—very passable. And this is first-rate salted pork. Or I can cut you some rashers of bacon and broil them, if you like. I am sorry there is no green stuff: the deliveries have been rather interrupted in the last few days! I cannot offer you anything to follow but butter and honey for your bread. Are you content?'

'Indeed yes,' said Gimli. 'The score is much reduced.'

The three were soon busy with their meal; and the two hobbits, unabashed, set to a second time. 'We must keep our guests company,' they said.

'You are full of courtesy this morning,' laughed Legolas. 'But maybe, if we had not arrived, you would already have been keeping one another company again.'

'Maybe; and why not?' said Pippin. 'We had foul fare with the Orcs, and little enough for days before that. It seems a long while since we could eat to heart's content.'

'It does not seem to have done you any harm,' said Aragorn. 'Indeed you look in the bloom of health.'

'Aye, you do indeed,' said Gimli, looking them up and down over the top of his cup. 'Why, your hair is twice as thick and curly as when we parted; and I would swear that you have both grown somewhat, if that is possible for hobbits of your age. This Treebeard at any rate has not starved you.'

'He has not,' said Merry. 'But Ents only drink, and drink is not enough for content. Treebeard's draughts may be nourishing, but one feels the need of something solid. And even *lembas* is none the worse for a change.'

'You have drunk of the waters of the Ents, have you?' said Legolas. 'Ah, then I think it is likely that Gimli's eyes do not deceive him. Strange songs have been sung of the draughts of Fangorn.'

'Many strange tales have been told about that land,' said Aragorn. 'I have never entered it. Come, tell me more about it, and about the Ents!'

'Ents,' said Pippin, 'Ents are—well Ents are all different for one thing. But their eyes now, their eyes are very odd.' He tried a few fumbling words that trailed off into silence. 'Oh, well,' he went on, 'you have seen some at a distance, already—they saw you at any rate, and reported that you were on the way—and you will see many others, I expect, before you leave here. You must form your own ideas.'

'Now, now!' said Gimli. 'We are beginning the story in the middle. I should like a tale in the right order, starting with that strange day when our fellowship was broken.'

'You shall have it, if there is time,' said Merry. 'But first—if you have finished eating—you shall fill your pipes and light up. And then for a little while we can pretend that we are all back safe at Bree again, or in Rivendell.'

He produced a small leather bag full of tobacco. 'We have heaps of it,' he said; 'and you can all pack as much as you wish, when we go. We did some salvage-work this morning, Pippin and I. There are lots of things floating about. It was Pippin who found two small barrels, washed up out of some cellar or store-house, I suppose. When we opened them, we found they were filled with this: as fine a pipe-weed as you could wish for, and quite unspoilt.'

Gimli took some and rubbed it in his palms and sniffed it. 'It feels good, and it smells good,' he said.

'It is good!' said Merry. 'My dear Gimli, it is Longbottom Leaf! There were the Hornblower brandmarks on the barrels, as plain as plain. How it came here, I can't imagine. For Saruman's private use, I fancy. I never knew that it went so far abroad. But it comes in handy now.'

'It would,' said Gimli, 'if I had a pipe to go with it. Alas, I lost mine in Moria, or before. Is there no pipe in all your plunder?'

'No, I am afraid not,' said Merry. 'We have not found any, not even here in the guardrooms. Saruman kept this dainty to himself, it seems. And I don't think it would be any use knocking on the doors of Orthanc to beg a pipe of him! We shall have to share pipes, as good friends must at a pinch.'

'Half a moment!' said Pippin. Putting his hand inside the breast of his jacket he pulled out a little soft wallet on a string. 'I keep a treasure or two near my skin, as precious as Rings to me. Here's one: my old wooden pipe. And here's another: an unused one. I have carried it a long way, though I don't know why. I never really expected to find any pipe-weed on the journey, when my own ran out. But now it comes in useful after all.' He held up a small pipe with a wide flattened bowl, and handed it to Gimli. 'Does that settle the score between us?' he said.

'Settle it!' cried Gimli. 'Most noble hobbit, it leaves me deep in your debt.'

'Well, I am going back into the open air, to see what the wind and sky are doing!' said Aragorn.

They went out and seated themselves upon the piled stones before the gateway. They could see far down into the valley now; the mists were lifting and floating away upon the breeze.

'Now let us take our ease here for a little!' said Aragorn. 'We will sit on the edge of ruin and talk, as Gandalf says, while he is busy elsewhere. I feel a weariness such as I have seldom felt before.' He wrapped his grey cloak about him, hiding his mail-shirt, and stretched out his long legs. Then he lay back and sent from his lips a thin stream of smoke.

'Look!' said Pippin. 'Strider the Ranger has come back!'

'He has never been away,' said Aragorn. 'I am Strider and Dúnadan too, and I belong both to Gondor and the North.'

They smoked in silence for a while, and the sun shone on them; slanting into the valley from among white clouds high in the West. Legolas lay still, looking up at the sun and sky with steady eyes, and singing softly to himself. At last he sat up. 'Come now!' he said. 'Time wears on, and the mists are blowing away, or would if you strange folk did not wreathe yourselves in smoke. What of the tale?'

'Well, my tale begins with waking up in the dark and finding myself all strung-up in an orc-camp,' said Pippin. 'Let me see, what is today?'

'The fifth of March in the Shire-reckoning,' said Aragorn. Pippin made some calculations on his fingers. 'Only nine days ago!' he said.* 'It seems a year since we were caught. Well, though half of it was like a bad dream, I reckon that three very horrible days followed. Merry will correct me, if I forget anything important: I am not going into

* Every month in the Shire-calendar had 30 days.

details: the whips and the filth and stench and all that; it does not bear remembering.' With that he plunged into an account of Boromir's last fight and the orc-march from Emyn Muil to the Forest. The others nodded as the various points were fitted in with their guesses.

'Here are some treasures that you let fall,' said Aragorn. 'You will be glad to have them back.' He loosened his belt from under his cloak, and took from it the two sheathed knives.

'Well!' said Merry. 'I never expected to see those again! I marked a few orcs with mine; but Uglúk took them from us. How he glared! At first I thought he was going to stab me, but he threw the things away as if they burned him.'

'And here also is your brooch, Pippin,' said Aragorn. 'I have kept it safe, for it is a very precious thing.'

'I know,' said Pippin. 'It was a wrench to let it go; but what else could I do?'

'Nothing else,' answered Aragorn. 'One who cannot cast away a treasure at need is in fetters. You did rightly.'

'The cutting of the bands on your wrists, that was smart work!' said Gimli. 'Luck served you there; but you seized your chance with both hands, one might say.'

'And set us a pretty riddle,' said Legolas. 'I wondered if you had grown wings!'

'Unfortunately not,' said Pippin. 'But you did not know about Grishnákh.' He shuddered and said no more, leaving Merry to tell of those last horrible moments: the pawing hands, the hot breath, and the dreadful strength of Grishnákh's hairy arms.

'All this about the Orcs of Mordor, or Lugbúrz as they call it, makes me uneasy,' said Aragorn. 'The Dark Lord already knew too much, and his servants also; and Grishnákh evidently sent some message across the River after the quarrel. The Red Eye will be looking towards Isengard. But Saruman at any rate is in a cleft stick of his own cutting.'

'Yes, whichever side wins, his outlook is poor,' said

Merry. 'Things began to go all wrong for him from the moment his Orcs set foot in Rohan.'

'We caught a glimpse of the old villain, or so Gandalf hints,' said Gimli. 'On the edge of the Forest.'

'When was that?' asked Pippin.

'Five nights ago,' said Aragorn.

'Let me see,' said Merry: 'five nights ago—now we come to a part of the story you know nothing about. We met Treebeard that morning after the battle; and that night we were at Wellinghall, one of his ent-houses. The next morning we went to Entmoot, a gathering of Ents, that is, and the queerest thing I have ever seen in my life. It lasted all that day and the next; and we spent the nights with an Ent called Quickbeam. And then late in the afternoon in the third day of their moot, the Ents suddenly blew up. It was amazing. The Forest had felt as tense as if a thunderstorm was brewing inside it: then all at once it exploded. I wish you could have heard their song as they marched.'

'If Saruman had heard it, he would be a hundred miles away by now, even if he had had to run on his own legs,' said Pippin.

> 'Though Isengard be strong and hard, as cold as stone
>   and bare as bone,
> We go, we go, we go to war, to hew the stone and break
>   the door!

There was very much more. A great deal of the song had no words, and was like a music of horns and drums. It was very exciting. But I thought it was only marching music and no more, just a song—until I got here. I know better now.'

'We came down over the last ridge into Nan Curunír, after night had fallen,' Merry continued. 'It was then that I first had the feeling that the Forest itself was moving behind us. I thought I was dreaming an entish dream, but Pippin had noticed it too. We were both frightened; but we did not find out more about it until later.

'It was the Huorns, or so the Ents call them in "short language". Treebeard won't say much about them, but I think they are Ents that have become almost like trees, at least to look at. They stand here and there in the wood or under its eaves, silent, watching endlessly over the trees; but deep in the darkest dales there are hundreds and hundreds of them, I believe.

'There is a great power in them, and they seem able to wrap themselves in shadow: it is difficult to see them moving. But they do. They can move very quickly, if they are angry. You stand still looking at the weather, maybe, or listening to the rustling of the wind, and then suddenly you find that you are in the middle of a wood with great groping trees all around you. They still have voices, and can speak with the Ents—that is why they are called Huorns, Treebeard says—but they have become queer and wild. Dangerous. I should be terrified of meeting them, if there were no true Ents about to look after them.

'Well, in the early night we crept down a long ravine into the upper end of the Wizard's Vale, the Ents with all their rustling Huorns behind. We could not see them, of course, but the whole air was full of creaking. It was very dark, a cloudy night. They moved at a great speed as soon as they had left the hills, and made a noise like a rushing wind. The Moon did not appear through the clouds, and not long after midnight there was a tall wood all round the north side of Isengard. There was no sign of enemies nor of any challenge. There was a light gleaming from a high window in the tower, that was all.

'Treebeard and a few more Ents crept on, right round to within sight of the great gates. Pippin and I were with him. We were sitting on Treebeard's shoulders, and I could feel the quivering tenseness in him. But even when they are roused, Ents can be very cautious and patient. They stood still as carved stones, breathing and listening.

'Then all at once there was a tremendous stir. Trumpets blared, and the walls of Isengard echoed. We thought that we had been discovered, and that battle was going to begin. But nothing of the sort. All Saruman's people were marching away. I don't know much about this war, or about the Horsemen of Rohan, but Saruman seems to have meant to finish off the king and all his men with one final blow. He emptied Isengard. I saw the enemy go: endless lines of marching Orcs; and troops of them mounted on great wolves. And there were battalions of Men, too. Many of them carried torches, and in the flare I could see their faces. Most of them were ordinary men, rather tall and dark-haired, and grim but not particularly evil-looking. But there were some others that were horrible: man-high, but with goblin-faces, sallow, leering, squint-eyed. Do you know, they reminded me at once of that Southerner at Bree; only he was not so obviously orc-like as most of these were.'

'I thought of him too,' said Aragorn. 'We had many of these half-orcs to deal with at Helm's Deep. It seems plain now that that Southerner was a spy of Saruman's; but whether he was working with the Black Riders, or for Saruman alone, I do not know. It is difficult with these evil folk to know when they are in league, and when they are cheating one another.'

'Well, of all sorts together, there must have been ten thousand at the very least,' said Merry. 'They took an hour to pass out of the gates. Some went off down the highway to the Fords, and some turned away and went eastward. A bridge has been built down there, about a mile away, where the river runs in a very deep channel. You could see it now, if you stood up. They were all singing with harsh voices, and laughing, making a hideous din. I thought things looked very black for Rohan. But Treebeard did not move. He said: "My business is with Isengard tonight, with rock and stone."

'But, though I could not see what was happening in the dark, I believe that Huorns began to move south, as soon as the gates were shut again. Their business was with Orcs I think. They were far down the valley in the morning; or at any rate there was a shadow there that one couldn't see through.

'As soon as Saruman had sent off all his army, our turn

came. Treebeard put us down, and went up to the gates, and began hammering on the doors, and calling for Saruman. There was no answer, except arrows and stones from the walls. But arrows are no use against Ents. They hurt them, of course, and infuriate them: like stinging flies. But an Ent can be stuck as full of orc-arrows as a pincushion, and take no serious harm. They cannot be poisoned, for one thing; and their skin seems to be very thick, and tougher than bark. It takes a very heavy axe-stroke to wound them seriously. They don't like axes. But there would have to be a great many axe-men to one Ent: a man that hacks once at an Ent never gets a chance of a second blow. A punch from an Ent-fist crumples up iron like thin tin.

'When Treebeard had got a few arrows in him, he began to warm up, to get positively "hasty", as he would say. He let out a great *hoom-hom,* and a dozen more Ents came striding up. An angry Ent is terrifying. Their fingers, and their toes, just freeze onto rock; and they tear it up like bread-crust. It was like watching the work of great tree-roots in a hundred years, all packed into a few moments.

'They pushed, pulled, tore, shook, and hammered; and *clang-bang, crash-crack,* in five minutes they had these huge gates just lying in ruin; and some were already beginning to eat into the walls, like rabbits in a sand-pit. I don't know what Saruman thought was happening; but anyway he did not know how to deal with it. His wizardry may have been falling off lately, of course; but anyway I think he has not much grit, not much plain courage alone in a tight place without a lot of slaves and machines and things, if you know what I mean. Very different from old Gandalf. I wonder if his fame was not all along mainly due to his cleverness in settling at Isengard.'

'No,' said Aragorn. 'Once he was as great as his fame made him. His knowledge was deep, his thought was subtle, and his hands marvellously skilled; and he had a power over the minds of others. The wise he could persuade, and the smaller folk he could daunt. That power he certainly still keeps. There are not many in Middle-earth that I should say were safe, if they were left alone to talk with him, even now when he has suffered a defeat. Gandalf, Elrond, and Galadriel, perhaps, now that his wickedness has been laid bare, but very few others.'

'The Ents are safe,' said Pippin. 'He seems at one time to have got round them, but never again. And anyway he did not understand them; and he made the great mistake of leaving them out of his calculations. He had no plan for them, and there was no time to make any, once they had set to work. As soon as our attack began, the few remaining rats in Isengard started bolting through every hole that the Ents made. The Ents let the Men go, after they had questioned them, two or three dozen only down at this end. I don't think many orc-folk, of any size, escaped. Not from the Huorns: there was a wood of them all round Isengard by that time, as well as those that had gone down the valley.

'When the Ents had reduced a large part of the southern walls to rubbish, and what was left of his people had bolted and deserted him, Saruman fled in a panic. He seems to have been at the gates when we arrived: I expect he came to watch his splendid army march out. When the Ents broke their way in, he left in a hurry. They did not spot him at first. But the night had opened out, and there was a great light of stars, quite enough for Ents to see by, and suddenly Quickbeam gave a cry: "The tree-killer, the tree-killer!" Quickbeam is a gentle creature, but he hates Saruman all the more fiercely for that: his people suffered cruelly from orc-axes. He leapt down the path from the inner gate, and he can move like a wind when he is roused. There was a pale figure hurrying away in and out of the shadows of the pillars, and it had nearly reached the stairs to the tower-door. But it was a near thing. Quickbeam was so hot after him, that he was within a step or two of being caught and strangled when he slipped in through the door.

'When Saruman was safe back in Orthanc, it was not long before he set some of his precious machinery to work.

By that time there were many Ents inside Isengard: some had followed Quickbeam, and others had burst in from the north and east; they were roaming about and doing a great deal of damage. Suddenly up came fires and foul fumes: the vents and shafts all over the plain began to spout and belch. Several of the Ents got scorched and blistered. One of them, Beechbone I think he was called, a very tall handsome Ent, got caught in a spray of some liquid fire and burned like a torch: a horrible sight.

'That sent them mad. I thought that they had been really roused before; but I was wrong. I saw what it was like at last. It was staggering. They roared and boomed and trumpeted, until stones began to crack and fall at the mere noise of them. Merry and I lay on the ground and stuffed our cloaks into our ears. Round and round the rock of Orthanc the Ents went striding and storming like a howling gale, breaking pillars, hurling avalanches of boulders down the shafts, tossing up huge slabs of stone into the air like leaves. The tower was in the middle of a spinning whirlwind. I saw iron posts and blocks of masonry go rocketing up hundreds of feet, and smash against the windows of Orthanc. But Treebeard kept his head. He had not had any burns, luckily. He did not want his folk to hurt themselves in their fury, and he did not want Saruman to escape out of some hole in the confusion. Many of the Ents were hurling themselves against the Orthanc-rock; but that defeated them. It is very smooth and hard. Some wizardry is in it, perhaps, older and stronger than Saruman's. Anyway they could not get a grip on it, or make a crack in it; and they were bruising and wounding themselves against it.

'So Treebeard went out into the ring and shouted. His enormous voice rose above all the din. There was a dead silence, suddenly. In it we heard a shrill laugh from a high window in the tower. That had a queer effect on the Ents. They had been boiling over; now they became cold, grim as ice, and quiet. They left the plain and gathered round Treebeard, standing quite still. He spoke to them for a little in their own language; I think he was telling them of a plan he had made in his old head long before. Then they just faded silently away in the grey light. Day was dawning by that time.

'They set a watch on the tower, I believe, but the watchers were so well hidden in shadows and kept so still, that I could not see them. The others went away north. All that day they were busy, out of sight. Most of the time we were left alone. It was a dreary day; and we wandered about a bit, though we kept out of the view of the windows of Orthanc, as much as we could: they stared at us so threateningly. A good deal of the time we spent looking for something to eat. And also we sat and talked, wondering what was happening away south in Rohan, and what had become of all the rest of our Company. Every now and then we could hear in the distance the rattle and fall of stone, and thudding noises echoing in the hills.

'In the afternoon we walked round the circle, and went to have a look at what was going on. There was a great shadowy wood of Huorns at the head of the valley, and another round the northern wall. We did not dare to go in. But there was a rending, tearing, noise of work going on inside. Ents and Huorns were digging great pits and trenches, making great pools and dams, gathering all the waters of the Isen and every other spring and stream that they could find. We left them to it.

'At dusk Treebeard came back to the gate. He was humming and booming to himself, and seemed pleased. He stood and stretched his great arms and legs and breathed deep. I asked him if he was tired.

' "Tired?" he said, "tired? Well no, not tired, but stiff. I need a good draught of Entwash. We have worked hard; we have done more stone-cracking and earth-gnawing today than we have done in many a long year before. But it is nearly finished. When night falls do not linger near this gate or in the old tunnel! Water may come through— and it will be foul water for a while, until all the filth of Saruman is washed away. Then Isen can run clean again." He began to pull down a bit more of the walls, in a leisurely sort of way, just to amuse himself.

'We were just wondering where it would be safe to lie and get some sleep, when the most amazing thing of all happened. There was the sound of a rider coming swiftly up the road. Merry and I lay quiet, and Treebeard hid himself in the shadows under the arch. Suddenly a great horse came striding up, like a flash of silver. It was getting dark, but I could see the rider's face clearly: it seemed to shine, and all his clothes were white. I just sat up, staring with my mouth open. I tried to call out, and couldn't.

'There was no need. He halted just by us and looked down at us. "Gandalf!" I said at last, but my voice was only a whisper. Did he say: "Hullo, Pippin! This is a pleasant surprise!"? No, indeed! He said: "Get up, you tom-fool of a Took! Where, in the name of wonder, in all this ruin is Treebeard? I want him. Quick!"

'Treebeard heard his voice and came out of the shadows at once; and there was a strange meeting. I was surprised, because neither of them seemed surprised at all. Gandalf obviously expected to find Treebeard here; and Treebeard might almost have been loitering about near the gates on purpose to meet him. Yet we had told the old Ent all about Moria. But then I remembered a queer look he gave us at the time. I can only suppose that he had seen Gandalf or had some news of him, but would not say anything in a hurry. "Don't be hasty" is his motto; but nobody, not even Elves, will say much about Gandalf's movements when he is not there.

' "Hoom! Gandalf!" said Treebeard. "I am glad you have come. Wood and water, stock and stone, I can master; but there is a wizard to manage here."

' "Treebeard," said Gandalf. "I need your help. You have done much, but I need more. I have about ten thousand Orcs to manage."

'Then those two went off and had a council together in some corner. It must have seemed very hasty to Treebeard, for Gandalf was in a tremendous hurry, and was already talking at a great pace, before they passed out of hearing. They were only away a matter of minutes, perhaps a quarter of an hour. Then Gandalf came back to us, and he seemed relieved, almost merry. He did say he was glad to see us, then.

'"But Gandalf," I cried, "where have you been? And have you seen the others?"

'"Wherever I have been, I am back," he answered in the genuine Gandalf manner. "Yes, I have seen some of the others. But news must wait. This is a perilous night, and I must ride fast. But the dawn may be brighter; and if so, we shall meet again. Take care of yourselves, and keep away from Orthanc! Good-bye!"

'Treebeard was very thoughtful after Gandalf had gone. He had evidently learnt a lot in a short time and was digesting it. He looked at us and said: "Hm, well, I find you are not such hasty folk as I thought. You said much less than you might, and no more than you should. Hm, this is a bundle of news and no mistake! Well, now Treebeard must get busy again."

'Before he went, we got a little news out of him; and it did not cheer us up at all. But for the moment we thought more about you three than about Frodo and Sam, or about poor Boromir. For we gathered that there was a great battle going on, or soon would be, and that you were in it, and might never come out of it.

'"Huorns will help," said Treebeard. Then he went away and we did not see him again until this morning.

'It was deep night. We lay on top of a pile of stone, and could see nothing beyond it. Mist or shadows blotted out everything like a great blanket all round us. The air seemed hot and heavy; and it was full of rustlings, creakings, and a murmur like voices passing. I think that hundreds more of the Huorns must have been passing by to help in the battle. Later there was a great rumble of thunder away south, and flashes of lightning far away across Rohan. Every now and then we could see mountain-peaks, miles and miles away, stab out suddenly, black and white, and then vanish. And behind us there were noises like thunder in hills, but different. At times the whole valley echoed.

'It must have been about midnight when the Ents broke

the dams and poured all the gathered waters through a
gap in the northern wall, down into Isengard. The Huorn-
dark had passed, and the thunder had rolled away. The
Moon was sinking behind the western mountains.

'Isengard began to fill up with black creeping streams
and pools. They glittered in the last light of the Moon, as
they spread over the plain. Every now and then the waters
found their way down into some shaft or spouthole. Great
white steams hissed up. Smoke rose in billows. There were
explosions and gusts of fire. One great coil of vapour went
whirling up, twisting round and round Orthanc, until it
looked like a tall peak of cloud, fiery underneath and
moonlit above. And still more water poured in, until at
last Isengard looked like a huge flat saucepan, all steaming
and bubbling.'

'We saw a cloud of smoke and steam from the south
last night, when we came to the mouth of Nan Curunír,'
said Aragorn. 'We feared that Saruman was brewing some
new devilry for us.'

'Not he!' said Pippin. 'He was probably choking and
not laughing any more. By the morning, yesterday morning, the water had sunk down into all the holes, and there
was a dense fog. We took refuge in that guardroom over
there; and we had rather a fright. The lake began to
overflow and pour out through the old tunnel, and the
water was rapidly rising up the steps. We thought we were
going to get caught like Orcs in a hole; but we found a
winding stair at the back of the store-room that brought
us out on top of the arch. It was a squeeze to get out, as the
passages had been cracked and half blocked with fallen
stone near the top. There we sat high up above the floods
and watched the drowning of Isengard. The Ents kept on
pouring in more water, till all the fires were quenched and
every cave filled. The fogs slowly gathered together and
steamed up into a huge umbrella of cloud: it must have
been a mile high. In the evening there was a great rainbow
over the eastern hills; and then the sunset was blotted out
by a thick drizzle on the mountain-sides. It all went very
quiet. A few wolves howled mournfully, far away. The Ents

stopped the inflow in the night, and sent the Isen back into its old course. And that was the end of it all.

'Since then the water has been sinking again. There must be outlets somewhere from the caves underneath, I think. If Saruman peeps out of any of his windows, it must look an untidy, dreary mess. We felt very lonely. Not even a visible Ent to talk to in all the ruin; and no news. We spent the night up on top there above the arch, and it was cold and damp and we did not sleep. We had a feeling that anything might happen at any minute. Saruman is still in his tower. There was a noise in the night like a wind coming up the valley. I think the Ents and Huorns that had been away came back then; but where they have all gone to now, I don't know. It was a misty, moisty morning when we climbed down and looked around again, and nobody was about. And that is about all there is to tell. It seems almost peaceful now after all the turmoil. And safer too, somehow, since Gandalf came back. I could sleep!'

They all fell silent for a while. Gimli re-filled his pipe. 'There is one thing I wonder about,' he said as he lit it with his flint and tinder: 'Wormtongue. You told Théoden he was with Saruman. How did he get there?'

'Oh yes, I forgot about him,' said Pippin. 'He did not get here till this morning. We had just lit the fire and had some breakfast when Treebeard appeared again. We heard him hooming and calling our names outside.

' "I have just come round to see how you are faring, my lads," he said; "and to give you some news. Huorns have come back. All's well; aye very well indeed!" he laughed, and slapped his thighs. "No more Orcs in Isengard, no more axes! And there will be folk coming up from the South before the day is old; some that you may be glad to see."

'He had hardly said that, when we heard the sound of hoofs on the road. We rushed out before the gates, and I stood and stared, half expecting to see Strider and Gandalf come riding up at the head of an army. But out of the mist there rode a man on an old tired horse; and he looked a queer twisted sort of creature himself. There was no one else. When he came out of the mist and suddenly saw all the ruin and wreckage in front of him, he sat and gaped, and his face went almost green. He was so bewildered that he did not seem to notice us at first. When he did, he gave a cry, and tried to turn his horse round and ride off. But Treebeard took three strides, put out a long arm, and lifted him out of the saddle. His horse bolted in terror, and he grovelled on the ground. He said he was Gríma, friend and counsellor of the king and had been sent with important messages from Théoden to Saruman.

' "No one else would dare to ride through the open land, so full of foul Orcs," he said, "so I was sent. And I have had a perilous journey, and I am hungry and weary. I fled far north out of my way, pursued by wolves."

'I caught the sidelong looks he gave to Treebeard, and I said to myself "liar". Treebeard looked at him in his long way for several minutes, till the wretched man was squirming on the floor. Then at last he said: "Ha, hm, I was expecting you, Master Wormtongue." The man started at that name. "Gandalf got here first. So I know as much about you as I need, and I know what to do with you. Put all the rats in one trap, said Gandalf; and I will. I am the master of Isengard now, but Saruman is locked in his tower; and you can go there and give him all the messages that you can think of."

' "Let me go, let me go!" said Wormtongue. "I know the way."

' "You knew the way, I don't doubt," said Treebeard. "But things have changed here a little. Go and see!"

'He let Wormtongue go, and he limped off through the arch, with us close behind, until he came inside the ring and could see all the floods that lay between him and Orthanc. Then he turned to us.

' "Let me go away!" he whined. "Let me go away! My messages are useless now."

' "They are indeed," said Treebeard. "But you have only two choices: to stay with me until Gandalf and your master arrive; or to cross the water. Which will you have?"

'The man shivered at the mention of his master, and put a foot into the water; but he drew back. "I cannot swim," he said.

' "The water is not deep," said Treebeard. "It is dirty, but that will not harm you, Master Wormtongue. In you go now!"

'With that the wretch floundered off into the flood. It rose up nearly to his neck before he got too far away for me to see him. The last I saw of him was clinging to some old barrel or piece of wood. But Treebeard waded after him, and watched his progress.

' "Well, he has gone in," he said when he returned. "I saw him crawling up the steps like a draggled rat. There is someone in the tower still: a hand came out and pulled him in. So there he is, and I hope the welcome is to his liking. Now I must go and wash myself clean of the slime. I'll be away up on the north side, if anyone wants to see me. There is no clean water down here fit for an Ent to drink, or to bathe in. So I will ask you two lads to keep a watch at the gate for the folk that are coming. There'll be the Lord of the Fields of Rohan, mark you! You must welcome him as well as you know how: his men have fought a great fight with the Orcs. Maybe, you know the right fashion of Men's words for such a lord, better than Ents. There have been many lords in the green fields in my time, and I have never learned their speech or their names. They will be wanting man-food, and you know all about that, I guess. So find what you think is fit for a king to eat, if you can." And that is the end of the story. Though I should like to know who this Wormtongue is. Was he really the king's counsellor?'

'He was,' said Aragorn; 'and also Saruman's spy and servant in Rohan. Fate has not been kinder to him than he deserves. The sight of the ruin of all that he thought so strong and magnificent must have been almost punishment enough. But I fear that worse awaits him.'

'Yes, I don't suppose Treebeard sent him to Orthanc out of kindness,' said Merry. 'He seemed rather grimly delighted with the business, and was laughing to himself when he went to get his bath and drink. We spent a busy time after that, searching the flotsam, and rummaging about. We found two or three store-rooms in different places nearby, above the flood-level. But Treebeard sent some Ents down, and they carried off a great deal of the stuff.

'"We want man-food for twenty-five," the Ents said, so you can see that somebody had counted your company carefully before you arrived. You three were evidently meant to go with the great people. But you would not have fared any better. We kept as good as we sent, I promise you. Better, because we sent no drink.

'"What about drink?" I said to the Ents.

'"There is water of Isen," they said, "and that is good enough for Ents and Men." But I hope that the Ents may have found time to brew some of their draughts from the mountain-springs, and we shall see Gandalf's beard curling when he returns. After the Ents had gone, we felt tired, and hungry. But we did not grumble—our labours had been well rewarded. It was through our search for man-food that Pippin discovered the prize of all the flotsam, those Hornblower barrels. "Pipe-weed is better after food," said Pippin; that is how the situation arose.'

'We understand it all perfectly now,' said Gimli.

'All except one thing,' said Aragorn: 'leaf from the Southfarthing in Isengard. The more I consider it, the more curious I find it. I have never been in Isengard, but I have journeyed in this land, and I know well the empty countries that lie between Rohan and the Shire. Neither goods nor folk have passed that way for many a long year, not openly. Saruman had secret dealings with someone in the Shire, I guess. Wormtongues may be found in other houses than King Théoden's. Was there a date on the barrels?'

'Yes,' said Pippin. 'It was the 1417 crop, that is last year's; no, the year before, of course, now: a good year.'

'Ah well, whatever evil was afoot is over now, I hope; or else it is beyond our reach at present,' said Aragorn.

'Yet I think I shall mention it to Gandalf, small matter though it may seem among his great affairs.'

'I wonder what he is doing,' said Merry. 'The afternoon is getting on. Let us go and look round! You can enter Isengard now at any rate, Strider, if you want to. But it is not a very cheerful sight.'

Chapter 10

The Voice of Saruman

They passed through the ruined tunnel and stood upon a heap of stones, gazing at the dark rock of Orthanc, and its many windows, a menace still in the desolation that lay all about it. The waters had now nearly all subsided. Here and there gloomy pools remained, covered with scum and wreckage; but most of the wide circle was bare again, a wilderness of slime and tumbled rock, pitted with blackened holes, and dotted with posts and pillars leaning drunkenly this way and that. At the rim of the shattered bowl there lay vast mounds and slopes, like the shingles cast up by a great storm; and beyond them the green and tangled valley ran up into the long ravine between the dark arms of the mountains. Across the waste they saw riders picking their way; they were coming from the north side, and already they were drawing near to Orthanc.

'There is Gandalf, and Théoden and his men!' said Legolas. 'Let us go and meet them!'

'Walk warily!' said Merry. 'There are loose slabs that may tilt up and throw you down into a pit, if you don't take care.'

They followed what was left of the road from the gates to Orthanc, going slowly, for the flag-stones were cracked and slimed. The riders, seeing them approach, halted under the shadow of the rock and waited for them. Gandalf rode forward to meet them.

'Well, Treebeard and I have had some interesting discussions, and made a few plans,' he said; 'and we have all had some much-needed rest. Now we must be going on again. I hope you companions have all rested, too, and refreshed yourselves?'

'We have,' said Merry. 'But our discussions began and

ended in smoke. Still we feel less ill-disposed towards Saruman than we did.'

'Do you indeed?' said Gandalf. 'Well, I do not. I have now a last task to do before I go: I must pay Saruman a farewell visit. Dangerous, and probably useless; but it must be done. Those of you who wish may come with me—but beware! And do not jest! This is not the time for it.'

'I will come,' said Gimli. 'I wish to see him and learn if he really looks like you.'

'And how will you learn that, Master Dwarf?' said Gandalf. 'Saruman could look like me in your eyes, if it suited his purpose with you. And are you yet wise enough to detect all his counterfeits? Well, we shall see, perhaps. He may be shy of showing himself before many different eyes together. But I have ordered all the Ents to remove themselves from sight, so perhaps we shall persuade him to come out.'

'What's the danger?' asked Pippin. 'Will he shoot at us, and pour fire out of the windows; or can he put a spell on us from a distance?'

'The last is most likely, if you ride to his door with a light heart,' said Gandalf. 'But there is no knowing what he can do, or may choose to try. A wild beast cornered is not safe to approach. And Saruman has powers you do not guess. Beware of his voice!'

They came now to the foot of Orthanc. It was black, and the rock gleamed as if it were wet. The many faces of the stone had sharp edges as though they had been newly chiselled. A few scorings, and small flake-like splinters near the base, were all the marks that it bore of the fury of the Ents.

On the eastern side, in the angle of two piers, there was a great door, high above the ground; and over it was a shuttered window, opening upon a balcony hedged with iron bars. Up to the threshold of the door there mounted a flight of twenty-seven broad stairs, hewn by some unknown art of the same black stone. This was the only entrance to the tower; but many tall windows were cut with deep embrasures in the climbing walls: far up they peered like little eyes in the sheer faces of the horns.

At the foot of the stairs Gandalf and the king dismounted. 'I will go up,' said Gandalf. 'I have been in Orthanc and I know my peril.'

'And I too will go up,' said the king. 'I am old, and fear no peril any more. I wish to speak with the enemy who has done me so much wrong. Éomer shall come with me, and see that my aged feet do not falter.'

'As you will,' said Gandalf. 'Aragorn shall come with me. Let the others await us at the foot of the stairs. They will hear and see enough, if there is anything to hear or see.'

'Nay!' said Gimli. 'Legolas and I wish for a closer view. We alone here represent our kindreds. We also will come behind.'

'Come then!' said Gandalf, and with that he climbed the steps, and Théoden went beside him.

The Riders of Rohan sat uneasily upon their horses, on either side of the stair, and looked up darkly at the great tower, fearing what might befall their lord. Merry and Pippin sat on the bottom step, feeling both unimportant and unsafe.

'Half a stick mile from here to the gate!' muttered Pippin. 'I wish I could slip off back to the guardroom unnoticed! What did we come for? We are not wanted.'

Gandalf stood before the door of Orthanc and beat on it with his staff. It rang with a hollow sound. 'Saruman, Saruman!' he cried in a loud commanding voice. 'Saruman come forth!'

For some time there was no answer. At last the window above the door was unbarred, but no figure could be seen at its dark opening.

'Who is it?' said a voice. 'What do you wish?'

Théoden started. 'I know that voice,' he said, 'and I curse the day when I first listened to it.'

'Go and fetch Saruman, since you have become his footman, Gríma Wormtongue!' said Gandalf. 'And do not waste our time!'

The window closed. They waited. Suddenly another voice spoke, low and melodious, its very sound an enchantment. Those who listened unwarily to that voice could seldom report the words that they heard; and if they did, they wondered, for little power remained in them. Mostly they remembered only that it was a delight to hear the voice speaking, all that it said seemed wise and reasonable, and desire awoke in them by swift agreement to seem wise themselves. When others spoke they seemed harsh and uncouth by contrast; and if they gainsaid the voice, anger was kindled in the hearts of those under the spell. For some the spell lasted only while the voice spoke to them, and when it spoke to another they smiled, as men do who see through a juggler's trick while others gape at it. For many the sound of the voice alone was enough to hold them enthralled; but for those whom it conquered the spell endured when they were far away, and ever they heard that soft voice whispering and urging them. But none were unmoved; none rejected its pleas and its commands without an effort of mind and will, so long as its master had control of it.

'Well?' it said now with gentle question. 'Why must you disturb my rest? Will you give me no peace at all by night or day?' Its tone was that of a kindly heart aggrieved by injuries undeserved.

They looked up, astonished, for they had heard no sound of his coming; and they saw a figure standing at the rail, looking down upon them: an old man, swathed in a great cloak, the colour of which was not easy to tell, for it changed if they moved their eyes or if he stirred. His face was long, with a high forehead, he had deep darkling eyes, hard to fathom, though the look that they now bore was grave and benevolent, and a little weary. His hair and beard were white, but strands of black still showed about his lips and ears.

'Like, and yet unlike,' muttered Gimli.

'But come now,' said the soft voice. 'Two at least of you I know by name. Gandalf I know too well to have much hope that he seeks help or counsel here. But you, Théoden Lord of the Mark of Rohan, are declared by your noble devices, and still more by the fair countenance of the house of Eorl. O worthy son of Thengel the Thrice-renowned! Why have you not come before, and as a friend? Much have I desired to see you, mightiest king of western lands, and especially in these latter years, to save you from the unwise and evil counsels that beset you! Is it yet too late? Despite the injuries that have been done to me, in which the men of Rohan, alas! have had some part, still I would save you, and deliver you from the ruin that draws nigh inevitably, if you ride upon this road which you have taken. Indeed I alone can aid you now.'

Théoden opened his mouth as if to speak, but he said nothing. He looked up at the face of Saruman with its dark solemn eyes bent down upon him, and then to Gandalf at his side; and he seemed to hesitate. Gandalf made no sign; but stood silent as stone, as one waiting patiently for some call that has not yet come. The Riders stirred at first, murmuring with approval of the words of Saruman; and then they too were silent, as men spell-bound. It seemed to them that Gandalf had never spoken so fair and fittingly to their lord. Rough and proud now seemed all his dealings with Théoden. And over their hearts crept a shadow, the fear of a great danger: the end of the Mark in a darkness to which Gandalf was driving them, while Saruman stood beside a door of escape, holding it half open so that a ray of light came through. There was a heavy silence.

It was Gimli the dwarf who broke in suddenly. 'The words of this wizard stand on their heads,' he growled, gripping the handle of his axe. 'In the language of Orthanc help means ruin, and having means slaying, that is plain. But we do not come here to beg.'

'Peace!' said Saruman, and for a fleeting moment his voice was less suave, and a light flickered in his eyes and was gone. 'I do not speak to you yet, Gimli Glóin's son,' he said. 'Far away is your home and small concern of yours are the troubles of this land. But it was not by design of your own that you became embroiled in them, and so I

will not blame such part as you have played—a valiant
one, I doubt not. But I pray you, allow me first to speak
with the King of Rohan, my neighbour, and once my friend.

'What have you to say, Théoden King? Will you have
peace with me, and all the aid that my knowledge, founded
in long years, can bring? Shall we make our counsels together against evil days, and repair our injuries with such
good will that our estates shall both come to fairer flower
than ever before?'

Still Théoden did not answer. Whether he strove with
anger or doubt none could say. Éomer spoke.

'Lord, hear me!' he said. 'Now we feel the peril that we
were warned of. Have we ridden forth to victory, only to
stand at last amazed by an old liar with honey on his
forked tongue? So would the trapped wolf speak to the
hounds, if he could. What aid can he give to you, forsooth?
All he desires is to escape from his plight. But will you
parley with this dealer in treachery and murder? Remember Théodred at the Ford and the grave of Háma in Helm's
Deep!'

'If we speak of poisoned tongues what shall we say of
yours, young serpent?' said Saruman, and the flash of his
anger was now plain to see. 'But come, Éomer Éomund's
son!' he went on in his soft voice again. 'To every man his
part. Valour in arms is yours, and you win high honour
thereby. Slay whom your lord names as enemies, and be
content. Meddle not in policies which you do not understand. But maybe, if you become a king, you will find
that he must choose his friends with care. The friendship
of Saruman and the power of Orthanc cannot be lightly
thrown aside, whatever grievances, real or fancied, may
lie behind. You have won a battle but not a war—and
that with help on which you cannot count again. You may
find the Shadow of the Wood at your own door next: it is
wayward, and senseless, and has no love for Men.

'But my lord of Rohan, am I to be called a murderer,
because valiant men have fallen in battle? If you go to war,
needlessly, for I did not desire it, then men will be slain. But
if I am a murderer on that account, then all the house of

Eorl is stained with murder; for they have fought many wars, and assailed many who defied them. Yet with some they have afterwards made peace, none the worse for being politic. I say, Théoden King: shall we have peace and friendship, you and I? It is ours to command.'

'We will have peace,' said Théoden at last thickly and with an effort. Several of the Riders cried out gladly. Théoden held up his hand. 'Yes, we will have peace,' he said, now in a clear voice, 'we will have peace, when you and all your works have perished—and the works of your dark master to whom you would deliver us. You are a liar, Saruman, and a corrupter of men's hearts. You hold out your hand to me, and I perceive only a finger of the claw of Mordor. Cruel and cold! Even if your war on me was just—as it was not, for were you ten times as wise you would have no right to rule me and mine for your own profit as you desired—even so, what will you say of your torches in Westfold and the children that lie dead there? And they hewed Háma's body before the gates of the Hornburg, after he was dead. When you hang from a gibbet at your window for the sport of your own crows, I will have peace with you and Orthanc. So much for the house of Eorl. A lesser son of great sires am I, but I do not need to lick your fingers. Turn elsewhither. But I fear your voice has lost its charm.'

The Riders gazed up at Théoden like men startled out of a dream. Harsh as an old raven's their master's voice sounded in their ears after the music of Saruman. But Saruman for a while was beside himself with wrath. He leaned over the rail as if he would smite the King with his staff. To some suddenly it seemed that they saw a snake coiling itself to strike.

'Gibbets and crows!' he hissed, and they shuddered at the hideous change. 'Dotard! What is the house of Eorl but a thatched barn where brigands drink in the reek, and their brats roll on the floor among the dogs? Too long have they escaped the gibbet themselves. But the noose comes, slow in the drawing, tight and hard in the end. Hang if you will!' Now his voice changed, as he slowly mastered himself. 'I know not why I have had the patience to speak to you. For I need you not, nor your little band of gallopers, as swift to fly as to advance, Théoden Horsemaster. Long ago I offered you a state beyond your merit and your wit. I have offered it again, so that those whom you mislead may clearly see the choice of roads. You give me brag and abuse. So be it. Go back to your huts!

'But you, Gandalf! For you at least I am grieved, feeling for your shame. How comes it that you can endure such company? For you are proud, Gandalf—and not without reason, having a noble mind and eyes that look both deep and far. Even now will you not listen to my counsel?'

Gandalf stirred, and looked up. 'What have you to say that you did not say at our last meeting?' he asked. 'Or, perhaps, you have things to unsay?'

Saruman paused. 'Unsay?' he mused, as if puzzled. 'Unsay? I endeavoured to advise you for your own good, but you scarcely listened. You are proud and do not love advice, having indeed a store of your own wisdom. But on that occasion you erred, I think, misconstruing my intentions wilfully. I fear that in my eagerness to persuade you, I lost patience. And indeed I regret it. For I bore you no ill-will; and even now I bear none, though you return to me in the company of the violent and the ignorant. How should I? Are we not both members of a high and ancient order, most excellent in Middle-earth? Our friendship would profit us both alike. Much we could still accomplish together, to heal the disorders of the world. Let us understand one another, and dismiss from thought these lesser folk! Let them wait on our decisions! For the common good I am willing to redress the past, and to receive you. Will you not consult with me? Will you not come up?'

So great was the power that Saruman exerted in this last effort that none that stood within hearing were unmoved. But now the spell was wholly different. They heard the gentle remonstrance of a kindly king with an erring but much-loved minister. But they were shut out, listening at a door to words not meant for them: ill-mannered children or stupid servants overhearing the elusive discourse of

their elders, and wondering how it would affect their lot. Of
loftier mould these two were made: reverend and wise. It
was inevitable that they should make alliance. Gandalf
would ascend into the tower, to discuss deep things beyond
their comprehension in the high chambers of Orthanc. The
door would be closed, and they would be left outside, dismissed to await allotted work or punishment. Even in the
mind of Théoden the thought took shape, like a shadow of
doubt: 'He will betray us; he will go—we shall be lost.'

Then Gandalf laughed. The fantasy vanished like a puff
of smoke.

'Saruman, Saruman!' said Gandalf still laughing. 'Saruman, you missed your path in life. You should have been
the king's jester and earned your bread, and stripes too,
by mimicking his counsellors. Ah me!' he paused, getting
the better of his mirth. 'Understand one another? I fear I
am beyond your comprehension. But you, Saruman, I
understand now too well. I keep a clearer memory of your
arguments, and deeds, than you suppose. When last I
visited you, you were the jailor of Mordor, and there I
was to be sent. Nay, the guest who has escaped from the
roof, will think twice before he comes back in by the
door. Nay, I do not think I will come up. But listen, Saruman, for the last time! Will you not come down? Isengard
has proved less strong than your hope and fancy made it.
So may other things in which you still have trust. Would
it not be well to leave it for a while? To turn to new
things, perhaps? Think well, Saruman! Will you not come
down?'

A shadow passed over Saruman's face; then it went
deathly white. Before he could conceal it, they saw through
the mask the anguish of a mind in doubt, loathing to stay
and dreading to leave its refuge. For a second he hesitated,
and no one breathed. Then he spoke, and his voice was
shrill and cold. Pride and hate were conquering him.

'Will I come down?' he mocked. 'Does an unarmed
man come down to speak with robbers out of doors? I can
hear you well enough here. I am no fool, and I do not trust
you, Gandalf. They do not stand openly on my stairs,

but I know where the wild wood-demons are lurking, at your command.'

'The treacherous are ever distrustful,' answered Gandalf wearily. 'But you need not fear for your skin. I do not wish to kill you, or hurt you, as you would know, if you really understood me. And I have the power to protect you. I am giving you a last chance. You can leave Orthanc, free—if you choose.'

'That sounds well,' sneered Saruman. 'Very much in the manner of Gandalf the Grey: so condescending, and so very kind. I do not doubt that you would find Orthanc commodious, and my departure convenient. But why should I wish to leave? And what do you mean by "free"? There are conditions, I presume?'

'Reasons for leaving you can see from your windows,' answered Gandalf. 'Others will occur to your thought. Your servants are destroyed and scattered; your neighbours you have made your enemies; and you have cheated your new master, or tried to do so. When his eye turns hither, it will be the red eye of wrath. But when I say "free", I mean "free": free from bond, of chain or command: to go where you will, even, even to Mordor, Saruman, if you desire. But you will first surrender to me the Key of Orthanc, and your staff. They shall be pledges of your conduct, to be returned later, if you merit them.'

Saruman's face grew livid, twisted with rage, and a red light was kindled in his eyes. He laughed wildly. 'Later!' he cried, and his voice rose to a scream. 'Later! Yes, when you also have the Keys of Barad-dûr itself, I suppose; and the crowns of seven kings, and the rods of the Five Wizards, and have purchased yourself a pair of boots many sizes larger than those that you wear now. A modest plan. Hardly one in which my help is needed! I have other things to do. Do not be a fool. If you wish to treat with me, while you have a chance, go away, and come back when you are sober! And leave behind these cut-throats and small rag-tag that dangle at your tail! Good day!' He turned and left the balcony.

'Come back, Saruman!' said Gandalf in a commanding

voice. To the amazement of the others, Saruman turned
again, and as if dragged against his will, he came slowly
back to the iron rail, leaning on it, breathing hard. His
face was lined and shrunken. His hand clutched his heavy
black staff like a claw.

'I did not give you leave to go,' said Gandalf sternly.
'I have not finished. You have become a fool, Saruman,
and yet pitiable. You might still have turned away from
folly and evil, and have been of service. But you choose to
stay and gnaw the ends of your old plots. Stay then! But I
warn you, you will not easily come out again. Not unless
the dark hands of the East stretch out to take you. Saruman!' he cried, and his voice grew in power and authority.
'Behold, I am not Gandalf the Grey, whom you betrayed. I am Gandalf the White, who has returned from
death. You have no colour now, and I cast you from the
order and from the Council.'

He raised his hand, and spoke slowly in a clear cold
voice. 'Saruman, your staff is broken.' There was a crack,
and the staff split asunder in Saruman's hand, and the
head of it fell down at Gandalf's feet. 'Go!' said Gandalf.
With a cry Saruman fell back and crawled away. At that
moment a heavy shining thing came hurtling down from
above. It glanced off the iron rail, even as Saruman left it,
and passing close to Gandalf's head, it smote the stair on
which he stood. The rail rang and snapped. The stair
cracked and splintered in glittering sparks. But the ball was
unharmed: it rolled on down the steps, a globe of crystal,
dark, but glowing with a heart of fire. As it bounded away
towards a pool Pippin ran after it and picked it up.

'The murderous rogue!' cried Éomer. But Gandalf was
unmoved. 'No, that was not thrown by Saruman,' he said;
'nor even at his bidding, I think. It came from a window
far above. A parting shot from Master Wormtongue, I
fancy, but ill aimed.'

'The aim was poor, maybe, because he could not make
up his mind which he hated more, you or Saruman,'
said Aragorn.

'That may be so,' said Gandalf. 'Small comfort will

those two have in their companionship: they will gnaw one another with words. But the punishment is just. If Wormtongue ever comes out of Orthanc alive, it will be more than he deserves.

'Here, my lad, I'll take that! I did not ask you to handle it,' he cried, turning sharply and seeing Pippin coming up the steps, slowly, as if he were bearing a great weight. He went down to meet him and hastily took the dark globe from the hobbit, wrapping it in the folds of his cloak. 'I will take care of this,' he said. 'It is not a thing that Saruman would have chosen to cast away.'

'But he may have other things to cast,' said Gimli. 'If that is the end of the debate, let us go out of stone's throw, at least!'

'It is the end,' said Gandalf. 'Let us go.'

They turned their backs on the doors of Orthanc, and went down. The riders hailed the king with joy, and saluted Gandalf. The spell of Saruman was broken: they had seen him come at call, and crawl away, dismissed.

'Well, that is done,' said Gandalf. 'Now I must find Treebeard and tell him how things have gone.'

'He will have guessed, surely?' said Merry. 'Were they likely to end any other way?'

'Not likely,' answered Gandalf, 'though they came to the balance of a hair. But I had reasons for trying; some merciful and some less so. First Saruman was shown that the power of his voice was waning. He cannot be both tyrant and counsellor. When the plot is ripe it remains no longer secret. Yet he fell into the trap, and tried to deal with his victims piece-meal, while others listened. Then I gave him a last choice and a fair one: to renounce both Mordor and his private schemes, and make amends by helping us in our need. He knows our need, none better. Great service he could have rendered. But he has chosen to withhold it, and keep the power of Orthanc. He will not serve, only command. He lives now in terror of the shadow of Mordor, and yet he still dreams of riding the storm. Unhappy fool! He will be devoured, if the power of the East stretches out its arms to Isengard. We cannot destroy Orthanc from without, but Sauron—who knows what he can do?'

'And what if Sauron does not conquer? What will you do to him?' asked Pippin.

'I? Nothing!' said Gandalf. 'I will do nothing to him. I do not wish for mastery. What will become of him? I cannot say. I grieve that so much that was good now festers in the tower. Still for us things have not gone badly. Strange are the turns of fortune! Often does hatred hurt itself! I fancy that, even if we had entered in, we could have found few treasures in Orthanc more precious than the thing which Wormtongue threw down at us.'

A shrill shriek, suddenly cut off, came from an open window high above.

'It seems that Saruman thinks so too,' said Gandalf. 'Let us leave them!'

They returned now to the ruins of the gate. Hardly had they passed out under the arch, when, from among the shadows of the piled stones where they had stood, Treebeard and a dozen other Ents came striding up. Aragorn, Gimli and Legolas gazed at them in wonder.

'Here are three of my companions, Treebeard,' said Gandalf. 'I have spoken of them, but you have not yet seen them.' He named them one by one.

The Old Ent looked at them long and searchingly, and spoke to them in turn. Last he turned to Legolas. 'So you have come all the way from Mirkwood, my good Elf? A very great forest it used to be!'

'And still is,' said Legolas. 'But not so great that we who dwell there ever tire of seeing new trees. I should dearly love to journey in Fangorn's Wood. I scarcely passed beyond the leaves of it, and I did not wish to turn back.'

Treebeard's eyes gleamed with pleasure. 'I hope you may have your wish, ere the hills be much older,' he said.

'I will come, if I have the fortune,' said Legolas. 'I have

made a bargain with my friend that, if all goes well, we will visit Fangorn together—by your leave.'

'Any Elf that comes with you will be welcome,' said Treebeard.

'The friend I speak of is not an Elf,' said Legolas; 'I mean Gimli, Glóin's son here.' Gimli bowed low, and the axe slipped from his belt and clattered on the ground.

'Hoom, hm! Ah now,' said Treebeard, looking dark-eyed at him. 'A dwarf and an axe-bearer! Hoom! I have good will to Elves; but you ask much. This is a strange friendship!'

'Strange it may seem,' said Legolas; 'but while Gimli lives I shall not come to Fangorn alone. His axe is not for trees, but for orc-necks, O Fangorn, Master of Fangorn's Wood. Forty-two he hewed in the battle.'

'Hoo! Come now!' said Treebeard. 'That is a better story! Well, well, things will go as they will; and there is no need to hurry to meet them. But now we must part for a while. Day is drawing to an end, yet Gandalf says you must go ere nightfall, and the Lord of the Mark is eager for his own house.'

'Yes, we must go, and go now,' said Gandalf. 'I fear that I must take your gatekeepers from you. But you will manage well enough without them.'

'Maybe I shall,' said Treebeard. 'But I shall miss them. We have become friends in so short a while that I think I must be getting hasty—growing backwards towards youth, perhaps. But there, they are the first new thing under Sun or Moon that I have seen for many a long, long day. I shall not forget them. I have put their names into the Long List. Ents will remember it.

> *Ents the earthborn, old as mountains,*
> *the wide-walkers, water drinking;*
> *and hungry as hunters, the Hobbit children,*
> *the laughing-folk, the little people,*

they shall remain friends as long as leaves are renewed. Fare you well! But if you hear news up in your pleasant land, in the Shire, send me word! You know what I mean: word or sight of the Entwives. Come yourselves if you can.'

'We will,' said Merry and Pippin together, and they turned away hastily. Treebeard looked at them, and was silent for a while, shaking his head thoughtfully. Then he turned to Gandalf.

'So Saruman would not leave?' he said. 'I did not think he would. His heart is as rotten as a black Huorn's. Still, if I were overcome and all my trees destroyed, I would not come while I had one dark hole left to hide in.'

'No,' said Gandalf. 'But you have not plotted to cover all the world with your trees and choke all other living things. But there it is, Saruman remains to nurse his hatred and weave again such webs as he can. He has the Key of Orthanc. But he must not be allowed to escape.'

'Indeed no! Ents will see to that,' said Treebeard. 'Saruman shall not set foot beyond the rock, without my leave. Ents will watch over him.'

'Good!' said Gandalf. 'That is what I hoped. Now I can go and turn to other matters with one care the less. But you must be wary. The waters have gone down. It will not be enough to put sentinels round the tower, I fear. I do not doubt that there were deep ways delved under Orthanc, and that Saruman hopes to go and come unmarked, before long. If you will undertake the labour, I beg you to pour in the waters again; and do so, until Isengard remains a standing pool, or you discover the outlets. When all the underground places are drowned, and the outlets blocked, then Saruman must stay upstairs and look out of the windows.'

'Leave it to the Ents!' said Treebeard. 'We shall search the valley from head to foot and peer under every pebble. Trees are coming back to live here, old trees, wild trees. The Watchwood we will call it. Not a squirrel will go here, but I shall know of it. Leave it to Ents! Until seven times the years in which he tormented us have passed, we shall not tire of watching him.'

Chapter 11

The Palantír

The sun was sinking behind the long western arm of the mountains when Gandalf and his companions, and the king with his Riders, set out again from Isengard. Gandalf took Merry behind him, and Aragorn took Pippin. Two of the king's men went on ahead, riding swiftly, and passed soon out of sight down into the valley. The others followed at an easy pace.

Ents in a solemn row stood like statues at the gate, with their long arms uplifted, but they made no sound. Merry and Pippin looked back, when they had passed some way down the winding road. Sunlight was still shining in the sky, but long shadows reached over Isengard: grey ruins falling into darkness. Treebeard stood alone there now, like the distant stump of an old tree: the hobbits thought of their first meeting, upon the sunny ledge far away on the borders of Fangorn.

They came to the pillar of the White Hand. The pillar was still standing, but the graven hand had been thrown down and broken into small pieces. Right in the middle of the road the long forefinger lay, white in the dusk, its red nail darkening to black.

'The Ents pay attention to every detail!' said Gandalf.

They rode on, and evening deepened in the valley.

'Are we riding far tonight, Gandalf?' asked Merry after a while. 'I don't know how you feel with small rag-tag dangling behind you; but the rag-tag is tired and will be glad to stop dangling and lie down.'

'So you heard that?' said Gandalf. 'Don't let it rankle! Be thankful no longer words were aimed at you. He had never met a hobbit before and did not know what kind of thing to say to you. He had his eyes on you. If it is any comfort to your pride, I should say that, at the moment, you and

246

Pippin are more in his thoughts than all the rest of us. Who you are; how you came there, and why; what you know; whether you were captured, and if so, how you escaped when all the Orcs perished—it is with those little riddles that the great mind of Saruman is troubled. A sneer from him, Meriadoc, is a compliment, if you feel honoured by his concern.'

'Thank you!' said Merry. 'But it is a greater honour to dangle at your tail, Gandalf. For one thing, in that position one has a chance of putting a question a second time. Are we riding far tonight?'

Gandalf laughed. 'A most unquenchable hobbit! All wizards should have a hobbit or two in their care—to teach them the meaning of the word, and to correct them. I beg your pardon. But I have given thought even to these simple matters. We will ride for a few hours, gently, until we come to the end of the valley. Tomorrow we must ride faster.

'When we came, we meant to go straight from Isengard back to the king's house at Edoras over the plains, a ride of some days. But we have taken thought and changed the plan. Messengers have gone ahead to Helm's Deep, to warn them that the king is returning tomorrow. He will ride from there with many men to Dunharrow by paths among the hills. From now on no more than two or three together are to go openly over the land, by day or night, when it can be avoided.'

'Nothing or a double helping is your way!' said Merry. 'I am afraid I was not looking beyond tonight's bed. Where and what are Helm's Deep and all the rest of it? I don't know anything about this country.'

'Then you'd best learn something, if you wish to understand what is happening. But not just now, and not from me: I have too many pressing things to think about.'

'All right, I'll tackle Strider by the camp-fire: he's less testy. But why all this secrecy? I thought we'd won the battle!'

'Yes, we have won, but only the first victory, and that in itself increases our danger. There was some link between

Isengard and Mordor, which I have not yet fathomed. How they exchanged news I am not sure; but they did so. The Eye of Barad-dûr will be looking impatiently towards the Wizard's Vale, I think; and towards Rohan. The less it sees the better.'

The road passed slowly, winding down the valley. Now further, and now nearer Isen flowed in its stony bed. Night came down from the mountains. All the mists were gone. A chill wind blew. The moon, now waxing round, filled the eastern sky with a pale cold sheen. The shoulders of the mountain to their right sloped down to bare hills. The wide plains opened grey before them.

At last they halted. Then they turned aside, leaving the highway and taking to the sweet upland turf again. Going westward a mile or so they came to a dale. It opened southward, leaning back into the slope of round Dol Baran, the last hill of the northern ranges, greenfooted, crowned with heather. The sides of the glen were shaggy with last year's bracken, among which the tight-curled fronds of spring were just thrusting through the sweet-scented earth. Thornbushes grew thick upon the low banks, and under them they made their camp, two hours or so before the middle of the night. They lit a fire in a hollow, down among the roots of a spreading hawthorn, tall as a tree, writhen with age, but hale in every limb. Buds were swelling at each twig's tip.

Guards were set, two at a watch. The rest, after they had supped, wrapped themselves in a cloak and blanket and slept. The hobbits lay in a corner by themselves upon a pile of old bracken. Merry was sleepy, but Pippin now seemed curiously restless. The bracken cracked and rustled, as he twisted and turned.

'What's the matter?' asked Merry. 'Are you lying on an ant-hill?'

'No,' said Pippin, 'but I'm not comfortable. I wonder how long it is since I slept in a bed?'

Merry yawned. 'Work it out on your fingers!' he said. 'But you must know how long it is since we left Lórien.'

'Oh, that!' said Pippin. 'I mean a real bed in a bedroom.'

'Well, Rivendell then,' said Merry. 'But I could sleep anywhere tonight.'

'You had the luck, Merry,' said Pippin softly, after a pause. 'You were riding with Gandalf.'

'Well, what of it?'

'Did you get any news, any information out of him?'

'Yes, a good deal. More than usual. But you heard it all or most of it; you were close by, and we were talking no secrets. But you can go with him tomorrow, if you think you can get more out of him—and if he'll have you.'

'Can I? Good! But he's close, isn't he? Not changed at all.'

'Oh yes, he is!' said Merry, waking up a little, and beginning to wonder what was bothering his companion. 'He has grown, or something. He can be both kinder and more alarming, merrier and more solemn than before, I think. He has changed; but we have not had a chance to see how much, yet. But think of the last part of that business with Saruman! Remember Saruman was once Gandalf's superior: head of the Council, whatever that may be exactly. He was Saruman the White. Gandalf is the White now. Saruman came when he was told, and his rod was taken; and then he was just told to go, and he went!'

'Well, if Gandalf has changed at all, then he's closer than ever that's all,' Pippin argued. 'That—glass ball, now. He seemed mighty pleased with it. He knows or guesses something about it. But does he tell us what? No, not a word. Yet I picked it up, and I saved it from rolling into a pool. *Here, I'll take that, my lad*—that's all. I wonder what it is? It felt so very heavy.' Pippin's voice fell very low as if he was talking to himself.

'Hullo!' said Merry. 'So that's what is bothering you? Now, Pippin my lad, don't forget Gildor's saying—the one Sam used to quote: *Do not meddle in the affairs of wizards, for they are subtle and quick to anger.*'

'But our whole life for months has been one long meddling in the affairs of wizards,' said Pippin. 'I should like a

bit of information as well as danger. I should like a look
at that ball.'

'Go to sleep!' said Merry. 'You'll get information
enough, sooner or later. My dear Pippin, no Took ever
beat a Brandybuck for inquisitiveness; but is this the
time, I ask you?'

'All right! What's the harm in my telling you what I
should like: a look at that stone? I know I can't have it,
with old Gandalf sitting on it, like a hen on an egg. But it
doesn't help much to get no more from you than a
you-can't-have-it-so-go-to-sleep!'

'Well, what else could I say?' said Merry. 'I'm sorry,
Pippin, but you really must wait till the morning. I'll be as
curious as you like after breakfast, and I'll help in any
way I can at wizard-wheedling. But I can't keep awake
any longer. If I yawn any more, I shall split at the ears.
Good night!'

Pippin said no more. He lay still now, but sleep remained far away; and it was not encouraged by the sound
of Merry breathing softly, asleep in a few minutes after
saying good night. The thought of the dark globe seemed
to grow stronger as all grew quiet. Pippin felt again its
weight in his hands, and saw again the mysterious red
depths into which he had looked for a moment. He tossed
and turned and tried to think of something else.

At last he could stand it no longer. He got up and
looked round. It was chilly, and he wrapped his cloak
about him. The moon was shining cold and white, down
into the dell, and the shadows of the bushes were black.
All about lay sleeping shapes. The two guards were not in
view: they were up on the hill, perhaps, or hidden in the
bracken. Driven by some impulse that he did not understand, Pippin walked softly to where Gandalf lay. He
looked down at him. The wizard seemed asleep, but with
lids not fully closed: there was a glitter of eyes under his
long lashes. Pippin stepped back hastily. But Gandalf
made no sign; and drawn forward once more, half against
his will, the hobbit crept up again from behind the wizard's

head. He was rolled in a blanket, with his cloak spread
over the top; and close beside him, between his right side
and his bent arm, there was a hummock, something round
wrapped in a dark cloth; his hand seemed only just to have
slipped off it to the ground.

Hardly breathing, Pippin crept nearer, foot by foot. At
last he knelt down. Then he put his hands out stealthily,
and slowly lifted the lump up: it did not seem quite so
heavy as he had expected. 'Only some bundle of oddments,
perhaps, after all,' he thought with a strange sense of relief;
but he did not put the bundle down again. He stood for a
moment clasping it. Then an idea came into his mind. He
tiptoed away, found a large stone, and came back.

Quickly now he drew off the cloth, wrapped the stone
in it and kneeling down, laid it back by the wizard's hand.
Then at last he looked at the thing that he had uncovered.
There it was: a smooth globe of crystal, now dark and
dead, lying bare before his knees. Pippin lifted it, covered
it hurriedly in his own cloak, and half turned to go back
to his bed. At that moment Gandalf moved in his sleep,
and muttered some words: they seemed to be in a strange
tongue; his hand groped out and clasped the wrapped
stone, then he sighed and did not move again.

'You idiotic fool!' Pippin muttered to himself. 'You're
going to get yourself into frightful trouble. Put it back
quick!' But he found now that his knees quaked, and he
did not dare to go near enough to the wizard to reach the
bundle. 'I'll never get it back now without waking him,' he
thought, 'not till I'm a bit calmer. So I may as well have a
look first. Not just here though!' He stole away, and sat
down on a green hillock not far from his bed. The moon
looked in over the edge of the dell.

Pippin sat with his knees drawn up and the ball between them. He bent low over it, looking like a greedy
child stooping over a bowl of food, in a corner away from
others. He drew his cloak aside and gazed at it. The air
seemed still and tense about him. At first the globe was
dark, black as jet, with the moonlight gleaming on its surface. Then there came a faint glow and stir in the heart

of it, and it held his eyes, so that now he could not look
away. Soon all the inside seemed on fire; the ball was
spinning, or the lights within were revolving. Suddenly the
lights went out. He gave a gasp and struggled; but he remained bent, clasping the ball with both hands. Closer and
closer he bent, and then became rigid; his lips moved
soundlessly for a while. Then with a strangled cry he fell
back and lay still.

The cry was piercing. The guards leapt down from the
banks. All the camp was soon astir.

'So this is the thief!' said Gandalf. Hastily he cast his
cloak over the globe where it lay. 'But you, Pippin! This is
a grievous turn to things!' He knelt by Pippin's body: the
hobbit was lying on his back, rigid, with unseeing eyes
staring up at the sky. 'The devilry! What mischief has he
done—to himself, and to all of us?' The wizard's face
was drawn and haggard.

He took Pippin's hand and bent over his face, listening
for his breath; then he laid his hands on his brow. The
hobbit shuddered. His eyes closed. He cried out; and sat
up, staring in bewilderment at all the faces round him,
pale in the moonlight.

'It is not for you, Saruman!' he cried in a shrill and
toneless voice, shrinking away from Gandalf. 'I will send
for it at once. Do you understand? Say just that!' Then
he struggled to get up and escape, but Gandalf held him
gently and firmly.

'Peregrin Took!' he said. 'Come back!'

The hobbit relaxed and fell back, clinging to the wizard's hand. 'Gandalf!' he cried. 'Gandalf! Forgive me!'

'Forgive you?' said the wizard. 'Tell me first what you
have done!'

'I, I took the ball and looked at it,' stammered Pippin;
'and I saw things that frightened me. And I wanted to go
away, but I couldn't. And then he came and questioned
me; and he looked at me, and, and, and that is all I remember.'

'That won't do,' said Gandalf sternly. 'What did you
see, and what did you say?'

Pippin shut his eyes and shivered, but said nothing. They all stared at him in silence, except Merry who turned away. But Gandalf's face was still hard. 'Speak!' he said.

In a low hesitating voice Pippin began again, and slowly his words grew clearer and stronger. 'I saw a dark sky, and tall battlements,' he said. 'And tiny stars. It seemed very far away and long ago, yet hard and clear. Then the stars went in and out—they were cut off by things with wings. Very big, I think, really; but in the glass they looked like bats wheeling round the tower. I thought there were nine of them. One began to fly straight towards me, getting bigger and bigger. It had a horrible—no, no! I can't say.

'I tried to get away, because I thought it would fly out; but when it had covered all the globe, it disappeared. Then *he* came. He did not speak so that I could hear words. He just looked, and I understood.

' "So you have come back? Why have you neglected to report for so long?"

'I did not answer. He said: "Who are you?" I still did not answer, but it hurt me horribly; and he pressed me, so I said: "A hobbit."

'Then suddenly he seemed to see me, and he laughed at me. It was cruel. It was like being stabbed with knives. I struggled. But he said: "Wait a moment! We shall meet again soon. Tell Saruman that this dainty is not for him. I will send for it at once. Do you understand? Say just that!"

'Then he gloated over me. I felt I was falling to pieces. No, no! I can't say any more. I don't remember anything else.'

'Look at me!' said Gandalf.

Pippin looked up straight into his eyes. The wizard held his gaze for a moment in silence. Then his face grew gentler, and the shadow of a smile appeared. He laid his hand softly on Pippin's head.

'All right!' he said. 'Say no more! You have taken no harm. There is no lie in your eyes, as I feared. But he did not speak long with you. A fool, but an honest fool,

you remain, Peregrin Took. Wiser ones might have done
worse in such a pass. But mark this! You have been saved,
and all your friends too, mainly by good fortune, as it is
called. You cannot count on it a second time. If he had
questioned you, then and there, almost certainly you would
have told all that you know, to the ruin of us all. But he
was too eager. He did not want information only: he
wanted *you,* quickly, so that he could deal with you in the
Dark Tower, slowly. Don't shudder! If you will meddle
in the affairs of wizards, you must be prepared to think of
such things. But come! I forgive you. Be comforted!
Things have not turned out as evilly as they might.'

He lifted Pippin gently and carried him back to his bed.
Merry followed, and sat down beside him. 'Lie there and
rest, if you can, Pippin!' said Gandalf. 'Trust me. If you
feel an itch in your palms again, tell me of it! Such
things can be cured. But anyway, my dear hobbit, don't
put a lump of rock under my elbow again! Now, I will
leave you two together for a while.'

With that Gandalf returned to the others, who were still
standing by the Orthanc-stone in troubled thought. 'Peril
comes in the night when least expected,' he said. 'We
have had a narrow escape!'

'How is the hobbit, Pippin?' asked Aragorn.

'I think all will be well now,' answered Gandalf. 'He
was not held long, and hobbits have an amazing power of
recovery. The memory, or the horror of it, will probably
fade quickly. Too quickly, perhaps. Will you, Aragorn,
take the Orthanc-stone and guard it? It is a dangerous
charge.'

'Dangerous indeed, but not to all,' said Aragorn. 'There
is one who may claim it by right. For this assuredly is the
palantír of Orthanc from the treasury of Elendil, set here
by the Kings of Gondor. Now my hour draws near. I will
take it.'

Gandalf looked at Aragorn, and then, to the surprise
of the others, he lifted the covered stone, and bowed as he
presented it.

'Receive it, lord!' he said: 'in earnest of other things that shall be given back. But if I may counsel you in the use of your own, do not use it—yet! Be wary!'

'When have I been hasty or unwary, who have waited and prepared for so many long years?' said Aragorn.

'Never yet. Do not then stumble at the end of the road,' answered Gandalf. 'But at the least keep this thing secret. You, and all others that stand here! The hobbit, Peregrin, above all should not know where it is bestowed. The evil fit may come on him again. For alas! he has handled it and looked in it, as should never have happened. He ought never to have touched it in Isengard, and there I should have been quicker. But my mind was bent on Saruman, and I did not guess the nature of the stone, until it was too late. Only now have I become sure of it.'

'Yes, there can be no doubt,' said Aragorn. 'At last we know the link between Isengard and Mordor, and how it worked. Much is explained.'

'Strange powers have our enemies, and strange weaknesses!' said Théoden. 'But it has long been said: *oft evil will shall evil mar.*'

'That many times is seen,' said Gandalf. 'But at this time we have been strangely fortunate. Maybe, I have been saved by this hobbit from a grave blunder. I had considered whether or not to probe this stone myself to find its uses. Had I done so, I should have been revealed to him myself. I am not ready for such a trial, if indeed I shall ever be so. But even if I found the power to withdraw myself, it would be disastrous for him to see me, yet —until the hour comes when secrecy will avail no longer.'

'That hour is now come, I think,' said Aragorn.

'Not yet,' said Gandalf. 'There remains a short while of doubt, which we must use. The Enemy, it is clear, thought that the stone was in Orthanc—why should he not? And that therefore the hobbit was captive there, driven to look in the glass for his torment by Saruman. That dark mind will be filled now with the voice and face of the hobbit and with expectation: it may take some time before he learns his error. We must snatch that time. We have been too leisurely. We must move. The neighbourhood of Isengard is no place now to linger in. I will ride ahead at once with Peregrin Took. It will be better for him than lying in the dark while others sleep.'

'I will keep Éomer and ten Riders,' said the king. 'They shall ride with me at early day. The rest may go with Aragorn and ride as soon as they have a mind.'

'As you will,' said Gandalf. 'But make all the speed you may to the cover of the hills, to Helm's Deep!'

At that moment a shadow fell over them. The bright moonlight seemed to be suddenly cut off. Several of the Riders cried out, and crouched, holding their arms above their heads, as if to ward off a blow from above: a blind fear and a deadly cold fell on them. Cowering they looked up. A vast winged shape passed over the moon like a black cloud. It wheeled and went north, flying at a speed greater than any wind of Middle-earth. The stars fainted before it. It was gone.

They stood up, rigid as stones. Gandalf was gazing up, his arms out and downwards, stiff, his hands clenched.

'Nazgûl!' he cried. 'The messenger of Mordor. The storm is coming. The Nazgûl have crossed the River! Ride, ride! Wait not for the dawn! Let not the swift wait for the slow! Ride!'

He sprang away, calling Shadowfax as he ran. Aragorn followed him. Going to Pippin, Gandalf picked him up in his arms. 'You shall come with me this time,' he said. 'Shadowfax shall show you his paces.' Then he ran to the place where he had slept. Shadowfax stood there already. Slinging the small bag which was all his luggage across his shoulders, the wizard leapt upon the horse's back. Aragorn lifted Pippin and set him in Gandalf's arms, wrapped in cloak and blanket.

'Farewell! Follow fast!' cried Gandalf. 'Away, Shadowfax!'

The great horse tossed his head. His flowing tail flicked in the moonlight. Then he leapt forward, spurning the earth, and was gone like the north wind from the mountains.

'A beautiful, restful night!' said Merry to Aragorn.
'Some folk have wonderful luck. He did not want to
sleep, and he wanted to ride with Gandalf—and there he
goes! Instead of being turned into a stone himself to stand
here forever as a warning.'

'If you had been the first to lift the Orthanc-stone, and
not he, how would it be now?' said Aragorn. 'You might
have done worse. Who can say? But now it is your luck
to come with me, I fear. At once. Go and get ready, and
bring anything that Pippin left behind. Make haste!'

Over the plains Shadowfax was flying, needing no urging and no guidance. Less than an hour had passed, and
they had reached the Fords of Isen and crossed them. The
Mound of the Riders and its cold spears lay grey behind
them.

Pippin was recovering. He was warm, but the wind in
his face was keen and refreshing. He was with Gandalf.
The horror of the stone and of the hideous shadow over
the moon was fading, things left behind in the mists of the
mountains or in a passing dream. He drew a deep breath.

'I did not know you rode bare-back, Gandalf,' he said.
'You haven't a saddle or a bridle!'

'I do not ride elf-fashion, except on Shadowfax,' said
Gandalf. 'But Shadowfax wiil have no harness. You do
not ride Shadowfax: he is willing to carry you—or not.
If he is willing, that is enough. It is then his business
to see that you remain on his back, unless you jump off
into the air.'

'How fast is he going?' asked Pippin. 'Fast by the wind,
but very smooth. And how light his footfalls are!'

'He is running now as fast as the swiftest horse could
gallop,' answered Gandalf; 'but that is not fast for him.
The land is rising a little here, and is more broken than
it was beyond the river. But see how the White Mountains
are drawing near under the stars! Yonder are the Thri-

hyrne peaks like black spears. It will not be long before we reach the branching roads and come to the Deeping Coomb, where the battle was fought two nights ago.'

Pippin was silent again for a while. He heard Gandalf singing softly to himself, murmuring brief snatches of rhyme in many tongues, as the miles ran under them. At last the wizard passed into a song of which the hobbit caught the words: a few lines came clear to his ears through the rushing of the wind:

> Tall ships and tall kings
> Three times three,
> What brought they from the foundered land
> Over the flowing sea?
> Seven stars and seven stones
> And one white tree.

'What are you saying, Gandalf?' asked Pippin.

'I was just running over some of the Rhymes of Lore in my mind,' answered the wizard. 'Hobbits, I suppose, have forgotten them, even those that they ever knew.'

'No, not all,' said Pippin. 'And we have many of our own, which wouldn't interest you, perhaps. But I have never heard this one. What is it about—the seven stars and seven stones?'

'About the *Palantíri* of the Kings of Old,' said Gandalf.

'And what are they?'

'The name meant *that which looks far away*. The Orthanc-stone was one.'

'Then it was made, not made'—Pippin hesitated—'by the Enemy?'

'No,' said Gandalf. 'Nor by Saruman. It is beyond his art, and beyond Sauron's too. The *palantíri* come from beyond Westernesse, from Eldamar. The Noldor made them. Fëanor himself, maybe, wrought them, in days so long ago that the time cannot be measured in years. But there is nothing that Sauron cannot turn to evil uses. Alas for Saruman! It was his downfall, as I now perceive. Perilous to us all are the devices of an art deeper than we possess ourselves. Yet he must bear the blame. Fool! to keep it secret, for his own profit. No word did he ever speak of it to any of the Council. It was not known to us that any of the *palantíri* had escaped the ruin of Gondor. Outside the Council it was not even remembered among Elves or Men that such things had ever been, save only in a Rhyme of Lore preserved among Aragorn's folk.'

'What did the Men of old use them for?' asked Pippin, delighted and astonished at getting answers to so many questions, and wondering how long it would last.

'To see far off, and to converse in thought with one another,' said Gandalf. 'In that way they long guarded and united the realm of Gondor. They set up stones at Minas Anor, and at Minas Ithil, and at Orthanc in the ring of Isengard. The chief and master of these was under the Dome of Stars at Osgiliath before its ruin. The others were far away. Few now know where, for no rhyme says. But in the House of Elrod it is told that they were at Annúminas, and Amon Sûl, and on the Tower Hills that look towards Mithlond in the Gulf of Lune where the grey ships lie.

'Each *palantír* spoke to each, but at Osgiliath they could survey them all together at one time. Now it appears that, as the rock of Orthanc has withstood the storms of time, so there the *palantír* of that tower has remained. But alone it could do nothing but see small images of things far off and days remote. Very useful, no doubt, that was to Saruman; yet it seems that he was not content. Further and further abroad he gazed, until he cast his gaze upon Barad-dûr. Then he was caught!

'Who knows where all those other stones now lie, broken, or buried, or drowned deep? But one at least Sauron must have obtained and mastered to his purposes. I guess that it was the Ithilstone, for he took Minas Ithil long ago and turned it into an evil place: Minas Morgul, it has become.

'Easy it is now to guess how quickly the roving eye of Saruman was trapped and held; and how ever since he has been persuaded from afar, and daunted when persuasion would not serve. The biter bit, the hawk under the eagle's foot, the spider in a steel web! How long, I wonder, has he been constrained to come often to his glass for inspection and instruction, and the Orthanc-stone so bent towards Barad-dûr that, if any save a will of adamant now looks into it, it will bear his mind and sight swiftly thither? And how it draws one to itself! Have I not felt it? Even now my heart desires to test my will upon it, to see if I could not wrench it from him and turn it where I would—to look across the wide seas of water and of time to Tirion the Fair, and perceive the unimaginable hand and mind of Fëanor at their work, while both the White Tree and the Golden were in flower!' He sighed and fell silent.

'I wish I had known all this before,' said Pippin. 'I had no notion of what I was doing.'

'Oh yes, you had,' said Gandalf. 'You knew you were behaving wrongly and foolishly; and you told yourself so, though you did not listen. I did not tell you all this before, because it is only by musing on all that has happened that I have at last understood, even as we ride together. But if I had spoken sooner, it would not have lessened your desire, or made it easier to resist. On the contrary! No, the burned hand teaches best. After that advice about fire goes to the heart.'

'It does,' said Pippin. 'If all the seven stones were laid out before me now, I should shut my eyes and put my hands in my pockets.'

'Good!' said Gandalf. 'That is what I hoped.'

'But I should like to know—' Pippin began.

'Mercy!' cried Gandalf. 'If the giving of information is to be the cure of your inquisitiveness, I shall spend all the rest of my days in answering you. What more do you want to know?'

'The names of all the stars, and of all living things, and the whole history of Middle-earth and Over-heaven and of the Sundering Seas,' laughed Pippin. 'Of course! What less? But I am not in a hurry tonight. At the moment I was just wondering about the black shadow. I heard you shout "messenger of Mordor". What was it? What could it do at Isengard?'

'It was a Black Rider on wings, a Nazgûl,' said Gandalf. 'It could have taken you away to the Dark Tower.'

'But it was not coming for me, was it?' faltered Pippin. 'I mean, it didn't know that I had. . . .'

'Of course not,' said Gandalf. 'It is two hundred leagues or more in straight flight from Barad-dûr to Orthanc, and even a Nazgûl would take a few hours to fly between them. But Saruman certainly looked in the stone since the orc-raid, and more of his secret thought, I do not doubt, has been read than he intended. A messenger has been sent to find out what he is doing. And after what has happened tonight another will come, I think, and swiftly. So Saruman will come to the last pinch of the vice that he has put his hand in. He has no captive to send. He has no stone to see with, and cannot answer the summons. Sauron will only believe that he is withholding the captive and refusing to use the stone. It will not help Saruman to tell the truth to the messenger. For Isengard may be ruined, yet he is still safe in Orthanc. So whether he will or no, he will appear a rebel. Yet he rejected us, so as to avoid that very thing! What he will do in such a plight, I cannot guess. He has power still, I think, while in Orthanc, to resist the Nine Riders. He may try to do so. He may try to trap the Nazgûl, or at least to slay the thing on which it now rides the air. In that case let Rohan look to its horses!

'But I cannot tell how it will fall out, well or ill for us. It may be that the counsels of the Enemy will be confused, or hindered by his wrath with Saruman. It may be that he will learn that I was there and stood upon the stairs of Orthanc—with hobbits at my tail. Or that an heir of Elendil lives and stood beside me. If Wormtongue was not deceived by the armour of Rohan, he would remember Aragorn and the title that he claimed. That is what I fear. And so we fly—not from danger but into greater danger. Every stride of Shadowfax bears you nearer to the Land of Shadow, Peregrin Took.'

Pippin made no answer, but clutched his cloak, as if a sudden chill had struck him. Grey land passed under them.

'See now!' said Gandalf. 'The Westfold dales are opening before us. Here we come back to the eastward road. The dark shadow yonder is the mouth of the Deeping Coomb. That way lies Aglarond and the Glittering Caves. Do not ask me about them. Ask Gimli, if you meet again, and for the first time you may get an answer longer than you wish. You will not see the caves yourself, not on this journey. Soon they will be far behind.'

'I thought you were going to stop at Helm's Deep!' said Pippin. 'Where are you going then?'

'To Minas Tirith, before the seas of war surround it.'

'Oh! And how far is that?'

'Leagues upon leagues,' answered Gandalf. 'Thrice as far as the dwellings of King Théoden, and they are more than a hundred miles east from here, as the messengers of Mordor fly. Shadowfax must run a longer road. Which will prove the swifter?

'We shall ride now till daybreak, and that is some hours away. Then even Shadowfax must rest, in some hollow of the hills: at Edoras, I hope. Sleep, if you can! You may see the first glimmer of dawn upon the golden roof of the House of Eorl. And in two days thence you shall see the purple shadow of Mount Mindolluin and the walls of the tower of Denethor white in the morning.

'Away now, Shadowfax! Run, greatheart, run as you have never run before! Now we are come to the lands where you were foaled, and every stone you know. Run now! Hope is in speed!'

Shadowfax tossed his head and cried aloud, as if a trumpet had summoned him to battle. Then he sprang forward. Fire flew from his feet; night rushed over him.

As he fell slowly into sleep, Pippin had a strange feeling: he and Gandalf were still as stone, seated upon the statue of a running horse, while the world rolled away beneath his feet with a great noise of wind.

BOOK IV

Chapter 1

The Taming of Sméagol

'Well, master, we're in a fix and no mistake,' said Sam Gamgee. He stood despondently with hunched shoulders beside Frodo, and peered out with puckered eyes into the gloom.

It was the third evening since they had fled from the Company, as far as they could tell: they had almost lost count of the hours during which they had climbed and laboured among the barren slopes and stones of the Emyn Muil, sometimes retracing their steps because they could find no way forward, sometimes discovering that they had wandered in a circle back to where they had been hours before. Yet on the whole they had worked steadily eastward, keeping as near as they could find a way to the outer edge of this strange twisted knot of hills. But always they found its outward faces sheer, high and impassable, frowning over the plain below; beyond its tumbled skirts lay livid festering marshes where nothing moved and not even a bird was to be seen.

The hobbits stood now on the brink of a tall cliff, bare and bleak, its feet wrapped in mist; and behind them rose the broken highlands crowned with drifting cloud. A chill wind blew from the East. Night was gathering over the shapeless lands before them; the sickly green of them was fading to a sullen brown. Far away to the right the Anduin, that had gleamed fitfully in sun-breaks during the day, was now hidden in shadow. But their eyes did not look beyond the River, back to Gondor, to their friends, to the lands of Men. South and east they stared to where, at the edge of the oncoming night, a dark line hung, like distant mountains of motionless smoke. Every now and again a tiny red gleam far away flickered upwards on the rim of earth and sky.

'What a fix!' said Sam. 'That's the one place in all the

lands we've ever heard of that we don't want to see any closer; and that's the one place we're trying to get to! And that's just where we can't get, nohow. We've come the wrong way altogether, seemingly. We can't get down; and if we did get down, we'd find all that green land a nasty bog, I'll warrant. Phew! Can you smell it?' He sniffed at the wind.

'Yes, I can smell it,' said Frodo, but he did not move, and his eyes remained fixed, staring out towards the dark line and the flickering flame. 'Mordor!' he muttered under his breath. 'If I must go there, I wish I could come there quickly and make an end!' He shuddered. The wind was chilly and yet heavy with an odour of cold decay. 'Well,' he said, at last withdrawing his eyes, 'we cannot stay here all night, fix or no fix. We must find a more sheltered spot, and camp once more; and perhaps another day will show us a path.'

'Or another and another and another,' muttered Sam. 'Or maybe no day. We've come the wrong way.'

'I wonder,' said Frodo. 'It's my doom, I think, to go to that Shadow yonder, so that a way will be found. But will good or evil show it to me? What hope we had was in speed. Delay plays into the Enemy's hands—and here I am: delayed. Is it the will of the Dark Tower that steers us? All my choices have proved ill. I should have left the Company long before, and come down from the North, east of the River and of the Emyn Muil, and so over the hard of Battle Plain to the passes of Mordor. But now it isn't possible for you and me alone to find a way back, and the Orcs are prowling on the east bank. Every day that passes is a precious day lost. I am tired, Sam. I don't know what is to be done. What food have we got left?'

'Only those, what d'you call 'em, *lembas*, Mr. Frodo. A fair supply, But they are better than naught, by a long bite. I never thought, though, when I first set tooth in them, that I should ever come to wish for a change. But I do now: a bit of plain bread, and a mug—aye, half a mug—of beer would go down proper. I've lugged my cooking-gear all the way from the last camp, and what use has it been? Naught to make a fire with, for a start; and naught to cook not even grass!'

They turned away and went down into a stony hollow. The westering sun was caught into clouds, and night came swiftly. They slept as well as they could for the cold, turn and turn about, in a nook among great jagged pinnacles of weathered rock; at least they were sheltered from the easterly wind.

'Did you see them again, Mr. Frodo?' asked Sam, as they sat, stiff and chilled, munching wafers of *lembas,* in the cold grey of early morning.

'No,' said Frodo. 'I've heard nothing, and seen nothing, for two nights now.'

'Nor me,' said Sam. 'Grrr! Those eyes did give me a turn! But perhaps we've shaken him off at last, the miserable slinker. Gollum! I'll give him *gollum* in his throat, if ever I get my hands on his neck.'

'I hope you'll never need to,' said Frodo. 'I don't know how he followed us; but it may be that he's lost us again, as you say. In this dry bleak land we can't leave many footprints, nor much scent, even for his snuffling nose.'

'I hope that's the way of it,' said Sam. 'I wish we could be rid of him for good!'

'So do I,' said Frodo; 'but he's not my chief trouble. I wish we could get away from these hills! I hate them. I feel all naked on the east side, stuck up here with nothing but the dead flats between me and that Shadow yonder. There's an Eye in it. Come on! We've got to get down to-day somehow.'

But that day wore on, and when afternoon faded towards evening they were still scrambling along the ridge and had found no way of escape.

Sometimes in the silence of that barren country they fancied that they heard faint sounds behind them, a stone falling, or the imagined step of flapping feet on the rock. But if they halted and stood still listening, they heard no more, nothing but the wind sighing over the edges of the stones—yet even that reminded them of breath softly hissing through sharp teeth.

All that day the outer ridge of the Emyn Muil had been bending gradually northward, as they struggled on. Along its brink there now stretched a wide tumbled flat of scored and weathered rock, cut every now and again by trench-like gullies that sloped steeply down to deep notches in the cliff-face. To find a path in these clefts, which were becoming deeper and more frequent, Frodo and Sam were driven to their left, well away from the edge, and they did not notice that for several miles they had been going slowly but steadily downhill: the cliff-top was sinking towards the level of the lowlands.

At last they were brought to a halt. The ridge took a sharper bend northward and was gashed by a deeper ravine. On the further side it reared up again, many fathoms at a single leap: a great grey cliff loomed before them, cut sheer down as if by a knife stroke. They could go no further forwards, and must turn now either west or east. But west would lead them only into more labour and delay, back towards the heart of the hills; east would take them to the outer precipice.

'There's nothing for it but to scramble down this gully, Sam,' said Frodo. 'Let's see what it leads to!'

'A nasty drop, I'll bet,' said Sam.

The cleft was longer and deeper than it seemed. Some way down they found a few gnarled and stunted trees, the first they had seen for days: twisted birch for the most part, with here and there a fir-tree. Many were dead and gaunt, bitten to the core by the eastern winds. Once in milder days there must have been a fair thicket in the ravine, but now, after some fifty yards, the trees came to an end, though old broken stumps straggled on almost to the cliff's brink. The bottom of the gully, which lay along the edge of a rock-fault, was rough with broken stone and slanted steeply down. When they came at last to the end of it, Frodo stooped and leaned out.

'Look!' he said. 'We must have come down a long way,

or else the cliff has sunk. It's much lower here than it was, and it looks easier too.'

Sam knelt beside him and peered reluctantly over the edge. Then he glanced up at the great cliff rising up, away on their left. 'Easier!' he grunted. 'Well, I suppose it's always easier getting down than up. Those as can't fly can jump!'

'It would be a big jump still,' said Frodo. 'About, well' —he stood for a moment measuring it with his eyes— 'about eighteen fathoms, I should guess. Not more.'

'And that's enough!' said Sam. 'Ugh! How I do hate looking down from a height! But looking's better than climbing.'

'All the same,' said Frodo, 'I think we could climb here; and I think we shall have to try. See—the rock is quite different from what it was a few miles back. It has slipped and cracked.'

The outer fall was indeed no longer sheer, but sloped outwards a little. It looked like a great rampart or sea-wall whose foundations had shifted, so that its courses were all twisted and disordered, leaving great fissures and long slanting edges that were in places almost as wide as stairs.

'And if we're going to try and get down, we had better try at once. It's getting dark early. I think there's a storm coming.'

The smoky blur of the mountains in the East was lost in a deeper blackness that was already reaching out westwards with long arms. There was a distant mutter of thunder borne on the rising breeze. Frodo sniffed the air and looked up doubtfully at the sky. He strapped his belt outside his cloak and tightened it, and settled his light pack on his back; then he stepped towards the edge. 'I'm going to try it,' he said.

'Very good!' said Sam gloomily. 'But I'm going first.'

'You?' said Frodo. 'What's made you change your mind about climbing?'

'I haven't changed my mind. But it's only sense: put the one lowest as is most likely to slip. I don't want to come down atop of you and knock you off—no sense in killing two with one fall.'

Before Frodo could stop him, he sat down, swung his legs over the brink, and twisted round, scrabbling with his toes for a foothold. It is doubtful if he ever did anything braver in cold blood, or more unwise.

'No, no! Sam, you old ass!' said Frodo. 'You'll kill yourself for certain, going over like that without even a look to see what to make for. Come back!' He took Sam under the armpits and hauled him up again. 'Now, wait a bit and be patient!' he said. Then he lay on the ground, leaning out and looking down; but the light seemed to be fading quickly, although the sun had not yet set. 'I think we could manage this,' he said presently. 'I could at any rate; and you could too, if you kept your head and followed me carefully.'

'I don't know how you can be so sure,' said Sam. 'Why! You can't see to the bottom in this light. What if you comes to a place where there's nowhere to put your feet or your hands?'

'Climb back, I suppose,' said Frodo.

'Easy said,' objected Sam. 'Better wait till morning and more light.'

'No! Not if I can help it,' said Frodo with a sudden strange vehemence. 'I grudge every hour, every minute. I'm going down to try it out. Don't you follow till I come back or call!'

Gripping the stony lip of the fall with his fingers he let himself gently down, until when his arms were almost at full stretch, his toes found a ledge. 'One step down!' he said. 'And this ledge broadens out to the right. I could stand there without a hold. I'll——' his words were cut short.

The hurrying darkness, now gathering great speed, rushed up from the East and swallowed the sky. There was a dry splitting crack of thunder right overhead. Searing lightning smote down into the hills. Then came a blast of savage wind, and with it, mingling with its roar, there came a high shrill shriek. The hobbits had heard just such a cry far away in the Marish as they fled from Hobbiton, and even there in the woods of the Shire it had frozen their blood. Out here in the waste its terror was far greater: it pierced them with cold blades of horror and despair, stopping heart and breath. Sam fell flat on his face. Involuntarily Frodo loosed his hold and put his hands over his head and ears. He swayed, slipped, and slithered downwards with a wailing cry.

Sam heard him and crawled with an effort to the edge. 'Master, master!' he called. 'Master!'

He heard no answer. He found he was shaking all over, but he gathered his breath, and once again he shouted: 'Master!' The wind seemed to blow his voice back into his throat, but as it passed, roaring up the gully and away over the hills, a faint answering cry came to his ears:

'All right, all right! I'm here. But I can't see.'

Frodo was calling with a weak voice. He was not actually very far away. He had slid and not fallen, and had come up with a jolt to his feet on a wider ledge not many yards lower down. Fortunately the rock-face at this point leaned well back and the wind had pressed him against the cliff, so that he had not toppled over. He steadied himself a little, laying his face against the cold stone, feeling his heart pounding. But either the darkness had grown complete, or else his eyes had lost their sight. All was black about him. He wondered if he had been struck blind. He took a deep breath.

'Come back! Come back!' he heard Sam's voice out of the blackness above.

'I can't,' he said. 'I can't see. I can't find any hold. I can't move yet.'

'What can I do, Mr. Frodo? What can I do?' shouted Sam, leaning out dangerously far. Why could not his master see? It was dim, certainly, but not as dark as all that. He could see Frodo below him, a grey forlorn figure splayed against the cliff. But he was far out of the reach of any helping hand.

There was another crack of thunder; and then the rain

came. In a blinding sheet, mingled with hail, it drove against the cliff, bitter cold.

'I'm coming down to you,' shouted Sam, though how he hoped to help in that way he could not have said.

'No, no! Wait!' Frodo called back, more strongly now. 'I shall be better soon. I feel better already. Wait! You can't do anything without a rope.'

'Rope!' cried Sam, talking wildly to himself in his excitement and relief. 'Well, if I don't deserve to be hung on the end of one as a warning to numbskulls! You're nowt but a ninnyhammer, Sam Gamgee: that's what the Gaffer said to me often enough, it being a word of his. Rope!'

'Stop chattering!' cried Frodo, now recovered enough to feel both amused and annoyed. 'Never mind your Gaffer! Are you trying to tell yourself you've got some rope in your pocket? If so, out with it!'

'Yes, Mr. Frodo, in my pack and all. Carried it hundreds of miles, and I'd clean forgotten it!'

'Then get busy and let an end down!'

Quickly Sam unslung his pack and rummaged in it. There indeed at the bottom was a coil of the silken-grey rope made by the folk of Lórien. He cast an end to his master. The darkness seemed to lift from Frodo's eyes, or else his sight was returning. He could see the grey line as it came dangling down, and he thought it had a faint silver sheen. Now that he had some point in the darkness to fix his eyes on, he felt less giddy. Leaning his weight forward, he made the end fast round his waist, and then he grasped the line with both hands.

Sam stepped back and braced his feet against a stump a yard or two from the edge. Half hauled, half scrambling, Frodo came up and threw himself on the ground.

Thunder growled and rumbled in the distance, and the rain was still falling heavily. The hobbits crawled away back into the gully; but they did not find much shelter there. Rills of water began to run down; soon they grew to a spate that splashed and fumed on the stones, and spouted out over the cliff like the gutters of a vast roof.

'I should have been half drowned down there, or washed

clean off,' said Frodo. 'What a piece of luck you had that rope!'

'Better luck if I'd thought of it sooner,' said Sam. 'Maybe you remember them putting the ropes in the boats, as we started off: in the elvish country. I took a fancy to it, and I stowed a coil in my pack. Years ago, it seems. "It may be a help in many needs," he said: Haldir, or one of those folk. And he spoke right.'

'A pity I didn't think of bringing another length,' said Frodo; 'but I left the Company in such a hurry and confusion. If only we had enough we could use it to get down. How long is your rope, I wonder?'

Sam paid it out slowly, measuring it with his arms: 'Five, ten, twenty, thirty ells, more or less,' he said.

'Who'd have thought it!' Frodo exclaimed.

'Ah! Who would?' said Sam. 'Elves are wonderful folk. It looks a bit thin, but it's tough; and soft as milk to the hand. Packs close too, and as light as light. Wonderful folk to be sure!'

'Thirty ells!' said Frodo considering. 'I believe it would be enough. If the storm passes before nightfall, I'm going to try it.'

'The rain's nearly given over already,' said Sam, 'but don't you go doing anything risky in the dim again, Mr. Frodo! And I haven't got over that shriek on the wind yet, if you have. Like a Black Rider it sounded—but one up in the air, if they can fly. I'm thinking we'd best lay up in this crack till night's over.'

'And I'm thinking that I won't spend a moment longer than I need, stuck up on this edge with the eyes of the Dark Country looking over the marshes,' said Frodo.

With that he stood up and went down to the bottom of the gully again. He looked out. Clear sky was growing in the East once more. The skirts of the storm were lifting, ragged and wet, and the main battle had passed to spread its great wings over the Emyn Muil, upon which the dark thought of Sauron brooded for a while. Thence it turned, smiting the vale of Anduin with hail and lightning, and casting its shadows upon Minas Tirith with threat of war.

Then, lowering in the mountains, and gathering its great spires, it rolled on slowly over Gondor and the skirts of Rohan, until far away the Riders on the plain saw its black towers moving behind the sun, as they rode into the West. But here, over the desert and the reeking marshes the deep blue sky of evening opened once more, and a few pallid stars appeared, like small white holes in the canopy above the crescent moon.

'It's good to be able to see again,' said Frodo, breathing deep. 'Do you know, I thought for a bit that I had lost my sight? From the lightning or something else worse. I could see nothing, nothing at all, until the grey rope came down. It seemed to shimmer somehow.'

'It does look sort of silver in the dark,' said Sam. 'Never noticed it before, though I can't remember as I've ever had it out since I first stowed it. But if you're so set on climbing, Mr. Frodo, how are you going to use it? Thirty ells, or say, about eighteen fathom: that's no more than your guess at the height of the cliff.'

Frodo thought for a while. 'Make it fast to that stump, Sam!' he said. 'Then I think you shall have your wish this time and go first. I'll lower you, and you need do no more than use your feet and hands to fend yourself off the rock. Though, if you put your weight on some of the ledges and give me a rest, it will help. When you're down, I'll follow. I feel quite myself again now.'

'Very well,' said Sam heavily. 'If it must be, let's get it over!' He took up the rope and made it fast over the stump nearest to the brink; then the other end he tied about his own waist. Reluctantly he turned and prepared to go over the edge a second time.

It did not, however, turn out half as bad as he had expected. The rope seemed to give him confidence, though he shut his eyes more than once when he looked down between his feet. There was one awkward spot, where there was no ledge and the wall was sheer and even undercut for a short space; there he slipped and swung out on the silver line. But Frodo lowered him slowly and steadily,

and it was over at last. His chief fear had been that the
rope-length would give out while he was still high up,
but there was still a good bight in Frodo's hands, when
Sam came to the bottom and called up: 'I'm down!'
His voice came up clearly from below, but Frodo could
not see him; his grey elven-cloak had melted into the
twilight.

Frodo took rather more time to follow him. He had the
rope about his waist and it was fast above, and he had
shortened it so that it would pull him up before he
reached the ground; still he did not want to risk a fall,
and he had not quite Sam's faith in this slender grey line.
He found two places, all the same, where he had to
trust wholly to it: smooth surfaces where there was no hold
even for his strong hobbit fingers and the ledges were
far apart. But at last he too was down.

'Well!' he cried. 'We've done it! We've escaped from
the Emyn Muil! And now what next, I wonder? Maybe we
shall soon be sighing for good hard rock under foot again.'

But Sam did not answer: he was staring back up the
cliff. 'Ninnyhammers!' he said. 'Noodles! My beautiful
rope! There it is tied to a stump, and we're at the bottom.
Just as nice a little stair for that slinking Gollum as we
could leave. Better put up a signpost to say which way
we've gone! I thought it seemed a bit too easy.'

'If you can think of any way we could have both used
the rope and yet brought it down with us, then you can
pass on to me ninnyhammer, or any other name your
Gaffer gave you,' said Frodo. 'Climb up and untie it and
let yourself down, if you want to!'

Sam scratched his head. 'No, I can't think how, begging
your pardon,' he said. 'But I don't like leaving it, and
that's a fact.' He stroked the rope's end and shook it
gently. 'It goes hard parting with anything I brought out of
the elf-country. Made by Galadriel herself, too, maybe.
Galadriel,' he murmured, nodding his head mournfully.
He looked up and gave one last pull to the rope as if in
farewell.

To the complete surprise of both the hobbits it came

loose. Sam fell over, and the long grey coils slithered silently down on top of him. Frodo laughed. 'Who tied the rope?' he said. 'A good thing it held as long as it did! To think that I trusted all my weight to your knot!'

Sam did not laugh. 'I may not be much good at climbing, Mr. Frodo,' he said in injured tones, 'but I do know something about rope and about knots. It's in the family, as you might say. Why, my grand-dad, and my uncle Andy after him, him that was the Gaffer's eldest brother, he had a rope-walk over by Tighfield many a year. And I put as fast a hitch over the stump as any one could have done, in the Shire or out of it.'

'Then the rope must have broken—frayed on the rock-edge, I expect,' said Frodo.

'I bet it didn't!' said Sam in an even more injured voice. He stooped and examined the ends. 'Nor it hasn't neither. Not a strand!'

'Then I'm afraid it must have been the knot,' said Frodo.

Sam shook his head and did not answer. He was passing the rope through his fingers thoughtfully. 'Have it your own way, Mr. Frodo,' he said at last, 'but I think the rope came off itself—when I called.' He coiled it up and stowed it lovingly in his pack.

'It certainly came,' said Frodo, 'and that's the chief thing. But now we've got to think of our next move. Night will be on us soon. How beautiful the stars are, and the Moon!'

'They do cheer the heart, don't they?' said Sam looking up. 'Elvish they are, somehow. And the Moon's growing. We haven't seen him for a night or two in this cloudy weather. He's beginning to give quite a light.'

'Yes,' said Frodo; 'but he won't be full for some days. I don't think we'll try the marshes by the light of half a moon.'

Under the first shadows of night they started out on the next stage of their journey. After a while Sam turned and looked back at the way they had come. The mouth of the gully was a black notch in the dim cliff. 'I'm glad we've got the rope,' he said. 'We've set a little puzzle for that footpad, anyhow. He can try his nasty flappy feet on those ledges!'

They picked their steps away from the skirts of the cliff, among a wilderness of boulders and rough stones, wet and slippery with the heavy rain. The ground still fell away sharply. They had not gone very far when they came upon a great fissure that yawned suddenly black before their feet. It was not wide, but it was too wide to jump across in the dim light. They thought they could hear water gurgling in its depths. It curved away on their left northward, back towards the hills, and so barred their road in that direction, at any rate while darkness lasted.

'We had better try a way back southward along the line of the cliff, I think,' said Sam. 'We might find some nook there, or even a cave or something.'

'I suppose so,' said Frodo. 'I'm tired, and I don't think I can scramble among stones much longer tonight—though I grudge the delay. I wish there was a clear path in front of us: then I'd go on till my legs gave way.'

They did not find the going any easier at the broken feet of the Emyn Muil. Nor did Sam find any nook or hollow to shelter in: only bare stony slopes frowned over by the cliff, which now rose again, higher and more sheer as they went back. In the end, worn out, they just cast themselves on the ground under the lee of a boulder lying not far from the foot of the precipice. There for some time they sat huddled mournfully together in the cold stony night, while sleep crept upon them in spite of all they could do to hold it off. The moon now rode high and clear. Its thin white light lit up the faces of the rocks and drenched the cold frowning walls of the cliff, turning all the wide looming darkness into a chill pale grey scored with black shadows.

'Well!' said Frodo, standing up and drawing his cloak more closely round him. 'You sleep for a bit Sam and take my blanket. I'll walk up and down on sentry for a while.' Suddenly he stiffened, and stooping he gripped Sam by the arm. 'What's that?' he whispered. 'Look over there on the cliff!'

Sam looked and breathed in sharply through his teeth. 'Ssss!' he said. 'That's what it is. It's that Gollum! Snakes and adders! And to think that I thought that we'd puzzle him with our bit of a climb! Look at him! Like a nasty crawling spider on a wall.'

Down the face of a precipice, sheer and almost smooth it seemed in the pale moonlight, a small black shape was moving with its thin limbs splayed out. Maybe its soft clinging hands and toes were finding crevices and holds that no hobbit could ever have seen or used, but it looked as if it was just creeping down on sticky pads, like some large prowling thing of insect-kind. And it was coming down head first, as if it was smelling its way. Now and again it lifted its head slowly, turning it right back on its long skinny neck, and the hobbits caught a glimpse of two small pale gleaming lights, its eyes that blinked at the moon for a moment and then were quickly lidded again.

'Do you think he can see us?' said Sam.

'I don't know,' said Frodo quietly, 'but I think not. It is hard even for friendly eyes to see these elven-cloaks: I cannot see you in the shadow even at a few paces. And I've heard that he doesn't like Sun or Moon.'

'Then why is he coming down just here?' asked Sam.

'Quietly, Sam!' said Frodo. 'He can smell us, perhaps. And he can hear as keen as Elves, I believe. I think he has heard something now: our voices probably. We did a lot of shouting away back there; and we were talking far too loudly until a minute ago.'

'Well, I'm sick of him,' said Sam. 'He's come once too often for me, and I'm going to have a word with him, if I can. I don't suppose we could give him the slip now anyway.' Drawing his grey hood well over his face, Sam crept stealthily towards the cliff.

'Careful!' whispered Frodo coming behind. 'Don't alarm him! He's much more dangerous than he looks.'

The black crawling shape was now three-quarters of the

way down, and perhaps fifty feet or less above the cliff's foot. Crouching stone-still in the shadow of a large boulder the hobbits watched him. He seemed to have come to a difficult passage or to be troubled about something. They could hear him snuffling, and now and again there was a harsh hiss of breath that sounded like a curse. He lifted his head, and they thought they heard him spit. Then he moved on again. Now they could hear his voice creaking and whistling.

'Ach, sss! Cautious, my precious! More haste less speed. We musstn't rissk our neck, musst we, precious? No, precious—*gollum*!' He lifted his head again, blinked at the moon, and quickly shut his eyes. 'We hate it,' he hissed. 'Nassty, nassty shivery light it is—sss—it spies on us, precious—it hurts our eyes.'

He was getting lower now and the hisses became sharper and clearer. 'Where iss it, where iss it: my precious, my precious? It's ours, it is, and we wants it. The thieves, the thieves, the filthy little thieves. Where are they with my precious? Curse them! We hates them.'

'It doesn't sound as if he knew we were here, does it?' whispered Sam. 'And what's his precious? Does he mean the——'

'Hsh!' breathed Frodo. 'He's getting near now, near enough to hear a whisper.'

Indeed Gollum had suddenly paused again, and his large head on its scrawny neck was lolling from side to side as if he was listening. His pale eyes were half unlidded. Sam restrained himself, though his fingers were twitching. His eyes, filled with anger and disgust, were fixed on the wretched creature as he now began to move again, still whispering and hissing to himself.

At last he was no more than a dozen feet from the ground, right above their heads. From that point there was a sheer drop, for the cliff was slightly undercut, and even Gollum could not find a hold of any kind. He seemed to be trying to twist round, so as to go legs first, when suddenly with a shrill whistling shriek he fell. As he did so, he curled his legs and arms up round him, like a spider whose descending thread is snapped.

Sam was out of his hiding in a flash and crossed the space between him and the cliff-foot in a couple of leaps. Before Gollum could get up, he was on top of him. But he found Gollum more than he bargained for, even taken like that, suddenly, off his guard after a fall. Before Sam could get a hold, long legs and arms were wound round him pinning his arms, and a clinging grip, soft but horribly strong, was squeezing him like slowly tightening cords; clammy fingers were feeling for his throat. Then sharp teeth bit into his shoulder. All he could do was to butt his hard round head sideways into the creature's face. Gollum hissed and spat, but he did not let go.

Things would have gone ill with Sam, if he had been alone. But Frodo sprang up, and drew Sting from its sheath. With his left hand he drew back Gollum's head by its thin lank hair, stretching its long neck, and forcing his pale venomous eyes to stare at the sky.

'Let go! Gollum,' he said. 'This is Sting. You have seen it before once upon a time. Let go, or you'll feel it this time! I'll cut your throat.'

Gollum collapsed and went as loose as wet string. Sam got up, fingering his shoulder. His eyes smouldered with anger, but he could not avenge himself: his miserable enemy lay grovelling on the stones whimpering.

'Don't hurt us! Don't let them hurt us, precious! They won't hurt us will they, nice little hobbitses? We didn't mean no harm, but they jumps on us like cats on poor mices, they did, precious. And we're so lonely, *gollum*. We'll be nice to them, very nice, if they'll be nice to us, won't we, yes, yess.'

'Well, what's to be done with it?' said Sam. 'Tie it up, so as it can't come sneaking after us no more, I say.'

'But that would kill us, kill us,' whimpered Gollum. 'Cruel little hobbitses. Tie us up in the cold hard lands and leave us, *gollum, gollum*.' Sobs welled up in his gobbling throat.

'No,' said Frodo. 'If we kill him, we must kill him outright. But we can't do that, not as things are. Poor wretch! He has done us no harm.'

'Oh hasn't he!' said Sam rubbing his shoulder. 'Anyway he meant to, *and* he means to, I'll warrant. Throttle us in our sleep, that's his plan.'

'I daresay,' said Frodo. 'But what he means to do is another matter.' He paused for a while in thought. Gollum lay still, but stopped whimpering. Sam stood glowering over him.

It seemed to Frodo then that he heard, quite plainly but far off, voices out of the past:

What a pity Bilbo did not stab the vile creature, when he had a chance!

Pity? It was Pity that stayed his hand. Pity, and Mercy: not to strike without need.

I do not feel any pity for Gollum. He deserves death.

Deserves death! I daresay he does. Many that live deserve death. And some die that deserve life. Can you give that to them? Then be not too eager to deal out death in the name of justice, fearing for your own safety. Even the wise cannot see all ends.

'Very well,' he answered aloud, lowering his sword. 'But still I am afraid. And yet, as you see, I will not touch the creature. For now that I see him, I do pity him.'

Sam stared at his master, who seemed to be speaking to some one who was not there. Gollum lifted his head.

'Yess, wretched we are, precious,' he whined. 'Misery misery! Hobbits won't kill us, nice hobbits.'

'No, we won't,' said Frodo. 'But we won't let you go, either. You're full of wickedness and mischief, Gollum. You will have to come with us, that's all, while we keep an eye on you. But you must help us, if you can. One good turn deserves another.'

'Yess, yes indeed,' said Gollum sitting up. 'Nice hobbits! We will come with them. Find them safe paths in the dark, yes we will. And where are they going in these cold hard lands, we wonders, yes we wonders?' He looked up at them, and a faint light of cunning and eagerness flickered for a second in his pale blinking eyes.

Sam scowled at him, and sucked his teeth; but he seemed to sense that there was something odd about his master's mood and that the matter was beyond argument. All the same he was amazed at Frodo's reply.

Frodo looked straight into Gollum's eyes which flinched and twisted away. 'You know that, or you guess well enough, Sméagol,' he said, quietly and sternly. 'We are going to Mordor, of course. And you know the way there, I believe.'

'Ach! sss!' said Gollum, covering his ears with his hands, as if such frankness, and the open speaking of the names, hurt him. 'We guessed, yes we guessed,' he whispered; 'and we didn't want them to go, did we? No, precious, not the nice hobbits. Ashes, ashes, and dust, and thirst there is; and pits, pits, pits, and Orcs, thousands of Orcses. Nice hobbits mustn't go to—sss—those places.'

'So you have been there?' Frodo insisted. 'And you're being drawn back there, aren't you?'

'Yess. Yess. No!' shrieked Gollum. 'Once, by accident it was, wasn't it, precious? Yes, by accident. But we won't go back, no, no!' Then suddenly his voice and language changed, and he sobbed in his throat, and spoke but not to them. 'Leave me alone, *gollum*! You hurt me. O my poor hands, *gollum*! I, we, I don't want to come back. I can't find it. I am tired. I, we can't find it, *gollum, gollum*, no, nowhere. They're always awake. Dwarves, Men, and Elves, terrible Elves with bright eyes. I can't find it. Ach!' He got up and clenched his long hand into a bony fleshless knot, shaking it towards the East. 'We won't!' he cried. 'Not for you.' Then he collapsed again. '*Gollum, gollum*,' he whimpered with his face to the ground. 'Don't look at us! Go away! Go to sleep!'

'He will not go away or go to sleep at your command, Sméagol,' said Frodo. 'But if you really wish to be free of him again, then you must help me. And that I fear means finding us a path towards him. But you need not go all the way, not beyond the gates of his land.'

Gollum sat up again and looked at him under his eye-lids. 'He's over there,' he cackled. 'Always there. Orcs will take you all the way. Easy to find Orcs east of the River. Don't ask Sméagol. Poor, poor Sméagol, he went away long ago. They took his Precious, and he's lost now.'

'Perhaps we'll find him again, if you come with us,' said Frodo.

'No, no, never! He's lost his Precious,' said Gollum.

'Get up!' said Frodo.

Gollum stood up and backed away against the cliff.

'Now!' said Frodo. 'Can you find a path easier by day or by night? We're tired; but if you choose the night, we'll start tonight.'

'The big lights hurt our eyes, they do,' Gollum whined. 'Not under the White Face, not yet. It will go behind the hills soon, yess. Rest a bit first, nice hobbits!'

'Then sit down,' said Frodo, 'and don't move!'

The hobbits seated themselves beside him, one on either side, with their backs to the stony wall, resting their legs. There was no need for any arrangement by word: they knew that they must not sleep for a moment. Slowly the moon went by. Shadows fell down from the hills, and all grew dark before them. The stars grew thick and bright in the sky above. No one stirred. Gollum sat with his legs drawn up, knees under chin, flat hands and feet splayed on the ground, his eyes closed; but he seemed tense, as if thinking or listening.

Frodo looked across at Sam. Their eyes met and they understood. They relaxed, leaning their heads back, and shutting their eyes or seeming to. Soon the sound of their soft breathing could be heard. Gollum's hands twitched a little. Hardly perceptibly his head moved to the left and the right, and first one eye and then the other opened a slit. The hobbits made no sign.

Suddenly, with startling agility and speed, straight off the ground with a jump like a grasshopper or a frog, Gollum bounded forward into the darkness. But that was just what Frodo and Sam had expected. Sam was on him before he had gone two paces after his spring. Frodo coming behind grabbed his leg and threw him.

'Your rope might prove useful again, Sam,' he said.

Sam got out the rope. 'And where were you off to in the cold hard lands, Mr. Gollum?' he growled. 'We wonders, aye, we wonders. To find some of your orc-friends, I warrant. You nasty treacherous creature. It's round your neck this rope ought to go, and a tight noose too.'

Gollum lay quiet and tried no further tricks. He did not answer Sam, but gave him a swift venomous look.

'All we need is something to keep a hold on him,' said Frodo. 'We want him to walk, so it's no good tying his legs—or his arms, he seems to use them nearly as much. Tie one end to his ankle, and keep a grip on the other end.'

He stood over Gollum, while Sam tied the knot. The result surprised them both. Gollum began to scream, a thin, tearing sound, very horrible to hear. He writhed, and tried to get his mouth to his ankle and bite the rope. He kept on screaming.

At last Frodo was convinced that he really was in pain; but it could not be from the knot. He examined it and found that it was not too tight, indeed hardly tight enough. Sam was gentler than his words. 'What's the matter with you?' he said. 'If you will try to run away, you must be tied; but we don't wish to hurt you.'

'It hurts us, it hurts us,' hissed Gollum. 'It freezes, it bites! Elves twisted it, curse them! Nasty cruel hobbits! That's why we tries to escape, of course it is, precious. We guessed they were cruel hobbits. They visits Elves, fierce Elves with bright eyes. Take it off us! It hurts us.'

'No, I will not take it off you,' said Frodo, 'not unless' —he paused a moment in thought—'not unless there is any promise you can make that I can trust.'

'We will swear to do what he wants, yes, yess,' said Gollum, still twisting and grabbing at his ankle. 'It hurts us.'

'Swear?' said Frodo.

'Sméagol,' said Gollum suddenly and clearly, opening

his eyes wide and staring at Frodo with a strange light.
'Sméagol will swear on the Precious.'

Frodo drew himself up, and again Sam was startled by
his words and his stern voice. 'On the Precious? How dare
you?' he said. 'Think!

One Ring to rule them all and in the Darkness bind them.

Would you commit your promise to that, Sméagol? It will
hold you. But it is more treacherous than you are. It may
twist your words. Beware!'

Gollum cowered. 'On the Precious, on the Precious!' he
repeated.

'And what would you swear?' asked Frodo.

'To be very very good,' said Gollum. Then crawling to
Frodo's feet he grovelled before him, whispering hoarsely:
a shudder ran over him, as if the words shook his very
bones with fear. 'Sméagol will swear never, never, to let
Him have it. Never! Sméagol will save it. But he must
swear on the Precious.'

'No! not on it,' said Frodo, looking down at him with
stern pity. 'All you wish is to see it and touch it, if you can,
though you know it would drive you mad. Not on it. Swear
by it, if you will. For you know where it is. Yes, you
know, Sméagol. It is before you.'

For a moment it appeared to Sam that his master had
grown and Gollum had shrunk: a tall stern shadow, a
mighty lord who hid his brightness in grey cloud, and at
his feet a little whining dog. Yet the two were in some
way akin and not alien: they could reach one another's
minds. Gollum raised himself and began pawing at Frodo,
fawning at his knees.

'Down! down!' said Frodo. 'Now speak your promise!'

'We promises, yes, I promise!' said Gollum. 'I will serve
the master of the Precious. Good master, good Sméagol,
gollum, gollum!' Suddenly he began to weep and bite at
his ankle again.

'Take the rope off, Sam!' said Frodo.

Reluctantly Sam obeyed. At once Gollum got up and

began prancing about, like a whipped cur whose master has patted it. From that moment a change, which lasted for some time, came over him. He spoke with less hissing and whining, and he spoke to his companions direct, not to his precious self. He would cringe and flinch, if they stepped near him or made any sudden movement, and he avoided the touch of their elven-cloaks; but he was friendly, and indeed pitifully anxious to please. He would cackle with laughter and caper, if any jest was made, or even if Frodo spoke kindly to him, and weep if Frodo rebuked him. Sam said little to him of any sort. He suspected him more deeply than ever, and if possible liked the new Gollum, the Sméagol, less than the old.

'Well, Gollum, or whatever it is we're to call you,' he said, 'now for it! The Moon's gone, and the night's going. We'd better start.'

'Yes, yes,' agreed Gollum, skipping about. 'Off we go! There's only one way across between the North-end and the South-end. I found it, I did. Orcs don't use it, Orcs don't know it. Orcs don't cross the Marshes, they go round for miles and miles. Very lucky you came this way. Very lucky you found Sméagol, yes. Follow Sméagol!'

He took a few steps away and looked back inquiringly, like a dog inviting them for a walk. 'Wait a bit, Gollum!' cried Sam. 'Not too far ahead now! I'm going to be at your tail, and I've got the rope handy.'

'No, no!' said Gollum. 'Sméagol promised.'

In the deep of night under hard clear stars they set off. Gollum led them back northward for a while along the way they had come; then he slanted to the right away from the steep edge of the Emyn Muil, down the broken stony slopes towards the vast fens below. They faded swiftly and softly into the darkness. Over all the leagues of waste before the gates of Mordor there was a black silence.

Chapter 2

The Passage of the Marshes

Gollum moved quickly, with his head and neck thrust forward, often using his hands as well as his feet. Frodo and Sam were hard put to it to keep up with him; but he seemed no longer to have any thought of escaping, and if they fell behind, he would turn and wait for them. After a time he brought them to the brink of the narrow gully that they had struck before; but they were now further from the hills.

'Here it is!' he cried. 'There is a way down inside, yes. Now we follows it—out, out away over there.' He pointed south and east towards the marshes. The reek of them came to their nostrils, heavy and foul even in the cool night air.

Gollum cast up and down along the brink, and at length he called to them. 'Here! We can get down here. Sméagol went this way once: I went this way, hiding from Orcs.'

He led the way, and following him the hobbits climbed down into the gloom. It was not difficult, for the rift was at this point only some fifteen feet deep and about a dozen across. There was running water at the bottom: it was in fact the bed of one of the many small rivers that trickled down from the hills to feed the stagnant pools and mires beyond. Gollum turned to the right, southward more or less, and splashed along with his feet in the shallow stony stream. He seemed greatly delighted to feel the water, and chuckled to himself, sometimes even croaking in a sort of song.

> *The cold hard lands*
> *they bites our hands,*
> *   they gnaws our feet.*
> *The rocks and stones*
> *are like old bones*

287

all bare of meat.
But stream and pool
is wet and cool:
so nice for feet!
And now we wish——

'Ha! ha! What does we wish?' he said, looking sidelong at the hobbits. 'We'll tell you,' he croaked. 'He guessed it long ago, Baggins guessed it.' A glint came into his eyes, and Sam catching the gleam in the darkness thought it far from pleasant.

Alive without breath;
as cold as death;
never thirsting, ever drinking;
clad in mail, never clinking.
Drowns on dry land,
thinks an island
is a mountain;
thinks a fountain
is a puff of air.
So sleek, so fair!
What a joy to meet!
We only wish
to catch a fish,
so juicy-sweet!

These words only made more pressing to Sam's mind a problem that had been troubling him from the moment when he understood that his master was going to adopt Gollum as a guide: the problem of food. It did not occur to him that his master might also have thought of it, but he supposed Gollum had. Indeed how had Gollum kept himself in all his lonely wandering? 'Not too well,' thought Sam. 'He looks fair famished. Not too dainty to try what hobbit tastes like, if there ain't no fish, I'll wager—supposing as he could catch us napping. Well, he won't: not Sam Gamgee for one.'

They stumbled along in the dark winding gully for a long time, or so it seemed to the tired feet of Frodo and Sam. The gully turned eastward, and as they went on it broadened and got gradually shallower. At last the sky above grew faint with the first grey of morning. Gollum had shown no signs of tiring, but now he looked up and halted.

'Day is near,' he whispered, as if Day was something that might overhear him and spring on him. 'Sméagol will stay here: I will stay here, and the Yellow Face won't see me.'

'We should be glad to see the Sun,' said Frodo, 'but we will stay here: we are too tired to go any further at present.'

'You are not wise to be glad of the Yellow Face,' said Gollum. 'It shows you up. Nice sensible hobbits stay with Sméagol. Orcs and nasty things are about. They can see a long way. Stay and hide with me!'

The three of them settled down to rest at the foot of the rocky wall of the gully. It was not much more than a tall man's height now, and at its base there were wide flat shelves of dry stone; the water ran in a channel on the other side. Frodo and Sam sat on one of the flats, resting their backs. Gollum paddled and scrabbled in the stream.

'We must take a little food,' said Frodo. 'Are you hungry, Sméagol? We have very little to share, but we will spare you what we can.'

At the word *hungry* a greenish light was kindled in Gollum's pale eyes, and they seemed to protrude further than ever from his thin sickly face. For a moment he relapsed into his old Gollum-manner. 'We are famisshed, yes famisshed we are, precious,' he said. 'What is it they eats? Have they nice fisshes?' His tongue lolled out between his sharp yellow teeth, licking his colourless lips.

'No, we have got no fish,' said Frodo. 'We have only got this'—he held up a wafer of *lembas*—'and water, if the water here is fit to drink.'

'Yess, yess, nice water,' said Gollum. 'Drink it, drink it, while we can! But what is it they've got, precious? Is it crunchable? Is it tasty?'

Frodo broke off a portion of a wafer and handed it to him on its leaf-wrapping. Gollum sniffed at the leaf and his face changed: a spasm of disgust came over it, and a hint of his old malice. 'Sméagol smells it!' he said. 'Leaves out of the elf-country, gah! They stinks. He climbed in those trees, and he couldn't wash the smell off his hands, my nice hands.' Dropping the leaf, he took a corner of the *lembas* and nibbled it. He spat, and a fit of coughing shook him.

'Ach! No!' he spluttered. 'You try to choke poor Sméagol. Dust and ashes, he can't eat that. He must starve. But Sméagol doesn't mind. Nice hobbits! Sméagol has promised. He will starve. He can't eat hobbits' food. He will starve. Poor thin Sméagol!'

'I'm sorry,' said Frodo; 'but I can't help you, I'm afraid. I think this food would do you good, if you would try. But perhaps you can't even try, not yet anyway.'

The hobbits munched their *lembas* in silence. Sam thought that it tasted far better, somehow, than it had for a good while: Gollum's behaviour had made him attend to its flavour again. But he did not feel comfortable. Gollum watched every morsel from hand to mouth, like an expectant dog by a diner's chair. Only when they had finished and were preparing to rest, was he apparently convinced that they had no hidden dainties that he could share in. Then he went and sat by himself a few paces away and whimpered a little.

'Look here!' Sam whispered to Frodo, not too softly: he did not really care whether Gollum heard him or not. 'We've got to get some sleep; but not both together with that hungry villain nigh, promise or no promise. Sméagol or Gollum, he won't change his habits in a hurry, I'll warrant. You go to sleep, Mr. Frodo, and I'll call you when I can't keep my eyelids propped up. Turn and about, same as before, while he's loose.'

'Perhaps you're right, Sam,' said Frodo speaking openly. 'There *is* a change in him, but just what kind of a change and how deep, I'm not sure yet. Seriously though, I don't think there is any need for fear—at present. Still watch if you wish. Give me about two hours, not more, and then call me.'

So tired was Frodo that his head fell forward on his breast and he slept, almost as soon as he had spoken the words. Gollum seemed no longer to have any fears. He curled up and went quickly to sleep, quite unconcerned. Presently his breath was hissing softly through his clenched teeth, but he lay still as stone. After a while, fearing that he would drop off himself, if he sat listening to his two companions breathing, Sam got up and gently prodded Gollum. His hands uncurled and twitched, but he made no other movement. Sam bent down and said *fissh* close to his ear, but there was no response, not even a catch in Gollum's breathing.

Sam scratched his head. 'Must really be asleep,' he muttered. 'And if I was like Gollum, he wouldn't wake up never again.' He restrained the thoughts of his sword and the rope that sprang to his mind, and went and sat down by his master.

When he woke up the sky above was dim, not lighter but darker than when they had breakfasted. Sam leapt to his feet. Not least from his own feeling of vigour and hunger, he suddenly understood that he had slept the daylight away, nine hours at least. Frodo was still fast asleep, lying now stretched on his side. Gollum was not to be seen. Various reproachful names for himself came to Sam's mind, drawn from the Gaffer's large paternal word-hoard; then it also occurred to him that his master had been right: there had for the present been nothing to guard against. They were at any rate both alive and unthrottled.

'Poor wretch!' he said half remorsefully. 'Now I wonder where he's got to?'

'Not far, not far!' said a voice above him. He looked up and saw the shape of Gollum's large head and ears against the evening sky.

'Here, what are you doing?' cried Sam, his suspicions coming back as soon as he saw that shape.

'Sméagol is hungry,' said Gollum. 'Be back soon.'

'Come back now!' shouted Sam. 'Hi! Come back!' But Gollum had vanished.

Frodo woke at the sound of Sam's shout and sat up, rubbing his eyes. 'Hullo!' he said. 'Anything wrong? What's the time?'

'I dunno,' said Sam. 'After sundown, I reckon. And he's gone off. Says he's hungry.'

'Don't worry!' said Frodo. 'There's no help for it. But he'll come back, you'll see. The promise will hold yet a while. And he won't leave his Precious, anyway.'

Frodo made light of it when he learned that they had slept soundly for hours with Gollum, and a very hungry Gollum too, loose beside them. 'Don't think of any of your Gaffer's hard names,' he said. 'You were worn out, and it has turned out well: we are now both rested. And we have a hard road ahead, the worst road of all.'

'About the food,' said Sam. 'How long's it going to take us to do this job? And when it's done, what are we going to do then? This waybread keeps you on your legs in a wonderful way, though it doesn't satisfy the innards proper, you might say: not to my feeling anyhow, meaning no disrespect to them as made it. But you have to eat some of it every day, and it doesn't grow. I reckon we've got enough to last, say, three weeks or so, and that with a tight belt and a light tooth, mind you. We've been a bit free with it so far.'

'I don't know how long we shall take to—to finish,' said Frodo. 'We were miserably delayed in the hills. But Samwise Gamgee, my dear hobbit—indeed, Sam my dearest hobbit, friend of friends—I do not think we need give thought to what comes after that. To *do the job* as you put it—what hope is there that we ever shall? And if we do, who knows what will come of that? If the One goes into the Fire, and we are at hand? I ask you, Sam, are we ever likely to need bread again? I think not. If we can nurse our limbs to bring us to Mount Doom, that is all we can do. More than I can, I begin to feel.'

Sam nodded silently. He took his master's hand and

bent over it. He did not kiss it, though his tears fell on it. Then he turned away, drew his sleeve over his nose, and got up, and stamped about, trying to whistle, and saying between the efforts: 'Where's that dratted creature?'

It was actually not long before Gollum returned; but he came so quietly that they did not hear him till he stood before them. His fingers and face were soiled with black mud. He was still chewing and slavering. What he was chewing, they did not ask or like to think.

'Worms or beetles or something slimy out of holes,' thought Sam. 'Brr! The nasty creature; the poor wretch!'

Gollum said nothing to them, until he had drunk deeply and washed himself in the stream. Then he came up to them, licking his lips. 'Better now,' he said. 'Are we rested? Ready to go on? Nice hobbits, they sleep beautifully. Trust Sméagol now? Very, very good.'

The next stage of their journey was much the same as the last. As they went on the gully became ever shallower and the slope of its floor more gradual. Its bottom was less stony and more earthy, and slowly its sides dwindled to mere banks. It began to wind and wander. That night drew to its end, but clouds were now over moon and star, and they knew of the coming of day only by the slow spreading of the thin grey light.

In a chill hour they came to the end of the water-course. The banks became moss-grown mounds. Over the last shelf of rotting stone the stream gurgled and fell down into a brown bog and was lost. Dry reeds hissed and rattled though they could feel no wind.

On either side and in front wide fens and mires now lay, stretching away southward and eastward into the dim half-light. Mists curled and smoked from dark and noisome pools. The reek of them hung stifling in the still air. Far away, now almost due south, the mountain-walls of Mordor loomed, like a black bar of rugged clouds floating above a dangerous fog-bound sea.

The hobbits were now wholly in the hands of Gollum.

They did not know, and could not guess in that misty light, that they were in fact only just within the northern borders of the marshes, the main expanse of which lay south of them. They could, if they had known the lands, with some delay have retraced their steps a little, and then turning east have come round over hard roads to the bare plain of Dagorlad: the field of the ancient battle before the gates of Mordor. Not that there was great hope in such a course. On that stony plain there was no cover, and across it ran the highways of the Orcs and the soldiers of the Enemy. Not even the cloaks of Lórien would have concealed them there.

'How do we shape our course now, Sméagol?' asked Frodo. 'Must we cross these evil-smelling fens?'

'No need, no need at all,' said Gollum. 'Not if hobbits want to reach the dark mountains and go to see Him very quick. Back a little, and round a little'—his skinny arm waved north and east—'and you can come on hard cold roads to the very gates of His country. Lots of His people will be there looking out for guests, very pleased to take them straight to Him, O yes. His Eye watches that way all the time. It caught Sméagol there, long ago.' Gollum shuddered. 'But Sméagol has used his eyes since then, yes, yes: I've used eyes and feet and nose since then. I know other ways. More difficult, not so quick; but better, if we don't want Him to see. Follow Sméagol! He can take you through the marshes, through the mists, nice thick mists. Follow Sméagol very carefully, and you may go a long way, quite a long way, before He catches you, yes perhaps.'

It was already day, a windless and sullen morning, and the marsh-reeks lay in heavy banks. No sun pierced the low clouded sky, and Gollum seemed anxious to continue the journey at once. So after a brief rest they set out again and were soon lost in a shadowy silent world, cut off from all view of the lands about, either the hills that they had left or the mountains that they sought. They went slowly in single file: Gollum, Sam, Frodo.

Frodo seemed the most weary of the three, and slow though they went, he often lagged. The hobbits soon found that what had looked like one vast fen was really an endless network of pools, and soft mires, and winding half-strangled water-courses. Among these a cunning eye and foot could thread a wandering path. Gollum certainly had that cunning, and needed all of it. His head on its long neck was ever turning this way and that, while he sniffed and muttered all the time to himself. Sometimes he would hold up his hand and halt them, while he went forward a little, crouching, testing the ground with fingers or toes, or merely listening with one ear pressed to the earth.

It was dreary and wearisome. Cold clammy winter still held sway in this forsaken country. The only green was the scum of livid weed on the dark greasy surfaces of the sullen waters. Dead grasses and rotting reeds loomed up in the mists like ragged shadows of long-forgotten summers.

As the day wore on the light increased a little, and the mists lifted, growing thinner and more transparent. Far above the rot and vapours of the world the Sun was riding high and golden now in a serene country with floors of dazzling foam, but only a passing ghost of her could they see below, bleared, pale, giving no colour and no warmth. But even at this faint reminder of her presence Gollum scowled and flinched. He halted their journey, and they rested, squatting like little hunted animals, in the borders of a great brown reed-thicket. There was a deep silence, only scraped on its surfaces by the faint quiver of empty seed-plumes, and broken grass-blades trembling in small air-movements that they could not feel.

'Not a bird!' said Sam mournfully.

'No, no birds,' said Gollum. 'Nice birds!' He licked his teeth. 'No birds here. There are snakeses, wormses, things in the pools. Lots of things, lots of nasty things. No birds,' he ended sadly. Sam looked at him with distaste.

So passed the third day of their journey with Gollum. Before the shadows of evening were long in happier lands, they went on again, always on and on with only brief halts. These they made not so much for rest as to help Gollum; for now even he had to go forward with great care, and he was sometimes at a loss for a while. They had come to the very midst of the Dead Marshes, and it was dark.

They walked slowly, stooping, keeping close in line, following attentively every move that Gollum made. The fens grew more wet, opening into wide stagnant meres, among which it grew more and more difficult to find the firmer places where feet could tread without sinking into gurgling mud. The travellers were light, or maybe none of them would ever have found a way through.

Presently it grew altogether dark; the air itself seemed black and heavy to breathe. When lights appeared Sam rubbed his eyes: he thought his head was going queer. He first saw one with the corner of his left eye, a wisp of pale sheen that faded away; but others appeared soon after: some like dimly shining smoke, some like misty flames flickering slowly above unseen candles; here and there they twisted like ghostly sheets unfurled by hidden hands. But neither of his companions spoke a word.

At last Sam could bear it no longer. 'What's all this, Gollum?' he said in a whisper. 'These lights? They're all round us now. Are we trapped? Who are they?'

Gollum looked up. A dark water was before him, and he was crawling on the ground, this way and that, doubtful of the way. 'Yes, they are all round us,' he whispered. 'The tricksy lights. Candles of corpses, yes, yes. Don't you heed them! Don't look! Don't follow them! Where's the master?'

Sam looked back and found that Frodo had lagged again. He could not see him. He went some paces back into the darkness, not daring to move far, or to call in more than a hoarse whisper. Suddenly he stumbled against Frodo, who was standing lost in thought, looking at the pale lights. His hands hung stiff at his sides; water and slime were dripping from them.

'Come, Mr. Frodo!' said Sam. 'Don't look at them! Gol-

lum says we mustn't. Let's keep up with him and get out
of this cursed place as quick as we can—if we can!'

'All right,' said Frodo, as if returning out of a dream.
'I'm coming. Go on!'

Hurrying forward again, Sam tripped, catching his foot
in some old root or tussock. He fell and came heavily on
his hands, which sank deep into sticky ooze, so that his
face was brought close to the surface of the dark mere.
There was a faint hiss, a noisome smell went up, the lights
flickered and danced and swirled. For a moment the water
below him looked like some window, glazed with grimy
glass, through which he was peering. Wrenching his hands
out of the bog, he sprang back with a cry. 'There are
dead things, dead faces in the water,' he said with horror. 'Dead faces!'

Gollum laughed. 'The Dead Marshes, yes, yes: that is
their name,' he cackled. 'You should not look in when
the candles are lit.'

'Who are they? What are they?' asked Sam shuddering,
turning to Frodo, who was now behind him.

'I don't know,' said Frodo in a dreamlike voice. 'But
I have seen them too. In the pools when the candles were
lit. They lie in all the pools, pale faces, deep deep under
the dark water. I saw them: grim faces and evil, and noble
faces and sad. Many faces proud and fair, and weeds
in their silver hair. But all foul, all rotting, all dead. A
fell light is in them.' Frodo hid his eyes in his hands. 'I
know not who they are; but I thought I saw there Men
and Elves, and Orcs beside them.'

'Yes, yes,' said Gollum. 'All dead, all rotten. Elves and
Men and Orcs. The Dead Marshes. There was a great battle long ago, yes, so they told him when Sméagol was
young, when I was young before the Precious came. It was
a great battle. Tall Men with long swords, and terrible
Elves, and Orcses shrieking. They fought on the plain for
days and months at the Black Gates. But the Marshes have
grown since then, swallowed up the graves; always creeping, creeping.'

'But that is an age and more ago,' said Sam. 'The

Dead can't be really there! Is it some devilry hatched in the Dark Land?'

'Who knows? Sméagol doesn't know,' answered Gollum. 'You cannot reach them, you cannot touch them. We tried once, yes, precious. I tried once; but you cannot reach them. Only shapes to see, perhaps, not to touch. No precious! All dead.'

Sam looked darkly at him and shuddered again, thinking that he guessed why Sméagol had tried to touch them. 'Well, I don't want to see them,' he said. 'Never again! Can't we get on and get away?'

'Yes, yes,' said Gollum. 'But slowly, very slowly. Very carefully! Or hobbits go down to join the Dead ones and light little candles. Follow Sméagol! Don't look at lights!'

He crawled away to the right, seeking for a path round the mere. They came close behind, stooping, often using their hands even as he did. 'Three precious little Gollums in a row we shall be, if this goes on much longer,' thought Sam.

At last they came to the end of the black mere, and they crossed it, perilously, crawling or hopping from one treacherous island tussock to another. Often they floundered, stepping or falling hands-first into waters as noisome as a cesspool, till they were slimed and fouled almost up to their necks and stank in one another's nostrils.

It was late in the night when at length they reached firmer ground again. Gollum hissed and whispered to himself, but it appeared that he was pleased: in some mysterious way, by some blended sense of feel, and smell, and uncanny memory for shapes in the dark, he seemed to know just where he was again, and to be sure of his road ahead.

'Now on we go!' he said. 'Nice hobbits! Brave hobbits! Very very weary, of course; so we are, my precious, all of us. But we must take master away from the wicked lights, yes, yes, we must.' With these words he started off again, almost at a trot, down what appeared to be a long lane between high reeds, and they stumbled after him as quickly as they could. But in a little while he stopped suddenly and sniffed the air doubtfully, hissing as if he was troubled or displeased again.

'What is it?' growled Sam, misinterpreting the signs. 'What's the need to sniff? The stink nearly knocks me down with my nose held. You stink, and master stinks; the whole place stinks.'

'Yes, yes, and Sam stinks!' answered Gollum. 'Poor Sméagol smells it, but good Sméagol bears it. Helps nice master. But that's no matter. The air's moving, change is coming. Sméagol wonders; he's not happy.'

He went on again, but his uneasiness grew, and every now and again he stood up to his full height, craning his neck eastward and southward. For some time the hobbits could not hear or feel what was troubling him. Then suddenly all three halted, stiffening and listening. To Frodo and Sam it seemed that they heard, far away, a long wailing cry, high and thin and cruel. They shivered. At the same moment the stirring of the air became perceptible to them; and it grew very cold. As they stood straining their ears, they heard a noise like a wind coming in the distance. The misty lights wavered, dimmed, and went out.

Gollum would not move. He stood shaking and gibbering to himself, until with a rush the wind came upon them, hissing and snarling over the marshes. The night became less dark, light enough for them to see, or half see, shapeless drifts of fog, curling and twisting as it rolled over them and passed them. Looking up they saw the clouds breaking and shredding; and then high in the south the moon glimmered out, riding in the flying wrack.

For a moment the sight of it gladdened the hearts of the hobbits; but Gollum cowered down, muttering curses on the White Face. Then Frodo and Sam, staring at the sky, breathing deeply of the fresher air, saw it come: a small cloud flying from the accursed hills; a black shadow loosed from Mordor; a vast shape winged and ominous. It scudded across the moon, and with a deadly cry went away westward, outrunning the wind in its fell speed.

They fell forward, grovelling heedlessly on the cold earth. But the shadow of horror wheeled and returned, passing lower now, right above them, sweeping the fen-reek with its ghastly wings. And then it was gone, flying back to Mordor with the speed of the wrath of Sauron; and behind it the wind roared away, leaving the Dead Marshes bare and bleak. The naked waste, as far as the eye could pierce, even to the distant menace of the mountains, was dappled with the fitful moonlight.

Frodo and Sam got up, rubbing their eyes, like children wakened from an evil dream to find the familiar night still over the world. But Gollum lay on the ground as if he had been stunned. They roused him with difficulty, and for some time he would not lift his face, but knelt forward on his elbows, covering the back of his head with his large flat hands.

'Wraiths!' he wailed. 'Wraiths on wings! The Precious is their master. They see everything, everything. Nothing can hide from them. Curse the White Face! And they tell Him everything. He sees, He knows. Ach, *gollum, gollum, gollum*!" It was not until the moon had sunk, westering far beyond Tol Brandir, that he would get up or make a move.

From that time on Sam thought that he sensed a change in Gollum again. He was more fawning and would-be friendly; but Sam surprised some strange looks in his eyes at times, especially towards Frodo; and he went back more and more into his old manner of speaking. And Sam had another growing anxiety. Frodo seemed to be weary, weary to the point of exhaustion. He said nothing, indeed he hardly spoke at all; and he did not complain, but he walked like one who carries a load, the weight of which is ever increasing; and he dragged along, slower and slower, so that Sam had often to beg Gollum to wait and not to leave their master behind.

In fact with every step towards the gates of Mordor Frodo felt the Ring on its chain about his neck grow more burdensome. He was now beginning to feel it as an actual weight dragging him earthwards. But far more he was troubled by the Eye: so he called it to himself. It was that more than the drag of the Ring that made him cower and stoop as he walked. The Eye: that horrible growing sense of a hostile will that strove with great power to pierce all shadows of cloud, and earth, and flesh, and to see you: to pin you under its deadly gaze, naked, immovable. So thin, so frail and thin, the veils were become that still warded it off. Frodo knew just where the present habitation and heart of that will now was: as certainly as a man can tell the direction of the sun with his eyes shut. He was facing it, and its potency beat upon his brow.

Gollum probably felt something of the same sort. But what went on in his wretched heart between the pressure of the Eye, and the lust of the Ring that was so near, and his grovelling promise made half in the fear of cold iron, the hobbits did not guess. Frodo gave no thought to it. Sam's mind was occupied mostly with his master, hardly noticing the dark cloud that had fallen on his own heart. He put Frodo in front of him now, and kept a watchful eye on every movement of his, supporting him if he stumbled, and trying to encourage him with clumsy words.

When day came at last the hobbits were surprised to see how much closer the ominous mountains had already drawn. The air was now clearer and colder, and though still far off, the walls of Mordor were no longer a cloudy menace on the edge of sight, but as grim black towers they frowned across a dismal waste. The marshes were at an end, dying away into dead peats and wide flats of dry cracked mud. The land ahead rose in long shallow slopes, barren and pitiless, towards the desert that lay at Sauron's gate.

While the grey light lasted, they cowered under a black stone like worms, shrinking, lest the winged terror should pass and spy them with its cruel eyes. The remainder of that journey was a shadow of growing fear in which memory could find nothing to rest upon. For two more nights they struggled on through the weary pathless land. The air, as it seemed to them, grew harsh, and filled with a bitter reek that caught their breath and parched their mouths.

At last, on the fifth morning since they took the road with Gollum, they halted once more. Before them dark in the dawn the great mountains reached up to roofs of smoke and cloud. Out from their feet were flung huge buttresses and broken hills that were now at the nearest scarce a dozen miles away. Frodo looked round in horror. Dreadful as the Dead Marshes had been, and the arid moors of the Noman-lands, more loathsome far was the country that the crawling day now slowly unveiled to his shrinking eyes. Even to the Mere of Dead Faces some haggard phantom of green spring could come; but here neither spring nor summer would ever come again. Here nothing lived, not even the leprous growths that feed on rottenness. The gasping pools were choked with ash and crawling muds, sickly white and grey, as if the mountains had vomited the filth of their entrails upon the lands about. High mounds of crushed and powdered rock, great cones of earth fire-blasted and poison-stained, stood like an obscene graveyard in endless rows, slowly revealed in the reluctant light.

They had come to the desolation that lay before Mordor: the lasting monument to the dark labour of its slaves that should endure when all their purposes were made void; a land defiled, diseased beyond all healing—unless the Great Sea should enter in and wash it with oblivion. 'I feel sick,' said Sam. Frodo did not speak.

For a while they stood there, like men on the edge of a sleep where nightmare lurks, holding it off, though they know that they can only come to morning through the shadows. The light broadened and hardened. The gasping pits and poisonous mounds grew hideously clear. The sun was up, walking among clouds and long flags of smoke, but even the sunlight was defiled. The hobbits had no welcome for that light; unfriendly it seemed, revealing them in their helplessness—little squeaking ghosts that wandered among the ash-heaps of the Dark Lord.

Too weary to go further they sought for some place where they could rest. For a while they sat without speaking under the shadow of a mound of slag; but foul fumes leaked out of it, catching their throats and choking them. Gollum was the first to get up. Spluttering and cursing he rose, and without a word or a glance at the hobbits he crawled away on all fours. Frodo and Sam crawled after him, until they came to a wide almost circular pit, high-banked upon the west. It was cold and dead, and a foul sump of oily many-coloured ooze lay at its bottom. In this evil hole they cowered, hoping in its shadow to escape the attention of the Eye.

The day passed slowly. A great thirst troubled them, but they drank only a few drops from their bottles—last filled in the gully, which now as they looked back in thought seemed to them a place of peace and beauty. The hobbits took it in turn to watch. At first, tired as they were, neither of them could sleep at all; but as the sun far away was climbing down into slow moving cloud, Sam dozed. It was Frodo's turn to be on guard. He lay back on the slope of the pit, but that did not ease the sense of burden that was on him. He looked up at the smoke-streaked sky and saw strange phantoms, dark riding shapes, and faces out of the past. He lost count of time, hovering between sleep and waking, until forgetfulness came over him.

Suddenly Sam woke up thinking that he heard his master calling. It was evening. Frodo could not have called, for he had fallen asleep, and had slid down nearly to the bottom of the pit. Gollum was by him. For a moment Sam thought that he was trying to rouse Frodo; then he saw that it was not so. Gollum was talking to himself. Sméagol was holding a debate with some other thought that used the same voice but made it squeak and hiss. A pale light and a green light alternated in his eyes as he spoke.

'Sméagol promised,' said the first thought.

'Yes, yes, my precious,' came the answer, 'we promised: to save our Precious, not to let Him have it—never.

But it's going to Him, yes, nearer every step. What's the hobbit going to do with it, we wonders, yes we wonders.'

'I don't know. I can't help it. Master's got it. Sméagol promised to help the master.'

'Yes, yes, to help the master: the master of the Precious. But if we was master, then we could help ourselves, yes, and still keep promises.'

'But Sméagol said he would be very very good. Nice hobbit! He took cruel rope off Sméagol's leg. He speaks nicely to me.'

'Very very good, eh, my precious? Let's be good, good as fish, sweet one, but to ourselfs. Not hurt the nice hobbit, of course, no, no.'

'But the Precious holds the promise,' the voice of Sméagol objected.

'Then take it,' said the other, 'and let's hold it ourselfs! Then we shall be master, *gollum*! Make the other hobbit, the nasty suspicious hobbit, make him crawl, yes, *gollum*!'

'But not the nice hobbit?'

'Oh no, not if it doesn't please us. Still he's a Baggins, my precious, yes, a Baggins. A Baggins stole it. He found it and he said nothing, nothing. We hates Bagginses.'

'No, not this Baggins.'

'Yes, every Baggins. All peoples that keep the Precious. We must have it!'

'But He'll see, He'll know. He'll take it from us!'

'He sees. He knows. He heard us make silly promises— against His orders, yes. Must take it. The Wraiths are searching. Must take it.'

'Not for Him!'

'No, sweet one. See, my precious: if we has it, then we can escape, even from Him, eh? Perhaps we grows very strong, stronger than Wraiths. Lord Sméagol? Gollum the Great? *The* Gollum! Eat fish every day, three times a day, fresh from the Sea. Most Precious Gollum! Must have it. We wants it, we wants it, we wants it!'

'But there's two of them. They'll wake too quick and kill us,' whined Sméagol in a last effort. 'Not now. Not yet.'

'We wants it! But'—and here there was a long pause,

as if a new thought had wakened. 'Not yet, eh? Perhaps not. She might help. She might, yes.'

'No, no! Not that way!' wailed Sméagol.

'Yes! We wants it! We wants it!'

Each time that the second thought spoke, Gollum's long hand crept out slowly, pawing towards Frodo, and then was drawn back with a jerk as Sméagol spoke again. Finally both arms, with long fingers flexed and twitching, clawed toward his neck.

Sam had lain still, fascinated by this debate, but watching every move that Gollum made from under his half-closed eye-lids. To his simple mind ordinary hunger, the desire to eat hobbits, had seemed the chief danger in Gollum. He realized now that it was not so: Gollum was feeling the terrible call of the Ring. The Dark Lord was *He,* of course; but Sam wondered who *She* was. One of the nasty friends the little wretch had made in his wanderings, he supposed. Then he forgot the point, for things had plainly gone far enough, and were getting dangerous. A great heaviness was in all his limbs, but he roused himself with an effort and sat up. Something warned him to be careful and not to reveal that he had overheard the debate. He let out a loud sigh and gave a huge yawn.

'What's the time?' he said sleepily.

Gollum sent out a long hiss through his teeth. He stood up for a moment, tense and menacing; and then he collapsed, falling forward on all fours and crawling up the bank of the pit. 'Nice hobbits. Nice Sam!' he said. 'Sleepy heads, yes, sleepy heads! Leave good Sméagol to watch! But it's evening. Dusk is creeping. Time to go.'

'High time!' thought Sam. 'And time we parted, too.' Yet it crossed his mind to wonder if indeed Gollum was not now as dangerous turned loose as kept with them. 'Curse him! I wish he was choked!' he muttered. He stumbled down the bank and roused his master.

Strangely enough, Frodo felt refreshed. He had been dreaming. The dark shadow had passed, and a fair vision had visited him in this land of disease. Nothing remained of it in his memory, yet because of it he felt glad and lighter of heart. His burden was less heavy on him. Gollum welcomed him with dog-like delight. He chuckled and chattered, cracking his long fingers, and pawing at Frodo's knees. Frodo smiled at him.

'Come!' he said. 'You have guided us well and faithfully. This is the last stage. Bring us to the Gate, and then I will not ask you to go further. Bring us to the Gate, and you may go where you wish—only not to our enemies.'

'To the Gate, eh?' Gollum squeaked, seeming surprised and frightened. 'To the Gate, master says! Yes, he says so. And good Sméagol does what he asks, O yes. But when we gets closer, we'll see perhaps, we'll see then. It won't look nice at all. O no! O no!'

'Go on with you!' said Sam. 'Let's get it over!'

In the falling dusk they scrambled out of the pit and slowly threaded their way through the dead land. They had not gone far before they felt once more the fear that had fallen on them when the winged shape swept over the marshes. They halted, cowering on the evil-smelling ground; but they saw nothing in the gloomy evening sky above, and soon the menace passed, high overhead, going maybe on some swift errand from Barad-dûr. After a while Gollum got up and crept forward again, muttering and shaking.

About an hour after midnight the fear fell on them a third time, but it now seemed more remote, as if it were passing far above the clouds, rushing with terrible speed into the West. Gollum, however, was helpless with terror, and was convinced that they were being hunted, that their approach was known.

'Three times!' he whimpered. 'Three times is a threat. They feel us here, they feel the Precious. The Precious is their master. We cannot go any further this way, no. It's no use, no use!'

Pleading and kind words were no longer of any avail. It was not until Frodo commanded him angrily and laid a hand on his sword-hilt that Gollum would get up again.

Then at last he rose with a snarl, and went before them like a beaten dog.

So they stumbled on through the weary end of the night, and until the coming of another day of fear they walked in silence with bowed heads, seeing nothing, and hearing nothing but the wind hissing in their ears.

Chapter 3

The Black Gate Is Closed

Before the next day dawned their journey to Mordor was over. The marshes and the desert were behind them. Before them, darkling against a pallid sky, the great mountains reared their threatening heads.

Upon the west of Mordor marched the gloomy range of Ephel Dúath, the Mountains of Shadow, and upon the north the broken peaks and barren ridges of Ered Lithui, grey as ash. But as these ranges approached one another, being indeed but parts of one great wall about the mournful plains of Lithlad and of Gorgoroth, and the bitter inland sea of Núrnen amidmost, they swung out long arms northward; and between these arms there was a deep defile. This was Cirith Gorgor, the Haunted Pass, the entrance to the land of the Enemy. High cliffs lowered upon either side, and thrust forward from its mouth were two sheer hills, black-boned and bare. Upon them stood the Teeth of Mordor, two towers strong and tall. In days long past they were built by the Men of Gondor in their pride and power, after the overthrow of Sauron and his flight, lest he should seek to return to his old realm. But the strength of Gondor failed, and men slept, and for long years the towers stood empty. Then Sauron returned. Now the watch-towers, which had fallen into decay, were repaired, and filled with arms, and garrisoned with ceaseless vigilance. Stony-faced they were, with dark window-holes staring north and east and west, and each window was full of sleepless eyes.

Across the mouth of the pass, from cliff to cliff, the Dark Lord had built a rampart of stone. In it there was a single gate of iron, and upon its battlement sentinels paced unceasingly. Beneath the hills on either side the rock was bored into a hundred caves and maggot-holes; there a host of orcs lurked, ready at a signal to issue forth like black ants going to war. None could pass the Teeth of Mordor and not feel their bite, unless they were summoned by Sauron, or knew the secret passwords that would open the Morannon, the black gate of his land.

The two hobbits gazed at the towers and the wall in despair. Even from a distance they could see in the dim light the movement of the black guards upon the wall, and the patrols before the gate. They lay now peering over the edge of a rocky hollow beneath the outstretched shadow of the northmost buttress of Ephel Dúath. Winging the heavy air in a straight flight a crow, maybe, would have flown but a furlong from their hiding-place to the black summit of the nearer tower. A faint smoke curled above it, as if fire smouldered in the hill beneath.

Day came, and the fallow sun blinked over the lifeless ridges of Ered Lithui. Then suddenly the cry of brazen-throated trumpets was heard: from the watch-towers they blared, and far away from hidden holds and outposts in the hills came answering calls; and further still, remote but deep and ominous, there echoed in the hollow land beyond the mighty horns and drums of Barad-dûr. Another dreadful day of fear and toil had come to Mordor; and the night-guards were summoned to their dungeons and deep halls, and the day-guards, evil-eyed and fell, were marching to their posts. Steel gleamed dimly on the battlement.

'Well, here we are!' said Sam. 'Here's the Gate, and it looks to me as if that's about as far as we are ever going to get. My word, but the Gaffer would have a thing or two to say, if he saw me now! Often said I'd come to a bad end, if I didn't watch my step, he did. But now I don't suppose I'll ever see the old fellow again. He'll miss his chance of *I told 'ee so, Sam*: more's the pity. He could go on telling me as long as he'd got breath, if only I could see his old face again. But I'd have to get a wash first, or he wouldn't know me.

'I suppose it's no good asking "what way do we go now?"

We can't go no further—unless we want to ask the Orcs for a lift.'

'No, no!' said Gollum. 'No use. We can't go further. Sméagol said so. He said: we'll go to the Gate, and then we'll see. And we do see. O yes, my precious, we do see. Sméagol knew hobbits could not go this way. O yes, Sméagol knew.'

'Then what the plague did you bring us here for?' said Sam, not feeling in the mood to be just or reasonable.

'Master said so. Master says: Bring us to the Gate. So good Sméagol does so. Master said so, wise master.'

'I did,' said Frodo. His face was grim and set, but resolute. He was filthy, haggard, and pinched with weariness, but he cowered no longer, and his eyes were clear. 'I said so, because I purpose to enter Mordor, and I know no other way. Therefore I shall go this way. I do not ask anyone to go with me.'

'No, no, master!' wailed Gollum, pawing at him, and seeming in great distress. 'No use that way! No use! Don't take the Precious to Him! He'll eat us all, if He gets it, eat all the world. Keep it, nice master, and be kind to Sméagol. Don't let Him have it. Or go away, go to nice places, and give it back to little Sméagol. Yes, yes, master: give it back, eh? Sméagol will keep it safe; he will do lots of good, especially to nice hobbits. Hobbits go home. Don't go to the Gate!'

'I am commanded to go to the land of Mordor, and therefore I shall go,' said Frodo. 'If there is only one way, then I must take it. What comes after must come.'

Sam said nothing. The look on Frodo's face was enough for him; he knew that words of his were useless. And after all he never had any real hope in the affair from the beginning; but being a cheerful hobbit he had not needed hope, as long as despair could be postponed. Now they were come to the bitter end. But he had stuck to his master all the way; that was what he had chiefly come for, and he would still stick to him. His master would not go to

Mordor alone. Sam would go with him—and at any rate they would get rid of Gollum.

Gollum, however, did not intend to be got rid of, yet. He knelt at Frodo's feet, wringing his hands and squeaking. 'Not this way, master!' he pleaded. 'There is another way. O yes indeed there is. Another way, darker, more difficult to find, more secret. But Sméagol knows it. Let Sméagol show you!'

'Another way!' said Frodo doubtfully, looking down at Gollum with searching eyes.

'Yess! Yess indeed! There *was* another way. Sméagol found it. Let's go and see if it's still there.'

'You have not spoken of this before.'

'No. Master did not ask. Master did not say what he meant to do. He does not tell poor Sméagol. He says: Sméagol, take me to the Gate—and then good-bye! Sméagol can run away and be good. But now he says: I purpose to enter Mordor this way. So Sméagol is very afraid. He does not want to lose nice master. And he promised, master made him promise, to save the Precious. But master is going to take it to Him, straight to the Black Hand, if master will go this way. So Sméagol must save them both, and he thinks of another way that there was, once upon a time. Nice master. Sméagol very good, always helps.'

Sam frowned. If he could have bored holes in Gollum with his eyes, he would have done. His mind was full of doubt. To all appearances Gollum was genuinely distressed and anxious to help Frodo. But Sam, remembering the overheard debate, found it hard to believe that the long submerged Sméagol had come out on top: that voice at any rate had not had the last word in the debate. Sam's guess was that the Sméagol and Gollum halves (or what in his own mind he called Slinker and Stinker) had made a truce and a temporary alliance: neither wanted the Enemy to get the Ring; both wished to keep Frodo from capture, and under their eye, as long as possible—at any rate as long as Stinker still had a chance of laying hands on his 'Precious'. Whether there really was another way into Mordor Sam doubted.

'And it's a good thing neither half of the old villain don't know what master means to do,' he thought. 'If he knew that Mr. Frodo is trying to put an end to his Precious for good and all, there'd be trouble pretty quick, I bet. Anyhow old Stinker is so frightened of the Enemy—and he's under orders of some kind from him, or was—that he'd give us away rather than be caught helping us; and rather than let his Precious be melted, maybe. At least that's my idea. And I hope the master will think it out carefully. He's as wise as any, but he's soft-hearted, that's what he is. It's beyond any Gamgee to guess what he'll do next.'

Frodo did not answer Gollum at once. While these doubts were passing through Sam's slow but shrewd mind, he stood gazing out towards the dark cliff of Cirith Gorgor. The hollow in which they had taken refuge was delved in the side of a low hill at some little height above a long trench-like valley that lay between it and the outer buttresses of the mountain. In the midst of the valley stood the black foundations of the western watchtower. By morning-light the roads that converged upon the Gate of Mordor could now be clearly seen, pale and dusty; one winding back northwards; another dwindling eastwards into the mists that clung about the feet of Ered Lithui; a third that ran towards him. As it bent sharply round the tower, it entered a narrow defile and passed not far below the hollow where he stood. Westward, to his right, it turned, skirting the shoulders of the mountains, and went off southwards into the deep shadows that mantled all the western sides of Ephel Dúath; beyond their sight it journeyed on into the narrow land between the mountains and the Great River.

As he gazed Frodo became aware that there was great stir and movement on the plain. It seemed as if whole armies were on the march, though for the most part they were hidden by the reeks and fumes drifting from the fens and wastes beyond. But here and there he caught the gleam of spears and helmets; and over the levels beside the roads horsemen could be seen riding in many companies. He remembered his vision from afar upon Amon Hen, so few days before, though now it seemed many years ago. Then he knew that the hope that had for one wild moment stirred in his heart was vain. The trumpets had not rung in challenge but in greeting. This was no assault upon the Dark Lord by the men of Gondor, risen like avenging ghosts from the graves of valour long passed away. These were Men of other race, out of the wide Eastlands, gathering to the summons of their Overlord; armies that had encamped before his Gate by night and now marched in to swell his mounting power. As if suddenly made fully aware of the peril of their position, alone, in the growing light of day, so near to this vast menace, Frodo quickly drew his frail grey hood close upon his head, and stepped down into the dell. Then he turned to Gollum.

'Sméagol,' he said, 'I will trust you once more. Indeed it seems that I must do so, and that it is my fate to receive help from you, where I least looked for it, and your fate to help me whom you long pursued with evil purpose. So far you have deserved well of me and have kept your promise truly. Truly, I say and mean,' he added with a glance at Sam, 'for twice now we have been in your power, and you have done no harm to us. Nor have you tried to take from me what you once sought. May the third time prove the best! But I warn you, Sméagol, you are in danger.'

'Yes, yes, master!' said Gollum. 'Dreadful danger! Sméagol's bones shake to think of it, but he doesn't run away. He must help nice master.'

'I did not mean the danger that we all share,' said Frodo. 'I mean a danger to yourself alone. You swore a promise by what you call the Precious. Remember that! It will hold you to it; but it will seek a way to twist it to your own undoing. Already you are being twisted. You revealed yourself to me just now, foolishly. *Give it back to Sméagol* you said. Do not say that again! Do not let that

thought grow in you! You will never get it back. But the
desire of it may betray you to a bitter end. You will never
get it back. In the last need, Sméagol, I should put on the
Precious; and the Precious mastered you long ago. If I,
wearing it, were to command you, you would obey, even
if it were to leap from a precipice or to cast yourself into
the fire. And such would be my command. So have a care,
Sméagol!'

Sam looked at his master with approval, but also with
surprise: there was a look in his face and a tone in his
voice that he had not known before. It had always been a
notion of his that the kindness of dear Mr. Frodo was of
such a high degree that it must imply a fair measure of
blindness. Of course, he also firmly held the incompatible
belief that Mr. Frodo was the wisest person in the world
(with the possible exception of Old Mr. Bilbo and of Gandalf). Gollum in his own way, and with much more excuse
as his acquaintance was much briefer, may have made a
similar mistake, confusing kindness and blindness. At any
rate this speech abashed and terrified him. He grovelled
on the ground and could speak no clear words but *nice
master*.

Frodo waited patiently for a while, then he spoke again
less sternly. 'Come now, Gollum or Sméagol if you wish,
tell me of this other way, and show me, if you can, what
hope there is in it, enough to justify me in turning aside
from my plain path. I am in haste.'

But Gollum was in a pitiable state, and Frodo's threat
had quite unnerved him. It was not easy to get any clear
account out of him, amid his mumblings and squeakings,
and the frequent interruptions in which he crawled on the
floor and begged them both to be kind to 'poor little
Sméagol'. After a while he grew a little calmer, and Frodo
gathered bit by bit that, if a traveller followed the road
that turned west of Ephel Dúath, he would come in time
to a crossing in a circle of dark trees. On the right a road
went down to Osgiliath and the bridges of the Anduin; in
the middle the road went on southwards.

'On, on, on,' said Gollum. 'We never went that way,

but they say it goes a hundred leagues, until you can see the Great Water that is never still. There are lots of fishes there, and big birds eat fishes: nice birds: but we never went there, alas no! we never had a chance. And further still there are more lands, they say, but the Yellow Face is very hot there, and there are seldom any clouds, and the men are fierce and have dark faces. We do not want to see that land.'

'No!' said Frodo. 'But do not wander from your road. What of the third turning?'

'O yes, O yes, there is a third way,' said Gollum. 'That is the road to the left. At once it begins to climb up, up, winding and climbing back towards the tall shadows. When it turns round the black rock, you'll see it, suddenly you'll see it above you, and you'll want to hide.'

'See it, see it? What will you see?'

'The old fortress, very old, very horrible now. We used to hear tales from the South, when Sméagol was young, long ago. O yes, we used to tell lots of tales in the evening, sitting by the banks of the Great River, in the willow-lands, when the River was younger too, *gollum, gollum.*' He began to weep and mutter. The hobbits waited patiently.

'Tales out of the South,' Gollum went on again, 'about the tall Men with the shining eyes, and their houses like hills of stone, and the silver crown of their King and his White Tree: wonderful tales. They built very tall towers, and one they raised was silver-white, and in it there was a stone like the Moon, and round it were great white walls. O yes, there were many tales about the Tower of the Moon.'

'That would be Minas Ithil that Isildur the son of Elendil built,' said Frodo. 'It was Isildur who cut off the finger of the Enemy.'

'Yes, He has only four on the Black Hand, but they are enough,' said Gollum shuddering. 'And He hated Isildur's city.'

'What does he not hate?' said Frodo. 'But what has the Tower of the Moon to do with us?'

'Well, master, there it was and there it is: the tall tower and the white houses and the wall; but not nice now, not beautiful. He conquered it long ago. It is a very terrible place now. Travellers shiver when they see it, they creep out of sight, they avoid its shadow. But master will have to go that way. That is the only other way. For the mountains are lower there, and the old road goes up and up, until it reaches a dark pass at the top, and then it goes down, down, again—to Gorgoroth.' His voice sank to a whisper and he shuddered.

'But how will that help us?' asked Sam. 'Surely the Enemy knows all about his own mountains, and that road will be guarded as close as this? The tower isn't empty, is it?'

'O no, not empty!' whispered Gollum. 'It seems empty, but it isn't, O no! Very dreadful things live there. Orcs, yes always Orcs; but worse things, worse things live there too. The road climbs right under the shadow of the walls and passes the gate. Nothing moves on the road that they don't know about. The things inside know: the Silent Watchers.'

'So that's your advice is it,' said Sam, 'that we should go another long march south, to find ourselves in the same fix or a worse one, when we get there, if we ever do?'

'No, no indeed,' said Gollum. 'Hobbits must see, must try to understand. He does not expect attack that way. His Eye is all round, but it attends more to some places than to others. He can't see everything all at once, not yet. You see, He has conquered all the country west of the Shadowy Mountains down to the River, and He holds the bridges now. He thinks no one can come to the Moon-tower without fighting big battle at the bridges, or getting lots of boats which they cannot hide and He will know about.'

'You seem to know a lot about what He's doing and thinking,' said Sam. 'Have you been talking to Him lately? Or just hobnobbing with Orcs?'

'Not nice hobbit, not sensible,' said Gollum, giving Sam an angry glance and turning to Frodo. 'Sméagol has talked to Orcs, yes of course, before he met master, and to many peoples: he has walked very far. And what he says now many peoples are saying. It's here in the North that the big danger is for Him, and for us. He will come out of the Black Gate one day, one day soon. That is the only way big armies can come. But away down west He is not afraid, and there are the Silent Watchers.'

'Just so!' said Sam, not to be put off. 'And so we are to walk up and knock at their gate and ask if we're on the right road for Mordor? Or are they too silent to answer? It's not sense. We might as well do it here, and save ourselves a long tramp.'

'Don't make jokes about it,' hissed Gollum. 'It isn't funny, O no! Not amusing. It's not sense to try and get into Mordor at all. But if master says *I must go* or *I will go*, then he must try some way. But he must not go to the terrible city, O no, of course not. That is where Sméagol helps, nice Sméagol, though no one tells him what it is all about. Sméagol helps again. He found it. He knows it.'

'What did you find?' asked Frodo.

Gollum crouched down and his voice sank to a whisper again. 'A little path leading up into the mountains; and then a stair, a narrow stair, O yes, very long and narrow. And then more stairs. And then'—his voice sank even lower—'a tunnel, dark tunnel; and at last a little cleft, and a path high above the main pass. It was that way that Sméagol got out of the darkness. But it was years ago. The path may have vanished now; but perhaps not, perhaps not.'

'I don't like the sound of it at all,' said Sam. 'Sounds too easy at any rate in the telling. If that path is still there, it'll be guarded too. Wasn't it guarded, Gollum?' As he said this, he caught or fancied he caught a green gleam in Gollum's eye. Gollum muttered and did not reply.

'Is it not guarded?' asked Frodo sternly. 'And did you *escape* out of the darkness, Sméagol? Were you not rather permitted to depart, upon an errand? That at least is what Aragorn thought, who found you by the Dead Marshes some years ago.'

'It's a lie!' hissed Gollum, and an evil light came into his eyes at the naming of Aragorn. 'He lied on me, yes he did. I did escape, all by my poor self. Indeed I was told to seek for the Precious; and I have searched and searched, of course I have. But not for the Black One. The Precious was ours, it was mine I tell you. I did escape.'

Frodo felt a strange certainty that in this matter Gollum was for once not so far from the truth as might be suspected; that he had somehow found a way out of Mordor, and at least believed that it was by his own cunning. For one thing, he noted that Gollum used *I*, and that seemed usually to be a sign, on its rare appearances, that some remnants of old truth and sincerity were for the moment on top. But even if Gollum could be trusted on this point, Frodo did not forget the wiles of the Enemy. The 'escape' may have been allowed or arranged, and well known in the Dark Tower. And in any case Gollum was plainly keeping a good deal back.

'I ask you again,' he said: 'is not this secret way guarded?'

But the name of Aragorn had put Gollum into a sullen mood. He had all the injured air of a liar suspected when for once he has told the truth, or part of it. He did not answer.

'Is it not guarded?' Frodo repeated.

'Yes, yes, perhaps. No safe places in this country,' said Gollum sulkily. 'No safe places. But master must try it or go home. No other way.' They could not get him to say more. The name of the perilous place and the high pass he could not tell, or would not.

Its name was Cirith Ungol, a name of dreadful rumour. Aragorn could perhaps have told them that name and its significance; Gandalf would have warned them. But they were alone, and Aragorn was far away, and Gandalf stood amid the ruin of Isengard and strove with Saruman, delayed by treason. Yet even as he spoke his last words to Saruman, and the Palantír crashed in fire upon the steps of Orthanc, his thought was ever upon Frodo and Sam-

wise, over the long leagues his mind sought for them in
hope and pity.

Maybe Frodo felt it, not knowing it, as he had upon
Amon Hen, even though he believed that Gandalf was
gone, gone forever into the shadow in Moria far away.
He sat upon the ground for a long while, silent, his head
bowed, striving to recall all that Gandalf had said to him.
But for this choice he could recall no counsel. Indeed
Gandalf's guidance had been taken from them too soon,
too soon, while the Dark Land was still very far away.
How they should enter it at the last Gandalf had not said.
Perhaps he could not say. Into the stronghold of the
Enemy in the North, into Dol Guldur, he had once
ventured. But into Mordor, to the Mountain of Fire and
to Barad-dûr, since the Dark Lord rose in power again,
had he ever journeyed there? Frodo did not think so. And
here he was a little halfling from the Shire, a simple hobbit of the quiet countryside, expected to find a way where
the great ones could not go, or dared not go. It was an
evil fate. But he had taken it on himself in his own sitting-
room in the far-off spring of another year, so remote now
that it was like a chapter in a story of the world's youth,
when the Trees of Silver and Gold were still in bloom.
This was an evil choice. Which way should he choose? And
if both led to terror and death, what good lay in choice?

The day drew on. A deep silence fell upon the little grey
hollow where they lay, so near to the borders of the land of
fear: a silence that could be felt, as if it were a thick veil
that cut them off from all the world about them. Above
them was a dome of pale sky barred with fleeting smoke,
but it seemed high and far away, as if seen through great
deeps of air heavy with brooding thought.

Not even an eagle poised against the sun would have
marked the hobbits sitting there, under the weight of doom,
silent, not moving, shrouded in their thin grey cloaks. For
a moment he might have paused to consider Gollum, a tiny
figure sprawling on the ground: there perhaps lay the
famished skeleton of some child of Men, its ragged gar-

ment still clinging to it, its long arms and legs almost bone-white and bone-thin: no flesh worth a peck.

Frodo's head was bowed over his knees, but Sam leaned back, with hands behind his head, staring out of his hood at the empty sky. At least for a long while it was empty. Then presently Sam thought he saw a dark bird-like figure wheel into the circle of his sight, and hover, and then wheel away again. Two more followed, and then a fourth. They were very small to look at, yet he knew, somehow, that they were huge, with a vast stretch of pinion, flying at a great height. He covered his eyes and bent forward, cowering. The same warning fear was on him as he had felt in the presence of the Black Riders, the helpless horror that had come with the cry in the wind and the shadow on the moon, though now it was not so crushing or compelling: the menace was more remote. But menace it was. Frodo felt it too. His thought was broken. He stirred and shivered, but he did not look up. Gollum huddled himself together like a cornered spider. The winged shapes wheeled, and stooped swiftly down, speeding back to Mordor.

Sam took a deep breath. 'The Riders are about again, up in the air,' he said in a hoarse whisper. 'I saw them. Do you think they could see us? They were very high up. And if they are Black Riders, same as before, then they can't see much by daylight, can they?'

'No, perhaps not,' said Frodo. 'But their steeds could see. And these winged creatures that they ride on now, they can probably see more than any other creature. They are like great carrion birds. They are looking for something: the Enemy is on the watch, I fear.'

The feeling of dread passed, but the enfolding silence was broken. For some time they had been cut off from the world, as if in an invisible island; now they were laid bare again, peril had returned. But still Frodo did not speak to Gollum or make his choice. His eyes were closed, as if he were dreaming, or looking inward into his heart and memory. At last he stirred and stood up, and it seemed that he was about to speak and to decide. But 'hark!' he said. 'What is that?'

A new fear was upon them. They heard singing and hoarse shouting. At first it seemed a long way off, but it drew nearer: it was coming towards them. It leaped into all their minds that the Black Wings had spied them and had sent armed soldiers to seize them: no speed seemed too great for these terrible servants of Sauron. They crouched, listening. The voices and the clink of weapons and harness was very close. Frodo and Sam loosened their small swords in their sheaths. Flight was impossible.

Gollum rose slowly and crawled insect-like to the lip of the hollow. Very cautiously he raised himself inch by inch, until he could peer over it between two broken points of stone. He remained there without moving for some time, making no sound. Presently the voices began to recede again, and then they slowly faded away. Far off a horn blew on the ramparts of the Morannon. Then quietly Gollum drew back and slipped down into the hollow.

'More Men going to Mordor,' he said in a low voice. 'Dark faces. We have not seen Men like these before, no, Sméagol has not. They are fierce. They have black eyes, and long black hair, and gold rings in their ears; yes, lots of beautiful gold. And some have red paint on their cheeks, and red cloaks; and their flags are red, and the tips of their spears; and they have round shields, yellow and black with big spikes. Not nice; very cruel wicked Men they look. Almost as bad as Orcs, and much bigger. Sméagol thinks they have come out of the South beyond the Great River's end: they came up that road. They have passed on to the Black Gate; but more may follow. Always more people coming to Mordor. One day all the peoples will be inside.'

'Were there any oliphaunts?' asked Sam, forgetting his fear in his eagerness for news of strange places.

'No, no oliphaunts. What are oliphaunts?' said Gollum.

Sam stood up, putting his hands behind his back (as he always did when 'speaking poetry') and began:

> Grey as a mouse,
> Big as a house,
> Nose like a snake,
> I make the earth shake,
> As I tramp through the grass;
> Trees crack as I pass.
> With horns in my mouth
> I walk in the South,
> Flapping big ears
> Beyond count of years
> I stump round and round,
> Never lie on the ground,
> Not even to die.
> Oliphaunt am I,
> Biggest of all,
> Huge, old, and tall.
> If ever you'd met me
> You wouldn't forget me.
> If you never do,
> You won't think I'm true;
> But old Oliphaunt am I,
> And I never lie.

'That,' said Sam, when he had finished reciting, 'that's a rhyme we have in the Shire. Nonsense maybe, and maybe not. But we have our tales too, and news out of the South, you know. In the old days hobbits used to go on their travels now and again. Not that many ever came back, and not that all they said was believed: *news from Bree*, and not *sure as Shiretalk*, as the sayings go. But I've heard tales of the big folk down away in the Sunlands. Swertings we call 'em in our tales; and they ride on oliphaunts, 'tis said, when they fight. They put houses and towers on the oliphauntses backs and all, and the oliphaunts throw rocks and trees at one another. So when you said "Men out of the South, all in red and gold," I said "were there any oliphaunts?" For if there was, I was going to take a look, risk or no. But now I don't suppose I'll ever see an oliphaunt. Maybe there ain't no such a beast.' He sighed.

'No, no oliphaunts,' said Gollum again. 'Sméagol has not heard of them. He does not want to see them. He does not want them to be. Sméagol wants to go away from here and hide somewhere safer. Sméagol wants master to go. Nice master, won't he come with Sméagol?'

Frodo stood up. He had laughed in the midst of all his cares when Sam trotted out the old fireside rhyme of *Oliphaunt,* and the laugh had released him from hesitation. 'I wish we had a thousand oliphaunts with Gandalf on a white one at their head,' he said. 'Then we'd break a way into this evil land, perhaps. But we've not; just our own tired legs, that's all. Well, Sméagol, the third turn may turn the best. I will come with you.'

'Good master, wise master, nice master!' cried Gollum in delight, patting Frodo's knees. 'Good master! Then rest now, nice hobbits, under the shadow of the stones, close under the stones! Rest and lie quiet, till the Yellow Face goes away. Then we can go quickly. Soft and quick as shadows we must be!'

Chapter 4

Of Herbs and Stewed Rabbit

For the few hours of daylight that were left they rested, shifting into the shade as the sun moved, until at last the shadow of the western rim of their dell grew long, and darkness filled all the hollow. Then they ate a little, and drank sparingly. Gollum ate nothing, but he accepted water gladly.

'Soon get more now,' he said, licking his lips. 'Good water runs down in streams to the Great River, nice water in the lands we are going to. Sméagol will get food there too, perhaps. He's very hungry, yes, *gollum*!' He set his two large flat hands on his shrunken belly, and a pale green light came into his eyes.

The dusk was deep when at length they set out, creeping over the westward rim of the dell, and fading like ghosts into the broken country on the borders of the road. The moon was now three nights from the full, but it did not climb over the mountains until nearly midnight, and the early night was very dark. A single red light burned high up in the Towers of the Teeth, but otherwise no sign could be seen or heard of the sleepless watch on the Morannon.

For many miles the red eye seemed to stare at them as they fled, stumbling through a barren stony country. They did not dare to take the road, but they kept it on their left, following its line as well as they could at a little distance. At last, when night was growing old and they were already weary, for they had taken only one short rest, the eye dwindled to a small fiery point and then vanished: they had turned the dark northern shoulder of the lower mountains and were heading southwards.

With hearts strangely lightened they now rested again, but not for long. They were not going quick enough for

Gollum. By his reckoning it was nearly thirty leagues from the Morannon to the cross-roads above Osgiliath, and he hoped to cover that distance in four journeys. So soon they struggled on once more, until the dawn began to spread slowly in the wide grey solitude. They had then walked almost eight leagues, and the hobbits could not have gone any further, even if they had dared.

The growing light revealed to them a land already less barren and ruinous. The mountains still loomed up ominously on their left, but near at hand they could see the southward road, now bearing away from the black roots of the hills and slanting westwards. Beyond it were slopes covered with sombre trees like dark clouds, but all about them lay a tumbled heathland, grown with ling and broom and cornel, and other shrubs that they did not know. Here and there they saw knots of tall pine-trees. The hearts of the hobbits rose again a little in spite of weariness: the air was fresh and fragrant, and it reminded them of the uplands of the Northfarthing far away. It seemed good to be reprieved, to walk in a land that had only been for a few years under the dominion of the Dark Lord and was not yet fallen wholly into decay. But they did not forget their danger, nor the Black Gate that was still all too near, hidden though it was behind the gloomy heights. They looked about for a hiding-place where they could shelter from evil eyes while the light lasted.

The day passed uneasily. They lay deep in the heather and counted out the slow hours, in which there seemed little change; for they were still under the shadows of the Ephel Dúath, and the sun was veiled. Frodo slept at times, deeply and peacefully, either trusting Gollum or too tired to trouble about him; but Sam found it difficult to do more than doze, even when Gollum was plainly fast asleep, whiffling and twitching in his secret dreams. Hunger, perhaps, more than mistrust kept him wakeful: he had begun to long for a good homely meal, 'something hot out of the pot'.

As soon as the land faded into a formless grey under coming night, they started out again. In a little while Gollum led them down onto the southward road; and after that they went on more quickly, though the danger was greater. Their ears were strained for the sound of hoof or foot on the road ahead, or following them from behind; but the night passed, and they heard no sound of walker or rider.

The road had been made in a long lost time, and for perhaps thirty miles below the Morannon it had been newly repaired, but as it went south the wild encroached upon it. The handiwork of Men of old could still be seen in its straight sure flight and level course: now and again it cut its way through hillside slopes, or leaped over a stream upon a wide shapely arch of enduring masonry; but at last all signs of stonework faded, save for a broken pillar here and there, peering out of bushes at the side, or old paving-stones still lurking amid weeds and moss. Heather and trees and bracken scrambled down and overhung the banks, or sprawled out over the surface. It dwindled at last to a country cart-road little used; but it did not wind: it held on its own sure course and guided them by the swiftest way.

So they passed into the northern marches of that land that Men once called Ithilien, a fair country of climbing woods and swift-falling streams. The night became fine under star and round moon, and it seemed to the hobbits that the fragrance of the air grew as they went forward; and from the blowing and muttering of Gollum it seemed that he noticed it too, and did not relish it. At the first signs of day they halted again. They had come to the end of a long cutting, deep, and sheer-sided in the middle, by which the road clove its way through a stony ridge. Now they climbed up the westward bank and looked abroad.

Day was opening in the sky, and they saw that the mountains were now much further off, receding eastward in a long curve that was lost in the distance. Before them, as they turned west, gentle slopes ran down into dim hazes far below. All about them were small woods of resinous trees, fir and cedar and cypress, and other kinds unknown in the Shire, with wide glades among them; and everywhere there was a wealth of sweet-smelling herbs and shrubs. The long journey from Rivendell had brought them far south of their own land, but not until now in this more sheltered region had the hobbits felt the change of clime. Here Spring was already busy about them: fronds pierced moss and mould, larches were green-fingered, small flowers were opening in the turf, birds were singing. Ithilien, the garden of Gondor now desolate, kept still a dishevelled dryad loveliness.

South and west it looked towards the warm lower vales of Anduin, shielded from the east by the Ephel Dúath and yet not under the mountain-shadow, protected from the north by the Emyn Muil, open to the southern airs and the moist winds from the Sea far away. Many great trees grew there, planted long ago, falling into untended age amid a riot of careless descendants; and groves and thickets there were of tamarisk and pungent terebinth, of olive and of bay; and there were junipers and myrtles; and thymes that grew in bushes, or with their woody creeping stems mantled in deep tapestries the hidden stones; sages of many kinds putting forth blue flowers, or red, or pale green; and marjorams and new-sprouting parsleys, and many herbs of forms and scents beyond the garden-lore of Sam. The grots and rocky walls were already starred with saxifrages and stonecrops. Primeroles and anemones were awake in the filbert-brakes; and asphodel and many lily-flowers nodded their half-opened heads in the grass: deep green grass beside the pools, where falling streams halted in cool hollows on their journey down to Anduin.

The travellers turned their backs on the road and went downhill. As they walked, brushing their way through bush and herb, sweet odours rose about them. Gollum coughed and retched; but the hobbits breathed deep, and suddenly Sam laughed, for heart's ease not for jest. They followed a stream that went quickly down before them. Presently it brought them to a small clear lake in a shallow dell: it lay

in the broken ruins of an ancient stone basin, the carven
rim of which was almost wholly covered with mosses and
rose-brambles; iris-swords stood in ranks about it, and
water-lily leaves floated on its dark, gently rippling surface;
but it was deep and fresh, and spilled ever softly out over a
stony lip at the far end.

Here they washed themselves and drank their fill at the
in-falling freshet. Then they sought for a resting-place, and
a hiding-place; for this land, fair-seeming still, was nonetheless now territory of the Enemy. They had not come
very far from the road, and yet even in so short a space
they had seen scars of the old wars, and the newer
wounds made by the Orcs and other foul servants of the
Dark Lord: a pit of uncovered filth and refuse; trees hewn
down wantonly and left to die, with evil runes or the fell
sign of the Eye cut in rude strokes on their bark.

Sam scrambling below the outfall of the lake, smelling
and touching the unfamiliar plants and trees, forgetful for
the moment of Mordor, was reminded suddenly of their
ever-present peril. He stumbled on a ring still scorched by
fire, and in the midst of it he found a pile of charred and
broken bones and skulls. The swift growth of the wild
with briar and eglantine and trailing clematis was already
drawing a veil over this place of dreadful feast and slaugh-
ter; but it was not ancient. He hurried back to his companions, but he said nothing: the bones were best left in
peace and not pawed and routed by Gollum.

'Let's find a place to lie up in,' he said. 'Not lower
down. Higher up for me.'

A little way back above the lake they found a deep
brown bed of last year's fern. Beyond it was a thicket of
dark-leaved bay-trees climbing up a steep bank that was
crowned with old cedars. Here they decided to rest and
pass the day, which already promised to be bright and
warm. A good day for strolling on their way along the
groves and glades of Ithilien; but though Orcs may shun
the sunlight, there were too many places here where they
could lie hid and watch; and other evil eyes were abroad:

Sauron had many servants. Gollum, in any case, would not move under the Yellow Face. Soon it would look over the dark ridges of the Ephel Dúath, and he would faint and cower in the light and heat.

Sam had been giving earnest thought to food as they marched. Now that the despair of the impassable Gate was behind him, he did not feel so inclined as his master to take no thought for their livelihood beyond the end of their errand; and anyway it seemed wiser to him to save the waybread of the Elves for worse times ahead. Six days or more had passed since he reckoned that they had only a bare supply for three weeks.

'If we reach the Fire in that time, we'll be lucky at this rate!' he thought. 'And we might be wanting to get back. We might!'

Besides, at the end of a long night-march, and after bathing and drinking, he felt even more hungry than usual. A supper, or a breakfast, by the fire in the old kitchen at Bagshot Row was what he really wanted. An idea struck him and he turned to Gollum. Gollum had just begun to sneak off on his own, and he was crawling away on all fours through the fern.

'Hi! Gollum!' said Sam. 'Where are you going? Hunting? Well, see here, old noser, you don't like our food, and I'd not be sorry for a change myself. Your new motto's *always ready to help*. Could you find anything fit for a hungry hobbit?'

'Yes, perhaps, yes,' said Gollum. 'Sméagol always helps, if they asks—if they asks nicely.'

'Right!' said Sam. 'I does ask. And if that isn't nice enough, I begs.'

Gollum disappeared. He was away some time, and Frodo after a few mouthfuls of *lembas* settled deep into the brown fern and went to sleep. Sam looked at him. The early daylight was only just creeping down into the shadows under the trees, but he saw his master's face very clearly, and his hands, too, lying at rest on the ground beside him. He was reminded suddenly of Frodo as he had lain, asleep in the house of Elrond, after his deadly wound. Then as he had kept watch Sam had noticed that at times a light seemed to be shining faintly within; but now the light was even clearer and stronger. Frodo's face was peaceful, the marks of fear and care had left it; but it looked old, old and beautiful, as if the chiselling of the shaping years was now revealed in many fine lines that had before been hidden, though the identity of the face was not changed. Not that Sam Gamgee put it that way to himself. He shook his head, as if finding words useless, and murmured: 'I love him. He's like that, and sometimes it shines through, somehow. But I love him, whether or no.'

Gollum returned quietly and peered over Sam's shoulder. Looking at Frodo, he shut his eyes and crawled away without a sound. Sam came to him a moment later and found him chewing something and muttering to himself. On the ground beside him lay two small rabbits, which he was beginning to eye greedily.

'Sméagol always helps,' he said. 'He has brought rabbits, nice rabbits. But master has gone to sleep, and perhaps Sam wants to sleep. Doesn't want rabbits now? Sméagol tries to help, but he can't catch things all in a minute.'

Sam, however, had no objection to rabbit at all, and said so. At least not to cooked rabbit. All hobbits, of course, can cook, for they begin to learn the art before their letters (which many never reach); but Sam was a good cook, even by hobbit reckoning, and he had done a good deal of the camp-cooking on their travels, when there was a chance. He still hopefully carried some of his gear in his pack: a small tinder-box, two small shallow pans, the smaller fitting into the larger; inside them a wooden spoon, a short two-pronged fork and some skewers were stowed; and hidden at the bottom of the pack in a flat wooden box a dwindling treasure, some salt. But he needed a fire, and other things besides. He thought for a bit, while he took out his knife, cleaned and whetted it, and began to dress the rabbits. He was not going to leave Frodo alone asleep even for a few minutes.

'Now, Gollum,' he said, 'I've another job for you. Go and fill these pans with water, and bring 'em back!'

'Sméagol will fetch water, yes,' said Gollum. 'But what does the hobbit want all that water for? He has drunk, he has washed.'

'Never you mind,' said Sam. 'If you can't guess, you'll soon find out. And the sooner you fetch the water, the sooner you'll learn. Don't you damage one of my pans, or I'll carve you into mincemeat.'

While Gollum was away Sam took another look at Frodo. He was still sleeping quietly, but Sam was now struck most by the leanness of his face and hands. 'Too thin and drawn he is,' he muttered. 'Not right for a hobbit. If I can get these coneys cooked, I'm going to wake him up.'

Sam gathered a pile of the driest fern, and then scrambled up the bank collecting a bundle of twigs and broken wood; the fallen branch of a cedar at the top gave him a good supply. He cut out some turves at the foot of the bank just outside the fern-brake, and made a shallow hole and laid his fuel in it. Being handy with flint and tinder he soon had a small blaze going. It made little or no smoke but gave off an aromatic scent. He was just stooping over his fire, shielding it and building it up with heavier wood, when Gollum returned, carrying the pans carefully and grumbling to himself.

He set the pans down, and then suddenly saw what Sam was doing. He gave a thin hissing shriek, and seemed to be both frightened and angry. 'Ach! Sss—no!' he cried. 'No! Silly hobbits, foolish, yes foolish! They mustn't do it!'

'Mustn't do what?' asked Sam in surprise.

'Not make the nassty red tongues,' hissed Gollum. 'Fire, fire! It's dangerous, yes it is. It burns, it kills. And it will bring enemies, yes it will.'

'I don't think so,' said Sam. 'Don't see why it should, if you don't put wet stuff on it and make a smother. But if it does, it does. I'm going to risk it, anyhow. I'm going to stew these coneys.'

'Stew the rabbits!' squealed Gollum in dismay. 'Spoil beautiful meat Sméagol saved for you, poor hungry Smé-

THE TWO TOWERS

agol! What for? What for, silly hobbit? They are young, they are tender, they are nice. Eat them, eat them!' He clawed at the nearest rabbit, already skinned and lying by the fire.

'Now, now!' said Sam. 'Each to his own fashion. Our bread chokes you, and raw coney chokes me. If you give me a coney, the coney's mine, see, to cook, if I have a mind. And I have. You needn't watch me. Go and catch another and eat it as you fancy—somewhere private and out o' my sight. Then you won't see the fire, and I shan't see you, and we'll both be the happier. I'll see the fire don't smoke, if that's any comfort to you.'

Gollum withdrew grumbling, and crawled into the fern. Sam busied himself with his pans. 'What a hobbit needs with coney,' he said to himself, 'is some herbs and roots, especially taters—not to mention bread. Herbs we can manage, seemingly.'

'Gollum!' he called softly. 'Third time pays for all. I want some herbs.' Gollum's head peeped out of the fern, but his looks were neither helpful nor friendly. 'A few bay-leaves, some thyme and sage, will do—before the water boils,' said Sam.

'No!' said Gollum. 'Sméagol is not pleased. And Sméagol doesn't like smelly leaves. He doesn't eat grasses or roots, no precious, not till he's starving or very sick, poor Sméagol.'

'Sméagol'll get into real true hot water, when this water boils, if he don't do as he's asked,' growled Sam. 'Sam'll put his head in it, yes precious. And I'd make him look for turnips and carrots, and taters too, if it was the time o' the year. I'll bet there's all sorts of good things running wild in this country. I'd give a lot for half a dozen taters.'

'Sméagol won't go, O no precious, not this time,' hissed Gollum. 'He's frightened, and he's very tired, and this hobbit's not nice, not nice at all. Sméagol won't grub for roots and carrotses and—taters. What's taters, precious, eh, what's taters?'

'Po—ta—toes,' said Sam. 'The Gaffer's delight, and rare good ballast for an empty belly. But you won't find any, so you needn't look. But be good Sméagol and fetch me the herbs, and I'll think better of you. What's more, if you turn over a new leaf, and keep it turned, I'll cook you some taters one of these days. I will: fried fish and chips served by S. Gamgee. You couldn't say no to that.'

'Yes, yes we could. Spoiling nice fish, scorching it. Give me fish *now*, and keep nassty chips!'

'Oh you're hopeless,' said Sam. 'Go to sleep!'

In the end he had to find what he wanted for himself; but he did not have to go far, not out of sight of the place where his master lay, still sleeping. For a while Sam sat musing, and tending the fire till the water boiled. The daylight grew and the air became warm; the dew faded off turf and leaf. Soon the rabbits cut up lay simmering in their pans with the bunched herbs. Almost Sam fell asleep as the time went by. He let them stew for close on an hour, testing them now and again with his fork, and tasting the broth.

When he thought all was ready he lifted the pans off the fire, and crept along to Frodo. Frodo half opened his eyes as Sam stood over him, and then he wakened from his dreaming: another gentle, unrecoverable dream of peace.

'Hullo, Sam!' he said. 'Not resting? Is anything wrong? What is the time?'

'About a couple of hours after daybreak,' said Sam, 'and nigh on half-past eight by Shire clocks, maybe. But nothing's wrong. Though it ain't quite what I'd call right: no stock, no onions, no taters. I've got a bit of a stew for you, and some broth, Mr. Frodo. Do you good. You'll have to sup it in your mug; or straight from the pan, when it's cooled a bit. I haven't brought no bowls, nor nothing proper-er.'

Frodo yawned and stretched. 'You should have been resting, Sam,' he said. 'And lighting a fire was dangerous in these parts. But I do feel hungry. Hmm! Can I smell it from here? What have you stewed?'

'A present from Sméagol,' said Sam: 'a brace o' young

coneys; though I fancy Gollum's regretting them now. But there's nought to go with them but a few herbs.'

Sam and his master sat just within the fern-brake and ate their stew from the pans, sharing the old fork and spoon. They allowed themselves half a piece of the elvish waybread each. It seemed a feast.

'Wheew! Gollum!' Sam called and whistled softly. 'Come on! Still time to change your mind. There's some left, if you want to try stewed coney.' There was no answer.

'Oh well, I suppose he's gone off to find something for himself. We'll finish it,' said Sam.

'And then you must take some sleep,' said Frodo.

'Don't you drop off, while I'm nodding, Mr. Frodo. I don't feel too sure of him. There's a good deal of Stinker— the bad Gollum, if you understand me—in him still, and it's getting stronger again. Not but what I think he'd try to throttle me first now. We don't see eye to eye, and he's not pleased with Sam, O no precious, not pleased at all.'

They finished, and Sam went off to the stream to rinse his gear. As he stood up to return, he looked back up the slope. At that moment he saw the sun rise out of the reek, or haze, or dark shadow, or whatever it was, that lay ever to the east, and it sent its golden beams down upon the trees and glades about him. Then he noticed a thin spiral of blue-grey smoke, plain to see as it caught the sunlight, rising from a thicket above him. With a shock he realized that this was the smoke from his little cooking-fire, which he had neglected to put out.

'That won't do! Never thought it would show like that!' he muttered, and he started to hurry back. Suddenly he halted and listened. Had he heard a whistle or not? Or was it the call of some strange bird? If it was a whistle, it did not come from Frodo's direction. There it went again from another place! Sam began to run as well as he could uphill.

He found that a small brand, burning away to its outer end, had kindled some fern at the edge of the fire, and the fern blazing up had set the turves smouldering. Hastily he stamped out what was left of the fire, scattered the ashes, and laid the turves on the hole. Then he crept back to Frodo.

'Did you hear a whistle, and what sounded like an answer?' he asked. 'A few minutes back. I hope it was only a bird, but it didn't sound quite like that: more like somebody mimicking a bird-call, I thought. And I'm afraid my bit of fire's been smoking. Now if I've gone and brought trouble, I'll never forgive myself. Nor won't have a chance, maybe!'

'Hush!' whispered Frodo. 'I thought I heard voices.'

The two hobbits trussed their small packs, put them on ready for flight, and then crawled deeper into the fern. There they crouched listening.

There was no doubt of the voices. They were speaking low and furtively, but they were near, and coming nearer. Then quite suddenly one spoke clearly close at hand.

'Here! Here is where the smoke came from!' it said. ' 'Twill be night at hand. In the fern, no doubt. We shall have it like a coney in a trap. Then we shall learn what kind of thing it is.'

'Aye, and what it knows!' said a second voice.

At once four men came striding through the fern from different directions. Since flight and hiding were no longer possible, Frodo and Sam sprang to their feet, putting back to back and whipping out their small swords.

If they were astonished at what they saw, their captors were even more astonished. Four tall Men stood there. Two had spears in their hands with broad bright heads. Two had great bows, almost of their own height, and great quivers of long green-feathered arrows. All had swords at their sides, and were clad in green and brown of varied hues, as if the better to walk unseen in the glades of Ithilien. Green gauntlets covered their hands, and their faces were hooded and masked with green, except for their eyes, which were very keen and bright. At once Frodo thought of Boromir, for these Men were like him in stature and bearing, and in their manner of speech.

'We have not found what we sought,' said one. 'But what have we found?'

'Not Orcs,' said another, releasing the hilts of his sword, which he had seized when he saw the glitter of Sting in Frodo's hand.

'Elves?' said a third, doubtfully.

'Nay! Not Elves,' said the fourth, the tallest, and as it appeared the chief among them. 'Elves do not walk in Ithilien in these days. And Elves are wondrous fair to look upon, or so 'tis said.'

'Meaning we're not, I take you,' said Sam. 'Thank you kindly. And when you've finished discussing us, perhaps you'll say who *you* are, and why you can't let two tired travellers rest.'

The tall green man laughed grimly. 'I am Faramir, Captain of Gondor,' he said. 'But there are no travellers in this land: only the servants of the Dark Tower, or of the White.'

'But we are neither,' said Frodo. 'And travellers we are, whatever Captain Faramir may say.'

'Then make haste to declare yourselves and your errand,' said Faramir. 'We have a work to do, and this is no time or place for riddling or parleying. Come! Where is the third of your company?'

'The third?'

'Yes, the skulking fellow that we saw with his nose in the pool down yonder. He had an ill-favoured look. Some spying breed of Orc, I guess, or a creature of theirs. But he gave us the slip by some fox-trick.'

'I do not know where he is,' said Frodo. 'He is only a chance companion met upon our road, and I am not answerable for him. If you come on him, spare him. Bring him or send him to us. He is only a wretched gangrel creature, but I have him under my care for a while. But as for us, we are Hobbits of the Shire, far to the North and West, beyond many rivers. Frodo son of Drogo is my name, and with me is Samwise son of Hamfast, a worthy hobbit in my service. We have come by long ways—out of Rivendell, or Imladris as some call it.' Here Faramir started and grew intent. 'Seven companions we had: one we lost at Moria, the others we left at Parth Galen above Rauros: two of my kin; a Dwarf there was also, and an Elf, and two Men. They were Aragorn; and Boromir, who said that he came out of Minas Tirith, a city in the South.'

'Boromir!' all the four men exclaimed.

'Boromir son of the Lord Denethor?' said Faramir, and a strange stern look came into his face. 'You came with him? That is news indeed, if it be true. Know, little strangers, that Boromir son of Denethor was High Warden of the White Tower, and our Captain-General: sorely do we miss him. Who are you then, and what had you to do with him? Be swift, for the Sun is climbing!'

'Are the riddling words known to you that Boromir brought to Rivendell?' Frodo replied.

> *Seek for the Sword that was Broken.*
> *In Imladris it dwells.*

'The words are known indeed,' said Faramir in astonishment. 'It is some token of your truth that you also know them.'

'Aragorn whom I named is the bearer of the Sword that was Broken,' said Frodo. 'And we are the Halflings that the rhyme spoke of.'

'That I see,' said Faramir thoughtfully. 'Or I see that it might be so. And what is Isildur's Bane?'

'That is hidden,' answered Frodo. 'Doubtless it will be made clear in time.'

'We must learn more of this,' said Faramir, 'and know what brings you so far east under the shadow of yonder——,' he pointed and said no name. 'But not now. We have business in hand. You are in peril, and you would not have gone far by field or road this day. There will be hard handstrokes nigh at hand ere the day is full. Then death, or swift flight back to Anduin. I will leave two to guard you, for your good and for mine. Wise man trusts not to chance-meeting on the road in this land. If I return, I will speak more with you.'

'Farewell!' said Frodo, bowing low. 'Think what you will, I am a friend of all enemies of the One Enemy. We would go with you, if we halfling folk could hope to serve you, such doughty men and strong as you seem, and if my errand permitted it. May the light shine on your swords!'

'The Halflings are courteous folk, whatever else they be,' said Faramir. 'Farewell!'

The hobbits sat down again, but they said nothing to one another of their thoughts and doubts. Close by, just under the dappling shadow of the dark bay-trees, two men remained on guard. They took off their masks now and again to cool them, as the day-heat grew, and Frodo saw that they were goodly men, pale-skinned, dark of hair, with grey eyes and faces sad and proud. They spoke together in soft voices, at first using the Common Speech, but after the manner of older days, and then changing to another language of their own. To his amazement, as he listened Frodo became aware that it was the Elven-tongue that they spoke, or one but little different; and he looked at them with wonder, for he knew then that they must be Dúnedain of the South, men of the line of the Lords of Westernesse.

After a while he spoke to them; but they were slow and cautious in answering. They named themselves Mablung and Damrod, soldiers of Gondor, and they were Rangers of Ithilien; for they were descended from folk who lived in Ithilien at one time, before it was overrun. From such men the Lord Denethor chose his forayers, who crossed the Anduin secretly (how or where, they would not say) to harry the Orcs and other enemies that roamed between the Ephel Dúath and the River.

'It is close on ten leagues hence to the east-shore of Anduin,' said Mablung, 'and we seldom come so far afield. But we have a new errand on this journey; we come to ambush the Men of Harad. Curse them!'

'Aye, curse the Southrons!' said Damrod. ' 'Tis said that there were dealings of old between Gondor and the kingdoms of the Harad in the Far South; though there was never friendship. In those days our bounds were away south beyond the mouths of Anduin, and Umbar, the nearest of their realms, acknowledged our sway. But that is long since. 'Tis many lives of Men since any passed to or fro between us. Now of late we have learned that the Enemy has been among them, and they are gone over to Him, or back to Him—they were ever ready to His will—as have so many also in the East. I doubt not that the days of Gondor are numbered, and the walls of Minas Tirith are doomed, so great is His strength and malice.'

'But still we will not sit idle and let Him do all as He would,' said Mablung. 'These cursed Southrons come now marching up the ancient roads to swell the hosts of the Dark Tower. Yea, up the very roads that craft of Gondor made. And they go ever more heedlessly, we learn, thinking that the power of their new master is great enough, so that the mere shadow of His hills will protect them. We come to teach them another lesson. Great strength of them was reported to us some days ago, marching north. One of their regiments is due by our reckoning to pass by, some time ere noon—up on the road above, where it passes through the cloven way. The road may pass, but they shall not! Not while Faramir is Captain. He leads now in all perilous ventures. But his life is charmed, or fate spares him for some other end.'

Their talk died down into a listening silence. All seemed still and watchful. Sam, crouched by the edge of the fernbrake, peered out. With his keen hobbit-eyes he saw that many more Men were about. He could see them stealing up the slopes, singly or in long files, keeping always to the shade of grove or thicket, or crawling, hardly visible in their brown and green raiment, through grass and brake. All were hooded and masked, and had gauntlets on their hands, and were armed like Faramir and his companions. Before long they had all passed and vanished. The sun rose till it neared the South. The shadow shrank.

'I wonder where that dratted Gollum is?' thought Sam, as he crawled back into deeper shade. 'He stands a fair

chance of being spitted for an Orc, or of being roasted by
the Yellow Face. But I fancy he'll look after himself.' He
lay down beside Frodo and began to doze.

He woke, thinking that he had heard horns blowing.
He sat up. It was now high noon. The guards stood alert
and tense in the shadow of the trees. Suddenly the horns
rang out louder and beyond mistake from above, over the
top of the slope. Sam thought that he heard cries and wild
shouting also, but the sound was faint, as if it came out
of some distant cave. Then presently the noise of fighting
broke out near at hand, just above their hiding-place. He
could hear plainly the ringing grate of steel on steel, the
clang of sword on iron cap, the dull beat of blade on
shield; men were yelling and screaming, and one clear
loud voice was calling *Gondor! Gondor!*

'It sounds like a hundred blacksmiths all smithying together,' said Sam to Frodo. 'They're as near as I want
them now.'

But the noise grew closer. 'They are coming!' cried
Damrod. 'See! Some of the Southrons have broken from
the trap and are flying from the road. There they go! Our
men after them, and the Captain leading.'

Sam, eager to see more, went now and joined the
guards. He scrambled a little way up into one of the larger
of the bay-trees. For a moment he caught a glimpse of
swarthy men in red running down the slope some way off
with green-clad warriors leaping after them, hewing them
down as they fled. Arrows were thick in the air. Then
suddenly straight over the rim of their sheltering bank, a
man fell, crashing through the slender trees, nearly on top
of them. He came to rest in the fern a few feet away, face
downward, green arrow-feathers sticking from his neck
below a golden collar. His scarlet robes were tattered,
his corslet of overlapping brazen plates was rent and
hewn, his black plaits of hair braided with gold were
drenched with blood. His brown hand still clutched the
hilt of a broken sword.

It was Sam's first view of a battle of Men against Men,

and he did not like it much. He was glad that he could not see the dead face. He wondered what the man's name was and where he came from; and if he was really evil of heart, or what lies or threats had led him on the long march from his home; and if he would not really rather have stayed there in peace—all in a flash of thought which was quickly driven from his mind. For just as Mablung stepped towards the fallen body, there was a new noise. Great crying and shouting. Amidst it Sam heard a shrill bellowing or trumpeting. And then a great thudding and bumping, like huge rams dinning on the ground.

'Ware! Ware!' cried Damrod to his companion. 'May the Valar turn him aside! Mûmak! Mûmak!'

To his astonishment and terror, and lasting delight, Sam saw a vast shape crash out of the trees and come careering down the slope. Big as a house, much bigger than a house, it looked to him, a grey-clad moving hill. Fear and wonder, maybe, enlarged him in the hobbit's eyes, but the Mûmak of Harad was indeed a beast of vast bulk, and the like of him does not walk now in Middle-earth; his kin that live still in latter days are but memories of his girth and majesty. On he came, straight towards the watchers, and then swerved aside in the nick of time, passing only a few yards away, rocking the ground beneath their feet: his great legs like trees, enormous sail-like ears spread out, long snout upraised like a huge serpent about to strike, his small red eyes raging. His upturned hornlike tusks were bound with bands of gold and dripped with blood. His trappings of scarlet and gold flapped about him in wild tatters. The ruins of what seemed a very war-tower lay upon his heaving back, smashed in his furious passage through the woods; and high upon his neck still desperately clung a tiny figure—the body of a mighty warrior, a giant among the Swertings.

On the great beast thundered, blundering in blind wrath through pool and thicket. Arrows skipped and snapped harmlessly about the triple hide of his flanks. Men of both sides fled before him, but many he overtook and crushed to the ground. Soon he was lost to view, still trumpeting and stamping far away. What became of him Sam never heard: whether he escaped to roam the wild for a time, until he perished far from his home or was trapped in some deep pit; or whether he raged on until he plunged in the Great River and was swallowed up.

Sam drew a deep breath. 'An Oliphaunt it was!' he said. 'So there are Oliphaunts, and I have seen one. What a life! But no one at home will ever believe me. Well, if that's over, I'll have a bit of sleep.'

'Sleep while you may,' said Mablung. 'But the Captain will return, if he is unhurt; and when he comes we shall depart swiftly. We shall be pursued as soon as news of our deed reaches the Enemy, and that will not be long.'

'Go quietly when you must!' said Sam. 'No need to disturb my sleep. I was walking all night.'

Mablung laughed. 'I do not think the Captain will leave you here, Master Samwise,' he said. 'But you shall see.'

Chapter 5

The Window on the West

It seemed to Sam that he had only dozed for a few minutes when he awoke to find that it was late afternoon and Faramir had come back. He had brought many men with him; indeed all the survivors of the foray were now gathered on the slope nearby, two or three hundred strong. They sat in a wide semicircle, between the arms of which Faramir was seated on the ground, while Frodo stood before him. It looked strangely like the trial of a prisoner.

Sam crept out from the fern, but no one paid any attention to him, and he placed himself at the end of the rows of men, where he could see and hear all that was going on. He watched and listened intently, ready to dash to his master's aid if needed. He could see Faramir's face, which was now unmasked: it was stern and commanding, and a keen wit lay behind his searching glance. Doubt was in the grey eyes that gazed steadily at Frodo.

Sam soon became aware that the Captain was not satisfied with Frodo's account of himself at several points: what part he had to play in the Company that set out from Rivendell; why he had left Boromir; and where he was now going. In particular he returned often to Isildur's Bane. Plainly he saw that Frodo was concealing from him some matter of great importance.

'But it was at the coming of the Halfling that Isildur's Bane should waken, or so one must read the words,' he insisted. 'If then you are the Halfling that was named, doubtless you brought this thing, whatever it may be, to the Council of which you speak, and there Boromir saw it. Do you deny it?'

Frodo made no answer. 'So!' said Faramir. 'I wish then to learn from you more of it; for what concerns Boromir concerns me. An orc-arrow slew Isildur, so far as old tales tell. But orc-arrows are plenty, and the sight of one would

343

not be taken as a sign of Doom by Boromir of Gondor. Had you this thing in keeping? It is hidden, you say; but is not that because you choose to hide it?'

'No, not because I choose,' answered Frodo. 'It does not belong to me. It does not belong to any mortal, great or small; though if any could claim it, it would be Aragorn son of Arathorn, whom I named, the leader of our Company from Moria to Rauros.'

'Why so, and not Boromir, prince of the City that the sons of Elendil founded?'

'Because Aragorn is descended in direct lineage, father to father, from Isildur Elendil's son himself. And the sword that he bears was Elendil's sword.'

A murmur of astonishment ran through all the ring of men. Some cried aloud: 'The sword of Elendil! The sword of Elendil comes to Minas Tirith! Great tidings!' But Faramir's face was unmoved.

'May be,' he said. 'But so great a claim will need to be established, and clear proofs will be required, should this Aragorn ever come to Minas Tirith. He had not come, nor any of your Company, when I set out six days ago.'

'Boromir was satisfied of that claim,' said Frodo. 'Indeed, if Boromir were here, he would answer all your questions. And since he was already at Rauros many days back, and intended then to go straight to your city, if you return, you may soon learn the answers there. My part in the Company was known to him, as to all the others, for it was appointed to me by Elrond of Imladris himself before the whole Council. On that errand I came into this country, but it is not mine to reveal to any outside the Company. Yet those who claim to oppose the Enemy would do well not to hinder it.'

Frodo's tone was proud, whatever he felt, and Sam approved of it; but it did not appease Faramir.

'So!' he said. 'You bid me mind my own affairs, and get me back home, and let you be. Boromir will tell all, when he comes. When he comes, say you! Were you a friend of Boromir?'

Vividly before Frodo's mind came the memory of Boromir's assault upon him, and for a moment he hesitated. Faramir's eyes watching him grew harder. 'Boromir was a valiant member of our Company,' said Frodo at length. 'Yes, I was his friend, for my part.'

Faramir smiled grimly. 'Then you would grieve to learn that Boromir is dead?'

'I would grieve indeed,' said Frodo. Then catching the look in Faramir's eyes, he faltered. 'Dead?' he said. 'Do you mean that he *is* dead, and that you knew it? You have been trying to trap me in words, playing with me? Or are you now trying to snare me with a falsehood?'

'I would not snare even an orc with a falsehood,' said Faramir.

'How then did he die, and how do you know of it? Since you say that none of the Company had reached the city when you left.'

'As to the manner of his death, I had hoped that his friend and companion would tell me how it was.'

'But he was alive and strong when we parted. And he lives still for all that I know. Though surely there are many perils in the world.'

'Many indeed,' said Faramir, 'and treachery not the least.'

Sam had been getting more and more impatient and angry at this conversation. These last words were more than he could bear, and bursting into the middle of the ring, he strode up to his master's side.

'Begging your pardon, Mr. Frodo,' he said, 'but this has gone on long enough. He's no right to talk to you so. After all you've gone through, as much for his good and all these great Men as for anyone else.

'See here, Captain!' He planted himself squarely in front of Faramir, his hands on his hips, and a look on his face as if he was addressing a young hobbit who had offered him what he called 'sauce' when questioned about visits to the orchard. There was some murmuring, but also some grins on the faces of the men looking on: the sight of their Captain sitting on the ground and eye to eye with a young hobbit, legs well apart, bristling with wrath, was one beyond their experience. 'See here!' he said. 'What are you driving at? Let's come to the point before all the Orcs of Mordor come down on us! If you think my master murdered this Boromir and then ran away, you've got no sense; but say it, and have done! And then let us know what you mean to do about it. But it's a pity that folk as talk about fighting the Enemy can't let others do their bit in their own way without interfering. He'd be mighty pleased, if he could see you now. Think he'd got a new friend, he would.'

'Patience!' said Faramir, but without anger. 'Do not speak before your master, whose wit is greater than yours. And I do not need any to teach me of our peril. Even so, I spare a brief time, in order to judge justly in a hard matter. Were I as hasty as you, I might have slain you long ago. For I am commanded to slay all whom I find in this land without the leave of the Lord of Gondor. But I do not slay man or beast needlessly, and not gladly even when it is needed. Neither do I talk in vain. So be comforted. Sit by your master, and be silent!'

Sam sat down heavily with a red face. Faramir turned to Frodo again. 'You asked how do I know that the son of Denethor is dead. Tidings of death have many wings. *Night oft brings news to near kindred,* 'tis said. Boromir was my brother.'

A shadow of sorrow passed over his face. 'Do you remember aught of special mark that the Lord Boromir bore with him among his gear?'

Frodo thought for a moment, fearing some further trap, and wondering how this debate would turn in the end. He had hardly saved the Ring from the proud grasp of Boromir, and how he would fare now among so many men, warlike and strong, he did not know. Yet he felt in his heart that Faramir, though he was much like his brother in looks, was a man less self-regarding, both sterner and wiser. 'I remember that Boromir bore a horn,' he said at last.

'You remember well, and as one who has in truth seen him,' said Faramir. 'Then maybe you can see it in your

mind's eye: a great horn of the wild ox of the East, bound
with silver, and written with ancient characters. That
horn the eldest son of our house has borne for many generations; and it is said that if it be blown at need anywhere within the bounds of Gondor, as the realm was of
old, its voice will not pass unheeded.

'Five days ere I set out on this venture, eleven days ago
at about this hour of the day, I heard the blowing of that
horn: from the northward it seemed, but dim, as if it were
but an echo in the mind. A boding of ill we thought it,
my father and I, for no tidings had we heard of Boromir
since he went away, and no watcher on our borders had
seen him pass. And on the third night after, another and a
stranger thing befell me.

'I sat at night by the waters of Anduin, in the grey dark
under the young pale moon, watching the ever-moving
stream; and the sad reeds were rustling. So do we ever
watch the shore nigh Osgiliath, which our enemies now
partly hold, and issue from it to harry our lands. But that
night all the world slept at the midnight hour. Then I saw,
or it seemed that I saw, a boat floating on the water,
glimmering grey, a small boat of a strange fashion with a
high prow, and there was none to row or steer it.

'An awe fell on me, for a pale light was round it. But I
rose and went to the bank, and began to walk out into the
stream, for I was drawn towards it. Then the boat turned
towards me, and stayed its pace, and floated slowly by
within my hand's reach, yet I durst not handle it. It
waded deep, as if it were heavily burdened, and it seemed
to me as it passed under my gaze that it was almost filled
with clear water, from which came the light; and lapped
in the water a warrior lay asleep.

'A broken sword was on his knee. I saw many wounds
on him. It was Boromir, my brother, dead. I knew his gear,
his sword, his beloved face. One thing only I missed: his
horn. One thing only I knew not: a fair belt, as it were of
linked golden leaves, about his waist. *Boromir!* I cried.
Where is thy horn? Whither goest thou? O Boromir! But
he was gone. The boat turned into the stream and passed

glimmering on into the night. Dreamlike it was, and yet no dream, for there was no waking. And I do not doubt that he is dead and has passed down the River to the Sea.'

'Alas!' said Frodo. 'That was indeed Boromir as I knew him. For the golden belt was given to him in Lothlórien by the Lady Galadriel. She it was that clothed us as you see us, in elven-grey. This brooch is of the same workmanship.' He touched the green and silver leaf that fastened his cloak beneath his throat.

Faramir looked closely at it. 'It is beautiful,' he said. 'Yes, 'tis work of the same craft. So then you passed through the Land of Lórien? Laurenlindórinan it was named of old, but long now it has lain beyond the knowledge of Men,' he added softly, regarding Frodo with a new wonder in his eyes. 'Much that was strange about you I begin now to understand. Will you tell me more? For it is a bitter thought that Boromir died, within sight of the land of his home.'

'No more can I say than I have said,' answered Frodo. 'Though your tale fills me with foreboding. A vision it was that you saw, I think, and no more, some shadow of evil fortune that has been or will be. Unless indeed it is some lying trick of the Enemy. I have seen the faces of fair warriors of old laid in sleep beneath the pools of the Dead Marshes, or seeming so by his foul arts.'

'Nay, it was not so,' said Faramir. 'For his works fill the heart with loathing; but my heart was filled with grief and pity.'

'Yet how could such a thing have happened in truth?' asked Frodo. 'For no boat could have been carried over the stony hills from Tol Brandir; and Boromir purposed to go home across the Entwash and the fields of Rohan. And yet how could any vessel ride the foam of the great falls and not founder in the boiling pools, though laden with water?'

'I know not,' said Faramir. 'But whence came the boat?'

'From Lórien,' said Frodo. 'In three such boats we

rowed down Anduin to the Falls. They also were of elven-work.'

'You passed through the Hidden Land,' said Faramir, 'but it seems that you little understood its power. If Men have dealings with the Mistress of Magic who dwells in the Golden Wood, then they may look for strange things to follow. For it is perilous for mortal man to walk out of the world of this Sun, and few of old came thence unchanged, 'tis said.

'Boromir, O Boromir!' he cried. *'What did she say to you, the Lady that dies not? What did she see? What woke in your heart then? Why went you ever to Laurelindórinan, and came not by your own road, upon the horses of Rohan riding home in the morning?'*

Then turning again to Frodo, he spoke in a quiet voice once more. 'To those questions I guess that you could make some answer, Frodo son of Drogo. But not here or now, maybe. But lest you still should think my tale a vision, I will tell you this. The horn of Boromir at least returned in truth, and not in seeming. The horn came, but it was cloven in two, as it were by axe or sword. The shards came severally to shore: one was found among the reeds where watchers of Gondor lay, northwards below the infalls of the Entwash; the other was found spinning on the flood by one who had an errand on the water. Strange chances, but murder will out, 'tis said.

'And now the horn of the elder son lies in two pieces upon the lap of Denethor, sitting in his high chair, waiting for news. And you can tell me nothing of the cleaving of the horn?'

'No, I did not know of it,' said Frodo. 'But the day when you heard it blowing, if your reckoning is true, was the day when we parted, when I and my servant left the Company. And now your tale fills me with dread. For if Boromir was then in peril and was slain, I must fear that all my companions perished too. And they were my kindred and my friends.

'Will you not put aside your doubt of me and let me go? I am weary, and full of grief, and afraid. But I have a deed to do, or attempt, before I too am slain. And the more need of haste, if we two halflings are all that remain of our fellowship.

'Go back, Faramir, valiant Captain of Gondor, and defend your city while you may, and let me go where my doom takes me.'

'For me there is no comfort in our speech together,' said Faramir; 'but you surely draw from it more dread than need be. Unless the people of Lórien themselves came to him, who arrayed Boromir as for a funeral? Not Orcs or servants of the Nameless. Some of your Company, I guess, live still.

'But whatever befell on the North March, you, Frodo, I doubt no longer. If hard days have made me any judge of Men's words and faces, then I may make a guess at Halflings! Though,' and now he smiled, 'there is something strange about you, Frodo, an elvish air, maybe. But more lies upon our words together than I thought at first. I should now take you back to Minas Tirith to answer there to Denethor, and my life will justly be forfeit, if I now choose a course that proves ill for my city. So I will not decide in haste what is to be done. Yet we must move hence without more delay.'

He sprang to his feet and issued some orders. At once the men who were gathered round him broke up into small groups, and went off this way and that, vanishing quickly into the shadows of the rocks and trees. Soon only Mablung and Damrod remained.

'Now you, Frodo and Samwise, will come with me and my guards,' said Faramir. 'You cannot go along the road southwards, if that was your purpose. It will be unsafe for some days, and always more closely watched after this affray than it has been yet. And you cannot, I think, go far today in any case, for you are weary. And so are we. We are going now to a secret place we have, somewhat less than ten miles from here. The Orcs and spies of the Enemy have not found it yet, and if they did, we could hold it long even against many. There we may lie up and rest for a while, and you with us. In the morning I will decide what is best for me to do, and for you.'

There was nothing for Frodo to do but to fall in with this request, or order. It seemed in any case a wise course for the moment, since this foray of the men of Gondor had made a journey in Ithilien more dangerous than ever.

They set out at once: Mablung and Damrod a little ahead, and Faramir with Frodo and Sam behind. Skirting the hither side of the pool where the hobbits had bathed, they crossed the stream, climbed a long bank, and passed into green-shadowed woodlands that marched ever downwards and westwards. While they walked, as swiftly as the hobbits could go, they talked in hushed voices.

'I broke off our speech together,' said Faramir, 'not only because time pressed, as Master Samwise had reminded me, but also because we were drawing near to matters that were better not debated openly before many men. It was for that reason that I turned rather to the matter of my brother and let be *Isildur's Bane*. You were not wholly frank with me, Frodo.'

'I told no lies, and of the truth all I could,' said Frodo.

'I do not blame you,' said Faramir. 'You spoke with skill in a hard place, and wisely, it seemed to me. But I learned or guessed more from you than your words said. You were not friendly with Boromir, or you did not part in friendship. You, and Master Samwise, too, I guess have some grievance. Now I loved him dearly, and would gladly avenge his death, yet I knew him well. *Isildur's Bane*— I would hazard that *Isildur's Bane* lay between you and was a cause of contention in your Company. Clearly it is a mighty heirloom of some sort, and such things do not breed peace among confederates, not if aught may be learned from ancient tales. Do I not hit near the mark?'

'Near,' said Frodo, 'but not in the gold. There was no contention in our Company, though there was doubt: doubt which way we should take from the Emyn Muil.

But be that as it may, ancient tales teach us also the peril of rash words concerning such things as—heirlooms.'

'Ah, then it is as I thought: your trouble was with Boromir alone. He wished this thing brought to Minas Tirith. Alas! it is a crooked fate that seals your lips who saw him last, and holds from me that which I long to know: what was in his heart and thought in his latest hours. Whether he erred or no, of this I am sure: he died well, achieving some good thing. His face was more beautiful even than in life.

'But, Frodo, I pressed you hard at first about *Isildur's Bane*. Forgive me! It was unwise in such an hour and place. I had not had time for thought. We had had a hard fight, and there was more than enough to fill my mind. But even as I spoke with you, I drew nearer to the mark, and so deliberately shot wider. For you must know that much is still preserved of ancient lore among the Rulers of the city that is not spread abroad. We of my house are not of the line of Elendil, though the blood of Númenor is in us. For we reckon back our line to Mardil, the good steward, who ruled in the king's stead when he went away to war. And that was King Eärnur, last of the line of Anárion, and childless, and he came never back. And the stewards have governed the city since that day, though it was many generations of Men ago.

'And this I remember of Boromir as a boy, when we together learned the tale of our sires and the history of our city, that always it displeased him that his father was not king. "How many hundreds of years needs it to make a steward a king, if the king returns not?" he asked. "Few years, maybe, in other places of less royalty," my father answered. "In Gondor ten thousand years would not suffice." Alas! poor Boromir. Does that not tell you something of him?'

'It does,' said Frodo. 'Yet always he treated Aragorn with honour.'

'I doubt it not,' said Faramir. 'If he were satisfied of Aragorn's claim, as you say, he would greatly reverence him. But the pinch had not yet come. They had not yet reached Minas Tirith or become rivals in her wars.

'But I stray. We in the house of Denethor know much ancient lore by long tradition, and there are moreover in our treasuries many things preserved: books and tablets writ on withered parchments, yea, and on stone, and on leaves of silver and of gold, in divers characters. Some none can now read; and for the rest, few ever unlock them. I can read a little in them, for I have had teaching. It was these records that brought the Grey Pilgrim to us. I first saw him when I was a child, and he has been twice or thrice since then.'

'The Grey Pilgrim?' said Frodo. 'Had he a name?'

'Mithrandir we called him in elf-fashion,' said Faramir, 'and he was content. *Many are my names in many countries,* he said. *Mithrandir among the Elves, Tharkûn to the Dwarves; Olórin I was in my youth in the West that is forgotten, in the South Incánus, in the North Gandalf; to the East I go not.*'

'Gandalf!' said Frodo. 'I thought it was he. Gandalf the Grey, dearest of counsellors. Leader of our Company. He was lost in Moria.'

'Mithrandir was lost!' said Faramir. 'An evil fate seems to have pursued your fellowship. It is hard indeed to believe that one of so great wisdom, and of power—for many wonderful things he did among us—could perish, and so much lore be taken from the world. Are you sure of this, and that he did not just leave you and depart where he would?'

'Alas! yes,' said Frodo. 'I saw him fall into the abyss.'

'I see that there is some great tale of dread in this,' said Faramir, 'which perhaps you may tell me in the evening-time. This Mithrandir was, I now guess, more than a lore-master: a great mover of the deeds that are done in our time. Had he been among us to consult concerning the hard words of our dream, he could have made them clear to us without need of messenger. Yet, maybe, he would not have done so, and the journey of Boromir was doomed. Mithrandir never spoke to us of what was to be, nor did he reveal his purposes. He got leave of Denethor, how I do not know, to look at the secrets of our treasury, and I learned a little of him, when he would teach (and that was seldom). Ever he would search and would question us above all else concerning the Great Battle that was fought upon Dagorlad in the beginning of Gondor, when He whom we do not name was overthrown. And he was eager for stories of Isildur, though of him we had less to tell; for nothing certain was ever known among us of his end.'

Now Faramir's voice sank to a whisper. 'But this much I learned, or guessed, and I have kept it ever secret in my heart since: that Isildur took somewhat from the hand of the Unnamed, ere he went away from Gondor, never to be seen among mortal men again. Here I thought was the answer to Mithrandir's questioning. But it seemed then a matter that concerned only the seekers after ancient learning. Nor when the riddling words of our dream were debated among us, did I think of *Isildur's Bane* as being this same thing. For Isildur was ambushed and slain by orc-arrows, according to the only legend that we knew, and Mithrandir had never told me more.

'What in truth this Thing is I cannot yet guess; but some heirloom of power and peril it must be. A fell weapon, perchance, devised by the Dark Lord. If it were a thing that gave advantage in battle, I can well believe that Boromir, the proud and fearless, often rash, ever anxious for the victory of Minas Tirith (and his own glory therein), might desire such a thing and be allured by it. Alas that ever he went on that errand! I should have been chosen by my father and the elders, but he put himself forward, as being the older and the hardier (both true), and he would not be stayed.

'But fear no more! I would not take this thing, if it lay by the highway. Not were Minas Tirith falling in ruin and I alone could save her, so, using the weapon of the Dark Lord for her good and my glory. No, I do not wish for such triumphs, Frodo son of Drogo.'

'Neither did the Council,' said Frodo. 'Nor do I. I would have nothing to do with such matters.'

'For myself,' said Faramir, 'I would see the White Tree in flower again in the courts of the kings, and the Silver Crown return, and Minas Tirith in peace: Minas Anor again as of old, full of light, high and fair, beautiful as a queen among other queens: not a mistress of many slaves, nay, not even a kind mistress of willing slaves. War must be, while we defend our lives against a destroyer who would devour all; but I do not love the bright sword for its sharpness, nor the arrow for its swiftness, nor the warrior for his glory. I love only that which they defend: the city of the Men of Númenor; and I would have her loved for her memory, her ancientry, her beauty, and her present wisdom. Not feared, save as men may fear the dignity of a man, old and wise.

'So fear me not! I do not ask you to tell me more. I do not even ask you to tell me whether I now speak nearer the mark. But if you will trust me, it may be that I can advise you in your present quest, whatever that be—yes, and even aid you.'

Frodo made no answer. Almost he yielded to the desire for help and counsel, to tell this grave young man, whose words seemed so wise and fair, all that was in his mind. But something held him back. His heart was heavy with fear and sorrow: if he and Sam were indeed, as seemed likely, all that was now left of the Nine Walkers, then he was in sole command of the secret of their errand. Better mistrust undeserved than rash words. And the memory of Boromir, of the dreadful change that the lure of the Ring had worked in him, was very present to his mind, when he looked at Faramir and listened to his voice: unlike they were, and yet also much akin.

They walked on in silence for a while, passing like grey and green shadows under the old trees, their feet making no sound; above them many birds sang, and the sun glistened on the polished roof of dark leaves in the evergreen woods of Ithilien.

Sam had taken no part in the conversation, though he had listened; and at the same time he had attended with his keen hobbit ears to all the soft woodland noises about them. One thing he had noted, that in all the talk the name of Gollum had not once come up. He was glad, though he felt that it was too much to hope that he would never hear it again. He soon became aware also that though they walked alone, there were many men close at hand: not only Damrod and Mablung flitting in and out of the shadows ahead, but others on either side, all making their swift secret way to some appointed place.

Once, looking suddenly back, as if some prickle of the skin told him that he was watched from behind, he thought he caught a brief glimpse of a small dark shape slipping behind a tree-trunk. He opened his mouth to speak and shut it again. 'I'm not sure of it,' he said to himself, 'and why should I remind them of the old villain, if they choose to forget him? I wish I could!'

So they passed on, until the woodlands grew thinner and the land began to fall more steeply. Then they turned aside again, to the right, and came quickly to a small river in a narrow gorge: it was the same stream that trickled far above out of the round pool, now grown to a swift torrent, leaping down over many stones in a deep-cloven bed, overhung with ilex and dark box-woods. Looking west they could see, below them in a haze of light, lowlands and broad meads, and glinting far off in the westering sun the wide waters of the Anduin.

'Here, alas! I must do you a discourtesy,' said Faramir. 'I hope you will pardon it to one who has so far made his orders give way to courtesy as not to slay you or to bind you. But it is a command that no stranger, not even one of Rohan that fights with us, shall see the path we now go with open eyes. I must blindfold you.'

'As you will,' said Frodo. 'Even the Elves do likewise at need, and blindfolded we crossed the borders of fair Lothlórien. Gimli the dwarf took it ill, but the hobbits endured it.'

'It is to no place so fair that I shall lead you,' said Faramir. 'But I am glad that you will take this willingly and not by force.'

He called softly and immediately Mablung and Damrod stepped out of the trees and came back to him. 'Blindfold these guests,' said Faramir. 'Securely, but not so as to discomfort them. Do not tie their hands. They will give their word not to try and see. I could trust them to shut their eyes of their own accord, but eyes will blink, if the feet stumble. Lead them so that they do not falter.'

With green scarves the two guards now bound up the hobbits' eyes, and drew their hoods down almost to their mouths; then quickly they took each one by the hand and went on their way. All that Frodo and Sam knew of this last mile of the road they learned from guessing in the dark. After a little they found that they were on a path descending steeply; soon it grew so narrow that they went in single file, brushing a stony wall on either side; their guards steered them from behind with hands laid firmly on their shoulders. Now and again they came to rough places and were lifted from their feet for a while, and then set down again. Always the noise of the running water was on their right hand, and it grew nearer and louder. At length they were halted. Quickly Mablung and Damrod turned them about, several times, and they lost all sense of direction. They climbed upwards a little: it seemed cold and the noise of the stream had become faint. Then they were picked up and carried down, down many steps, and round a corner. Suddenly they heard the water again, loud now, rushing and splashing. All round them it seemed, and they felt a fine rain on their hands and cheeks. At last they were set on their feet once more. For a moment they stood so, half fearful, blindfold, not knowing where they were; and no one spoke.

Then came the voice of Faramir close behind. 'Let them see!' he said. The scarves were removed and their hoods drawn back, and they blinked and gasped.

They stood on a wet floor of polished stone, the doorstep, as it were, of a rough-hewn gate of rock opening dark behind them. But in front a thin veil of water was hung, so near that Frodo could have put an outstretched arm into it. It faced westward. The level shafts of the setting sun behind beat upon it, and the red light was broken into many flickering beams of ever-changing colour. It was as if they stood at the window of some elven-tower, curtained with threaded jewels of silver and gold, and ruby, sapphire and amethyst, all kindled with an unconsuming fire.

'At least by good chance we came at the right hour to reward you for your patience,' said Faramir. 'This is the Window of the Sunset, Henneth Annûn, fairest of all the falls of Ithilien, land of many fountains. Few strangers have ever seen it. But there is no kingly hall behind to match it. Enter now and see!'

Even as he spoke the sun sank, and the fire faded in the flowing water. They turned and passed under the low forbidding arch. At once they found themselves in a rock-chamber, wide and rough, with an uneven stooping roof. A few torches were kindled and cast a dim light on the glistening walls. Many men were already there. Others were still coming in by twos and threes through a dark narrow door on one side. As their eyes grew accustomed to the gloom the hobbits saw that the cave was larger than they had guessed and was filled with great store of arms and victuals.

'Well, here is our refuge,' said Faramir. 'Not a place of great ease, but here you may pass the night in peace. It is dry at least, and there is food, though no fire. At one time the water flowed down through this cave and out of the arch, but its course was changed further up the gorge, by workmen of old, and the stream sent down in a fall of doubled height over the rocks far above. All the ways into this grot were then sealed against the entry of water or aught else, all save one. There are now but two ways out: that passage yonder by which you entered blindfold, and through the Window-curtain into a deep bowl filled with knives of stone. Now rest a while, until the evening meal is set.'

The hobbits were taken to a corner and given a low bed to lie on, if they wished. Meanwhile men busied themselves about the cave, quietly and in orderly quickness. Light tables were taken from the walls and set up on trestles and laden with gear. This was plain and unadorned for the most part, but all well and fairly made: round platters, bowls and dishes of glazed brown clay or turned boxwood, smooth and clean. Here and there was a cup or basin of polished bronze; and a goblet of plain silver was set by the Captain's seat in the middle of the inmost table.

Faramir went about among the men, questioning each as he came in, in a soft voice. Some came back from the pursuit of the Southrons; others, left behind as scouts near the road, came in latest. All the Southrons had been accounted for, save only the great mûmak: what happened to him none could say. Of the enemy no movement could be seen; not even an orc-spy was abroad.

'You saw and heard nothing, Anborn?' Faramir asked of the latest comer.

'Well, no, lord,' said the man. 'No Orc at least. But I saw, or thought I saw, something a little strange. It was getting deep dusk, when the eyes make things greater than they should be. So perhaps it may have been no more than a squirrel.' Sam pricked up his ears at this. 'Yet if so, it was a black squirrel, and I saw no tail. 'Twas like a shadow on the ground, and it whisked behind a tree-trunk when I drew nigh and went up aloft as swift as any squirrel could. You will not have us slay wild beasts for no purpose, and it seemed no more, so I tried no arrow. It was too dark for sure shooting anyway, and the creature was gone into the gloom of the leaves in a twinkling. But I stayed for a while, for it seemed strange, and then I hastened back. I thought I heard the thing hiss at me from high above as I turned away. A large squirrel, maybe. Perhaps under the shadow of the Unnamed some of the beasts of Mirkwood are wandering hither to our woods. They have black squirrels there, 'tis said.'

'Perhaps,' said Faramir. 'But that would be an ill omen, if it were so. We do not want the escapes of Mirkwood in Ithilien.' Sam fancied that he gave a swift glance towards the hobbits as he spoke; but Sam said nothing. For a while he and Frodo lay back and watched the torchlight, and the men moving to and fro speaking in hushed voices. Then suddenly Frodo fell asleep.

Sam struggled with himself, arguing this way and that. 'He may be all right,' he thought, 'and then he may not. Fair speech may hide a foul heart.' He yawned. 'I could sleep for a week, and I'd be better for it. And what can I do, if I do keep awake, me all alone, and all these great Men about? Nothing, Sam Gamgee; but you've got to keep awake all the same.' And somehow he managed it. The light faded from the cave door, and the grey veil of falling water grew dim and was lost in gathering shadow. Always the sound of water went on, never changing its note, morning or evening or night. It murmured and whispered of sleep. Sam stuck his knuckles in his eyes.

Now more torches were being lit. A cask of wine was broached. Storage barrels were being opened. Men were fetching water from the fall. Some were laving their hands in basins. A wide copper bowl and a white cloth were brought to Faramir and he washed.

'Wake our guests,' he said, 'and take them water. It is time to eat.'

Frodo sat up and yawned and stretched. Sam, not used to being waited on, looked with some surprise at the tall man who bowed, holding a basin of water before him.

'Put it on the ground, master, if you please!' he said. 'Easier for me and you.' Then to the astonishment and amusement of the Men he plunged his head into the cold water and splashed his neck and ears.

'Is it the custom in your land to wash the head before supper?' said the man who waited on the hobbits.

'No, before breakfast,' said Sam. 'But if you're short of sleep cold water on the neck's like rain on a wilted lettuce.

There! Now I can keep awake long enough to eat a bit.'

They were led then to seats beside Faramir; barrels covered with pelts and high enough above the benches of the Men for their convenience. Before they ate, Faramir and all his men turned and faced west in a moment of silence. Faramir signed to Frodo and Sam that they should do likewise.

'So we always do,' he said, as they sat down: 'we look towards Númenor that was, and beyond to Elvenhome that is, and to that which is beyond Elvenhome and will ever be. Have you no such custom at meat?'

'No,' said Frodo, feeling strangely rustic and untutored. 'But if we are guests, we bow to our host, and after we have eaten we rise and thank him.'

'That we do also,' said Faramir.

After so long journeying and camping, and days spent in the lonely wild, the evening meal seemed a feast to the hobbits: to drink pale yellow wine, cool and fragrant, and eat bread and butter, and salted meats, and dried fruits, and good red cheese, with clean hands and clean knives and plates. Neither Frodo nor Sam refused anything that was offered, nor a second, nor indeed a third helping. The wine coursed in their veins and tired limbs, and they felt glad and easy of heart as they had not done since they left the land of Lórien.

When all was done Faramir led them to a recess at the back of the cave, partly screened by curtains; and a chair and two stools were brought there. A little earthenware lamp burned in a niche.

'You may soon desire to sleep,' he said, 'and especially good Samwise, who would not close his eyes before he ate—whether for fear of blunting the edge of a noble hunger, or for fear of me, I do not know. But it is not good to sleep too soon after meat, and that following a fast. Let us talk a while. On your journey from Rivendell there must have been many things to tell. And you, too, would perhaps wish to learn something of us and the lands where

you now are. Tell me of Boromir my brother, and of old
Mithrandir, and of the fair people of Lothlórien.'

Frodo no longer felt sleepy and he was willing to talk.
But though the food and wine had put him at his ease, he
had not lost all his caution. Sam was beaming and humming to himself, but when Frodo spoke he was at first
content to listen, only occasionally venturing to make an
exclamation of agreement.

Frodo told many tales, yet always he steered the matter
away from the quest of the Company and from the Ring,
enlarging rather on the valiant part Boromir had played
in all their adventures, with the wolves of the wild, in the
snows under Caradhras, and in the mines of Moria where
Gandalf fell. Faramir was most moved by the story of the
fight on the bridge.

'It must have irked Boromir to run from Orcs,' he said,
'or even from the fell thing you name, the Balrog—even
though he was the last to leave.'

'He was the last,' said Frodo, 'but Aragorn was forced
to lead us. He alone knew the way after Gandalf's fall. But
had there not been us lesser folk to care for, I do not think
that either he or Boromir would have fled.'

'Maybe, it would have been better had Boromir fallen
there with Mithrandir,' said Faramir, 'and not gone on to
the fate that waited above the falls of Rauros.'

'Maybe. But tell me now of your own fortunes,' said
Frodo, turning the matter aside once again. 'For I would
learn more of Minas Ithil and Osgiliath, and Minas Tirith
the long-enduring. What hope have you for that city in
your long war?'

'What hope have we?' said Faramir. 'It is long since we
had any hope. The sword of Elendil, if it returns indeed,
may rekindle it, but I do not think that it will do more than
put off the evil day, unless other help unlooked-for also
comes, from Elves or Men. For the Enemy increases and
we decrease. We are a failing people, a springless autumn.

'The Men of Númenor were settled far and wide on the
shores and seaward regions of the Great Lands, but for
the most part they fell into evils and follies. Many became

enamoured of the Darkness and the black arts; some were given over wholly to idleness and ease, and some fought among themselves, until they were conquered in their weakness by the wild men.

'It is not said that evil arts were ever practised in Gondor, or that the Nameless One was ever named in honour there; and the old wisdom and beauty brought out of the West remained long in the realm of the sons of Elendil the Fair, and they linger there still. Yet even so it was Gondor that brought about its own decay, falling by degrees into dotage, and thinking that the Enemy was asleep, who was only banished not destroyed.

'Death was ever present, because the Númenoreans still, as they had in their old kingdom, and so lost it, hungered after endless life unchanging. Kings made tombs more splendid than houses of the living, and counted old names in the rolls of their descent dearer than the names of sons. Childless lords sat in aged halls musing on heraldry; in secret chambers withered men compounded strong elixirs, or in high cold towers asked questions of the stars. And the last king of the line of Anárion had no heir.

'But the stewards were wiser and more fortunate. Wiser, for they recruited the strength of our people from the sturdy folk of the seacoast, and from the hardy mountaineers of Ered Nimrais. And they made a truce with the proud peoples of the North, who often had assailed us, men of fierce valour, but our kin from afar off, unlike the wild Easterlings or the cruel Haradrim.

'So it came to pass in the days of Cirion the Twelfth Steward (and my father is the six and twentieth) that they rode to our aid and at the great Field of Celebrant they destroyed our enemies that had seized our northern provinces. These are the Rohirrim, as we name them, masters of horses, and we ceded to them the fields of Calenardhon that are since called Rohan; for that province had long been sparsely peopled. And they became our allies, and have ever proved true to us, aiding us at need, and guarding our northern marches and the Gap of Rohan.

'Of our lore and manners they have learned what they

would, and their lords speak our speech at need; yet for the most part they hold by the ways of their own fathers and to their own memories, and they speak among themselves their own North tongue. And we love them: tall men and fair women, valiant both alike, golden-haired, bright-eyed, and strong; they remind us of the youth of Men, as they were in the Elder Days. Indeed it is said by our lore-masters that they have from of old this affinity with us that they are come from those same Three Houses of Men as were the Númenoreans in their beginning; not from Hador the Goldenhaired, the Elf-friend, maybe, yet from such of his sons and people as went not over Sea into the West, refusing the call.

'For so we reckon Men in our lore, calling them the High, or Men of the West, which were Númenoreans; and the Middle Peoples, Men of the Twilight, such as are the Rohirrim and their kin that dwell still far in the North; and the Wild, the Men of Darkness.

'Yet now, if the Rohirrim are grown in some ways more like to us, enhanced in arts and gentleness, we too have become more like to them, and can scarce claim any longer the title High. We are become Middle Men, of the Twilight, but with memory of other things. For as the Rohirrim do, we now love war and valour as things good in themselves, both a sport and an end; and though we still hold that a warrior should have more skills and knowledge than only the craft of weapons and slaying, we esteem a warrior, nonetheless, above men of other crafts. Such is the need of our days. So even was my brother, Boromir: a man of prowess, and for that he was accounted the best man in Gondor. And very valiant indeed he was: no heir of Minas Tirith has for long years been so hardy in toil, so onward into battle, or blown a mightier note on the Great Horn.' Faramir sighed and fell silent for a while.

'You don't say much in all your tales about the Elves, sir,' said Sam, suddenly plucking up courage. He had noted that Faramir seemed to refer to Elves with reverence, and this even more than his courtesy, and his food and wine, had won Sam's respect and quieted his suspicions.

'No indeed, Master Samwise,' said Faramir, 'for I am not learned in Elven-lore. But there you touch upon another point in which we have changed, declining from Númenor to Middle-earth. For as you may know, if Mithrandir was your companion and you have spoken with Elrond, the Edain, the Fathers of the Númenoreans, fought beside the Elves in the first wars, and were rewarded by the gift of the kingdom in the midst of the Sea, within sight of Elvenhome. But in Middle-earth Men and Elves became estranged in the days of darkness, by the arts of the Enemy, and by the slow changes of time in which each kind walked further down their sundered roads. Men now fear and misdoubt the Elves, and yet know little of them. And we of Gondor grow like other Men, like the men of Rohan; for even they, who are foes of the Dark Lord, shun the Elves and speak of the Golden Wood with dread.

'Yet there are among us still some who have dealings with the Elves when they may, and ever and anon one will go in secret to Lórien, seldom to return. Not I. For I deem it perilous now for mortal man wilfully to seek out the Elder People. Yet I envy you that have spoken with the White Lady.'

'The Lady of Lórien! Galadriel!' cried Sam. 'You should see her, indeed you should, sir. I am only a hobbit, and gardening's my job at home, sir, if you understand me, and I'm not much good at poetry—not at making it: a bit of a comic rhyme, perhaps, now and again, you know, but not real poetry—so I can't tell you what I mean. It ought to be sung. You'd have to get Strider, Aragorn that is, or old Mr. Bilbo, for that. But I wish I could make a song about her. Beautiful she is, sir! Lovely! Sometimes like a great tree in flower, sometimes like a white daffadowndilly, small and slender like. Hard as di'monds, soft as moonlight. Warm as sunlight, cold as frost in the stars. Proud and far-off as a snow-mountain, and as merry as any lass I ever saw with daisies in her hair in springtime. But that's a lot o' nonsense, and all wide of my mark.'

'Then she must be lovely indeed,' said Faramir. "Peril-ously fair.'

'I don't know about *perilous*,' said Sam. 'It strikes me that folk takes their peril with them into Lórien, and finds it there because they've brought it. But perhaps you could call her perilous, because she's so strong in herself. You, you could dash yourself to pieces on her, like a ship on a rock; or drownd yourself, like a hobbit in a river. But neither rock nor river would be to blame. Now Boro——' He stopped and went red in the face.

'Yes? *Now Boromir* you would say?' said Faramir. 'What would you say? He took his peril with him?'

'Yes sir, begging your pardon, and a fine man as your brother was, if I may say so. But you've been warm on the scent all along. Now I watched Boromir and listened to him, from Rivendell all down the road—looking after my master, as you'll understand, and not meaning any harm to Boromir—and it's my opinion that in Lórien he first saw clearly what I guessed sooner: what he wanted. From the moment he first saw it he wanted the Enemy's Ring!'

'Sam!' cried Frodo aghast. He had fallen deep into his own thoughts for a while, and came out of them suddenly and too late.

'Save me!' said Sam turning white, and then flushing scarlet. 'There I go again! *When ever you open your big mouth you put your foot in it* the Gaffer used to say to me, and right enough. O dear, O dear!

'Now look here, sir!' He turned, facing up to Faramir with all the courage that he could muster. 'Don't you go taking advantage of my master because his servant's no better than a fool. You've spoken very handsome all along, put me off my guard, talking of Elves and all. But *hand-some is as handsome does* we say. Now's a chance to show your quality.'

'So it seems,' said Faramir, slowly and very softly, with a strange smile. 'So that is the answer to all the riddles! The One Ring that was thought to have perished from the world. And Boromir tried to take it by force? And you es-caped? And ran all the way—to me! And here in the wild

I have you: two halflings, and a host of men at my call, and
the Ring of Rings. A pretty stroke of fortune! A chance for
Faramir, Captain of Gondor, to show his quality! Ha!' He
stood up, very tall and stern, his grey eyes glinting.

Frodo and Sam sprang from their stools and set themselves side by side with their backs to the wall, fumbling
for their sword-hilts. There was a silence. All the men in
the cave stopped talking and looked towards them in wonder. But Faramir sat down again in his chair and began
to laugh quietly, and then suddenly became grave again.

'Alas for Boromir! It was too sore a trial!' he said. 'How
you have increased my sorrow, you two strange wanderers
from a far country, bearing the peril of Men! But you are
less judges of Men than I of Halflings. We are truth-speak-
ers, we men of Gondor. We boast seldom, and then per-
form, or die in the attempt. *Not if I found it on the
highway would I take it* I said. Even if I were such a man
as to desire this thing, and even though I knew not clearly
what this thing was when I spoke, still I should take those
words as a vow, and be held by them.

'But I am not such a man. Or I am wise enough to know
that there are some perils from which a man must flee. Sit
at peace! And be comforted, Samwise. If you seem to have
stumbled, think that it was fated to be so. Your heart is
shrewd as well as faithful, and saw clearer than your eyes.
For strange though it may seem, it was safe to declare this
to me. It may even help the master that you love. It shall
turn to his good, if it is in my power. So be comforted.
But do not even name this thing again aloud. Once is
enough.'

The hobbits came back to their seats and sat very quiet.
Men turned back to their drink and their talk, perceiving that their captain had had some jest or other with the
little guests, and that it was over.

'Well, Frodo, now at last we understand one another,'
said Faramir. 'If you took this thing on yourself, unwilling,
at others' asking, then you have pity and honour from me.
And I marvel at you: to keep it hid and not to use it. You

are a new people and a new world to me. Are all your kin
of like sort? Your land must be a realm of peace and
content, and there must gardeners be in high honour.'

'Not all is well there,' said Frodo, 'but certainly gardeners are honoured.'

'But folk must grow weary there, even in their gardens,
as do all things under the Sun of this world. And you are
far from home and wayworn. No more tonight. Sleep, both
of you—in peace, if you can. Fear not! I do not wish to see
it, or touch it, or know more of it than I know (which
is enough), lest peril perchance waylay me and I fall lower
in the test than Frodo son of Drogo. Go now to rest—but
first tell me only, if you will, whither you wish to go, and
what to do. For I must watch, and wait, and think. Time
passes. In the morning we must each go swiftly on the
ways appointed to us.'

Frodo had felt himself trembling as the first shock of
fear passed. Now a great weariness came down on him like
a cloud. He could dissemble and resist no longer.

'I was going to find a way into Mordor,' he said faintly.
'I was going to Gorgoroth. I must find the Mountain of Fire
and cast the thing into the gulf of Doom. Gandalf said so.
I do not think I shall ever get there.'

Faramir stared at him for a moment in grave astonishment. Then suddenly he caught him as he swayed, and
lifting him gently, carried him to the bed and laid him
there, and covered him warmly. At once he fell into a
deep sleep.

Another bed was set beside him for his servant. Sam
hesitated for a moment, then bowing very low: 'Good
night, Captain, my lord,' he said. 'You took the chance,
sir.'

'Did I so?' said Faramir.

'Yes sir, and showed your quality: the very highest.'

Faramir smiled. 'A pert servant, Master Samwise. But
nay: the praise of the praiseworthy is above all rewards.
Yet there was naught in this to praise. I had no lure or
desire to do other than I have done.'

'Ah well, sir,' said Sam, 'you said my master had an

elvish air; and that was good and true. But I can say this: you have an air too, sir, that reminds me of, of—well, Gandalf, of wizards.'

'Maybe,' said Faramir. 'Maybe you discern from far away the air of Númenor. Good night!'

Chapter 6

The Forbidden Pool

Frodo woke to find Faramir bending over him. For a second old fears seized him and he sat up and shrank away.

'There is nothing to fear,' said Faramir.

'Is it morning already?' said Frodo yawning.

'Not yet, but night is drawing to an end, and the full moon is setting. Will you come and see it? Also there is a matter on which I desire your counsel. I am sorry to rouse you from sleep, but will you come?'

'I will,' said Frodo, rising and shivering a little as he left the warm blanket and pelts. It seemed cold in the fireless cave. The noise of the water was loud in the stillness. He put on his cloak and followed Faramir.

Sam, waking suddenly by some instinct of watchfulness, saw first his master's empty bed and leapt to his feet. Then he saw two dark figures, Frodo and a man, framed against the archway, which was now filled with a pale white light. He hurried after them, past rows of men sleeping on mattresses along the way. As he went by the cave-mouth he saw that the Curtain was now become a dazzling veil of silk and pearls and silver thread: melting icicles of moonlight. But he did not pause to admire it, and turning aside he followed his master through the narrow doorway in the wall of the cave.

They went first along a black passage, then up many wet steps, and so came to a small flat landing cut in the stone and lit by the pale sky, gleaming high above through a long deep shaft. From here two flights of steps led: one going on, as it seemed, up onto the high bank of the stream; the other turning away to the left. This they followed. It wound its way up like a turret-stair.

At last they came out of the stony darkness and looked

about. They were on a wide flat rock without rail or parapet. At their right, eastwards, the torrent fell, splashing
over many terraces, and then, pouring down a steep race,
it filled a smooth-hewn channel with a dark force of water
flecked with foam, and curling and rushing almost at their
feet it plunged sheer over the edge that yawned upon their
left. A man stood there, near the brink, silent, gazing
down.

Frodo turned to watch the sleek necks of the water as
they curved and dived. Then he lifted his eyes and gazed
far away. The world was quiet and cold, as if dawn were
near. Far off in the West the full moon was sinking, round
and white. Pale mists shimmered in the great vale below:
a wide gulf of silver fume, beneath which rolled the cool
night-waters of the Anduin. A black darkness loomed
beyond, and in it glinted, here and there, cold, sharp,
remote, white as the teeth of ghosts, the peaks of Ered
Nimrais, the White Mountains of the Realm of Gondor,
tipped with everlasting snow.

For a while Frodo stood there on the high stone, and a
shiver ran through him, wondering if anywhere in the
vastness of the nightlands his old companions walked or
slept, or lay dead shrouded in mist. Why was he brought
here out of forgetful sleep?

Sam was eager for an answer to the same question and
could not refrain himself from muttering, for his master's
ear alone as he thought: 'It's a fine view, no doubt, Mr.
Frodo, but chilly to the heart, not to mention the bones!
What's going on?'

Faramir heard and answered. 'Moonset over Gondor.
Fair Ithil, as he goes from Middle-earth, glances upon the
white locks of old Mindolluin. It is worth a few shivers. But
that is not what I brought you to see—though as for you,
Samwise, you were not brought, and do but pay the
penalty of your watchfulness. A draught of wine shall
amend it. Come, look now!'

He stepped up beside the silent sentinel on the dark
edge, and Frodo followed. Sam hung back. He already felt
insecure enough on this high wet platform. Faramir and

Frodo looked down. Far below them they saw the white waters pour into a foaming bowl, and then swirl darkly about a deep oval basin in the rocks, until they found their way out again through a narrow gate, and flowed away, fuming and chattering, into calmer and more level reaches. The moonlight still slanted down to the fall's foot and gleamed on the ripples of the basin. Presently Frodo was aware of a small dark thing on the near bank, but even as he looked at it, it dived and vanished just beyond the boil and bubble of the fall, cleaving the black water as neatly as an arrow or an edgewise stone.

Faramir turned to the man at his side. 'Now what would you say that it is, Anborn? A squirrel, or a king-fisher? Are there black kingfishers in the night-pools of Mirkwood?'

' 'Tis not a bird, whatever else it be,' answered Anborn. 'It has four limbs and dives manwise; a pretty mastery of the craft it shows, too. What is it at? Seeking a way up be-hind the Curtain to our hidings? It seems we are discovered at last. I have my bow here, and I have posted other archers, nigh as good marksmen as myself, on either bank. We wait only for your command to shoot, Captain.'

'Shall we shoot?' said Faramir, turning quickly to Frodo.

Frodo did not answer for a moment. Then 'No!' he said. 'No! I beg you not to.' If Sam had dared, he would have said 'Yes,' quicker and louder. He could not see, but he guessed well enough from their words what they were looking at.

'You know, then, what this thing is?' said Faramir. 'Come, now you have seen, tell me why it should be spared. In all our words together you have not once spoken of your gangrel companion, and I let him be for the time. He could wait till he was caught and brought before me. I sent my keenest huntsmen to seek him, but he slipped them, and they had no sight of him till now, save Anborn here, once at dusk yesterevening. But now he has done worse trespass than only to go coney-snaring in the up-lands: he has dared to come to Henneth Annûn, and his life is forfeit. I marvel at the creature: so secret and so sly as he is, to come sporting in the pool before our very window. Does he think that men sleep without watch all night? Why does he so?'

'There are two answers, I think,' said Frodo. 'For one thing, he knows little of Men, and sly though he is, your refuge is so hidden that perhaps he does not know that Men are concealed here. For another, I think he is allured here by a mastering desire, stronger than his caution.'

'He is lured here, you say?' said Faramir in a low voice. 'Can he, does he then know of your burden?'

'Indeed yes. He bore it himself for many years.'

'*He* bore it?' said Faramir, breathing sharply in his wonder. 'This matter winds itself ever in new riddles. Then he is pursuing it?'

'Maybe. It is precious to him. But I did not speak of that.'

'What then does the creature seek?'

'Fish,' said Frodo. 'Look!'

They peered down at the dark pool. A little black head appeared at the far end of the basin, just out of the deep shadow of the rocks. There was a brief silver glint, and a swirl of tiny ripples. It swam to the side, and then with marvellous agility a froglike figure climbed out of the water and up the bank. At once it sat down and began to gnaw at the small silver thing that glittered as it turned: the last rays of the moon were now falling behind the stony wall at the pool's end.

Faramir laughed softly. 'Fish!' he said. 'It is a less perilous hunger. Or maybe not: fish from the pool of Henneth Annûn may cost him all he has to give.'

'Now I have him at the arrow-point,' said Anborn. 'Shall I not shoot, Captain? For coming unbidden to this place death is our law.'

'Wait, Anborn,' said Faramir. 'This is a harder matter than it seems. What have you to say now, Frodo? Why should we spare.'

'The creature is wretched and hungry,' said Frodo, 'and unaware of his danger. And Gandalf, your Mithrandir, he would have bidden you not to slay him for that reason, and for others. He forbade the Elves to do so. I do not know clearly why, and of what I guess I cannot speak openly out here. But this creature is in some way bound up with my errand. Until you found us and took us, he was my guide.'

'Your guide!' said Faramir. 'The matter becomes ever stranger. I would do much for you, Frodo, but this I cannot grant: to let this sly wanderer go free at his own will from here, to join you later if it please him, or to be caught by Orcs and tell all he knows under threat of pain. He must be slain or taken. Slain, if he be not taken very swiftly. But how can this slippery thing of many guises be caught, save by a feathered shaft?'

'Let me go down quietly to him,' said Frodo. 'You may keep your bows bent, and shoot me at least, if I fail. I shall not run away.'

'Go then and be swift!' said Faramir. 'If he comes off alive, he should be your faithful servant for the rest of his unhappy days. Lead Frodo down to the bank, Anborn, and go softly. The thing has a nose and ears. Give me your bow.'

Anborn grunted and led the way down the winding stair to the landing, and then up the other stair, until at last they came to a narrow opening shrouded with thick bushes. Passing silently through, Frodo found himself on the top of the southern bank above the pool. It was now dark and the falls were pale and grey, reflecting only the lingering moonlight of the western sky. He could not see Gollum. He went forward a short way and Anborn came softly behind him.

'Go on!' he breathed in Frodo's ear. 'Have a care to your right. If you fall in the pool, then no one but your fishing friend can help you. And forget not that there are bowmen near at hand, though you may not see them.'

Frodo crept forward, using his hands Gollum-like to feel his way and to steady himself. The rocks were for the most part flat and smooth but slippery. He halted listening. At first he could hear no sound but the unceasing rush of the fall behind him. Then presently he heard, not far ahead, a hissing murmur.

'Fissh, nice fissh. White Face has vanished, my precious, at last, yes. Now we can eat fish in peace. No, not in peace, precious. For Precious is lost; yes. Dirty hobbits, nasty hobbits. Gone and left us, *gollum;* and Precious is gone. Only poor Sméagol all alone. No Precious. Nasty Men, they'll take it, steal my Precious. Thieves. We hates them. Fissh, nice fissh. Makes us strong. Makes eyes bright, fingers tight, yes. Throttle them, precious. Throttle them all, yes, if we gets chances. Nice fissh. Nice fissh!'

So it went on, almost as unceasing as the waterfall, only interrupted by a faint noise of slavering and gurgling. Frodo shivered, listening with pity and disgust. He wished it would stop, and that he never need hear that voice again. Anborn was not far behind. He could creep back and ask him to get the huntsmen to shoot. They would probably get close enough, while Gollum was gorging and off his guard. Only one true shot, and Frodo would be rid of the miserable voice forever. But no, Gollum had a claim on him now. The servant has a claim on the master for service, even service in fear. They would have foundered in the Dead Marshes but for Gollum. Frodo knew, too, somehow, quite clearly that Gandalf would not have wished it.

'Sméagol!' he said softly.

'Fissh, nice fissh,' said the voice.

'Sméagol!' he said, a little louder. The voice stopped.

'Sméagol, Master has come to look for you. Master is here. Come, Sméagol!' There was no answer but a soft hiss, as of intaken breath.

'Come, Sméagol!' said Frodo. 'We are in danger. Men will kill you, if they find you here. Come quickly, if you wish to escape death. Come to Master!'

'No!' said the voice. 'Not nice Master. Leaves poor Sméagol and goes with new friends. Master can wait. Sméagol hasn't finished.'

'There's no time,' said Frodo. 'Bring fish with you. Come!'

'No! Must finish fish.'

'Sméagol!' said Frodo desperately. 'Precious will be angry. I shall take Precious, and I shall say: make him swallow the bones and choke. Never taste fish again. Come, Precious is waiting!'

There was a sharp hiss. Presently out of the darkness Gollum came crawling on all fours, like an erring dog called to heel. He had a half-eaten fish in his mouth and another in his hand. He came close to Frodo, almost nose to nose, and sniffed at him. His pale eyes were shining. Then he took the fish out of his mouth and stood up.

'Nice Master!' he whispered. 'Nice hobbit, come back to poor Sméagol. Good Sméagol comes. Now let's go, go quickly, yes. Through the trees, while the Faces are dark. Yes, come, let's go!'

'Yes, we'll go soon,' said Frodo. 'But not at once. I will go with you as I promised. I promised again. But not now. You are not safe yet. I will save you, but you must trust me.'

'We must trust Master?' said Gollum doubtfully. 'Why? Why not go at once? Where is the other one, the cross rude hobbit? Where is he?'

'Away up there,' said Frodo, pointing to the waterfall. 'I am not going without him. We must go back to him.' His heart sank. This was too much like trickery. He did not really fear that Faramir would allow Gollum to be killed, but he would probably make him prisoner and bind him; and certainly what Frodo did would seem a treachery to the poor treacherous creature. It would probably be impossible ever to make him understand or believe that Frodo had saved his life in the only way he could. What else could he do?—to keep faith, as near as might be, with both sides. 'Come!' he said. 'Or the Precious will be angry. We are going back now, up the stream. Go on, go on, you go in front!'

Gollum crawled along close to the brink for a little way, snuffling and suspicious. Presently he stopped and raised his head. 'Something's there!' he said. 'Not a hobbit.' Suddenly he turned back. A green light was flickering in his bulging eyes. 'Masster, masster!' he hissed. 'Wicked!

Tricksy! False!' He spat and stretched out his long arms with white snapping fingers.

At that moment the great black shape of Anborn loomed up behind him and came down on him. A large strong hand took him in the nape of the neck and pinned him. He twisted round like lightning, all wet and slimy as he was, wriggling like an eel, biting and scratching like a cat. But two more men came up out of the shadows.

'Hold still!' said one. 'Or we'll stick you as full of pins as a hedgehog. Hold still!'

Gollum went limp, and began to whine and weep. They tied him, none too gently.

'Easy, easy!' said Frodo. 'He has no strength to match you. Don't hurt him, if you can help it. He'll be quieter, if you don't. Sméagol! They won't hurt you. I'll go with you, and you shall come to no harm. Not unless they kill me too. Trust Master!'

Gollum turned and spat at him. The men picked him up, put a hood over his eyes, and carried him off.

Frodo followed them, feeling very wretched. They went through the opening behind the bushes, and back, down the stairs and passages, into the cave. Two or three torches had been lit. Men were stirring. Sam was there, and he gave a queer look at the limp bundle that the men carried. 'Got him?' he said to Frodo.

'Yes. Well no, I didn't get him. He came to me, because he trusted me at first, I'm afraid. I did not want him tied up like this. I hope it will be all right; but I hate the whole business.'

'So do I,' said Sam. 'And nothing will ever be all right where that piece of misery is.'

A man came and beckoned to the hobbits, and took them to the recess at the back of the cave. Faramir was sitting there in his chair, and the lamp had been rekindled in its niche above his head. He signed to them to sit down on the stools beside him. 'Bring wine for the guests,' he said. 'And bring the prisoner to me.'

The wine was brought, and then Anborn came carrying Gollum. He removed the cover from Gollum's head and set him on his feet, standing behind him to support him. Gollum blinked, hooding the malice of his eyes with their heavy pale lids. A very miserable creature he looked, dripping and dank, smelling of fish (he still clutched one in his hand); his sparse locks were hanging like rank weed over his bony brows, his nose was snivelling.

'Loose us! Loose us!' he said. 'The cord hurts us, yes it does, it hurts us, and we've done nothing.'

'Nothing?' said Faramir, looking at the wretched creature with a keen glance, but without any expression in his face either of anger, or pity, or wonder. 'Nothing? Have you never done anything worthy of binding or of worse punishment? However, that is not for me to judge, happily. But tonight you have come where it is death to come. The fish of this pool are dearly bought.'

Gollum dropped the fish from his hand. 'Don't want fish,' he said.

'The price is not set on the fish,' said Faramir. 'Only to come here and look on the pool bears the penalty of death. I have spared you so far at the prayer of Frodo here, who says that of him at least you have deserved some thanks. But you must also satisfy me. What is your name? Whence do you come? And whither do you go? What is your business?'

'We are lost, lost,' said Gollum. 'No name, no business, no Precious, nothing. Only empty. Only hungry: yes, we are hungry. A few little fishes, nasty bony little fishes, for a poor creature, and they say death. So wise they are; so just, so very just.'

'Not very wise,' said Faramir. 'But just: yes perhaps, as just as our little wisdom allows. Unloose him, Frodo!' Faramir took a small nail-knife from his belt and handed it to Frodo. Gollum, misunderstanding the gesture, squealed and fell down.

'Now, Sméagol!' said Frodo. 'You must trust me. I will not desert you. Answer truthfully, if you can. It will do you good not harm.' He cut the cords on Gollum's wrists and ankles and raised him to his feet.

'Come hither!' said Faramir. 'Look at me! Do you know the name of this place? Have you been here before?'

Slowly Gollum raised his eyes and looked unwillingly into Faramir's. All light went out of them, and they stared bleak and pale for a moment into the clear unwavering eyes of the man of Gondor. There was a still silence. Then Gollum dropped his head and shrank down, until he was squatting on the floor, shivering. 'We doesn't know and we doesn't want to know,' he whimpered. 'Never came here; never come again.'

'There are locked doors and closed windows in your mind, and dark rooms behind them,' said Faramir. 'But in this I judge that you speak the truth. It is well for you. What oath will you swear never to return; and never to lead any living creature hither by word or sign?'

'Master knows,' said Gollum with a sidelong glance at Frodo. 'Yes, he knows. We will promise Master, if he saves us. We'll promise to It, yes.' He crawled to Frodo's feet. 'Save us, nice Master!' he whined. 'Sméagol promises to Precious, promises faithfully. Never come again, never speak, no never! No, precious, no!'

'Are you satisfied?' said Faramir.

'Yes,' said Frodo. 'At least, you must either accept this promise or carry out your law. You will get no more. But I promised that if he came to me, he should not be harmed. And I would not be proved faithless.'

Faramir sat for a moment in thought. 'Very good,' he said at last. 'I surrender you to your master, to Frodo son of Drogo. Let him declare what he will do with you!'

'But, Lord Faramir,' said Frodo bowing, 'you have not yet declared your will concerning the said Frodo, and until that is made known, he cannot shape his plans for himself or his companions. Your judgement was postponed until the morning; but that is now at hand.'

'Then I will declare my doom,' said Faramir. 'As for you, Frodo, in so far as lies in me under higher authority, I declare you free in the realm of Gondor to the furthest of its ancient bounds; save only that neither you nor any that go with you have leave to come to this place unbidden. This doom shall stand for a year and a day, and then cease, unless you shall before that term come to Minas Tirith and present yourself to the Lord and Steward of the City. Then I will entreat him to confirm what I have done and to make it lifelong. In the meantime, whomsoever you take under your protection shall be under my protection and under the shield of Gondor. Are you answered?'

Frodo bowed low. 'I am answered,' he said, 'and I place myself at your service, if that is of any worth to one so high and honourable.'

'It is of great worth,' said Faramir. 'And now, do you take this creature, this Sméagol, under your protection?'

'I do take Sméagol under my protection,' said Frodo. Sam sighed audibly; and not at the courtesies, of which, as any hobbit would, he thoroughly approved. Indeed in the Shire such a matter would have required a great many more words and bows.

'Then I say to you,' said Faramir, turning to Gollum, 'you are under doom of death; but while you walk with Frodo you are safe for our part. Yet if ever you be found by any man of Gondor astray without him, the doom shall fall. And may death find you swiftly, within Gondor or without, if you do not well serve him. Now answer me: whither would you go? You were his guide, he says. Whither were you leading him?' Gollum made no reply.

'This I will not have secret,' said Faramir. 'Answer me, or I will reverse judgement!' Still Gollum did not answer.

'I will answer for him,' said Frodo. 'He brought me to the Black Gate, as I asked; but it was impassable.'

'There is no open gate into the Nameless Land,' said Faramir.

'Seeing this, we turned aside and came by the Southward road,' Frodo continued; 'for he said that there is, or there may be, a path near to Minas Ithil.'

'Minas Morgul,' said Faramir.

'I do not know clearly,' said Frodo; 'but the path climbs, I think, up into the mountains on the northern side of that vale where the old city stands. It goes up to a high cleft and so down to——that which is beyond.'

'Do you know the name of that high pass?' said Faramir.

'No,' said Frodo.

'It is called Cirith Ungol.' Gollum hissed sharply and began muttering to himself. 'Is not that its name?' said Faramir turning to him.

'No!' said Gollum, and then he squealed, as if something had stabbed him. 'Yes, yes, we heard the name once. But what does the name matter to us? Master says he must get in. So we must try some way. There is no other way to try, no.'

'No other way?' said Faramir. 'How do you know that? And who has explored all the confines of that dark realm?' He looked long and thoughtfully at Gollum. Presently he spoke again. 'Take this creature away, Anborn. Treat him gently, but watch him. And do not you, Sméagol, try to dive into the falls. The rocks have such teeth there as would slay you before your time. Leave us now and take your fish!'

Anborn went out and Gollum went cringing before him. The curtain was drawn across the recess.

'Frodo, I think you do very unwisely in this,' said Faramir. 'I do not think you should go with this creature. It is wicked.'

'No, not altogether wicked,' said Frodo.

'Not wholly, perhaps,' said Faramir; 'but malice eats it like a canker, and the evil is growing. He will lead you to no good. If you will part with him, I will give him safe-conduct and guidance to any point on the borders of Gondor that he may name.'

'He would not take it,' said Frodo. 'He would follow after me as he long has done. And I have promised many times to take him under my protection and to go where he led. You would not ask me to break faith with him?'

'No,' said Faramir. 'But my heart would. For it seems less evil to counsel another man to break troth than to do so oneself, especially if one sees a friend bound unwitting to his own harm. But no—if he will go with you, you must now endure him. But I do not think you are holden to go to Cirith Ungol, of which he has told you less than he knows. That much I perceived clearly in his mind. Do not go to Cirith Ungol!'

'Where then shall I go?' said Frodo. 'Back to the Black Gate and deliver myself up to the guard? What do you know against this place that makes its name so dreadful?'

'Nothing certain,' said Faramir. 'We of Gondor do not ever pass east of the Road in these days, and none of us younger men has ever done so, nor has any of us set foot upon the Mountains of Shadow. Of them we know only old report and the rumour of bygone days. But there is some dark terror that dwells in the passes above Minas Morgul. If Cirith Ungol is named, old men and masters of lore will blanch and fall silent.

'The valley of Minas Morgul passed into evil very long ago, and it was a menace and a dread while the banished Enemy dwelt yet far away, and Ithilien was still for the most part in our keeping. As you know, that city was once a strong place, proud and fair, Minas Ithil, the twin sister of our own city. But it was taken by fell men whom the Enemy in his first strength had dominated, and who wandered homeless and masterless after his fall. It is said that their lords were men of Númenor who had fallen into dark wickedness; to them the Enemy had given rings of power, and he had devoured them: living ghosts they were become, terrible and evil. After his going they took Minas Ithil and dwelt there, and they filled it, and all the valley about, with decay: it seemed empty and was not so, for a shapeless fear lived within the ruined walls. Nine Lords there were, and after the return of their Master, which they aided and prepared in secret, they grew strong again. Then the Nine Riders issued forth from the gates of horror, and we could not withstand them. Do not approach their citadel. You will be espied. It is a place of sleepless malice, full of lidless eyes. Do not go that way!'

'But where else will you direct me?' said Frodo. 'You cannot yourself, you say, guide me to the mountains, nor over them. But over the mountains I am bound, by solemn undertaking to the Council, to find a way or perish in the seeking. And if I turn back, refusing the road in its bitter end, where then shall I go among Elves or Men? Would you have me come to Gondor with this Thing, the Thing that drove your brother mad with desire? What spell would it work in Minas Tirith? Shall there be two cities of Minas Morgul, grinning at each other across a dead land filled with rottenness?'

'I would not have it so,' said Faramir.

'Then what would you have me do?'

'I know not. Only I would not have you go to death or to torment. And I do not think that Mithrandir would have chosen this way.'

'Yet since he is gone, I must take such paths as I can find. And there is no time for long searching,' said Frodo.

'It is a hard doom and a hopeless errand,' said Faramir. 'But at the least, remember my warning: beware of this guide, Sméagol. He has done murder before now. I read it in him.' He sighed.

'Well, so we meet and part, Frodo son of Drogo. You have no need of soft words: I do not hope to see you again on any other day under this Sun. But you shall go now with my blessing upon you, and upon all your people. Rest a little while food is prepared for you.

'I would gladly learn how this creeping Sméagol became possessed of the Thing of which we speak, and how he lost it, but I will not trouble you now. If ever beyond hope you return to the lands of the living and we re-tell our tales, sitting by a wall in the sun, laughing at old grief, you shall tell me then. Until that time, or some other time beyond the vision of the Seeing-stones of Númenor, farewell!'

He rose and bowed low to Frodo, and drawing the curtain passed out into the cave.

Chapter 7

Journey to the Cross-Roads

Frodo and Sam returned to their beds and lay there in silence resting for a little, while men bestirred themselves and the business of the day began. After a while water was brought to them, and then they were led to a table where food was set for three. Faramir broke his fast with them. He had not slept since the battle on the day before, yet he did not look weary.

When they had finished they stood up. 'May no hunger trouble you on the road,' said Faramir. 'You have little provision, but some small store of food fit for travellers I have ordered to be stowed in your packs. You will have no lack of water as you walk in Ithilien, but do not drink of any stream that flows from Imlad Morgul, the valley of Living Death. This also I must tell you. My scouts and watchers have all returned, even some that have crept within sight of the Morannon. They all find a strange thing. The land is empty. Nothing is on the road, and no sound of foot, or horn, or bowstring is anywhere to be heard. A waiting silence broods above the Nameless Land. I do not know what this portends. But the time draws swiftly to some great conclusion. Storm is coming. Hasten while you may! If you are ready, let us go. The Sun will soon rise above the shadow.'

The hobbits' packs were brought to them (a little heavier than they had been), and also two stout staves of polished wood, shod with iron, and with carven heads through which ran plaited leathern thongs.

'I have no fitting gifts to give you at our parting,' said Faramir; 'but take these staves. They may be of service to those who walk or climb in the wild. The men of the White Mountains use them; though these have been cut down to your height and newly shod. They are made of the fair tree *lebethron,* beloved of the woodwrights of Gondor,

and a virtue has been set upon them of finding and returning. May that virtue not wholly fail under the Shadow into
which you go!'

The hobbits bowed low. 'Most gracious host,' said
Frodo, 'it was said to me by Elrond Halfelven that I should
find friendship upon the way, secret and unlooked for.
Certainly I looked for no such friendship as you have
shown. To have found it turns evil to great good.'

Now they made ready to depart. Gollum was brought
out of some corner or hiding-hole, and he seemed better
pleased with himself than he had been, though he kept
close to Frodo and avoided the glance of Faramir.

'Your guide must be blindfolded,' said Faramir, 'but
you and your servant Samwise I release from this, if you
wish.'

Gollum squealed, and squirmed, and clutched at Frodo,
when they came to bind his eyes; and Frodo said: 'Blindfold us all three, and cover up my eyes first, and then perhaps he will see that no harm is meant.' This was done,
and they were led from the cave of Henneth Annûn. After
they had passed the passages and stairs they felt the cool
morning air, fresh and sweet, about them. Still blind they
went on for some little time, up and then gently down. At
last the voice of Faramir ordered them to be uncovered.

They stood under the boughs of the woods again. No
noise of the falls could be heard, for a long southward
slope lay now between them and the ravine in which the
stream flowed. To the west they could see light through
the trees, as if the world came there to a sudden end, at a
brink looking out only onto sky.

'Here is the last parting of our ways,' said Faramir. 'If
you take my counsel, you will not turn eastward yet. Go
straight on, for thus you will have the cover of the woodland for many miles. On your west is an edge where the
lands falls into the great vales, sometimes suddenly and
sheer, sometimes in long hillsides. Keep near to this edge
and the skirts of the forest. In the beginning of your journey you may walk under daylight, I think. The land

dreams in a false peace, and for a while all evil is withdrawn. Fare you well, while you may!'

He embraced the hobbits then, after the manner of his people, stooping, and placing his hands upon their shoulders, and kissing their foreheads. 'Go with the good will of all good men!' he said.

They bowed to the ground. Then he turned and without looking back he left them and went to his two guards that stood at a little distance away. They marvelled to see with what speed these greenclad men now moved, vanishing almost in the twinkling of an eye. The forest where Faramir had stood seemed empty and drear, as if a dream had passed.

Frodo sighed and turned back southward. As if to mark his disregard of all such courtesy, Gollum was scrabbling in the mould at the foot of a tree. 'Hungry again already?' thought Sam. 'Well, now for it again!'

'Have they gone at last?' said Gollum. 'Nassty wicked Men! Sméagol's neck still hurts him, yes it does. Let's go!'

'Yes, let us go,' said Frodo. 'But if you can only speak ill of those who showed you mercy, keep silent!'

'Nice Master!' said Gollum. 'Sméagol was only joking. Always forgives, he does, yes, yes, even nice Master's little trickses. Oh yes, nice Master, nice Sméagol!'

Frodo and Sam did not answer. Hoisting their packs and taking their staves in hand, they passed on into the woods of Ithilien.

Twice that day they rested and took a little of the food provided by Faramir: dried fruits and salted meat, enough for many days; and bread enough to last while it was still fresh. Gollum ate nothing.

The sun rose and passed overhead unseen, and began to sink, and the light through the trees to the west grew golden; and always they walked in cool green shadow, and all about them was silence. The birds seemed all to have flown away or to have fallen dumb.

Darkness came early to the silent woods, and before the fall of night they halted, weary, for they had walked

seven leagues or more from Henneth Annûn. Frodo lay
and slept away the night on the deep mould beneath an ancient tree. Sam beside him was more uneasy: he woke
many times, but there was never a sign of Gollum, who had
slipped off as soon as the others had settled to rest.
Whether he had slept by himself in some hole nearby, or
had wandered restlessly prowling through the night, he
did not say; but he returned with the first glimmer of light,
and roused his companions.

'Must get up, yes they must!' he said. 'Long ways to go
still, south and east. Hobbits must make haste!'

That day passed much as the day before had gone, except that the silence seemed deeper; the air grew heavy,
and it began to be stifling under the trees. It felt as if
thunder was brewing. Gollum often paused, sniffing the
air, and then he would mutter to himself and urge them to
greater speed.

As the third stage of their day's march drew on and
afternoon waned, the forest opened out, and the trees became larger and more scattered. Great ilexes of huge girth
stood dark and solemn in wide glades with here and there
among them hoary ash-trees, and giant oaks just putting
out their brown-green buds. About them lay long launds of
green grass dappled with celandine and anemones, white
and blue, now folded for sleep; and there were acres
populous with the leaves of woodland hyacinths: already
their sleek bell-stems were thrusting through the mould.
No living creature, beast or bird, was to be seen, but in
these open places Gollum grew afraid, and they walked
now with caution, flitting from one long shadow to another.

Light was fading fast when they came to the forest-end.
There they sat under an old gnarled oak that sent its
roots twisting like snakes down a steep crumbling bank. A
deep dim valley lay before them. On its further side the
woods gathered again, blue and grey under the sullen
evening, and marched on southwards. To the right the
Mountains of Gondor glowed, remote in the West, under a
fire-flecked sky. To the left lay darkness: the towering

walls of Mordor; and out of that darkness the long valley came, falling steeply in an ever-widening trough towards the Anduin. At its bottom ran a hurrying stream: Frodo could hear its stony voice coming up through the silence; and beside it on the hither side a road went winding down like a pale ribbon, down into chill grey mists that no gleam of sunset touched. There it seemed to Frodo that he descried far off, floating as it were on a shadowy sea, the high dim tops and broken pinnacles of old towers forlorn and dark.

He turned to Gollum. 'Do you know where we are?' he said.

'Yes, Master. Dangerous places. This is the road from the Tower of the Moon, Master, down to the ruined city by the shores of the River. The ruined city, yes, very nasty place, full of enemies. We shouldn't have taken Men's advice. Hobbits have come a long way out of the path. Must go east now, away up there.' He waved his skinny arm towards the darkling mountains. 'And we can't use this road. Oh no! Cruel peoples come this way, down from the Tower.'

Frodo looked down onto the road. At any rate nothing was moving on it now. It appeared lonely and forsaken, running down to empty ruins in the mist. But there was an evil feeling in the air, as if things might indeed be passing up and down that eyes could not see. Frodo shuddered as he looked again at the distant pinnacles now dwindling into night, and the sound of the water seemed cold and cruel: the voice of Morgulduin, the polluted stream that flowed from the Valley of the Wraiths.

'What shall we do?' he said. 'We have walked long and far. Shall we look for someplace in the woods behind where we can lie hidden?'

'No good hiding in the dark,' said Gollum. 'It's in day that hobbits must hide now, yes in day.'

'Oh come!' said Sam. 'We must rest for a bit, even if we get up again in the middle of the night. There'll still be hours of dark then, time enough for you to take us a long march, if you know the way.'

Gollum reluctantly agreed to this, and he turned back towards the trees, working eastward for a while along the straggling edges of the wood. He would not rest on the ground so near the evil road and after some debate they all climbed up into the crotch of a large holm-oak, whose thick branches springing together from the trunk made a good hiding-place and a fairly comfortable refuge. Night fell and it grew altogether dark under the canopy of the tree. Frodo and Sam drank a little water and ate some bread and dried fruit, but Gollum at once curled up and went to sleep. The hobbits did not shut their eyes.

It must have been a little after midnight when Gollum woke up: suddenly they were aware of his pale eyes unlidded gleaming at them. He listened and sniffed, which seemed, as they had noticed before, his usual method of discovering the time of night.

'Are we rested? Have we had beautiful sleep?' he said. 'Let's go!'

'We aren't, and we haven't,' growled Sam. 'But we'll go if we must.'

Gollum dropped at once from the branches of the tree onto all fours, and the hobbits followed more slowly.

As soon as they were down they went on again with Gollum leading, eastwards, up the dark sloping land. They could see little, for the night was now so deep that they were hardly aware of the stems of trees before they stumbled against them. The ground became more broken and walking was more difficult, but Gollum seemed in no way troubled. He led them through thickets and wastes of brambles; sometimes round the lip of a deep cleft or dark pit, sometimes down into black bush-shrouded hollows and out again; but if ever they went a little downward, always the further slope was longer and steeper. They were climbing steadily. At their first halt they looked back, and they could dimly perceive the roofs of the forest they had left behind, lying like a vast dense shadow, a darker night under the dark blank sky. There seemed to be a great blackness looming slowly out of the East, eating up the faint blurred stars. Later the sinking moon escaped from the pursuing cloud, but it was ringed all about with a sickly yellow glare.

At last Gollum turned to the hobbits. 'Day soon,' he said. 'Hobbits must hurry. Not safe to stay in the open in these places. Make haste!'

He quickened his pace, and they followed him wearily. Soon they began to climb up onto a great hog-back of land. For the most part it was covered with a thick growth of gorse and whortleberry, and low tough thorns, though here and there clearings opened, the scars of recent fires. The gorse-bushes became more frequent as they got nearer the top; very old and tall they were, gaunt and leggy below but thick above, and already putting out yellow flowers that glimmered in the gloom and gave a faint sweet scent. So tall were the spiny thickets that the hobbits could walk upright under them, passing through long dry aisles carpeted with a deep prickly mould.

On the further edge of this broad hill-back they stayed their march and crawled for hiding underneath a tangled knot of thorns. Their twisted boughs, stooping to the ground, were overridden by a clambering maze of old briars. Deep inside there was a hollow hall, raftered with dead branch and bramble, and roofed with the first leaves and shoots of spring. There they lay for a while, too tired yet to eat; and peering out through the holes in the covert they watched for the slow growth of day.

But no day came, only a dead brown twilight. In the East there was a dull red glare under the lowering cloud: it was not the red of dawn. Across the tumbled lands between, the mountains of the Ephel Dúath frowned at them, black and shapeless below where night lay thick and did not pass away, above with jagged tops and edges outlined hard and menacing against the fiery glow. Away to their right a great shoulder of the mountains stood out, dark and black amid the shadows, thrusting westward.

'Which way do we go from here?' asked Frodo. 'Is that the opening of—of the Morgul Valley, away over there beyond that black mass?'

'Need we think about it yet?' said Sam. 'Surely we're not going to move any more today, if day it is?'

'Perhaps not, perhaps not,' said Gollum. 'But we must go soon, to the Cross-roads. Yes, to the Cross-roads. That's the way over there, yes, Master.'

The red glare over Mordor died away. The twilight deepened as great vapours rose in the East and crawled above them. Frodo and Sam took a little food and then lay down, but Gollum was restless. He would not eat any of their food, but he drank a little water and then crawled about under the bushes, sniffing and muttering. Then suddenly he disappeared.

'Off hunting, I suppose,' said Sam and yawned. It was his turn to sleep first, and he was soon deep in a dream. He thought he was back in the Bag End garden looking for something; but he had a heavy pack on his back, which made him stoop. It all seemed very weedy and rank somehow, and thorns and bracken were invading the beds down near the bottom hedge.

'A job of work for me, I can see; but I'm so tired,' he kept on saying. Presently he remembered what he was looking for. 'My pipe!' he said, and with that he woke up.

'Silly!' he said to himself, as he opened his eyes and wondered why he was lying down under the hedge. 'It's in your pack all the time!' Then he realized, first that the pipe might be in his pack but he had no leaf, and next that he was hundreds of miles from Bag End. He sat up. It seemed to be almost dark. Why had his master let him sleep on out of turn, right on till evening?

'Haven't you had no sleep, Mr. Frodo?' he said. 'What's the time? Seems to be getting late!'

'No it isn't,' said Frodo. 'But the day is getting darker instead of lighter: darker and darker. As far as I can tell, it isn't midday yet, and you've only slept for about three hours.'

'I wonder what's up,' said Sam. 'Is there a storm coming? If so it's going to be the worst there ever was. We shall wish we were down a deep hole, not just stuck under a hedge.' He listened. 'What's that? Thunder, or drums, or what is it?'

'I don't know,' said Frodo. 'It's been going on for a good while now. Sometimes the ground seems to tremble, sometimes it seems to be the heavy air throbbing in your ears.'

Sam looked round. 'Where's Gollum?' he said. 'Hasn't he come back yet?'

'No,' said Frodo. 'There's not been a sign or sound of him.'

'Well, I can't abide him,' said Sam. 'In fact, I've never taken anything on a journey that I'd have been less sorry to lose on the way. But it would be just like him, after coming all these miles, to go and get lost now, just when we shall need him most—that is, if he's ever going to be any use, which I doubt.'

'You forget the Marshes,' said Frodo. 'I hope nothing has happened to him.'

'And I hope he's up to no tricks. And anyway I hope he doesn't fall into other hands, as you might say. Because if he does, we shall soon be in for trouble.'

At that moment a rolling and rumbling noise was heard again, louder now and deeper. The ground seemed to quiver under their feet. 'I think we are in for trouble anyhow,' said Frodo. 'I'm afraid our journey is drawing to an end.'

'Maybe,' said Sam; 'but *where there's life there's hope,* as my Gaffer used to say; *and need of vittles,* as he mostways used to add. You have a bite, Mr. Frodo, and then a bit of sleep.'

The afternoon, as Sam supposed it must be called, wore on. Looking out from the covert he could see only a dun, shadowless world, fading slowly into a featureless, colourless gloom. It felt stifling but not warm. Frodo slept unquietly, turning and tossing, and sometimes murmuring. Twice Sam thought he heard him speaking Gandalf's name. The time seemed to drag interminably. Suddenly

Sam heard a hiss behind him, and there was Gollum on all fours, peering at them with gleaming eyes.

'Wake up, wake up! Wake up, sleepies!' he whispered. 'Wake up! No time to lose. We must go, yes, we must go at once. No time to lose!'

Sam stared at him suspiciously: he seemed frightened or excited. 'Go now? What's your little game? It isn't time yet. It can't be tea-time even, leastways not in decent places where there is tea-time.'

'Silly!' hissed Gollum. 'We're not in decent places. Time's running short, yes, running fast. No time to lose. We must go. Wake up, Master, wake up!' He clawed at Frodo; and Frodo, startled out of sleep, sat up suddenly and seized him by the arm. Gollum tore himself loose and backed away.

'They mustn't be silly,' he hissed. 'We must go. No time to lose!' And nothing more could they get out of him. Where he had been, and what he thought was brewing to make him in such a hurry, he would not say. Sam was filled with deep suspicion, and showed it; but Frodo gave no sign of what was passing in his mind. He sighed, hoisted his pack, and prepared to go out into the ever-gathering darkness.

Very stealthily Gollum led them down the hillside, keeping under cover wherever it was possible, and running, almost bent to the ground, across any open space; but the light was now so dim that even a keen-eyed beast of the wild could scarcely have seen the hobbits, hooded, in their grey cloaks, nor heard them, walking as warily as the little people can. Without the crack of a twig or the rustle of a leaf they passed and vanished.

For about an hour they went on, silently, in single file, oppressed by the gloom and by the absolute stillness of the land, broken only now and again by the faint rumbling as of thunder far away or drum-beats in some hollow of the hills. Down from their hiding-place they went, and then turning south they steered as straight a course as Gollum could find across a long broken slope that leaned up towards the mountains. Presently, not far ahead, looming up like a black wall, they saw a belt of trees. As they drew nearer they became aware that these were of vast size, very ancient it seemed, and still towering high, though their tops were gaunt and broken, as if tempest and lightning-blast had swept across them, but had failed to kill them or to shake their fathomless roots.

'The Cross-roads, yes,' whispered Gollum, the first words that had been spoken since they left their hiding-place. 'We must go that way.' Turning eastward now, he led them up the slope; and then suddenly there it was before them: the Southward Road, winding its way about the outer feet of the mountains, until presently it plunged into the great ring of trees.

'This is the only way,' whispered Gollum. 'No paths beyond the road. No paths. We must go to the Cross-roads. But make haste! Be silent!'

As furtively as scouts within the encampment of their enemies, they crept down onto the road, and stole along its westward edge under the stony bank, grey as the stones themselves, and soft-footed as hunting cats. At length they reached the trees, and found that they stood in a great roofless ring, open in the middle to the sombre sky; and the spaces between their immense boles were like the great dark arches of some ruined hall. In the very centre four ways met. Behind them lay the road to the Morannon; before them it ran out again upon its long journey south; to their right the road from old Osgiliath came climbing up, and crossing, passed out eastward into darkness: the fourth way, the road they were to take.

Standing there for a moment filled with dread Frodo became aware that a light was shining; he saw it glowing on Sam's face beside him. Turning towards it, he saw, beyond an arch of boughs, the road to Osgiliath running almost as straight, as a stretched ribbon down, down, into the West. There, far away, beyond sad Gondor now overwhelmed in shade, the Sun was sinking, finding at last the hem of the great slow-rolling pall of cloud, and falling in an ominous fire towards the yet unsullied Sea. The brief glow fell upon a huge sitting figure, still and solemn as the great stone kings of Argonath. The years had gnawed it, and violent hands had maimed it. Its head was gone, and in its place was set in mockery a round rough-hewn stone, rudely painted by savage hands in the likeness of a grinning face with one large red eye in the midst of its forehead. Upon its knees and mighty chair, and all about the pedestal, were idle scrawls mixed with the foul symbols that the maggot-folk of Mordor used.

Suddenly, caught by the level beams, Frodo saw the old king's head: it was lying rolled away by the roadside. 'Look, Sam!' he cried, startled into speech. 'Look! The king has got a crown again!'

The eyes were hollow and the carven beard was broken, but about the high stern forehead there was a coronal of silver and gold. A trailing plant with flowers like small white stars had bound itself across the brows as if in reverence for the fallen king, and in the crevices of his stony hair yellow stonecrop gleamed.

'They cannot conquer forever!' said Frodo. And then suddenly the brief glimpse was gone. The Sun dipped and vanished, and as if at the shuttering of a lamp, black night fell.

Chapter 8

The Stairs of Cirith Ungol

Gollum was tugging at Frodo's cloak and hissing with fear and impatience. 'We must go,' he said. 'We mustn't stand here. Make haste!'

Reluctantly Frodo turned his back on the West and followed as his guide led him, out into the darkness of the East. They left the ring of trees and crept along the road towards the mountains. This road, too, ran straight for a while, but soon it began to bend away southwards, until it came right under the great shoulder of rock that they had seen from the distance. Black and forbidding it loomed above them, darker than the dark sky behind. Crawling under its shadow the road went on, and rounding it sprang east again and began to climb steeply.

Frodo and Sam were plodding along with heavy hearts, no longer able to care greatly about their peril. Frodo's head was bowed; his burden was dragging him down again. As soon as the great Cross-roads had been passed, the weight of it, almost forgotten in Ithilien, had begun to grow once more. Now, feeling the way become steep before his feet, he looked wearily up; and then he saw it, even as Gollum had said that he would: the city of the Ringwraiths. He cowered against the stony bank.

A long-tilted valley, a deep gulf of shadow, ran back far into the mountains. Upon the further side, some way within the valley's arms, high on a rocky seat upon the black knees of the Ephel Dúath, stood the walls and tower of Minas Morgul. All was dark about it, earth and sky, but it was lit with light. Not the imprisoned moonlight welling through the marble walls of Minas Ithil long ago, Tower of the Moon, fair and radiant in the hollow of the hills. Paler indeed than the moon ailing in some slow eclipse was the light of it now, wavering and blowing like a noisome exhalation of decay, a corpse-light, a light that illuminated nothing. In the walls and tower windows showed, like countless black holes looking inward into emptiness; but the topmost course of the tower revolved slowly, first one way and then another, a huge ghostly head leering into the night. For a moment the three companions stood there, shrinking, staring up with unwilling eyes. Gollum was the first to recover. Again he pulled at their cloaks urgently, but he spoke no word. Almost he dragged them forward. Every step was reluctant, and time seemed to slow its pace, so that between the raising of a foot and the setting of it down minutes of loathing passed.

So they came slowly to the white bridge. Here the road, gleaming faintly, passed over the stream in the midst of the valley, and went on, winding deviously up towards the city's gate: a black mouth opening in the outer circle of the northward walls. Wide flats lay on either bank, shadowy meads filled with pale white flowers. Luminous these were too, beautiful and yet horrible of shape, like the demented forms in an uneasy dream; and they gave forth a faint sickening charnel-smell; an odour of rottenness filled the air. From mead to mead the bridge sprang. Figures stood there at its head, carven with cunning in forms human and bestial, but all corrupt and loathsome. The water flowing beneath was silent, and it steamed, but the vapour that rose from it, curling and twisting about the bridge, was deadly cold. Frodo felt his senses reeling and his mind darkening. Then suddenly, as if some force were at work other than his own will, he began to hurry, tottering forward, his groping hands held out, his head lolling from side to side. Both Sam and Gollum ran after him. Sam caught his master in his arms, as he stumbled and almost fell, right on the threshold of the bridge.

'Not that way! No, not that way!' whispered Gollum, but the breath between his teeth seemed to tear the heavy stillness like a whistle, and he cowered to the ground in terror.

'Hold up, Mr. Frodo!' muttered Sam in Frodo's ear.

'Come back! Not that way. Gollum says not, and for once
I agree with him.'

Frodo passed his hand over his brow and wrenched his
eyes away from the city on the hill. The luminous tower
fascinated him, and he fought the desire that was on him
to run up the gleaming road towards its gate. At last with
an effort he turned back, and as he did so, he felt the
Ring resisting him, dragging at the chain about his neck
and his eyes too, as he looked away, seemed for the moment to have been blinded. The darkness before him
was impenetrable.

Gollum, crawling on the ground like a frightened ani-
mal, was already vanishing into the gloom. Sam, supporting and guiding his stumbling master, followed after him
as quickly as he could. Not far from the near bank of the
stream there was a gap in the stone-wall beside the road.
Through this they passed, and Sam saw that they were on
a narrow path that gleamed faintly at first, as the main
road did, until climbing above the meads of deadly flower
it faded and went dark, winding its crooked way up into
the northern sides of the valley.

Along this path the hobbits trudged, side by side, unable
to see Gollum in front of them, except when he turned
back to beckon them on. Then his eyes shone with a green-
white light, reflecting the noisome Morgul-sheen perhaps,
or kindled by some answering mood within. Of that deadly
gleam and of the dark eyeholes Frodo and Sam were always conscious, ever glancing fearfully over their shoulders,
and ever dragging their eyes back to find the darkening path. Slowly they laboured on. As they rose above the
stench and vapours of the poisonous stream their breath
became easier and their heads clearer; but now their
limbs were deadly tired, as if they had walked all night
under a burden, or had been swimming long against a
heavy tide of water. At last they could go no further
without a halt.

Frodo stopped and sat down on a stone. They had now
climbed up to the top of a great hump of bare rock. Ahead
of them there was a bay in the valley-side, and round the

head of this the path went on, no more than a wide ledge with a chasm on the right; across the sheer southward face of the mountain it crawled upwards, until it disappeared into the blackness above.

'I must rest a while, Sam,' whispered Frodo. 'It's heavy on me, Sam lad, very heavy. I wonder how far I can carry it? Anyway I must rest before we venture on to that.' He pointed to the narrow way ahead.

'Sssh! ssh!' hissed Gollum hurrying back to them. 'Sssh!' His fingers were on his lips and he shook his head urgently. Tugging at Frodo's sleeve, he pointed towards the path; but Frodo would not move.

'Not yet,' he said, 'not yet.' Weariness and more than weariness oppressed him; it seemed as if a heavy spell was laid on his mind and body. 'I must rest,' he muttered.

At this Gollum's fear and agitation became so great that he spoke again, hissing behind his hand, as if to keep the sound from unseen listeners in the air. 'Not here, no. Not rest here. Fools! Eyes can see us. When they come to the bridge they will see us. Come away! Climb, climb! Come!'

'Come, Mr. Frodo,' said Sam. 'He's right again. We can't stay here.'

'All right,' said Frodo in a remote voice, as of one speaking half asleep. 'I will try.' Wearily he got to his feet.

But it was too late. At that moment the rock quivered and trembled beneath them. The great rumbling noise, louder than ever before, rolled in the ground and echoed in the mountains. Then with searing suddenness there came a great red flash. Far beyond the eastern mountains it leapt into the sky and splashed the lowering clouds with crimson. In that valley of shadow and cold deathly light it seemed unbearably violent and fierce. Peaks of stone and ridges like notched knives sprang out in staring black against the uprushing flame in Gorgoroth. Then came a great crack of thunder.

And Minas Morgul answered. There was a flare of livid lightnings: forks of blue flame springing up from the tower and from the encircling hills into the sullen clouds. The

earth groaned; and out of the city there came a cry.
Mingled with harsh high voices as of birds of prey, and the
shrill neighing of horses wild with rage and fear, there
came a rending screech, shivering, rising swiftly to a piercing pitch beyond the range of hearing. The hobbits wheeled
round towards it, and cast themselves down, holding their
hands upon their ears.

As the terrible cry ended, falling back through a long
sickening wail to silence, Frodo slowly raised his head.
Across the narrow valley, now almost on a level with his
eyes, the walls of the evil city stood, and its cavernous gate,
shaped like an open mouth with gleaming teeth, was
gaping wide. And out of the gate an army came.

All that host was clad in sable, dark as the night.
Against the wan walls and the luminous pavement of the
road Frodo could see them, small black figures in rank
upon rank, marching swiftly and silently, passing outwards
in an endless stream. Before them went a great cavalry of
horsemen moving like ordered shadows, and at their head
was one greater than all the rest: a Rider, all black,
save that on his hooded head he had a helm like a crown
that flickered with a perilous light. Now he was drawing
near the bridge below, and Frodo's staring eyes followed
him, unable to wink or to withdraw. Surely there was the
Lord of the Nine Riders returned to earth to lead his
ghastly host to battle? Here, yes here indeed was the
haggard king whose cold hand had smitten down the Ring-
bearer with his deadly knife. The old wound throbbed
with pain and a great chill spread towards Frodo's heart.

Even as these thoughts pierced him with dread and
held him bound as with a spell, the Rider halted suddenly,
right before the entrance of the bridge, and behind him
all the host stood still. There was a pause, a dead silence.
Maybe it was the Ring that called to the Wraith-lord, and
for a moment he was troubled, sensing some other power
within his valley. This way and that turned the dark head
helmed and crowned with fear, sweeping the shadows with
its unseen eyes. Frodo waited, like a bird at the approach
of a snake, unable to move. And as he waited, he felt

more urgent than ever before, the command that he should put on the Ring. But great as the pressure was, he felt no inclination now to yield to it. He knew that the Ring would only betray him, and that he had not, even if he put it on, the power to face the Morgul-king—not yet. There was no longer any answer to that command in his own will, dismayed by terror though it was, and he felt only the beating upon him of a great power from outside. It took his hand, and as Frodo watched with his mind, not willing it but in suspense (as if he looked on some old story far away), it moved the hand inch by inch towards the chain upon his neck. Then his own will stirred; slowly it forced the hand back and set it to find another thing, a thing lying hidden near his breast. Cold and hard it seemed as his grip closed on it: the phial of Galadriel, so long treasured, and almost forgotten till that hour. As he touched it, for a while all thought of the Ring was banished from his mind. He sighed and bent his head.

At that moment the Wraith-king turned and spurred his horse and rode across the bridge, and all his dark host followed him. Maybe the elven-hoods defied his unseen eyes, and the mind of his small enemy, being strengthened, had turned aside his thought. But he was in haste. Already the hour had struck, and at his great Master's bidding he must march with war into the West.

Soon he had passed, like a shadow into shadow, down the winding road, and behind him still the black ranks crossed the bridge. So great an army had never issued from that vale since the days of Isildur's might; no host so fell and strong in arms had yet assailed the fords of Anduin; and yet it was but one and not the greatest of the hosts that Mordor now sent forth.

Frodo stirred. And suddenly his heart went out to Faramir. 'The storm has burst at last,' he thought. 'This great array of spears and swords is going to Osgiliath. Will Faramir get across in time? He guessed it, but did he know the hour? And who can now hold the fords when the King of the Nine Riders comes? And other armies will come. I am too late. All is lost. I tarried on the way. All is lost. Even if my errand is performed, no one will ever know. There will be no one I can tell. It will be in vain.' Overcome with weakness he wept. And still the host of Morgul crossed the bridge.

Then at a great distance, as if it came out of memories of the Shire, some sunlit early morning, when the day called and doors were opening, he heard Sam's voice speaking. 'Wake up, Mr. Frodo! Wake up!' Had the voice added: 'Your breakfast is ready,' he would hardly have been surprised. Certainly Sam was urgent. 'Wake up, Mr. Frodo! They're gone,' he said.

There was a dull clang. The gates of Minas Morgul had closed. The last rank of spears had vanished down the road. The tower still grinned across the valley, but the light was fading in it. The whole city was falling back into a dark brooding shade, and silence. Yet still it was filled with watchfulness.

'Wake up, Mr. Frodo! They're gone, and we'd better go too. There's something still alive in that place, something with eyes, or a seeing mind, if you take me; and the longer we stay in one spot, the sooner it will get on to us. Come on, Mr. Frodo!'

Frodo raised his head, and then stood up. Despair had not left him, but the weakness had passed. He even smiled grimly, feeling now as clearly as a moment before he had felt the opposite, that what he had to do, he had to do, if he could, and that whether Faramir or Aragorn or Elrond or Galadriel or Gandalf or anyone else ever knew about it was beside the purpose. He took his staff in one hand and the phial in his other. When he saw that the clear light was already welling through his fingers, he thrust it into his bosom and held it against his heart. Then turning from the city of Morgul, now no more than a grey glimmer across a dark gulf, he prepared to take the upward road.

Gollum, it seemed, had crawled off along the ledge into the darkness beyond, when the gates of Minas Morgul opened, leaving the hobbits where they lay. He now came creeping back, his teeth chattering and his fingers snapping.

'Foolish! Silly!' he hissed. 'Make haste! They mustn't think danger has passed. It hasn't. Make haste!'

They did not answer, but they followed him onto the climbing ledge. It was little to the liking of either of them, not even after facing so many other perils; but it did not last long. Soon the path reached a rounded angle where the mountain-side swelled out again, and there it suddenly entered a narrow opening in the rock. They had come to the first stair that Gollum had spoken of. The darkness was almost complete, and they could see nothing much beyond their hands' stretch; but Gollum's eyes shone pale, several feet above, as he turned back towards them.

'Careful!' he whispered. 'Steps. Lots of steps. Must be careful!'

Care was certainly needed. Frodo and Sam at first felt easier, having now a wall on either side, but the stairway was almost as steep as a ladder, and as they climbed up and up, they became more and more aware of the long black fall behind them. And the steps were narrow, spaced unevenly, and often treacherous: they were worn and smooth at the edges, and some were broken, and some cracked as foot was set upon them. The hobbits struggled on, until at last they were clinging with desperate fingers to the steps ahead, and forcing their aching knees to bend and straighten; and ever as the stair cut its way deeper into the sheer mountain the rocky walls rose higher and higher above their heads.

At length, just as they felt that they could endure no more, they saw Gollum's eyes peering down at them again. 'We're up,' he whispered. 'First stair's past. Clever hobbits to climb so high, very clever hobbits. Just a few more little steps and that's all, yes.'

Dizzy and very tired Sam, and Frodo following him, crawled up the last step, and sat down rubbing their legs and knees. They were in a deep dark passage that seemed still to go up before them, though at a gentler slope and without steps. Gollum did not let them rest long.

'There's another stair still,' he said. 'Much longer stair. Rest when we get to the top of next stair. Not yet.'

Sam groaned. 'Longer, did you say?' he asked.

'Yes, yess, longer,' said Gollum. 'But not so difficult. Hobbits have climbed the Straight Stair. Next comes the Winding Stair.'

'And what after that?' said Sam.

'We shall see,' said Gollum softly. 'O yes, we shall see!'

'I thought you said there was a tunnel,' said Sam. 'Isn't there a tunnel or something to go through?'

'O yes, there's a tunnel,' said Gollum. 'But hobbits can rest before they try that. If they get through that, they'll be nearly at the top. Very nearly, if they get through. O yes!'

Frodo shivered. The climb had made him sweat, but now he felt cold and clammy, and there was a chill draught in the dark passage, blowing down from the invisible heights above. He got up and shook himself. 'Well, let's go on!' he said. 'This is no place to sit in.'

The passage seemed to go on for miles, and always the chill air flowed over them, rising as they went on to a bitter wind. The mountains seemed to be trying with their deadly breath to daunt them, to turn them back from the secrets of the high places, or to blow them away into the darkness behind. They only knew that they had come to the end, when suddenly they felt no wall at their right hand. They could see very little. Great black shapeless masses and deep grey shadows loomed above them and about them, but now and again a dull red light flickered up under the lowering clouds, and for a moment they were aware of tall peaks, in front and on either side, like pillars holding up a vast sagging roof. They seemed to have climbed up many hundreds of feet, onto a wide shelf. A cliff was on their left and a chasm on their right.

Gollum led the way close under the cliff. For the present they were no longer climbing, but the ground was now more broken and dangerous in the dark, and there were blocks and lumps of fallen stone in the way. Their going

was slow and cautious. How many hours had passed
since they had entered the Morgul Vale neither Sam nor
Frodo could any longer guess. The night seemed endless.

At length they were once more aware of a wall looming up, and once more a stairway opened before them.
Again they halted, and again they began to climb. It was a
long and weary ascent; but this stairway did not delve into
the mountain-side. Here the huge cliff-face sloped backwards, and the path like a snake wound to and fro across
it. At one point it crawled sideways right to the edge of the
dark chasm, and Frodo glancing down saw below him as a
vast deep pit the great ravine at the head of the Morgul
Valley. Down in its depths glimmered like a glow-worm
thread the wraith-road from the dead city to the Nameless Pass. He turned hastily away.

Still on and up the stairway bent and crawled, until at
last with a final flight, short and straight, it climbed out
again onto another level. The path had veered away from
the main pass in the great ravine, and it now followed its
own perilous course at the bottom of a lesser cleft among
the higher regions of the Ephel Dúath. Dimly the hobbits
could discern tall piers and jagged pinnacles of stone on
either side, between which were great crevices and fissures blacker than the night, where forgotten winters had
gnawed and carved the sunless stone. And now the red
light in the sky seemed stronger; though they could not tell
whether a dreadful morning were indeed coming to this
place of shadow, or whether they saw only the flame
of some great violence of Sauron in the torment of Gorgoroth beyond. Still far ahead, and still high above, Frodo,
looking up, saw, as he guessed, the very crown of this
bitter road. Against the sullen redness of the eastern sky a
cleft was outlined in the topmost ridge, narrow, deep-
cloven between two black shoulders; and on either shoulder was a horn of stone.

He paused and looked more attentively. The horn upon
the left was tall and slender; and in it burned a red light,
or else the red light in the land beyond was shining through

a hole. He saw now: it was a black tower poised above the outer pass. He touched Sam's arm and pointed.

'I don't like the look of that!' said Sam. 'So this secret way of yours is guarded after all,' he growled, turning to Gollum. 'As you knew all along, I suppose?'

'All ways are watched, yes,' said Gollum. 'Of course they are. But hobbits must try some way. This may be least watched. Perhaps they've all gone away to big battle, perhaps!'

'Perhaps,' grunted Sam. 'Well, it still seems a long way off, and a long way up before we get there. And there's still the tunnel. I think you ought to rest now, Mr. Frodo. I don't know what time of day or night it is, but we've kept going for hours and hours.'

'Yes, we must rest,' said Frodo. 'Let us find some corner out of the wind, and gather our strength—for the last lap.' For so he felt it to be. The terrors of the land beyond, and the deed to be done there, seemed remote, too far off yet to trouble him. All his mind was bent on getting through or over this impenetrable wall and guard. If once he could do that impossible thing, then somehow the errand would be accomplished, or so it seemed to him in that dark hour of weariness, still labouring in the stony shadows under Cirith Ungol.

In a dark crevice between two great piers of rock they sat down: Frodo and Sam a little way within, and Gollum crouched upon the ground near the opening. There the hobbits took what they expected would be their last meal before they went down into the Nameless Land, maybe the last meal they would ever eat together. Some of the food of Gondor they ate, and wafers of the waybread of the Elves, and they drank a little. But of their water they were sparing and took only enough to moisten their dry mouths.

'I wonder when we'll find water again?' said Sam. 'But I suppose even over there they drink? Orcs drink, don't they?'

'Yes, they drink,' said Frodo. 'But do not let us speak of that. Such drink is not for us.'

'Then all the more need to fill our bottles,' said Sam. 'But there isn't any water up here; not a sound or a trickle have I heard. And anyway Faramir said we were not to drink any water in Morgul.'

'No water flowing out of Imlad Morgul, were his words,' said Frodo. 'We are not in that valley now, and if we came on a spring it would be flowing into it and not out of it.'

'I wouldn't trust it,' said Sam, 'not till I was dying of thirst. There's a wicked feeling about this place.' He sniffed. 'And a smell, I fancy. Do you notice it? A queer kind of a smell, stuffy. I don't like it.'

'I don't like anything here at all,' said Frodo, 'step or stone, breath or bone. Earth, air and water all seem accursed. But so our path is laid.'

'Yes, that's so,' said Sam. 'And we shouldn't be here at all, if we'd known more about it before we started. But I suppose it's often that way. The brave things in the old tales and songs, Mr. Frodo: adventures, as I used to call them. I used to think that they were things the wonderful folk of the stories went out and looked for, because they wanted them, because they were exciting and life was a bit dull, a kind of a sport, as you might say. But that's not the way of it with the tales that really mattered, or the ones that stay in the mind. Folk seem to have been just landed in them, usually—their paths were laid that way, as you put it. But I expect they had lots of chances, like us, of turning back, only they didn't. And if they had, we shouldn't know, because they'd have been forgotten. We hear about those as just went on—and not all to a good end, mind you; at least not to what folk inside a story and not outside it call a good end. You know, coming home, and finding things all right, though not quite the same—like old Mr. Bilbo. But those aren't always the best tales to hear, though they may be the best tales to get landed in! I wonder what sort of a tale we've fallen into?'

'I wonder,' said Frodo. 'But I don't know. And that's the

way of a real tale. Take any one that you're fond of. You may know, or guess, what kind of a tale it is, happy-ending or sad-ending, but the people in it don't know. And you don't want them to.'

'No, sir, of course not. Beren now, he never thought he was going to get that Silmaril from the Iron Crown in Thangorodrim, and yet he did, and that was a worse place and a blacker danger than ours. But that's a long tale, of course, and goes on past the happiness and into grief and beyond it—and the Silmaril went on and came to Eärendil. And why, sir, I never thought of that before! We've got —you've got some of the light of it in that star-glass that the Lady gave you! Why, to think of it, we're in the same tale still! It's going on. Don't the great tales never end?'

'No, they never end as tales,' said Frodo. 'But the people in them come, and go when their part's ended. Our part will end later—or sooner.'

'And then we can have some rest and some sleep,' said Sam. He laughed grimly. 'And I mean just that, Mr. Frodo. I mean plain ordinary rest, and sleep, and waking up to a morning's work in the garden. I'm afraid that's all I'm hoping for all the time. All the big important plans are not for my sort. Still, I wonder if we shall ever be put into songs or tales. We're in one, of course; but I mean: put into words, you know, told by the fireside, or read out of a great big book with red and black letters, years and years afterwards. And people will say: "Let's hear about Frodo and the Ring!" And they'll say: "Yes, that's one of my favourite stories. Frodo was very brave, wasn't he, dad?" "Yes, my boy, the famousest of the hobbits, and that's saying a lot." '

'It's saying a lot too much,' said Frodo, and he laughed, a long clear laugh from his heart. Such a sound had not been heard in those places since Sauron came to Middle-earth. To Sam suddenly it seemed as if all the stones were listening and the tall rocks leaning over them. But Frodo did not heed them; he laughed again. 'Why, Sam,' he said, 'to hear you somehow makes me as merry as if the story was already written. But you've left out one of the chief characters: Samwise the stouthearted. "I want to hear more about Sam, dad. Why didn't they put in more of his talk, dad? That's what I like, it makes me laugh. And Frodo wouldn't have got far without Sam, would he, dad?" '

'Now, Mr. Frodo,' said Sam, 'you shouldn't make fun. I was serious.'

'So was I,' said Frodo, 'and so I am. We're going on a bit too fast. You and I, Sam, are still stuck in the worst places of the story, and it is all too likely that some will say at this point: "Shut the book now, dad; we don't want to read any more." '

'Maybe,' said Sam, 'but I wouldn't be one to say that. Things done and over and made into part of the great tales are different. Why, even Gollum might be good in a tale, better than he is to have by you, anyway. And he used to like tales himself once, by his own account. I wonder if he thinks he's the hero or the villain?

'Gollum!' he called. 'Would you like to be the hero— now where's he got to again?'

There was no sign of him at the mouth of their shelter nor in the shadows near. He had refused their food, though he had, as usual, accepted a mouthful of water; and then he had seemed to curl up for a sleep. They had supposed that one at any rate of his objects in his long absence the day before had been to hunt for food to his own liking; and now he had evidently slipped off again while they talked. But what for this time?

'I don't like his sneaking off without saying,' said Sam. 'And least of all now. He can't be looking for food up here, not unless there's some kind of rock he fancies. Why, there isn't even a bit of moss!'

'It's no good worrying about him now,' said Frodo. 'We couldn't have got so far, not even within sight of the pass, without him, and so we'll have to put up with his ways. If he's false, he's false.'

'All the same, I'd rather have him under my eye,' said Sam. 'All the more so, if he's false. Do you remember he never would say if this pass was guarded or no? And

now we see a tower there—and it may be deserted, and
it may not. Do you think he's gone to fetch them, Orcs
or whatever they are?'

'No, I don't think so,' answered Frodo. 'Even if he's up
to some wickedness, and I suppose that's not unlikely. .
don't think it's that: not to fetch Orcs, or any servants of
the Enemy. Why wait till now, and go through all the
labour of the climb, and come so near the land he fears?
He could probably have betrayed us to Orcs many times
since we met him. No, if it's anything, it will be some little
private trick of his own that he thinks is quite secret.'

'Well, I suppose you're right, Mr. Frodo,' said Sam.
'Not that it comforts me mightily. I don't make no mistake: I don't doubt he'd hand me over to Orcs as gladly as
kiss his hand. But I was forgetting—his Precious. No, I
suppose the whole time it's been *The Precious for poor
Sméagol*. That's the one idea in all his little schemes, if he
has any. But how bringing us up here will help him in that
is more than I can guess.'

'Very likely he can't guess himself,' said Frodo. 'And I
don't think he's got just one plain scheme in his muddled
head. I think he really is in part trying to save the Precious
from the Enemy, as long as he can. For that would be the
last disaster for himself too, if the Enemy got it. And in the
other part, perhaps, he's just biding his time and waiting on chance.'

'Yes, Slinker and Stinker, as I've said before,' said Sam.
'But the nearer they get to the Enemy's land the more like
Stinker Slinker will get. Mark my words: if ever we get to
the pass, he won't let us really take the precious thing
over the border without making some kind of trouble.'

'We haven't got there yet,' said Frodo.

'No, but we'd better keep our eyes skinned till we do. If
we're caught napping, Stinker will come out on top pretty
quick. Not but what it would be safe for you to have a wink
now, master. Safe, if you lay close to me. I'd be dearly
glad to see you have a sleep. I'd keep watch over you; and
anyway, if you lay near, with my arm round you, no one
could come pawing you without your Sam knowing it.'

'Sleep!' said Frodo and sighed, as if out of a desert he had seen a mirage of cool green. 'Yes, even here I could sleep.'

'Sleep then, master! Lay your head in my lap.'

And so Gollum found them hours later, when he returned, crawling and creeping down the path out of the gloom ahead. Sam sat propped against the stone, his head dropping sideways and his breathing heavy. In his lap lay Frodo's head, drowned deep in sleep; upon his white forehead lay one of Sam's brown hands, and the other lay softly upon his master's breast. Peace was in both their faces.

Gollum looked at them. A strange expression passed over his lean hungry face. The gleam faded from his eyes, and they went dim and grey, old and tired. A spasm of pain seemed to twist him, and he turned away, peering back up towards the pass, shaking his head, as if engaged in some interior debate. Then he came back, and slowly putting out a trembling hand, very cautiously he touched Frodo's knee—but almost the touch was a caress. For a fleeting moment, could one of the sleepers have seen him, they would have thought that they beheld an old weary hobbit, shrunken by the years that had carried him far beyond his time, beyond friends and kin, and the fields and streams of youth, an old starved pitiable thing.

But at that touch Frodo stirred and cried out softly in his sleep, and immediately Sam was wide awake. The first thing he saw was Gollum—'pawing at master,' as he thought.

'Hey you!' he said roughly. 'What are you up to?'

'Nothing, nothing,' said Gollum softly. 'Nice Master!'

'I daresay,' said Sam. 'But where have you been to— sneaking off and sneaking back, you old villain?'

Gollum withdrew himself, and a green glint flickered under his heavy lids. Almost spider-like he looked now, crouched back on his bent limbs, with his protruding eyes. The fleeting moment had passed, beyond recall. 'Sneaking, sneaking!' he hissed. 'Hobbits always so polite, yes. O nice hobbits! Sméagol brings them up secret ways that nobody else could find. Tired he is, thirsty he is, yes thirsty; and he guides them and he searches for paths, and they say *sneak, sneak*. Very nice friends, O yes my precious, very nice.'

Sam felt a bit remorseful, though not more trustful. 'Sorry,' he said. 'I'm sorry, but you startled me out of my sleep. And I shouldn't have been sleeping, and that made me a bit sharp. But Mr. Frodo, he's that tired, I asked him to have a wink; and well, that's how it is. Sorry. But where *have* you been to?'

'Sneaking,' said Gollum, and the green glint did not leave his eyes.

'O very well,' said Sam, 'have it your own way! I don't suppose it's so far from the truth. And now we'd better all be sneaking along together. What's the time? Is it today or tomorrow?'

'It's tomorrow,' said Gollum, 'or this was tomorrow when hobbits went to sleep. Very foolish, very dangerous—if poor Sméagol wasn't sneaking about to watch.'

'I think we shall get tired of that word soon,' said Sam. 'But never mind. I'll wake master up.' Gently he smoothed the hair back from Frodo's brow, and bending down spoke softly to him.

'Wake up, Mr. Frodo! Wake up!'

Frodo stirred and opened his eyes, and smiled, seeing Sam's face bending over him. 'Calling me early aren't you, Sam?' he said. 'It's dark still!'

'Yes it's always dark here,' said Sam. 'But Gollum's come back, Mr. Frodo, and he says it's tomorrow. So we must be walking on. The last lap.'

Frodo drew a deep breath and sat up. 'The last lap!' he said. 'Hullo, Sméagol! Found any food? Have you had any rest?'

'No food, no rest, nothing for Sméagol,' said Gollum. 'He's a sneak.'

Sam clicked his tongue, but restrained himself.

'Don't take names to yourself, Sméagol,' said Frodo. 'It's unwise, whether they are true or false.'

'Sméagol has to take what's given him,' answered Gollum. 'He was given that name by kind Master Samwise, the hobbit that knows so much.'

Frodo looked at Sam. 'Yes sir,' he said. 'I did use the word, waking up out of my sleep sudden and all and finding him at hand. I said I was sorry, but I soon shan't be.'

'Come, let it pass then,' said Frodo. 'But now we seem to have come to the point, you and I, Sméagol. Tell me. Can we find the rest of the way by ourselves? We're in sight of the pass, of a way in, and if we can find it now, then I suppose our agreement can be said to be over. You have done what you promised, and you're free: free to go back to food and rest, wherever you wish to go, except to servants of the Enemy. And one day I may reward you, I or those that remember me.'

'No, no, not yet,' Gollum whined. 'O no! They can't find the way themselves, can they? O no indeed. There's the tunnel coming. Sméagol must go on. No rest. No food. Not yet.'

Chapter 9

Shelob's Lair

It may indeed have been daytime now, as Gollum said, but the hobbits could see little difference, unless, perhaps, the heavy sky above was less utterly black, more like a great roof of smoke; while instead of the darkness of deep night, which lingered still in cracks and holes, a grey blurring shadow shrouded the stony world about them. They passed on, Gollum in front and the hobbits now side by side, up the long ravine between the piers and columns of torn and weathered rock, standing like huge unshapen statues on either hand. There was no sound. Some way ahead, a mile or so, perhaps, was a great grey wall, a last huge upthrusting mass of mountain-stone. Darker it loomed, and steadily it rose as they approached, until it towered up high above them, shutting out the view of all that lay beyond. Deep shadow lay before its feet. Sam sniffed the air.

'Ugh! That smell!' he said. 'It's getting stronger and stronger.'

Presently they were under the shadow, and there in the midst of it they saw the opening of a cave. 'This is the way in,' said Gollum softly. 'This is the entrance of the tunnel.' He did not speak its name: Torech Ungol, Shelob's Lair. Out of it came a stench, not the sickly odour of decay in the meads of Morgul, but a foul reek, as if filth unnameable were piled and hoarded in the dark within.

'Is this the only way, Sméagol?' said Frodo.

'Yes, yes,' he answered. 'Yes, we must go this way now.'

'D'you mean to say you've been through this hole?' said Sam. 'Phew! But perhaps you don't mind bad smells.'

Gollum's eyes glinted. 'He doesn't know what we minds, does he, precious? No, he doesn't. But Sméagol can bear things. Yes. He's been through, O yes, right through. It's the only way.'

'And what makes the smell, I wonder,' said Sam. 'It's like—well, I wouldn't like to say. Some beastly hole of the Orcs, I'll warrant, with a hundred years of their filth in it.'

'Well,' said Frodo, 'Orcs or no, if it's the only way, we must take it.'

Drawing a deep breath they passed inside. In a few steps they were in utter and impenetrable dark. Not since the lightless passages of Moria had Frodo or Sam known such darkness, and if possible here it was deeper and denser. There, there were airs moving, and echoes, and a sense of space. Here the air was still, stagnant, heavy, and sound fell dead. They walked as it were in a black vapour wrought of veritable darkness itself that, as it was breathed, brought blindness not only to the eyes but to the mind, so that even the memory of colours and of forms and of any light faded out of thought. Night always had been, and always would be, and night was all.

But for a while they could still feel, and indeed the senses of their feet and fingers at first seemed sharpened almost painfully. The walls felt, to their surprise, smooth, and the floor, save for a step now and again, was straight and even, going ever up at the same stiff slope. The tunnel was high and wide, so wide that, though the hobbits walked abreast, only touching the side-walls with their outstretched hands, they were separated, cut off alone in the darkness.

Gollum had gone in first and seemed to be only a few steps ahead. While they were still able to give heed to such things, they could hear his breath hissing and gasping just in front of them. But after a time their senses became duller, both touch and hearing seemed to grow numb, and they kept on, groping, walking, on and on, mainly by the force of the will with which they had entered, will to go through and desire to come at last to the high gate beyond.

Before they had gone very far, perhaps, but time and distance soon passed out of his reckoning, Sam on the right, feeling the wall, was aware that there was an opening at the side: for a moment he caught a faint breath of some air less heavy, and then they passed it by.

'There's more than one passage here,' he whispered with an effort: it seemed hard to make his breath give any sound. 'It's as orc-like a place as ever there could be!'

After that, first he on the right, and then Frodo on the left, passed three or four such openings, some wider, some smaller; but there was as yet no doubt of the main way, for it was straight, and did not turn, and still went steadily up. But how long was it, how much more of this would they have to endure, or could they endure? The breathlessness of the air was growing as they climbed; and now they seemed often in the blind dark to sense some resistance thicker than the foul air. As they thrust forward they felt things brush against their heads, or against their hands, long tentacles, or hanging growths perhaps: they could not tell what they were. And still the stench grew. It grew, until almost it seemed to them that smell was the only clear sense left to them, and that was for their torment. One hour, two hours, three hours: how many had they passed in this lightless hole? Hours—days, weeks rather. Sam left the tunnel-side and shrank towards Frodo, and their hands met and clasped, and so together they still went on.

At length Frodo, groping along the left-hand wall, came suddenly to a void. Almost he fell sideways into the emptiness. Here was some opening in the rock far wider than any they had yet passed; and out of it came a reek so foul, and a sense of lurking malice so intense, that Frodo reeled. And at that moment Sam too lurched and fell forwards.

Fighting off both the sickness and the fear, Frodo gripped Sam's hand. 'Up!' he said in a hoarse breath without voice. 'It all comes from here, the stench and the peril. Now for it! Quick!'

Calling up his remaining strength and resolution, he dragged Sam to his feet, and forced his own limbs to move. Sam stumbled beside him. One step, two steps, three steps—at last six steps. Maybe they had passed the dread ful unseen opening, but whether that was so or not, suddenly it was easier to move, as if some hostile will for the moment had released them. They struggled on, still hand in hand.

But almost at once they came to a new difficulty. The tunnel forked, or so it seemed, and in the dark they could not tell which was the wider way, or which kept nearer to the straight. Which should they take, the left, or the right? They knew of nothing to guide them, yet a false choice would almost certainly be fatal.

'Which way has Gollum gone?' panted Sam. 'And why didn't he wait?'

'Sméagol!' said Frodo, trying to call. 'Sméagol!' But his voice croaked, and the name fell dead almost as it left his lips. There was no answer, not an echo, not even a tremor of the air.

'He's really gone this time, I fancy,' muttered Sam. 'I guess this is just exactly where he meant to bring us. Gollum! If ever I lay hands on you again, you'll be sorry for it.'

Presently, groping and fumbling in the dark, they found that the opening on the left was blocked: either it was a blind, or else some great stone had fallen in the passage. 'This can't be the way,' Frodo whispered. 'Right or wrong, we must take the other.'

'And quick!' Sam panted. 'There's something worse than Gollum about. I can feel something looking at us.'

They had not gone more than a few yards when from behind them came a sound, startling and horrible in the heavy padded silence: a gurgling, bubbling noise, and a long venomous hiss. They wheeled round, but nothing could be seen. Still as stones they stood, staring, waiting for they did not know what.

'It's a trap!' said Sam, and he laid his hand upon the hilt of his sword; and as he did so, he thought of the darkness of the barrow whence it came. 'I wish old Tom was near us now!' he thought. Then, as he stood, darkness about him and a blackness of despair and anger in his heart, it seemed to him that he saw a light; a light in his mind, almost unbearably bright at first, as a sun-ray to the eyes of one long hidden in a windowless pit. Then the light became colour: green, gold, silver, white. Far off, as in a little picture drawn by elven-fingers, he saw the Lady Galadriel standing on the grass in Lórien, and gifts were in her hands. *And you, Ring-bearer,* he heard her say, remote but clear, *for you I have prepared this.*

The bubbling hiss drew nearer, and there was a creaking as of some great jointed thing that moved with slow purpose in the dark. A reek came on before it. 'Master, master!' cried Sam, and life and urgency came back into his voice. 'The Lady's gift! The star-glass! A light to you in dark places, she said it was to be. The star-glass!'

'The star-glass?' muttered Frodo, as one answering out of sleep, hardly comprehending. 'Why yes! Why had I forgotten it? *A light when all other lights go out!* And now indeed light alone can help us.'

Slowly his hand went to his bosom, and slowly he held aloft the Phial of Galadriel. For a moment it glimmered, faint as a rising star struggling in heavy earthward mists, and then as its power waxed, and hope grew in Frodo's mind, it began to burn, and kindled to a silver flame, a minute heart of dazzling light, as though Eärendil had himself come down from the high sunset paths with the last Silmaril upon his brow. The darkness receded from it, until it seemed to shine in the centre of a globe of airy crystal, and the hand that held it sparkled with white fire.

Frodo gazed in wonder at this marvellous gift that he had so long carried, not guessing its full worth and potency. Seldom had he remembered it on the road, until they came to Morgul Vale, and never had he used it for fear of its revealing light. *Aiya Eärendil Elenion Ancalima!* he cried, and knew not what he had spoken; for it seemed that another voice spoke through his, clear, untroubled by the foul air of the pit.

But other potencies there are in Middle-earth, powers of night, and they are old and strong. And She that walked in the darkness had heard the Elves cry that cry far back in the deeps of time, and she had not heeded it, and it did

not daunt her now. Even as Frodo spoke he felt a great
malice bent upon him, and a deadly regard considering
him. Not far down the tunnel, between them and the
opening where they had reeled and stumbled, he was
aware of eyes growing visible, two great clusters of many-
windowed eyes—the coming menace was unmasked at
last. The radiance of the star-glass was broken and thrown
back from their thousand facets, but behind the glitter a
pale deadly fire began steadily to glow within, a flame
kindled in some deep pit of evil thought. Monstrous and
abominable eyes they were, bestial and yet filled with
purpose and with hideous delight, gloating over their prey
trapped beyond all hope of escape.

Frodo and Sam, horror-stricken, began slowly to back
away, their own gaze held by the dreadful stare of those
baleful eyes; but as they backed so the eyes advanced.
Frodo's hand wavered, and slowly the Phial drooped.
Then suddenly, released from the holding spell to run a
little while in vain panic for the amusement of the eyes,
they both turned and fled together; but even as they ran
Frodo looked back and saw with terror that at once the
eyes came leaping up behind. The stench of death was like
a cloud about him.

'Stand! stand!' he cried desperately. 'Running is no use.'
Slowly the eyes crept nearer.

'Galadriel!' he called, and gathering his courage he lifted
up the Phial once more. The eyes halted. For a moment
their regard relaxed, as if some hint of doubt troubled
them. Then Frodo's heart flamed within him, and without
thinking what he did, whether it was folly or despair or
courage, he took the Phial in his left hand, and with his
right hand drew his sword. Sting flashed out, and the
sharp elven-blade sparkled in the silver light, but at its
edges a blue fire flicked. Then holding the star aloft and
the bright sword advanced, Frodo, hobbit of the Shire,
walked steadily down to meet the eyes.

They wavered. Doubt came into them as the light approached. One by one they dimmed, and slowly they drew

back. No brightness so deadly had ever afflicted them before. From sun and moon and star they had been safe underground, but now a star had descended into the very earth. Still it approached, and the eyes began to quail. One by one they all went dark; they turned away, and a great bulk, beyond the light's reach, heaved its huge shadow in between. They were gone.

'Master, master!' cried Sam. He was close behind, his own sword drawn and ready. 'Stars and glory! But the Elves would make a song of that, if ever they heard of it! And may I live to tell them and hear them sing. But don't go on, master! Don't go down to that den! Now's our only chance. Now let's get out of this foul hole!'

And so back they turned once more, first walking and then running; for as they went the floor of the tunnel rose steeply, and with every stride they climbed higher above the stenches of the unseen lair, and strength returned to limb and heart. But still the hatred of the Watcher lurked behind them, blind for a while, perhaps, but undefeated, still bent on death. And now there came a flow of air to meet them, cold and thin. The opening, the tunnel's end, at last it was before them. Panting, yearning for a roofless place, they flung themselves forward; and then in amazement they staggered, tumbling back. The outlet was blocked with some barrier, but not of stone: soft and a little yielding it seemed, and yet strong and impervious; air filtered through, but not a glimmer of any light. Once more they charged and were hurled back.

Holding aloft the Phial Frodo looked and before him he saw a greyness which the radiance of the star-glass did not pierce and did not illuminate, as if it were a shadow that being cast by no light, no light could dissipate. Across the width and height of the tunnel a vast web was spun, orderly as the web of some huge spider, but denser-woven and far greater, and each thread was as thick as rope.

Sam laughed grimly. 'Cobwebs!' he said. 'Is that all? Cobwebs! But what a spider! Have at 'em, down with 'em!'

In a fury he hewed at them with his sword, but the

thread that he struck did not break. It gave a l[...]
then sprang back like a plucked bowstring, turni[...]
blade and tossing up both sword and arm. Three t[...]es
Sam struck with all his force, and at last one single cord
of all the countless cords snapped and twisted, curling
and whipping through the air. One end of it lashed Sam's
hand, and he cried out in pain, starting back and drawing
his hand across his mouth.

'It will take days to clear the road like this,' he said.
'What's to be done? Have those eyes come back?'

'No, not to be seen,' said Frodo. 'But I still feel that they
are looking at me, or thinking about me: making some
other plan, perhaps. If this light were lowered, or if it
failed, they would quickly come again.'

'Trapped in the end!' said Sam bitterly, his anger rising again above weariness and despair. 'Gnats in a net.
May the curse of Faramir bite that Gollum and bite him
quick!'

'That would not help us now,' said Frodo. 'Come! Let
us see what Sting can do. It is an elven-blade. There were
webs of horror in the dark ravines of Beleriand where it
was forged. But you must be the guard and hold back the
eyes. Here, take the star-glass. Do not be afraid. Hold it
up and watch!'

Then Frodo stepped up to the great grey net, and
hewed it with a wide sweeping stroke, drawing the bitter
edge swiftly across a ladder of close-strung cords, and at
once springing away. The blue-gleaming blade shore
through them like a scythe through grass, and they leaped
and writhed and then hung loose. A great rent was made.

Stroke after stroke he dealt, until at last all the web
within his reach was shattered, and the upper portion
blew and swayed like a loose veil in the incoming wind.
The trap was broken.

'Come!' cried Frodo. 'On! On!' Wild joy at their escape
from the very mouth of despair suddenly filled all his
mind. His head whirled as with a draught of potent wine.
He sprang out, shouting as he came.

It seemed light in that dark land to his eyes that had passed through the den of night. The great smokes had risen and grown thinner, and the last hours of a sombre day were passing; the red glare of Mordor had died away in sullen gloom. Yet it seemed to Frodo that he looked upon a morning of sudden hope. Almost, he had reached the summit of the wall. Only a little higher now. The cleft, Cirith Ungol, was before him, a dim notch in the black ridge, and the horns of rock darkling in the sky on either side. A short race, a sprinter's course, and he would be through!

'The pass, Sam!' he cried, not heeding the shrillness of his voice, that released from the choking airs of the tunnel rang out now high and wild. 'The pass! Run, run, and we'll be through—through before anyone can stop us!'

Sam came up behind as fast as he could urge his legs; but glad as he was to be free, he was uneasy, and as he ran, he kept on glancing back at the dark arch of the tunnel, fearing to see eyes, or some shape beyond his imagining, spring out in pursuit. Too little did he or his master know of the craft of Shelob. She had many exits from her lair.

There agelong she had dwelt, an evil thing in spider-form, even such as once of old had lived in the Land of the Elves in the West that is now under the Sea, such as Beren fought in the Mountains of Terror in Doriath, and so came to Lúthien upon the green sward amid the hemlocks in the moonlight long ago. How Shelob came there, flying from ruin, no tale tells, for out of the Dark Years few tales have come. But still she was there, who was there before Sauron, and before the first stone of Barad-dûr; and she served none but herself, drinking the blood of Elves and Men, bloated and grown fat with endless brooding on her feasts, weaving webs of shadow; for all living things were her food, and her vomit darkness. Far and wide her lesser broods, bastards of the miserable mates, her own offspring, that she slew, spread from glen to glen, from the Ephel Dúath to the eastern hills, to Dol Guldur and the fastnesses of Mirkwood. But none could rival her, Shelob the Great, last child of Ungoliant to trouble the unhappy world.

Already, years before, Gollum had beheld her, Sméagol who pried into all dark holes, and in past days he had bowed and worshipped her, and the darkness of her evil will walked through all the ways of his weariness beside him, cutting him off from light and from regret. And he had promised to bring her food. But her lust was not his lust. Little she knew of or cared for towers, or rings, or anything devised by mind or hand, who only desired death for all others, mind and body, and for herself a glut of life, alone, swollen till the mountains could no longer hold her up and the darkness could not contain her.

But that desire was yet far away, and long now had she been hungry, lurking in her den, while the power of Sauron grew, and light and living things forsook his borders; and the city in the valley was dead, and no Elf or Man came near, only the unhappy Orcs. Poor food and wary. But she must eat, and however busily they delved new winding passages from the pass and from their tower, ever she found some way to snare them. But she lusted for sweeter meat. And Gollum had brought it to her.

'We'll see, we'll see,' he said often to himself, when the evil mood was on him, as he walked the dangerous road from Emyn Muil to Morgul Vale, 'we'll see. It may well be, O yes, it may well be that when She throws away the bones and the empty garments, we shall find it, we shall get it, the Precious, a reward for poor Sméagol who brings nice food. And we'll save the Precious, as we promised. O yes. And when we've got it safe, then She'll know it, O yes, then we'll pay Her back, my precious. Then we'll pay every one back!'

So he thought in an inner chamber of his cunning, which he still hoped to hide from her, even when he had come to her again and had bowed low before her while his companions slept.

And as for Sauron: he knew where she lurked. It pleased him that she should dwell there hungry but un-abated in malice, a more sure watch upon that ancient path into his land than any other that his skill could have devised. And Orcs, they were useful slaves, but he had them in plenty. If now and again Shelob caught them to stay her appetite, she was welcome: he could spare them. And sometimes as a man may cast a dainty to his cat (*his cat* he calls her, but she owns him not) Sauron would send her prisoners that he had not better uses for: he would have them driven to her hole, and report brought back to him of the play she made.

So they both lived, delighting in their own devices, and feared no assault, nor wrath, nor any end of their wickedness. Never yet had any fly escaped from Shelob's webs, and the greater now was her rage and hunger.

But nothing of this evil which they had stirred up against them did poor Sam know, except that a fear was growing on him, a menace which he could not see; and such a weight did it become that it was a burden to him to run, and his feet seemed leaden.

Dread was round him, and enemies before him in the pass, and his master was in a fey mood running heedlessly to meet them. Turning his eyes away from the shadow behind and the deep gloom beneath the cliff upon his left, he looked ahead, and he saw two things that increased his dismay. He saw that the sword which Frodo still held unsheathed was glittering with blue flame; and he saw that though the sky behind was now dark, still the window in the tower was glowing red.

'Orcs!' he muttered. 'We'll never rush it like this. There's Orcs about, and worse than Orcs.' Then returning quickly to his long habit of secrecy, he closed his hand about the precious Phial which he still bore. Red with his own living blood his hand shone for a moment, and then he thrust the revealing light deep into a pocket near his breast and drew his elven-cloak about him. Now he tried to quicken his pace. His master was gaining on him; already he was some twenty strides ahead, flitting on like a shadow; soon he would be lost to sight in that grey world.

Hardly had Sam hidden the light of the star-glass when she came. A little way ahead and to his left he saw suddenly, issuing from a black hole of shadow under the cliff, the most loathly shape that he had ever beheld, horrible beyond the horror of an evil dream. Most like a spider she was, but huger than the great hunting beasts, and more terrible than they because of the evil purpose in her remorseless eyes. Those same eyes that he had thought daunted and defeated, there they were lit with a fell light again, clustering in her out-thrust head. Great horns she had, and behind her short stalk-like neck was her huge swollen body, a vast bloated bag, swaying and sagging between her legs; its great bulk was black, blotched with livid marks, but the belly underneath was pale and luminous and gave forth a stench. Her legs were bent, with great knobbed joints high above her back, and hair that stuck out like steel spines, and at each leg's end there was a claw.

As soon as she had squeezed her soft squelching body and its folded limbs out of the upper exit from her lair, she moved with a horrible speed, now running on her creaking legs, now making a sudden bound. She was between Sam and his master. Either she did not see Sam, or she avoided him for the moment as the bearer of the light, and fixed all her intent upon one prey, upon Frodo, bereft of his Phial, running heedless up the path, unaware yet of his peril. Swiftly he ran, but Shelob was swifter; in a few leaps she would have him.

Sam gasped and gathered all his remaining breath to shout. 'Look out behind!' he yelled. 'Look out, master! I'm'—but suddenly his cry was stifled.

A long clammy hand went over his mouth and another caught him by the neck, while something wrapped itself about his legs. Taken off his guard he toppled backwards into the arms of his attacker.

'Got him!' hissed Gollum in his ear. 'At last, my precious, we've got him, yes, the nassty hobbit. We takes this one. She'll get the other. O yes, Shelob will get him, not Sméagol: he promised; he won't hurt Master at all. But

he's got you, you nassty filthy little sneak!' He spat on
Sam's neck.

Fury at the treachery, and desperation at the delay
when his master was in deadly peril, gave to Sam a sudden violence and strength that was far beyond anything
that Gollum had expected from this slow stupid hobbit, as
he thought him. Not Gollum himself could have twisted
more quickly or more fiercely. His hold on Sam's mouth
slipped, and Sam ducked and lunged forward again, trying
to tear away from the grip on his neck. His sword was still
in his hand, and on his left arm, hanging by its thong, was
Faramir's staff. Desperately he tried to turn and stab his
enemy. But Gollum was too quick. His long right arm shot
out, and he grabbed Sam's wrist: his fingers were like a
vice; slowly and relentlessly he bent the hand down and
forward, till with a cry of pain Sam released the sword and
it fell to the ground; and all the while Gollum's other
hand was tightening on Sam's throat.

Then Sam played his last trick. With all his strength he
pulled away and got his feet firmly planted; then suddenly
he drove his legs against the ground and with his whole
force hurled himself backwards.

Not expecting even this simple trick from Sam, Gollum
fell over with Sam on top, and he received the weight of the
sturdy hobbit in his stomach. A sharp hiss came out of him,
and for a second his hand upon Sam's throat loosened;
but his fingers still gripped the sword-hand. Sam tore
himself forward and away, and stood up, and then quickly
he wheeled away to his right, pivoted on the wrist held by
Gollum. Laying hold of the staff with his left hand, Sam
swung it up, and down it came with a whistling crack on
Gollum's outstretched arm, just below the elbow.

With a squeal Gollum let go. Then Sam waded in; not
waiting to change the staff from left to right he dealt another savage blow. Quick as a snake Gollum slithered
aside, and the stroke aimed at his head fell across his
back. The staff cracked and broke. That was enough for
him. Grabbing from behind was an old game of his, and
seldom had he failed in it. But this time, misled by spite,

he had made the mistake of speaking and gloating before he had both hands on his victim's neck. Everything had gone wrong with his beautiful plan, since that horrible light had so unexpectedly appeared in the darkness. And now he was face to face with a furious enemy, little less than his own size. The fight was not for him. Sam swept up his sword from the ground and raised it. Gollum squealed, and springing aside onto all fours, he jumped away in one big bound like a frog. Before Sam could reach him, he was off, running with amazing speed back towards the tunnel.

Sword in hand Sam went after him. For the moment he had forgotten everything else but the red fury in his brain and the desire to kill Gollum. But before he could overtake him, Gollum was gone. Then as the dark hole stood before him and the stench came out to meet him, like a clap of thunder the thought of Frodo and the monster smote upon Sam's mind. He spun round, and rushed wildly up the path, calling and calling his master's name. He was too late. So far Gollum's plot had succeeded.

Chapter 10

The Choices of Master Samwise

Frodo was lying face upward on the ground and the monster was bending over him, so intent upon her victim that she took no heed of Sam and his cries, until he was close at hand. As he rushed up he saw that Frodo was already bound in cords, wound about him from ankle to shoulder, and the monster with her great forelegs was beginning half to lift, half to draw his body away.

On the near side of him lay, gleaming on the ground, his elven-blade, where it had fallen useless from his grasp. Sam did not wait to wonder what was to be done, or whether he was brave, or loyal, or filled with rage. He sprang forward with a yell, and seized his master's sword in his left hand. Then he charged. No onslaught more fierce was ever seen in the savage world of beasts, where some desperate small creature armed with little teeth, alone, will spring upon a tower of horn and hide that stands above its fallen mate.

Disturbed as if out of some gloating dream by his small yell she turned slowly the dreadful malice of her glance upon him. But almost before she was aware that a fury was upon her greater than any she had known in countless years, the shining sword bit upon her foot and shore away the claw. Sam sprang in, inside the arches of her legs, and with a quick upthrust of his other hand stabbed at the clustered eyes upon her lowered head. One great eye went dark.

Now the miserable creature was right under her, for the moment out of the reach of her sting and of her claws. Her vast belly was above him with its putrid light, and the stench of it almost smote him down. Still his fury held for one more blow, and before she could sink upon him, smothering him and all his little impudence of courage,

428

he slashed the bright elven-blade across her with desperate strength.

But Shelob was not as dragons are, no softer spot had she save only her eyes. Knobbed and pitted with corruption was her age-old hide, but ever thickened from within with layer on layer of evil growth. The blade scored it with a dreadful gash, but those hideous folds could not be pierced by any strength of men, not though Elf or Dwarf should forge the steel or the hand of Beren or of Túrin wield it. She yielded to the stroke, and then heaved up the great bag of her belly high above Sam's head. Poison frothed and bubbled from the wound. Now splaying her legs she drove her huge bulk down on him again. Too soon. For Sam still stood upon his feet, and dropping his own sword, with both hands he held the elven-blade point upwards, fending off that ghastly roof; and so Shelob, with the driving force of her own cruel will, with strength greater than any warrior's hand, thrust herself upon a bitter spike. Deep, deep it pricked, as Sam was crushed slowly to the ground.

No such anguish had Shelob ever known, or dreamed of knowing, in all her long world of wickedness. Not the doughtiest soldier of old Gondor, nor the most savage Orc entrapped, had ever thus endured her, or set blade to her beloved flesh. A shudder went through her. Heaving up again, wrenching away from the pain, she bent her writhing limbs beneath her and sprang backwards in a convulsive leap.

Sam had fallen to his knees by Frodo's head, his senses reeling in the foul stench, his two hands still gripping the hilt of the sword. Through the mist before his eyes he was aware dimly of Frodo's face, and stubbornly he fought to master himself and to drag himself out of the swoon that was upon him. Slowly he raised his head and saw her, only a few paces away, eyeing him, her beak drabbling a spittle of venom, and a green ooze trickling from below her wounded eye. There she crouched, her shuddering belly splayed upon the ground, the great bows of her legs quivering, as she gathered herself for another spring—this time to crush and sting to death: no little bite of poison to still the struggling of her meat; this time to slay and then to rend.

Even as Sam himself crouched, looking at her, seeing his death in her eyes, a thought came to him, as if some remote voice had spoken, and he fumbled in his breast with his left hand, and found what he sought: cold and hard and solid it seemed to his touch in a phantom world of horror, the Phial of Galadriel.

'Galadriel!' he said faintly, and then he heard voices far off but clear: the crying of the Elves as they walked under the stars in the beloved shadows of the Shire, and the music of the Elves as it came through his sleep in the Hall of Fire in the house of Elrond.

Gilthoniel A Elbereth!

And then his tongue was loosed and his voice cried in a language which he did not know:

> *A Elbereth Gilthoniel*
> *o menel palan-díriel,*
> *le nallon sí di'nguruthos!*
> *A tíro nin, Fanuilos!*

And with that he staggered to his feet and was Samwise the hobbit, Hamfast's son, again.

'Now come, you filth!' he cried. 'You've hurt my master, you brute, and you'll pay for it. We're going on; but we'll settle with you first. Come on, and taste it again!'

As if his indomitable spirit had set its potency in motion, the glass blazed suddenly like a white torch in his hand. It flamed like a star that leaping from the firmament sears the dark air with intolerable light. No such terror out of heaven had ever burned in Shelob's face before. The beams of it entered into her wounded head and scored it with unbearable pain, and the dreadful infection of light spread from eye to eye. She fell back beating the air with her forelegs, her sight blasted by inner lightnings, her mind in agony. Then turning her maimed head away, she rolled aside and began to crawl, claw by claw, towards the opening in the dark cliff behind.

Sam came on. He was reeling like a drunken man, but he came on. And Shelob, cowed at last, shrunken in defeat, jerked and quivered as she tried to hasten from him. She reached the hole, and squeezing down, leaving a trail of green-yellow slime, she slipped in, even as Sam hewed a last stroke at her dragging legs. Then he fell to the ground.

Shelob was gone; and whether she lay long in her lair, nursing her malice and her misery, and in slow years of darkness healed herself from within, rebuilding her clustered eyes, until with hunger like death she spun once more her dreadful snares in the glens of the Mountains of Shadow, this tale does not tell.

Sam was left alone. Wearily, as the evening of the Nameless Land fell upon the place of battle, he crawled back to his master.

'Master, dear master,' he said, but Frodo did not speak. As he had run forward, eager, rejoicing to be free, Shelob with hideous speed had come behind and with one swift stroke had stung him in the neck. He lay now pale, and heard no voice, and did not move.

'Master, dear master!' said Sam, and through a long silence waited, listening in vain.

Then as quickly as he could he cut away the binding cords and laid his head upon Frodo's breast and to his mouth, but no stir of life could he find, nor feel the faintest flutter of the heart. Often he chafed his master's hands and feet, and touched his brow, but all were cold.

'Frodo, Mr. Frodo!' he called. 'Don't leave me here alone! It's your Sam calling. Don't go where I can't follow! Wake up, Mr. Frodo! O wake up, Frodo, me dear, me dear. Wake up!'

Then anger surged over him, and he ran about his master's body in a rage, stabbing the air, and smiting the stones, and shouting challenges. Presently he came back, and bending looked at Frodo's face, pale beneath him in the dusk. And suddenly he saw that he was in the picture that was revealed to him in the mirror of Galadriel in Lórien: Frodo with a pale face lying fast asleep under a great dark cliff. Or fast asleep he had thought then. 'He's dead!' he said. 'Not asleep, dead!' And as he said it, as if the words had set the venom to its work again, it seemed to him that the hue of the face grew livid green.

And then black despair came down on him, and Sam bowed to the ground, and drew his grey hood over his head, and night came into his heart, and he knew no more.

When at last the blackness passed, Sam looked up and shadows were about him; but for how many minutes or hours the world had gone dragging on he could not tell. He was still in the same place, and still his master lay beside him dead. The mountains had not crumbled nor the earth fallen into ruin.

'What shall I do, what shall I do?' he said. 'Did I come all this way with him for nothing?' And then he remembered his own voice speaking words that at the time he did not understand himself, at the beginning of their journey: *I have something to do before the end. I must see it through, sir, if you understand.*

'But what can I do? Not leave Mr. Frodo dead, unburied on the top of the mountains, and go home? Or go on? Go on?' he repeated, and for a moment doubt and fear shook him. 'Go on? Is that what I've got to do? And leave him?'

Then at last he began to weep; and going to Frodo he composed his body, and folded his cold hands upon his breast, and wrapped his cloak about him; and he laid his own sword at one side, and the staff that Faramir had given at the other.

'If I'm to go on,' he said, 'then I must take your sword, by your leave, Mr. Frodo, but I'll put this one to lie by you, as it lay by the old king in the barrow; and you've got your beautiful mithril coat from old Mr. Bilbo. And your star-glass, Mr. Frodo, you did lend it to me and I'll need it, for I'll be always in the dark now. It's too good for me,

d the Lady gave it to you, but maybe she'd under-
and. Do *you* understand, Mr. Frodo? I've got to go on.'

But he could not go, not yet. He knelt and held Frodo's
and and could not release it. And time went by and still
knelt, holding his master's hand, and in his heart
eping a debate.

Now he tried to find strength to tear himself away and
o on a lonely journey—for vengeance. If once he could
, his anger would bear him down all the roads of the
orld, pursuing, until he had him at last: Gollum. Then
ollum would die in a corner. But that was not what he
d set out to do. It would not be worth while to leave his
aster for that. It would not bring him back. Nothing
ould. They had better both be dead together. And that
o would be a lonely journey.

He looked on the bright point of the sword. He thought
the places behind where there was a black brink
d an empty fall into nothingness. There was no escape
at way. That was to do nothing, not even to grieve.
hat was not what he had set out to do. 'What am I
do then?' he cried again, and now he seemed plainly
know the hard answer: *see it through.* Another lonely
urney, and the worst.

'What? Me, alone, go to the Crack of Doom and all?'
e quailed still, but the resolve grew. 'What? *Me* take the
ing from *him?* The Council gave it to him.'

But the answer came at once: 'And the Council gave
m companions, so that the errand should not fail. And
u are the last of all the Company. The errand must not
l.'

'I wish I wasn't the last,' he groaned. 'I wish old Gan-
lf was here, or somebody. Why am I left all alone to
ake up my mind? I'm sure to go wrong. And it's not for
e to go taking the Ring, putting myself forward.'

'But you haven't put yourself forward; you've been put
rward. And as for not being the right and proper person,
y, Mr. Frodo wasn't, as you might say, nor Mr. Bilbo.
ey didn't choose themselves.'

'Ah well, I must make up my own mind. I will make up. But I'll be sure to go wrong: that'd be Sam Gamgee a over.

'Let me see now: if we're found here, or Mr. Frodo' found, and that Thing's on him, well, the Enemy will g it. And that's the end of us all, of Lórien, and Rivendel and the Shire and all. And there's no time to lose, or it' be the end anyway. The war's begun, and more tha likely things are all going the Enemy's way already. N chance to go back with It and get advice or permissior No, it's sit here till they come and kill me over master body, and gets It; or take It and go.' He drew a dee breath. 'Then take It, it is!'

He stooped. Very gently he undid the clasp at the nec and slipped his hand inside Frodo's tunic; then with h other hand raising the head, he kissed the cold forehea and softly drew the chain over it. And then the head la quietly back again in rest. No change came over the sti face, and by that more than by other tokens Sam wa convinced at last that Frodo had died and laid aside th Quest.

'Good-bye, master, my dear!' he murmured. 'Forgi your Sam. He'll come back to this spot when the job's dor —if he manages it. And then he'll not leave you agair Rest you quiet till I come; and may no foul creature con anigh you! And if the Lady could hear me and give me or wish, I would wish to come back and find you agair Good-bye!'

And then he bent his own neck and put the chain upo it, and at once his head was bowed to the ground wit the weight of the Ring, as if a great stone had been strur on him. But slowly, as if the weight became less, or ne strength grew in him, he raised his head, and then with great effort got to his feet and found that he could wal and bear his burden. And for a moment he lifted up th Phial and looked down at his master, and the light burne gently now with the soft radiance of the evening-star i summer, and in that light Frodo's face was fair of ht

gain, pale but beautiful with an elvish beauty, as of one
who has long passed the shadows. And with the bitter
omfort of that last sight Sam turned and hid the light and
tumbled on into the growing dark.

He had not far to go. The tunnel was some way behind;
he Cleft a couple of hundred yards ahead, or less. The
ath was visible in the dusk, a deep rut worn in ages of
assage, running now gently up in a long trough with
liffs on either side. The trough narrowed rapidly. Soon
am came to a long flight of broad shallow steps. Now the
rc-tower was right above him, frowning black, and in it
he red eye glowed. Now he was hidden in the dark shadow
nder it. He was coming to the top of the steps and was in
he Cleft at last.

'I've made up my mind,' he kept saying to himself. But
e had not. Though he had done his best to think it out,
what he was doing was altogether against the grain of his
ature. 'Have I got it wrong?' he muttered. 'What ought
to have done?'

As the sheer sides of the Cleft closed about him, before
e reached the actual summit, before he looked at last
n the path descending into the Nameless Land, he
urned. For a moment, motionless in intolerable doubt, he
ooked back. He could still see, like a small blot in the
athering gloom, the mouth of the tunnel; and he thought
e could see or guess where Frodo lay. He fancied there
as a glimmer on the ground down there, or perhaps it was
ome trick of his tears, as he peered out at that high stony
lace where all his life had fallen in ruin.

'If only I could have my wish, my one wish,' he sighed,
o go back and find him!' Then at last he turned to the
ad in front and took a few steps: the heaviest and the
ost reluctant he had ever taken.

Only a few steps; and now only a few more and he
ould be going down and would never see that high place
gain. And then suddenly he heard cries and voices. He
ood still as stone. Orc-voices. They were behind him and

before him. A noise of tramping feet and harsh shouts
Orcs were coming up to the Cleft from the far side, from
some entry to the tower, perhaps. Tramping feet and
shouts behind. He wheeled round. He saw small red lights
torches, winking away below there as they issued from the
tunnel. At last the hunt was up. The red eye of the tower
had not been blind. He was caught.

Now the flicker of approaching torches and the clink of
steel ahead was very near. In a minute they would reach
the top and be on him. He had taken too long in making up
his mind, and now it was no good. How could he escape,
or save himself, or save the Ring? The Ring. He was not
aware of any thought or decision. He simply found himself drawing out the chain and taking the Ring in his
hand. The head of the orc-company appeared in the Cleft
right before him. Then he put it on.

The world changed, and a single moment of time was
filled with an hour of thought. At once he was aware that
hearing was sharpened while sight was dimmed, but otherwise than in Shelob's lair. All things about him now were
not dark but vague; while he himself was there in a grey
hazy world, alone, like a small black solid rock, and the
Ring, weighing down his left hand, was like an orb of
hot gold. He did not feel invisible at all, but horribly and
uniquely visible; and he knew that somewhere an Eye was
searching for him.

He heard the crack of stone, and the murmur of water
far off in Morgul Vale; and down away under the rock the
bubbling misery of Shelob, groping, lost in some blind
passage; and voices in the dungeons of the tower; and the
cries of the Orcs as they came out of the tunnel; and
deafening, roaring in his ears, the crash of the feet and
the rending clamour of the Orcs before him. He shrank
against the cliff. But they marched up like a phantom
company, grey distorted figures in a mist, only dreams of
fear with pale flames in their hands. And they passed him
by. He cowered, trying to creep away into some cranny
and to hide.

He listened. The Orcs from the tunnel and the others marching down had sighted one another, and both parties were now hurrying and shouting. He heard them both clearly, and he understood what they said. Perhaps the Ring gave understanding of tongues, or simply understanding, especially of the servants of Sauron its maker, so that if he gave heed, he understood and translated the thought to himself. Certainly the Ring had grown greatly in power as it approached the places of its forging; but one thing it did not confer, and that was courage. At present Sam still thought only of hiding, of lying low till all was quiet again; and he listened anxiously. He could not tell how near the voices were, the words seemed almost in his ears.

'Hola! Gorbag! What are you doing up here? Had enough of war already?'

'Orders, you lubber. And what are you doing, Shagrat? Tired of lurking up there? Thinking of coming down to fight?'

'Orders to you. I'm in command of this pass. So speak civil. What's your report?'

'Nothing.'

'Hai! hai! yoi!' A yell broke into the exchanges of the leaders. The Orcs lower down had suddenly seen something. They began to run. So did the others.

'Hai! Hola! Here's something! Lying right in the road. A spy, a spy!' There was a hoot of snarling horns and a babel of baying voices.

With a dreadful stroke Sam was wakened from his lowering mood. They had seen his master. What would they do? He had heard tales of the Orcs to make the blood run cold. It could not be borne. He sprang up. He flung the Quest and all his decisions away, and fear and doubt with them. He knew now where his place was and had been: at his master's side, though what he could do there was not clear. Back he ran down the steps, down the path towards Frodo.

'How many are there?' he thought. 'Thirty or forty from
the tower at least, and a lot more than that from down be
low, I guess. How many can I kill before they get me
They'll see the flame of the sword, as soon as I draw i
and they'll get me sooner or later. I wonder if any song wi
ever mention it: How Samwise fell in the High Pass an
made a wall of bodies round his master. No, no song. C
course not, for the Ring'll be found, and there'll be n
more songs. I can't help it. My place is by Mr. Frodo. The
must understand that—Elrond and the Council, and th
great Lords and Ladies with all their wisdom. Their plan
have gone wrong. I can't be their Ring-bearer. Not withou
Mr. Frodo.'

But the Orcs were out of his dim sight now. He had ha
no time to consider himself, but now he realized that h
was weary, weary almost to exhaustion: his legs woul
not carry him as he wished. He was too slow. The pat
seemed miles long. Where had they all got to in the mist

There they were again! A good way ahead still. .
cluster of figures round something lying on the ground;
few seemed to be darting this way and that, bent like dog
on a trail. He tried to make a spurt.

'Come on, Sam!' he said, 'or you'll be too late again
He loosened the sword in its sheath. In a minute he woul
draw it, and then——

There was a wild clamour, hooting and laughing, a
something was lifted from the ground. 'Ya hoi! Ya har
hoi! Up! Up!'

Then a voice shouted: 'Now off! The quick way. Bac
to the Undergate! She'll not trouble us tonight by all th
signs.' The whole band of orc-figures began to move. For
in the middle were carrying a body high on their shou
ders. 'Ya hoi!'

They had taken Frodo's body. They were off. He cou
not catch them up. Still he laboured on. The Orcs reache
the tunnel and were passing in. Those with the burden we
first, and behind them there was a good deal of strugglir

and jostling. Sam came on. He drew the sword, a flicker of blue in his wavering hand, but they did not see it. Even as he came panting up, the last of them vanished into the black hole.

For a moment he stood, gasping, clutching his breast. Then he drew his sleeve across his face, wiping away the grime, and sweat, and tears. 'Curse the filth!' he said, and sprang after them into the darkness.

It no longer seemed very dark to him in the tunnel, rather it was as if he had stepped out of a thin mist into a heavier fog. His weariness was growing but his will hardened all the more. He thought he could see the light of torches a little way ahead, but try as he would, he could not catch them up. Orcs go fast in tunnels, and this tunnel they knew well; for in spite of Shelob they were forced to use it often as the swiftest way from the Dead City over the mountains. In what far-off time the main tunnel and the great round pit had been made, where Shelob had taken up her abode in ages past, they did not know; but many byways they had themselves delved about it on either side, so as to escape the lair in their goings to and fro on the business of their masters. Tonight they did not intend to go far down, but were hastening to find a side-passage that led back to their watch-tower on the cliff. Most of them were gleeful, delighted with what they had found and seen, and as they ran they gabbled and yammered after the fashion of their kind. Sam heard the noise of their harsh voices, flat and hard in the dead air, and he could distinguish two voices from among all the rest: they were louder, and nearer to him. The captains of the two parties seemed to be bringing up the rear, debating as they went.

'Can't you stop your rabble making such a racket, Shagrat?' grunted the one. 'We don't want Shelob on us.'

'Go on, Gorbag! Yours are making more than half the noise,' said the other. 'But let the lads play! No need to worry about Shelob for a bit, I reckon. She's sat on a nail, it seems, and we shan't cry about that. Didn't you see: a

nasty mess all the way back to that cursed crack of hers
If we've stopped it once, we've stopped it a hundred times
So let 'em laugh. And we've struck a bit of luck at last: go
something that Lugbúrz wants.'

'Lugbúrz wants it, eh? What is it, d'you think? Elvish
it looked to me, but undersized. What's the danger in a
thing like that?'

'Don't know till we've had a look.'

'Oho! So they haven't told you what to expect? They
don't tell us all they know, do they? Not by half. But the
can make mistakes, even the Top Ones can.'

'Sh, Gorbag!' Shagrat's voice was lowered, so that even
with his strangely sharpened hearing Sam could only jus
catch what was said. 'They may, but they've got eyes an
ears everywhere; some among my lot, as like as not. Bu
there's no doubt about it, they're troubled about something
The Nazgûl down below are, by your account; and Lug
búrz is too. Something nearly slipped.'

'Nearly, you say!' said Gorbag.

'All right,' said Shagrat, 'but we'll talk of that later
Wait till we get to the Under-way. There's a place ther
where we can talk a bit, while the lads go on.'

Shortly afterwards Sam saw the torches disappear. The
there was a rumbling noise, and just as he hurried up, a
bump. As far as he could guess the Orcs had turned an
gone into the very opening which Frodo and he had trie
and found blocked. It was still blocked.

There seemed to be a great stone in the way, but th
Orcs had got through somehow, for he could hear the
voices on the other side. They were still running alon
deeper and deeper into the mountain, back towards th
tower. Sam felt desperate. They were carrying off his ma
ter's body for some foul purpose and he could not follow
He thrust and pushed at the block, and he threw himse
against it, but it did not yield. Then not far inside, or so h
thought, he heard the two captains' voices talking agai
He stood still listening for a while, hoping perhaps to lear
something useful. Perhaps Gorbag, who seemed to belon

to Minas Morgul, would come out, and he could then slip
in.

'No, I don't know,' said Gorbag's voice. 'The messages
go through quicker than anything could fly, as a rule. But
I don't enquire how it's done. Safest not to. Grr! Those
Nazgûl give me the creeps. And they skin the body off you
as soon as look at you, and leave you all cold in the dark
on the other side. But He likes 'em; they're His favourites
nowadays, so it's no use grumbling. I tell you, it's no game
serving down in the city.'

'You should try being up here with Shelob for company,'
said Shagrat.

'I'd like to try somewhere where there's none of 'em.
But the war's on now, and when that's over things may be
easier.'

'It's going well, they say.'

'They would,' grunted Gorbag. 'We'll see. But anyway,
if it does go well, there would be a lot more room. What
d'you say?—if we get a chance, you and me'll slip off and
set up somewhere on our own with a few trusty lads, somewhere where there's good loot nice and handy, and no big
bosses.'

'Ah!' said Shagrat. 'Like old times.'

'Yes,' said Gorbag. 'But don't count on it. I'm not easy
in my mind. As I said, the Big Bosses, ay,' his voice sank
almost to a whisper, 'ay, even the Biggest, can make mistakes. Something nearly slipped, you say. I say, something *has* slipped. And we've got to look out. Always the
poor Uruks to put slips right, and small thanks. But don't
forget: the enemies don't love us any more than they love
Him, and if they get topsides on Him, we're done too.
But see here: when were you ordered out?'

'About an hour ago, just before you saw us. A message
came: *Nazgûl uneasy. Spies feared on Stairs. Double
vigilance. Patrol to head of Stairs.* I came at once.'

'Bad business,' said Gorbag. 'See here—our Silent
Watchers were uneasy more than two days ago, that I
know. But my patrol wasn't ordered out for another day,
nor any message sent to Lugbúrz either: owing to the Great

Signal going up, and the High Nazgûl going off to the war and all that. And then they couldn't get Lugbúrz to pay attention for a good while, I'm told.'

'The Eye was busy elsewhere, I suppose,' said Shagrat. 'Big things going on away west, they say.'

'I daresay,' growled Gorbag. 'But in the meantime enemies have got up the Stairs. And what were you up to? You're supposed to keep watch, aren't you, special orders or no? What are you for?'

'That's enough! Don't try and teach me my job. We were awake all right. We knew there were funny things going on.'

'Very funny!'

'Yes, very funny: lights and shouting and all. But Shelob was on the go. My lads saw her and her Sneak.'

'Her Sneak? What's that?'

'You must have seen him: little thin black fellow; like a spider himself, or perhaps more like a starved frog. He's been here before. Came *out* of Lugbúrz the first time, years ago, and we had word from High Up to let him pass. He's been up the Stairs once or twice since then, but we've left him alone: seems to have some understanding with Her Ladyship. I suppose he's no good to eat: she wouldn't worry about words from High Up. But a fine guard you keep in the valley: he was up here a day before all this racket. Early last night we saw him. Anyway my lads reported that Her Ladyship was having some fun, and that seemed good enough for me, until the message came. I thought her Sneak had brought her a toy, or that you'd perhaps sent her a present, a prisoner of war or something. I don't interfere when she's playing. Nothing gets by Shelob when she's on the hunt.'

'Nothing, say you! Didn't you use your eyes back there? I tell you I'm not easy in my mind. Whatever came up the Stairs, *did* get by. It cut her web and got clean out of the hole. That's something to think about!'

'Ah well, but she got him in the end, didn't she?'

'*Got* him? Got *who*? This little fellow? But if he was the only one, then she'd have had him off to her larder long before, and there he'd be now. And if Lugbúrz wanted him, *you'd* have to go and get him. Nice for you. But there was more than one.'

At this point Sam began to listen more attentively and pressed his ear against the stone.

'Who cut the cords she'd put round him, Shagrat? Same one as cut the web. Didn't you see that? And who stuck a pin into Her Ladyship? Same one, I reckon. And where is he? Where is he, Shagrat?'

Shagrat made no reply.

'You may well put your thinking cap on, if you've got one. It's no laughing matter. No one, *no* one has ever stuck a pin in Shelob before, as you should know well enough. There's no grief in that; but think—there's someone loose hereabouts as is more dangerous than any other damned rebel that ever walked since the bad old times, since the great Siege. Something *has* slipped.'

'And what is it then?' growled Shagrat.

'By all the signs, Captain Shagrat, I'd say there's a large warrior loose, Elf most likely, with an elf-sword anyway, and an axe as well maybe; and he's loose in your bounds, too, and you've never spotted him. Very funny indeed!' Gorbag spat. Sam smiled grimly at this description of himself.

'Ah well, you always did take a gloomy view,' said Shagrat. 'You can read the signs how you like, but there may be other ways to explain them. Anyhow, I've got watchers at every point, and I'm going to deal with one thing at a time. When I've had a look at the fellow we *have* caught, then I'll begin to worry about something else.'

'It's my guess you won't find much in that little fellow,' said Gorbag. 'He may have had nothing to do with the real mischief. The big fellow with the sharp sword doesn't seem to have thought him worth much anyhow—just left him lying: regular elvish trick.'

'We'll see. Come on now! We've talked enough. Let's go and have a look at the prisoner!'

'What are you going to do with him? Don't forget I

spotted him first. If there's any game, me and my lads mus
be in it.'

'Now, now,' growled Shagrat, 'I have my orders. And
it's more than my belly's worth, or yours, to break 'em
Any trespasser found by the guard is to be held at the
tower. Prisoner is to be stripped. Full description of every
article, garment, weapon, letter, ring, or trinket is to be
sent to Lugbúrz at once, and to Lugbúrz *only*. And the
prisoner is to be kept safe and intact, under pain of death
for every member of the guard, until He sends or comes
Himself. That's plain enough, and that's what I'm going
to do.'

'Stripped, eh?' said Gorbag. 'What, teeth, nails, hair
and all?'

'No, none of that. He's for Lugbúrz, I tell you. He's
wanted safe and whole.'

'You'll find that difficult,' laughed Gorbag. 'He's nothing but carrion now. What Lugbúrz will do with such stuff
I can't guess. He might as well go in the pot.'

'You fool,' snarled Shagrat. 'You've been talking very
clever, but there's a lot you don't know, though most
other folk do. You'll be for the pot or for Shelob, if you
don't take care. Carrion! Is that all you know of Her
Ladyship? When she binds with cords, she's after meat.
She doesn't eat dead meat, nor suck cold blood. This fellow
isn't dead!'

Sam reeled, clutching at the stone. He felt as if the whole
dark world was turning upside down. So great was the
shock that he almost swooned, but even as he fought to
keep a hold on his senses, deep inside him he was aware
of the comment: 'You fool, he isn't dead, and your heart
knew it. Don't trust your head, Samwise, it is not the best
part of you. The trouble with you is that you never really
had any hope. Now what is to be done?' For the moment
nothing, but to prop himself against the unmoving stone
and listen, listen to the vile orc-voices.

'Garn!' said Shagrat. 'She's got more than one poison.

When she's hunting, she just gives 'em a dab in the neck and they go as limp as boned fish, and then she has her way with them. D'you remember old Ufthak? We lost him for days. Then we found him in a corner; hanging up he was, but he was wide awake and glaring. How we laughed! She'd forgotten him, maybe, but we didn't touch him—no good interfering with Her. Nar—this little filth, he'll wake up, in a few hours; and beyond feeling a bit sick for a bit, he'll be all right. Or would be, if Lugbúrz would let him alone. And of course, beyond wondering where he is and what's happened to him.'

'And what's going to happen to him,' laughed Gorbag. 'We can tell him a few stories at any rate, if we can't do anything else. I don't suppose he's ever been in lovely Lugbúrz, so he may like to know what to expect. This is going to be more funny than I thought. Let's go!'

'There's going to be no fun, I tell you,' said Shagrat. 'And he's got to be kept safe, or we're all as good as dead.'

'All right! But if I were you, I'd catch the big one that's loose, before you send in any report to Lugbúrz. It won't sound too pretty to say you've caught the kitten and let the cat escape.'

The voices began to move away. Sam heard the sound of feet receding. He was recovering from his shock, and now a wild fury was on him. 'I got it all wrong!' he cried. 'I knew I would. Now they've got him, the devils; the filth! Never leave your master, never, never: that was my right rule. And I knew it in my heart. May I be forgiven! Now I've got to get back to him. Somehow, somehow!'

He drew his sword again and beat on the stone with the hilts, but it only gave out a dull sound. The sword, however, blazed so brightly now that he could see dimly in its light. To his surprise he noticed that the great block was shaped like a heavy door, and was less than twice his own height. Above it was a dark blank space between the top and the low arch of the opening. It was probably only meant to be a stop against the intrusion of Shelob, fastened on the inside with some latch or bolt beyond the

reach of her cunning. With his remaining strength Sam
leaped and caught the top, scrambled up, and dropped;
and then he ran madly, sword blazing in hand, round
a bend and up a winding tunnel.

The news that his master was still alive roused him to
a last effort beyond thought of weariness. He could not
see anything ahead, for this new passage twisted and
turned constantly; but he thought he was catching the two
Orcs up: their voices were growing nearer again. Now
they seemed quite close.

'That's what I'm going to do,' said Shagrat in angry
tones. 'Put him right up in the top chamber.'

'What for?' growled Gorbag. 'Haven't you any lock-ups
down below?'

'He's going out of harm's way, I tell you,' answered
Shagrat. 'See? He's precious. I don't trust all my lads, and
none of yours; nor you neither, when you're mad for
fun. He's going where I want him, and where you won't
come, if you don't keep civil. Up to the top, I say. He'll be
safe there.'

'Will he?' said Sam. 'You're forgetting the great big elvish warrior that's loose!' And with that he raced round
the last corner, only to find that by some trick of the tunnel, or of the hearing which the Ring gave him, he had
misjudged the distance.

The two orc-figures were still some way ahead. He could
see them now, black and squat against a red glare. The
passage ran straight at last, up an incline; and at the end,
wide open, were great double doors, leading probably to
deep chambers far below the high horn of the tower. Already the Orcs with their burden had passed inside. Gorbag
and Shagrat were drawing near the gate.

Sam heard a burst of hoarse singing, blaring of horns
and banging of gongs, a hideous clamour. Gorbag and
Shagrat were already on the threshold.

Sam yelled and brandished Sting, but his little voice was
drowned in the tumult. No one heeded him.

The great doors slammed to. Boom. The bars of iron

ell into place inside. Clang. The gate was shut. Sam hurled
imself against the bolted brazen plates and fell senseless
o the ground. He was out in the darkness. Frodo was alive
ut taken by the Enemy.

Here ends the second part of the history of the War of the Ring.
The third part tells of the last defence against the Shadow, and
he end of the mission of the Ring-bearer in THE RETURN OF
HE KING.